ROMANCE FROM JANELLE TAYLOR

ANYTHING FOR LOVE   (0-8217-4992-7, $5.99)

DESTINY MINE   (0-8217-5185-9, $5.99)

CHASE THE WIND   (0-8217-4740-1, $5.99)

MIDNIGHT SECRETS   (0-8217-5280-4, $5.99)

MOONBEAMS AND MAGIC   (0-8217-0184-4, $5.99)

SWEET SAVAGE HEART   (0-8217-5276-6, $5.99)

SOME LIKE IT HOTTER

Deb Stover

Pinnacle Books
Kensington Publishing Corp.

http://www.pinnaclebooks.com

PINNACLE BOOKS are published by

Kensington Publishing Corp.
850 Third Avenue
New York, NY 10022

Pinnacle and the P logo Reg. U.S. Pat. & TM Off.

First Printing: April, 1997
10 9 8 7 6 5 4 3 2 1

Printed in the United States of America

For Dad, Mom, Dave, Barbi, Bonnie, and Ben.

Special thanks to Laura, Paula, Pam, and Karen, who were there to help me make it work, and to David Kuamoo, for giving this manuscript a policeman's seal of approval.

Laura Kenner, Sam, and Lilly, meet me at Bean's Place— I'm buying.

Chapter One

"I'll bet Dirty Harry never had to do this," Mike Faricy said, leaning back against the worn vinyl upholstery.

"I hear that." Barney aimed his binoculars toward the three-story building again.

Parked in a lonely alley behind a waterfront warehouse, the Chevy was more like a prison cell than a car. Darkness settled over the sleeping city of Natchez like a shroud; a thick bank of fog from the river blotted out the stars. The streetlights appeared as nothing more than faint golden halos in the unseasonably cool, moisture-laden air.

Trying to fill the boring hours with happier thoughts, Mike allowed himself a smile. Barney and Carrie's great news more than compensated for the gloomy ambiance. "Man, this is great—I'm going to be an uncle," Mike said, feeling himself warm from within. His sister, Carrie, had been trying for years to have a baby. Finally, it looked as if her dream might come true. "Let's see, today's June twentieth, so when's the baby due?"

"Sometime in early March." Barney gave a satisfied grunt, keeping his curly head turned toward the dark building as he spoke. "I hate stakeouts."

"Yeah. Me, too." Mike sighed. "Having a brother-in-law for my partner's bad enough. I can just imagine what having an expectant father around is going to be like."

"It'll be far freakin' out, and you know it." Barney chuckled low in his throat, never interrupting his surveillance of the still-dark building. "You don't suppose Milton's men are going to let us down again tonight, do you?"

"Nah." Mike shifted in his seat to peer toward the building. "If they do, it'll be embarrassing as hell after all the trouble we had convincing the state police this was Milton's point of operation."

"A little town like Natchez sure as hell isn't the most likely spot." Barney shot Mike a crooked grin, barely visible in the increasing darkness. "Yeah, Mike, I'd say after ten days of this crap, it's past time for them to come out and play."

"That's for sure."

"So, you think the kid'll be as good-lookin' as his old man?"

Mike chuckled, ignoring his partner's indignant grunt as he turned to face the warehouse again. "I don't know, Barney. I think Carrie'd prefer he take after his Uncle Mike."

"In your dreams."

They laughed quietly, nervously, continuing to stare in silence at the building.

Nothing happened. Minutes turned into hours. Well after midnight Mike was ready to call their shift another waste of time when a van, headlights off, pulled into the alley adjacent to the warehouse. "Hot damn." A few minutes later, light filled an upstairs window.

"It's about time," Barney whispered, drawing his gun from his shoulder holster and releasing the safety.

Mike mimicked his partner's actions, sharing Barney's obvious excitement. "This is one crack shipment that isn't going to find its way to the streets." Barney didn't have to respond—Mike knew they both felt the same way. Group think became automatic after all the years they'd worked together.

"Milton's mine."

"Don't be an ass." Mike reached for his partner's arm. "That kid's death wasn't your fault and you know it."

Barney sat quietly for several seconds, then released a sigh. "I know, but if my last collar had stuck, Milton would've been locked up ... and that kid would be getting ready for his frigging prom about now."

Mike nodded, knowing this wasn't the time to press. "I'll call for backup."

"Do that." Barney turned toward the warehouse again.

Mike reached for the radio and wasted precious seconds waiting for the frequency to clear, then he called for backup. Every time they were on the brink of busting Milton's operation, something always interfered. The drug lord had more than his share of luck, but he was pure pond scum.

"Ready?"

"Yeah," Mike whispered, climbing from the dark car. Barney'd permanently disabled the dome light to allow them to get out of the car without tipping off the bad guys. He and Barney were the white hats, out to see justice done, to preserve the American way. But this wasn't a game like the cops and robbers they'd played together as children.

This was for keeps.

"Cover me, Mike," Barney whispered over his shoulder, breaking silently for the open alley before his partner could stop him.

"Barney, damn you. Wait for backup," Mike whispered fiercely—futilely—then darted from the sidewalk, adrenaline pumping through his body. He flattened himself against the cold brick building across the alley, squinting to get his bearings through the thick fog. Barney had always been the brave one—foolishly so, on more than one occasion.

But now Barney was an expectant father. Mike couldn't let anything happen to his brother-in-law. That would devastate Carrie, especially now.

One of them had to keep his head, and it sure as hell wouldn't be Barney. History'd proven that. Mike's brother-in-law hadn't earned the status of most-decorated cop in the department from practicing common sense. Mike had to be the voice of reason.

Scary thought.

Barney—the horse's ass—was walking right through the

side entrance as if he paid the mortgage, the taxes, and had the only key. Mike clenched his teeth, feeling his jaw twitch as he watched the slight shifting of light near the doorway where Barney slipped stealthily inside.

With the bad guys.

Cautiously, Mike scanned the street. Nothing. Where was their backup? *Damn.* Releasing the breath he'd been holding, he darted across the alley, thankful for his black athletic shoes, dark jeans and denim jacket. He was quiet and invisible in the night.

Quiet and invisible was the only way to be on a night like this.

There was an edge to the evening that Mike had felt before, and he didn't like it. Instincts became lifelines to cops over the years, and separated the veterans from the rookies.

Tonight, for some insane reason, Mike felt like a rookie.

Pausing outside the door Barney'd slipped through, Mike waited for his breathing to slow, listening for sounds from inside. What the hell was Barney doing in there?

Panic wasn't Mike's way, but tonight he had to struggle against it. The stakes had gone up, and suddenly he almost wished Barney hadn't shared his good news.

Why couldn't he shake the cold sense of dread that had crawled inside him like a deadly snake?

I hate this.

The door was open, allowing Mike to squeeze through noiselessly. He had to find Barney. Some deep feeling of urgency coursed through him, driving him to seek out his partner before . . .

A cold sweat popped out on his forehead as he eased his way along a dark hall toward the stairs. Weapon drawn, Mike kept his back against the wall to guide him until he reached the metal stair railing, then he gripped it with one hand, continuing to clutch his gun in the other.

"You son of a bitch!" The shout echoed down the dark stairwell.

Mike took the steps two at a time, reaching the top as a gun exploded on the other side of the door. His blood turned to ice. He froze, his free hand clutching the doorknob.

Always wait for backup.

Swallowing his fear, he ignored all the standard rules of precaution as he turned the knob and opened the door. More darkness greeted him on the other side, but he knew he was no longer alone. A subtle alteration in the blackness divulged another's presence.

Barney?

"Stupid cop," the raspy voice—definitely not Barney's— taunted from across the hallway. "Dead cop."

Mike dropped to a low crouch, taking aim on the shifting silhouette. What dead cop? Did the thug mean him?

Or Barney?

A flash from the man's gun pinpointed his location as a spray of bullets blasted into the wall just above Mike's head. Splintered plaster showered him as he scooted to his left, hoping to confuse the gunman.

Where's Barney? Mike couldn't risk accidentally shooting his partner. He took careful aim and waited for the man to fire another round, praying his adversary would miss again.

Both guns discharged almost simultaneously, followed by the welcome thud of a falling body. Mike lurched to the right, coming into contact with something warm and solid on the floor.

Mike's heart hammered dangerously loud as he remained alert to a possible counter attack from his enemy. He felt the shape on the floor with his free hand.

A body.

Swallowing the lump in his throat, Mike moved his hand along the supine form, finding warm, sticky blood where there should have been a neck. He struggled against exploding panic, glancing once toward the area where his opponent had fallen. There was no movement, no sound.

Cautiously, he reached into his pocket and withdrew the penlight hooked to his key ring. After flipping it on, he shined the small light on the body.

Barney.

''Oh, God.'' Mike sucked in a breath to kill his rising nausea as he searched his brother-in-law's face above the wound. Sightless eyes stared up at the ceiling.

Lowering the beam, Mike confirmed that CPR would be pointless. Barney's throat and neck were blown wide open— no chance that his heart would beat again.

You dumb son of a bitch. I told you to wait for backup. He sucked in a breath and struggled for control. *How the hell am I going to tell . . . Carrie?*

Barney—his childhood playmate. His partner. Carrie's husband. Mike's kid sister was a widow because of Milton and his apes.

A gaping wound in his own throat would've been easier— better—than this. *God, not Barney.*

The sound of running feet came from the far end of the hall, then a door burst open. Three men carrying large flashlights— and even bigger guns—emerged, stopping to take in the carnage.

''Holy shit. Somebody got Joe,'' a man said, sweeping the floor with his flashlight. ''Milton said we wouldn't have no trouble tonight.''

''Looks like plenty trouble to me,'' another man said.

This wasn't his backup.

Mike eased back against the door, reminding himself that Barney was beyond help. Besides, Carrie sure as hell didn't need to lose her husband and brother on the same night.

''There!''

Knowing he'd been spotted, Mike leapt to his feet. Forcing the image of Barney's lifeless eyes from his mind, he sailed down the metal staircase, just ahead of the bullets fired by his pursuers. He sprinted out the side door and out into the alley.

He had to get to the car. Hell, Barney had the only set of keys.

Men thundered down the metal stairs inside the building as Mike started to run. They wouldn't stop until they had him.

Just like Barney.

Barney.

He ran down the street with his pistol still clutched in his

fist, sweat and tears streaming down his face. *Calm down Mike.*
Need to find a phone. Need to think. Let somebody know what
happened. Barney, you bastard. Milton, I'll get you, I swear.

He didn't know or care where he ran—it didn't matter.

They were getting closer.

Mike rounded a corner on the rain-slick street, desperately
searching for a place to hide. To think he and Barney's planned
to put the biggest crime boss in the state of Mississippi behind
bars for the rest of his natural days.

Now all that mattered was survival.

His lungs felt as if they would burst. His heart battered the
walls of his chest. This pace was killing him.

But to stop meant *certain* death.

No matter how far he ran in the misty streets, the footsteps
were never far behind. A car joined in the chase, careening
after him through the fog. Even the cover of darkness couldn't
protect him.

Mike paused at the corner, recognizing the huge old house
across the street. No one ever went inside the antebellum mansion on the outskirts of town. Everyone in Mississippi knew—
thought—it was haunted.

The second story windows stared back at him like harbingers
of disaster.

Get a grip, Mike.

Barney wouldn't have been afraid. Besides, Mike didn't
believe in ghosts. He'd seen too much real life—and death—
to start believing in nonsense at this late date.

Clenching his teeth, he looked over his shoulder. He couldn't
see his pursuers, but he heard them. In only a matter of minutes
they'd have him, unless he could manage to become invisible.

Picturing his sister's smiling face when she and Barney'd
told him their good news, he knew what he had to do. In
desperation, he ducked beneath the board which had been nailed
to the broken gate, then darted across the overgrown lawn.
When he reached the porch of the run-down mansion, he
dropped to his knees and waited in the shadows.

The gang members congregated on the walk just outside the
gate. Mike's lungs burned for air, but he denied them the luxury

awhile longer. He had to make sure his enemies were gone before he dared make too much noise. High humidity and cool temperatures turned the air into a conduit for sound. His oxygen-starved senses would have to wait awhile longer.

Because if they caught him, he wouldn't need to concern himself with trivial matters like oxygen.

He listened while the threesome compared notes with the driver of the Thunderbird that had stopped beside them.

"Where the hell'd he go?" one voice demanded.

"Man, Milton's gonna have our asses for this."

"More'n our asses."

"Shit! We gotta find this dude."

"We gotta go back and get rid of the other one."

"Yeah, get in. The fish are hungry."

Barney. Mike closed his eyes. Even if he managed to escape from Milton's goons tonight, they'd catch up with him sooner or later. Every thug in town knew Faricy and Sloane. As soon as the killers figured out Barney's identity, they'd know exactly where to look for Mike.

He was as good as dead right now.

Fish fodder.

"One of us has gotta hang around here," the driver said. "Just in case he's hidin' out, waiting for us to leave."

Great.

"I ain't stayin' here by myself, man. Everybody knows that old house is haunted."

"Haunted?" The driver chuckled, a menacing sound on the night air. "You're full of shit, Billy. Now stay here and keep your eyes open. We gotta take out that piece of shit or we'll be feedin' the fish. Got it?"

"Yeah." The man ordered to remain grumbled incoherently as the others climbed into the car and it sped away.

Mike glanced behind him at the dilapidated house. He had to get inside and rest for a while. The guy thought the house was haunted. Perfect. For tonight, it would be haunted.

By Mike Faricy.

Once the sun came up, he'd find his way to Carrie.

He watched until the man crossed the street and vanished

into the alley, then Mike crept quietly around to the side of the house. He passed by a few boarded windows, hesitating to jiggle a couple of doorknobs. No luck. Everything was locked up tight, though he couldn't imagine why. It wasn't as if the place was on the hit list of any local burglars. In fact, no one ever went near the place.

Except maybe on Halloween.

When he found the French doors on the west side, his luck changed. The old lock was easily picked and soon the right side swung open on squeaky hinges.

Mike held his breath—what little he had—wondering if any of Milton's men might still be in the area. Every sound could be the last one he ever made or heard. He had to be more careful; his sister needed him.

Once the door closed against the damp outside air, he heaved a sigh of relief and gulped precious, dusty air into his starving lungs. Regaining some of his strength, he walked across a broad expanse of wood flooring, forcing the image of Barney's face from his mind with every step. The place was huge.

Looking up, he realized the area he now stood in must be at least three stories high. Dark shapes defined what he suspected were doors and stair rails as he turned in a circle.

Yeah, like I care.

Brushing cobwebs from his face and hair, he sought a place where he would be able to see all the possible entrances, then lowered himself to the dirty floor to lean against the wall. A deathly silence permeated the huge structure, making him shudder as he waited for his pulse to slow to something the normal side of critical. He shoved his weapon in its holster.

"Dammit, Barney." A lump formed in Mike's throat, threatening to gag him if he didn't release the grief boiling inside him. His gut burned as he struggled against the stinging tears behind his eyes.

A faint sound drifted to his ears, momentarily distracting him from his misery as he gazed around the dark room. It was distant, muted. He strained to listen more closely, trying to identify the sound.

Music.

Yeah, right. Maybe a funeral dirge.

Insistent tears pricked his eyes again. He hadn't cried since second grade, when he and Carrie'd first learned about their parents' car accident.

They were dead—just like Barney.

All he and Carrie had now was each other.

He closed his eyes against memories of the night he'd just survived. Remembering the blood, his partner's dead eyes, bile again rose in his throat. He'd seen more than his share of mutilated bodies in various stages of decay in his life, but this was different. Barney'd been more than a brother-in-law—he'd been like a *real* brother. A soul mate.

How was Mike ever going to break the news to his sister? He should never have let her marry a cop.

Barney was dead. Gone. No amount of hindsight, twenty-twenty or not, would bring him back.

The music suddenly ended as mysteriously as it had begun. An awesome silence filled the old mansion, crawling right inside Mike to incite his agony. The only sound he heard now was the heavy thud of his heart, beating out the tempo of sadness and dread. Fear. Terror.

His Dirty Harry Callahan imitation only went so far, then the real Mike Faricy came out to play.

God, not now. He had to be superhuman.

Mike blinked, trying to focus in the dusty darkness. No sound, no movements. He was alone. Then what had he heard? Where had the music come from? As if on cue, muted sounds again drifted to his ears. Closing his eyes for only a moment, he focused on the noise. Definitely music—no doubt about it. A piano.

Was he losing his mind?

The music continued, fluctuating from faintly distinguishable to almost silent. It was real.

Breathing very slowly, Mike suspected he inhaled more dust than oxygen, but it didn't matter. He'd erupt internally before he'd let himself sneeze.

Seconds ticked by as he continued to search the room. The only distinguishable shapes were the French doors, where faint surreal light came through. His gaze was drawn to that light, where the gray fog played tricks behind the dirty glass.

What was that?

His heart pounded louder, faster as he watched the minimal movement of light and gray outside the doors. A darker, more solid shape stirred beyond the glass, then paused to turn toward him.

A face—a man—stared through the French doors.

They'd found him—he was a dead man.

Milton's flunky had mustered his courage, after all. Slowly, Mike reached across his chest and inside his open jacket. The hard butt of his gun offered a false sense of security. Mike knew he couldn't possibly win against all of Milton's men.

Still, he'd die trying.

The doorknob rattled, then the French doors slowly squeaked open. Mike swallowed hard, preparing himself to do battle again.

"Come on out, Mike," the man said in a deep, self-assured voice. "I mean you no harm. I'm here to help you."

Help, my ass. That voice couldn't possibly belong to the one Milton's men had left behind. True, Mike had called for backup, but they wouldn't be looking for him in this dump. Besides, he knew everyone on the force and, despite the darkness, Mike felt positive this guy wasn't one of them.

"Hiding is pointless. I can see you."

It was a trick. Mike ground his teeth together, itching to pull the trigger. Suddenly, the need for revenge overpowered common sense. Mike felt a rush of hatred, so powerful it overtook all sense of reason. Like a slow but insidious poison, revulsion seeped through his veins.

Scrambling to his feet, he lunged toward the silhouette in the darkness, still clutching his weapon in his right hand. With lightning reflexes, the man gripped Mike's wrist with one hand.

"You ready to talk now, Mike?"

The man's bone-wrenching grip dug through Mike's skin and straight to the marrow. Forced to his knees, then immobilized, Mike clenched his teeth, struggling against the urge to drop his gun in surrender to this strange and powerful enemy. "Who the devil are you?"

The man chuckled—the sound echoed mockingly through the vast emptiness. "Ah, now that's an interesting choice of words. I probably should thank you for the promotion."

Mike shook his head, trying to determine which words the man found interesting. "Go ahead and kill me—get it over with, you bastard."

"Oh, rest assured, I've been called worse." The man sighed, then jerked Mike's wrist until his gun flew across the room as if propelled by some invisible force. "Your weapon is useless against me."

"Oh, yeah? Why don't we give it a try? I'd like to see for myself."

The intruder laughed again, a sick, menacing sound that made Mike shudder. "There isn't enough time for that."

"I've got all night," Mike said steadily.

"And I have tonight *and* eternity." The man sounded bored with life. "Trust me, even that isn't enough time."

Mike shook his head as his own mad laughter consumed him, shaking the foundations of his sanity. This was too damned much. Why the hell didn't his captor just kill him and get it over with—put him out of his misery?

What about Carrie?

"Yes, what about your darling sister, Mike?"

Mike's laughter died an instant death as he jerked his head around to stare through the darkness at the creep who still imprisoned his wrist. He blinked several times, continuing to gape at this strange man. "How—"

"There's something you want. My boss sent me here because I know there's some way I can be of . . . service to you," he said in an infuriatingly calm voice, though there was an intensity to it that belied his more obvious attempt at sincerity. "All you have to do is name it, Mike, and it's yours."

"Something I want?" Mike swallowed hard, feeling strangely desperate to reveal his need. It was a need more powerful and insistent than any he'd known in his entire life.

It was almost as if this man drew it from him—reached right inside his core and yanked the truth from him.

"Yeah, there's something I want, but you can't give it to me. Nobody can," Mike confessed before he could stop himself. "I'd give anything . . ." What the hell did he have to lose?

"Anything at all to—shall we say—*turn back the clock?*" His voice took on a mesmerizing song-like quality, luring Mike into a trusting state.

"Turn back the clock?" Mike echoed, trying to resist being sucked in by this guy's hypnotic voice, but it was a constant battle. There was an odd, powerful presence about him, more significant than the superhuman strength which enabled him to hold Mike powerless at his feet.

"Of course." The peculiar man gave a dramatic sigh. "Really, Mike, how else can we undo *all* that's happened tonight?"

"What . . . ?" A cold sweat popped out on his forehead. "You're frigging nuts, man."

"Let's see—today's June twentieth, so all we have to do is make it June nineteenth. Right?"

"Sure. Just snap your fingers and make it yesterday." Mike squeezed his eyes shut for a moment. God, how he wished he could really do just that. If only he could go back in time to stop what had happened, to make Barney live again.

"So be it."

Fool! he chided himself, trying to regain control of his thoughts and actions. No one could undo the horrible events of this night. Not even God.

The man suddenly threw his head back and laughed out loud. It was a terrifying sound. Monstrous.

A streak of lightning illuminated the mansion, sending dancing sparks to the tips of the man's fiery hair. For a brief moment, Mike's gaze locked with his. The man's eyes were—

Impossible.

Another lightning bolt revealed the truth. The man's eyes were red, glowing with a feral power that left Mike paralyzed. The flesh around his mouth tingled and he felt hollow inside.

Now, even in darkness, those red eyes glowed, holding Mike prisoner in his own body.

He had to fight this, whatever it was. This madman wanted something, and every instinct in Mike's body screamed in favor of escape.

Every instinct but one.

His need for revenge.

Common sense rallied, trying to seize control for a flickering moment. Mike jerked his wrist, but the stranger held him fast.

"I don't know who the hell you are or what you want, and I really don't give a rat's ass," Mike lied, unconvincing even to his own ears.

"Mike, Mike," the man said with that same taunting, strangely soothing tone. He was like a used car salesman moving in for the kill. "I'm here to give you your heart's desire—what you want more than anything else. I'm going to allow you to go back in time." He chuckled quietly. "You said you'd give anything . . ."

A sense of foreboding filled Mike, but he forced it into submission. "Yeah, anything. Everything." His voice sounded hoarse, barely more than a strangled whisper. Why was he buying into this jerk's sick game? Then the brilliance of those red eyes intensified, forcing Mike's doubts to whither beneath an onslaught of fierce hunger.

Blood-lust.

He would have his revenge. Satisfaction. And more importantly . . . Barney would live to raise his child. Madness claimed him and Mike barked a derisive, and strangely victorious, laugh. Though the bastard hadn't yet spoken the words, here it was, out in the open at last. Mike knew.

"Yeah, hotshot. Even my worthless, fucking soul!"

Chapter Two

"Lord have mercy!"

The frantic words and running footsteps shot right through Abigail Kingsley, making her sit upright in bed with a start. She clutched her mended gown to her throat. The voice belonged to her friend and servant—nothing to fear there. The woman's tone, however, created a tremor in Abigail's very soul, awakening memories best forgotten.

Hurried footsteps sounded in the hallway as she threw back the patchwork quilt and swung her legs to the floor. She stood just as her bedroom door burst open and Rosalie rushed inside.

Perspiration dampened the woman's dark face; tendrils of black hair had crept from the coiled braid at the top of her head, framing her wide, frightened eyes with wiry curls.

"What is it?" Abigail swallowed the lump in her throat, reminding herself that the war was over. Her fears were unfounded.

Weren't they?

"There's a man, Miss Abigail," Rosalie whispered urgently, her eyes widening further. "In the great hall."

"A man?"

"A stranger."

"What's he doing?"

Rosalie shrugged and shook her head. "Sleepin' on the floor, but he near scared me outta two years' growth."

Abigail squeezed her eyes shut and said a quick prayer. "Lord, please don't let him be another Yankee." She opened her eyes and cast a furtive glance at her servant.

"Or a hungry soldier from either army," Rosalie added, pressing her lips together in a thin line. "We done fed enough of them from both sides."

Abigail nodded, trying not to think about the knot of hunger in the pit of her own stomach. Over the course of the war, she'd grown accustomed to never having quite enough to eat. Provided Wade had adequate nourishment to sustain his growing body, she would survive. Her priorities were clear and simple.

But right now, there was a man in the great hall.

Asleep, thank God. With any luck, she had time to dress before having to confront the intruder. Abigail rushed to the corner and pulled a simple muslin frock from a peg, then draped it over a cane-backed chair while she removed her nightgown. After slipping the faded blue work dress over her head, she splashed her face with water to clear the sleep from her eyes. She needed her wits about her this morning.

"Who is he, Rosalie?" she asked hopefully, hurriedly buttoning her bodice. "Is it someone we know? One of the Monroes, maybe?"

"No, Miss Abigail. I done told you he's a stranger." Rosalie's young face was thin and her expression anxious. "This ain't nobody I ever seen before."

Abigail's stomach gave a lurch. "Listen, I want you to go to Wade's room and sneak outside with him while I find out who the man is . . . and what he wants."

"I ain't gonna let you go down there by yourself." Rosalie folded her arms across her chest and thrust her lower lip out stubbornly. "Your daddy's last words was tellin' me to take care of you."

Abigail's heart swelled with love for this young woman, more friend than servant. They were only two months apart in age, yet Abigail felt years older. "I'm asking you to stay with Wade. Please?"

Rosalie's lower lip, so stubborn a moment ago, now trembled and a lonely tear trickled down her coffee-colored cheek. "Yes, Miss Abigail."

"Thank you." Abigail reached out and hugged Rosalie, then ushered her out the door. She watched until Rosalie disappeared through the door across the hall, then Abigail rushed to retrieve her father's pistol from behind the bureau.

"Dear God, I hope I never really need to use this thing." She fought rising panic and won, throwing her shoulders back and lifting her chin. "Again."

She rushed to her bedroom door and caught a glimpse of herself in the mirror. Stunned by her appearance, Abigail froze for a fleeting moment. She looked like a wild woman, with her dark hair having worked itself free of its nightly braid. It hung in ripples to her waist, uncombed and frightfully shocking even to her. Her gaze dropped to the reflection of the old dueling pistol clutched in her hand, reminding her with a start that a stranger lurked downstairs.

Biting her lower lip, she turned to the open door and peered into the hall. She found nothing but peeling wallpaper and the tattered remnants of the Persian carpet runner which had once been a great source of pride to her mother. Somewhat grateful her mother wasn't alive to see the decline of her home, Abigail drew a deep breath and concealed the gun within the folds of her skirt as she tiptoed toward the wide staircase.

One step at a time, constantly sweeping the great hall with her frightened gaze, Abigail made her way down. Why hadn't she extracted more information? Abigail didn't even know exactly where her servant had seen the stranger.

Foolish, Abigail, she chided, clutching the bannister with her free hand while her gaze continued to dart about the great hall. Where was he? Could Rosalie have imagined the stranger?

No. Something very real had incited Rosalie's fear.

Something terrifying.

A stranger in the house.

A man.

Abigail bridled the trepidation which threatened to diminish what little courage she'd managed to muster, and scanned the room again for any sign of movement.

The sun was just now peeking above the horizon, replacing faint gray with brilliant colors spilling through the broken glass in the east windows. A mosaic of pinks, violets, yellows, and blues splayed across the great hall, creating long shadows along the broad expanse of bare floor.

A streak of darker pink caught her eye. Abigail's wary gaze followed the stripe to the opposite side of the room near the piano and the twin staircase. Something dark punctuated the end of the brilliant pink—a shape on the floor.

It moved.

It moaned.

God, give me strength, but please . . . do hurry. Abigail's palms perspired, making the heavy gun slip in her hand. Using her free hand, she adjusted the gun's weight and tightened her grip, then inched her way toward the shape. Rosalie'd been correct—it was a man.

A stranger.

Steadily, she approached him. He lay on his side with his back to her. His hair was light brown and worn very short. His chest rose and fell steadily with his regular breathing, interrupted by an occasional moan.

Her gaze traveled slowly along his length as he slept. Broad shoulders tapered to a slender waist and hips. His legs were long, encased in snug-fitting trousers.

Blue.

A Yankee?

She looked again—her heart thundered so fast she could probably dance a reel to its rhythm. Yes, they were blue, but not the blue wool of a Union Army uniform. Perhaps he wasn't a Yankee, after all.

Following the seam of his trousers downward, she paused. The strangest shoes she'd ever seen encased his rather large feet. They were black and even from this distance she felt certain they'd feel soft to the touch. Soldiers wore sturdy boots or nothing. With increasing frequency, nothing was the norm for the young men she'd fed and nursed back to health during their homeward journeys.

He groaned again, then flopped onto his back. Abigail gasped and retreated a step, nearly dropping the gun still hidden within the folds of her skirt. Groaning again, he brought one large, tanned hand to his forehead, furrowing his face as if in great pain.

Was he injured?

She looked again for any sign of illness or injury. This man appeared to be in far better condition than his predecessors. Still, there was something amiss—she felt certain of it.

His lips parted in a grimace and he bent his left knee, then his right. His free hand rested across his flat midsection. A wide leather belt with a silver buckle encircled his waist. Shamelessly, she shifted her attention lower. For a fleeting, scandalous moment, her gaze lingered.

Compared to the sickly, ragtag soldiers who'd trudged along the river, trying desperately to make their way home, this man bloomed with vigor.

She felt selfish and awful for taking pleasure in finding a man whose flesh had not been torn, whose bones seemed intact. Even asleep on her floor, he exuded strength.

Virility.

"Goodness," she whispered, as a flash of heat flooded her face. She inched closer, leaning slightly over him to stare down at his face.

This was the face of a man who'd seen much of life—not all good, she suspected. Fine lines etched the corners of his closed eyes. Dark lashes rested gently against his cheeks, in direct contrast to the hard contours of his sculpted features. His nose was a little crooked, but rather than diminish his appeal, it gave him a rakish quality she couldn't help but admire.

Lowering her gaze, she looked at his mouth—full lips relaxed in slumber. Dark beard stubble marred his complexion, though a few scars revealed this was a far from flawless face anyway. He wasn't perfect, but he was more impressive than any man had a right to be these days.

He obviously hadn't fought in the war, or if he had, he'd

fared much better than the men she'd seen these past weeks. But in which army had he served?

If he'd served.

The possibility that this healthy stranger could be a dangerous criminal crept back into Abigail's mind. She must seize control of her wayward thoughts. Rosalie and Wade were waiting for her to make sure they were safe.

Well, there was only one way to make certain.

Nudging him in the ribs with her bare toe, Abigail tightened her grip on the heavy pistol. He shifted very slightly and turned toward her, pinning her foot beneath his arm.

Then she saw it.

He had a gun.

God, please don't make me have to shoot him. The thought of pulling the trigger and taking another human life, even in self-defense, nauseated her. *Not again, God. Please, never again.*

Her foot numbed beneath his weight. Wriggling her toes, she eased her appendage out from under him until she liberated it, never shifting her gaze from the gun he wore strapped across his broad chest. With a sigh, she prepared to take a step back from him when his hand snaked out to grab her bare ankle in a brutal grip.

"Who the hell are you?" he growled.

"Unhand me!"

It was a woman.

Mike blinked several times to clear his vision. His head felt as if a novice neurosurgeon had performed a lobotomy on him for practice.

And botched it.

She tried to wrench her foot free, but he tightened his grip in response. Memories tore at him, every bit as fierce as her jerking and twisting. She tried once to kick him with her other foot, but he foiled her efforts with one quick tug, depositing her on the floor at his side.

She went after him with both feet then. "Hey, settle down."

Mike shifted himself into a semi-sitting position. "Chill, lady and let me think."

"Let go of me!" she shouted, still struggling.

"No way—not until I figure out what the hell happened to me last night." Mike swallowed hard. His mouth tasted like the morning after a forty-eight-hour drunk.

Then he remembered and his stomach lurched—his pulse could have outrun the Bionic Man. *Damn.* He closed his eyes against reality. Barney.

Barney was dead.

With a sinking feeling in his heart, Mike's eyes flew open. Another memory plucked at his sanity—he was really losing it. As his gaze swept the room, images of the evening past became clearer. Undeniable.

Had he truly sold his soul? This was crazy—the stuff of cheap horror films. But the image of the laughing man with the red eyes refused to leave Mike's mind. It was as vivid as the mental picture of Barney's sightless eyes staring up at the warehouse ceiling.

Dead eyes.

Mike's gut gave a decisive twist of protest. Not Barney.

Again, he saw Barney's face beneath his narrow penlight beam. Dead.

Really dead.

"Oh, God," he muttered, squeezing his eyes shut against the pain, which only served to intensify the images in his mind.

And this woman. Who was she? How did she fit into this insanity? She was still now. He ventured a glance at her face. She sat staring at him with wide blue eyes.

Nearly paralyzed with grief, Mike stared at her for several minutes. His mind wanted to deny the brutal facts, and the handiest defense mechanism at the moment was concentrating on this strange woman.

"Who are you?" he croaked, trying unsuccessfully to moisten his dry lips. His tongue felt like sandpaper.

"I . . ." She lowered her gaze for a moment, then lifted her chin and looked right into his eyes. "I believe you're the one who should be answering questions, sir. You *are* trespassing."

"Trespassing?" Mike chuckled, then coughed, never releasing her ankles. "In this dump?"

She bristled visibly and renewed her efforts to kick him. "Let me go!"

"Will you stop kicking me . . . and just tell me your name?"

"No, sir. I will not." She kicked both her feet, yanking against his tight hold. Suddenly, she ceased her efforts. "Abigail Kingsley. Now let me go," she whispered. "Please?"

Her chin quivered very slightly. *Great.* The last thing in the world he needed this morning was a crying woman on his hands. Of course, when he broke the news to Carrie . . .

"Damn."

She whimpered.

"Don't . . . don't cry." He winced, releasing both her ankles simultaneously. "I'm not going to hurt you. There's been enough of that already."

He wasn't surprised when she scooted away until several feet of scarred wood flooring separated them. She held one hand at an odd angle in her lap. Had she injured it when he jerked her feet out from under her?

"You—who are you?" she asked in a quivery voice. "Why are you here?"

"Mike Faricy. What am I doing here? Damned if I know." Mike sat up straight and dragged his fingers through his hair. "I have to go now anyway. The place is all yours."

Again, he saw the image of that strange man. It must have been a dream.

A nightmare.

He shot the woman a suspicious glance. "Are we the only ones here? I mean—are we alone?" The unintentionally sharp edge to his voice made her shift farther away. "I'm sorry. I thought there was a man here last night."

She furrowed her brow and shook her head very slowly. "You're the only man here, sir . . . and you shouldn't be."

"No." He chuckled cynically. "You're right. I shouldn't be." What the hell happened to him last night? First Barney, then . . .

The devil?

Bitter laughter skipped over his tongue and filled the room. So he sold his soul? For what? For something impossible. This was a sick day for Mike Faricy. Sick, sick, sick.

Staggering to his feet, he fought the urge to throw something. Anything. He wanted to break things.

Milton's neck, for starters.

Think, Mike. Obviously, he must've come in here last night and passed out from exhaustion. That devil business had been nothing but a bad dream.

If only Barney's death could be so simply explained. How he wished he could pull off a television miracle, like Bobby Ewing in the shower after a full season's absence from "*Dallas.*" If only he could walk over to Barney and Carrie's house and find them eating breakfast in their sunny kitchen.

Maybe.

He looked down at his hands, flexing his fingers and examining them. Reddish brown stains edged his fingernails.

Blood.

Barney's blood.

"Oh, God." He dragged a deep breath that sounded more like a sob. "He's dead."

"Dead?"

When he met her gaze, he saw a combination of emotions flicker across her face. Fear. Compassion. Confusion. Pity?

Yes, he should be pitied. Any man desperate enough to imagine having sold his soul to the devil deserved pity. *Get a grip, Mike. You're a real basket case.*

"Who's dead?"

Unable to answer, Mike looked at her again—*really* looked at her. She was a knockout.

She had enough hair to make wigs for all the fancy ladies in the Daughters of the Confederacy. A wild mane of midnight curls surrounded her small face. Her cheeks were flushed pink and her chin slightly pointed. A few freckles garnished her slightly upturned nose, and her mouth . . .

Those lips looked moist and soft.

Kissable.

Damn. Despite the numbed state of his emotions, Mike

couldn't prevent his body's instinctive response to the sight of a beautiful woman. It didn't matter that his mind continuously struggled against the horrors of last night. His libido just didn't give a damn.

But he did.

Mike's head started to pound as guilt overshadowed desire. Here he stood, thinking about sex while his sister was about to learn that her husband was dead. That their baby would grow up without a father . . .

"Look, I don't know who you are or what you're doing here," he said steadily, then paused to swallow the lump in his throat. "It doesn't really matter anyway. I have to be going now. You have a nice day, ma'am."

He turned toward the door, then froze. How the hell was he going to do this? Just walk up to Carrie and blurt it out? *Hey, Sis. Sorry, but Barney got shot and they dumped his body in the river.*

Dropping his chin to his chest, Mike squeezed his eyes shut. Carrie needed him—he had to get his act together. "I . . . I'm sorry."

He heard her scramble to her feet behind him, and when he half-turned, expecting to find her gone, he was stunned to find her walking slowly toward him. She looked nervous— frightened.

That was understandable. He must look like the dev—

Devil. There it was again. He lifted his hand to scratch the back of his neck, but a sharp pain in his wrist gave him pause. Flexing his hand, he held it out in front of him and examined his wrist. He rotated it to check the inside . . . and froze.

Fingerprints.

Purple, finger-shaped marks ringed his wrist. His heart lurched and a buzzing sound started in his head. "Holy Mother of—"

"Sir?"

He jerked his head around to face her, only a few feet away from him. "Did you see him?" Mike demanded, taking two long strides toward her. He stopped in front of her and looked down into her frightened eyes. "Tell me. Did you see the man?"

"I . . . I told you there was no other man." Her voice quivered. "Please. You said you were leaving."

"I can't—not yet." He studied her face. She was hiding something. Reflexively, he reached out and grabbed her upper arms with both hands. "Tell me what happened. Where did he go? Who was he?"

Panic thundered through his veins, intent on destroying the filament of sanity remaining to him.

She shook her head and a tear slid down her left cheek. "I don't know who you're talking about," she whispered. "Please, release me."

Mike's gaze dropped to her open collar. She'd obviously been in a hurry this morning, because the front of her old-fashioned dress was buttoned crooked, gaping open to reveal the tops of her full breasts.

Sweat popped from every pore on his body and his blood supply took a detour straight to his crotch. A hairpin curve sign couldn't do justice to the situation in which his responsive body suddenly found itself.

His explosive physical reaction to her stunned him. How could he want a woman this fiercely when his entire world had been turned upside down?

Though he told himself it was insanity, he burned to touch this woman in every intimate way he could imagine, and he could imagine plenty. That hair. Those breasts. Her lips . . .

He was on fire.

"You're beautiful," he whispered, feeling her flinch at his words.

"Please . . . ?"

Something in her voice drew him back to reality, away from the dark pit of insanity which beckoned to him, giving false promises of miracles and respite from his grief.

Horse shit.

Barney was dead and there'd been no devil's minion here to bargain with last night. He dropped his hands to his sides.

"I'm . . . sorry," he whispered, then drew a ragged breath. "I really have to go. I didn't mean to frighten you."

"Why did you come here?"

He met her gaze, surprised she'd spoken again. "To hide." He chuckled and shook his head, turning away from her again to the French doors he'd entered last night. "I was running for my miserable life."

Silence.

He looked at her over his shoulder. "You don't believe me, do you?" Rolling his eyes in disbelief, he muttered, "It doesn't matter."

Very slowly, he approached the doors and reached for the handle. Time to face Carrie. He'd postponed this as long as possible.

He gave the handle a sharp twist, amazed when it swung open easily, no squeaking or groaning like last night. A sudden suspicion shot through him and he turned to scan the room again.

It was clean.

Last night, the cobwebs and dust had been so thick he could scarcely breathe. This was nuts. Though much of the furniture was badly in need of replacement, everything was immaculate. Even the floor, though scarred, had a clean sheen to it.

"Weird." He raked his hand through his hair, wincing as his bruised wrist reminded him again of his nightmare. *Dammit, nightmares don't leave bruises behind.* He looked down at his wrist again. The marks were still there.

Enough. Drawing a deep breath, he stepped outside and froze.

If he ever tried to explain what he saw, the brass would have him kicked off the force for good. The department would have no problem having him declared unstable for this one.

"Where the hell is Natchez?"

She approached quietly and stepped outside to stand beside him on the porch. He glanced once at her from the corner of his eye. "Natchez?" she echoed. "About three miles downriver, where it's always been."

Mike whirled around to stare at her—his pulse had just

darted from the starting gate at Churchill Downs. "What did you say?"

He towered over her by several inches, but right now all he wanted were answers. Turning to gaze out across the open field and forests surrounding the house, he shook his head. "I don't get it. Where the hell'd the damned city go?"

"Sir, I really think you should go now." She took a step back toward the open door behind them.

Mike's throat swelled, threatening to cut off his breath. Perspiration drenched his body and he had to take a leak so bad he could taste it. He was tired, uncomfortable, confused as hell, and depressed—not a good combination. "Don't mess with me, lady," he warned. "I asked a simple question, and I damned well want an answer."

She stiffened, lifting her chin a notch to glower at him. "I've had all of your foul language I'm going to tolerate this morning, sir." With a toss of her head, she whirled around and stomped back inside.

Mike ground his teeth together and reached one hand out to grab her arm. As he pulled her around to face him, she lifted the hand she'd been holding at the strange angle, leveling a huge antique gun straight at his gut.

"Don't make me use this," she pleaded, her voice betraying her fear. "I promised God I'd never kill another man, but I swear—"

"*Another* man?" The absurdity of his situation made Mike laugh. He couldn't help it.

She must have thought him certifiable. Maybe he was. One thing he knew for sure—in all his years as a cop, if he'd ever aimed his gun at someone who started laughing like he was, he'd probably have shot them. Hell, shooting him would be merciful at this point. He'd totally lost his mind anyway. What good would he be to Carrie in this condition?

"I have no idea what you find so amusing, sir," she said, taking another step toward the open door, "but I would appreciate it if you would leave here at once."

Mike's laughter faded away as he continued to stare at her. "Oh, I'd love to, lady." He shrugged. "But I don't know where the hell I am, or how to get to Natchez. Hell, I should *be* right on the edge of town.''

He turned to stare out across the countryside again. ''This is wild.''

Placing a fist on each hip, he counseled himself on the wisdom of turning his back on a presumably loaded gun, but decided it really didn't matter if she shot him. He couldn't be any worse off than he already was, losing his mind.

He saw nothing but trees, grass, birds, a squirrel, and a few flowers. ''Amazing.''

''Please, go.''

He turned slowly to face her again. ''I told you, I don't know where to go.'' He swallowed and tried to ignore the burning in his eyes. How could he find Carrie to tell her about Barney if he didn't know where he was? Couldn't God have let him keep his sanity long enough to help his baby sister?

Anything to turn back the clock . . .

He shook his head, trying to rid himself of the memory. That hellish nightmare tormented him again.

I'm here to give you your heart's desire, Mike.

''No.'' He pressed his hands over his ears. ''No, this can't be happening.''

Let's see . . . today is June twentieth, so all we have to do is make it June nineteenth. Right?

The memory was vivid—a blade, honed to a deadly edge. He hadn't imagined that conversation, though he sure as hell could've been mistaken about the identity of the bastard. He'd probably been nothing more than some sick creep playing games with Mike's mind. That was all. The devil?

Hell, no.

He met her gaze again, not bothering to check to see if she still held the gun. He knew without looking that she did.

He had to ask. It was insane—*he* was insane. Still, he had to hear someone say the words. He needed confirmation that he was still alive—still sane.

Just in case.

''What . . . day is it?'' he asked, noticing the slight flicker of concern sweep across her face. *Yes, pity me, pretty lady. Anything—as long as you answer me.* "Please?"

"It's Monday."

Mike slowly shook his head. "No, please." He released the breath he didn't realize he'd been holding. "The date. I know it's June, but I've lost track . . ."

She took another step back, narrowing her eyes in open suspicion. "If I tell you, will you leave?"

He nodded. "The *date?*" His voice was hoarse, cracking with tension. Did he believe in this hocus pocus stuff? Could he have really sold his soul? Did he want it to be true?

Yeah, if it'll bring Barney back.

"Tell—me—the—*date!*"

"It's June nineteenth."

"Nineteenth," he echoed. A dull roar began in Mike's head, surpassing the buzz he'd heard earlier. Had he heard her correctly? No—impossible. It couldn't be.

"Are you sure?" he demanded, wondering how he could be overheard above the noise in his head. Then his gaze took in her strange attire again and an even more bizarre possibility struck him. *Oh, God—it couldn't be.* "What . . . year is it?"

"Are you . . . all right, sir?"

Her voice sounded as if they were talking inside a tin can. He shook his head to rid himself of the deafening roar, but it grew louder. "Just tell me the year, dammit!"

"1865."

A face appeared in his mind, surrounded by darkness. He saw nothing but that hideous face with glowing red eyes.

A laughing face.

The devil's face.

Abigail had never seen anyone move as fast as Mr. Faricy did as he ran away from the house. "What in heaven's name . . . ?" She stared after the retreating figure, wondering what nightmare had summoned terror in a grown man.

Resisting the urge to sag to the porch floor in relief, she shook her head, then turned to go inside. She should call upstairs

to let Rosalie know it was safe for her to bring Wade down
now, but she hesitated. It might be best to wait until she was
certain the man wouldn't return.

A ludicrous impulse to run after him and bring him back,
to offer him comfort and try to help Mr. Faricy through his
turmoil surfaced, but she quickly quelled it. Something about
the stranger tugged at her heart, and other regions of her body
that had little or nothing to do with altruism.

More than a few years had passed since a handsome man
last wreaked havoc on Abigail Kingsley's demeanor. Yet the
strange, tormented soul who'd passed through her home this
morning, touched a part of her she'd thought dead and buried
long ago.

Before the war, when she'd been young and untroubled,
eager to live life in all its splendor, she had suitors. Many
young men from the county called on her, and some of them
even asked her father for her hand in marriage.

There had been a few stolen kisses in Mama's rose garden
with Tom Monroe. With a flash of heat to her face, she recalled
another time when Andrew Montague had not only kissed her
with his mouth open, but had also allowed his hand to brazenly
brush against her breast.

Though she'd harbored no ardent romantic notions toward
Andrew, her perplexing reaction to that incident had been terrifying yet wondrous. In her youthful curiosity, she'd relished
the moment of experimentation, the barest hint of what could
be . . .

Hopes, dreams, a young girl's desires, had all come to a
brusque standstill in the spring of 1861 when the world as she
knew it ceased to exist. Now, years later, she'd once again
discovered the sweet ache of desire deep in her belly. When
the mysterious Mr. Faricy's gaze had roamed over her face and
down her throat to linger at her bosom, a fierce throb of longing
had caught her unprepared.

And terrified her at the same time.

Her heart smarted from the pain she'd seen so vividly in his
eyes. She couldn't help but believe that gazing into his eyes
this morning was like looking into his very essence. For some

reason, she felt a connection to the strange man. The need to help him through his problems coursed through her anew.

No. She mustn't dwell on the enigmatic Mr. Faricy any longer. Such irrational thoughts would be the ruination of her yet. It was impractical and downright improper for her to harbor such fancies for a perfect—albeit slightly damaged—stranger.

"Enough of this, Abigail." She hurried to the kitchen, pausing briefly to glance out the window, surprised to find her son and Rosalie outside. They'd obviously left the house by the back stairway while she dealt with the intruder. It was just as well. She needed to delay facing Wade's constant hunger awhile longer.

Abigail rummaged through the pantry, trying not to remember the days when everything she could possibly want to eat had been readily available. If her craving was for something exotic, her father had invariably arranged for it to be brought from New Orleans.

Now *anything* nourishing and filling would be considered a delicacy in the Kingsley household. Alas, a bit of cornmeal in a metal canister was all her foraging managed to produce.

"Cornbread again." She looked forlornly into the tin container. If only it could be *real* cornbread with all the proper ingredients it might be more tolerable. This would be nothing more than a barely edible fried paste of cornmeal and water.

"And this is the very last." She had no choice. A trip to Natchez to spend the few coins she'd managed to cache was unavoidable. She could delay no longer.

"Miss Abigail," Rosalie called, pausing to scrape her feet on the back porch before entering the kitchen. "You ain't gonna believe this. Look here what Wade done found. Ain't them beauties?"

A small smiling face emerged from behind Rosalie's skirt as Abigail moved closer to inspect the treasures gingerly removed from the girl's voluminous pockets. A perfect pair of brown-speckled eggs sat in Rosalie's outstretched hands.

"Eggs?" Abigail looked at her two-year-old son in confusion. "You found these, Wade? Where?"

"Barn." The little boy moved from behind Rosalie, pride evident in his deportment. "Me find."

Rosalie smiled. "I told him they was for eatin', but I don't think he believed me."

Of course, Wade had never even seen an egg. Abigail nodded when he looked at her with a question in his eyes. "Yes, Wade. If we cook these, you can eat them. They're good." *Very good.*

He pointed to the eggs, then to his mouth.

Abigail met Rosalie's dark glittering gaze, noticing a tear trickle unheeded down her friend's cheek. At this moment, like so many others, Abigail felt that strong sense of family—a desperate need for the three of them to remain together, no matter what. Rosalie's tears were bittersweet. Their gazes locked—words were unnecessary.

Wade would not go hungry this morning.

Abigail laughed and cried at the same time as she knelt beside her son and gathered his small, warm frame against her. "Wade, we'll scramble them for you. I promise you'll like it."

Nodding, a grin lit his face—a face lacking the roundness typical in most children his age. If only she hadn't lost her milk so early, perhaps he wouldn't be so thin. Maybelle, the midwife from the neighboring plantation, had assured Abigail that was normal for a woman not receiving enough to eat.

Abigail would have given everything within her power to continue feeding her son by any possible means. "Scrambled it is, then." Her throat felt full, tight.

Forcing a smile, she touched his soft cheek with the tips of her fingers. "Very special scrambled eggs for the best egg-hunter in Mississippi."

Rosalie chuckled as Abigail straightened and took the precious eggs from her friend's open hands. "Thank you," Abigail whispered, steeling herself against the threatening tears.

As she turned to take a small wooden bowl from the shelf above the stove, Rosalie said, "It's a good thing I don't like eggs myself."

Abigail's heart swelled with love for her lifelong friend as Rosalie walked over to the counter and cracked the eggs open, depositing their sunny yolks in the bowl. Rosalie beat them with the only fork which hadn't been stolen by scavengers or raiders.

Feeling a tiny tug on the back of her skirt, Abigail glanced down at her son. His soft brown eyes were round with curiosity. "Mama, too?"

Her breath snagged in her throat at his words. Mama would love to eat eggs, salty ham, biscuits, thick red-eye gravy, grits . . .

No, stop! She was breaking her rule for the second time this morning by thinking about the impossible. "No, Mama's not hungry for eggs today, Wade," she lied, stroking his blond curls.

He seemed satisfied with her explanation, so Abigail took his hand and led him to the scarred table while Rosalie poured the beaten eggs into the skillet and stood guard over them as if they were more valuable than gold. In a way, they were.

There she went again with her dreaming. Biting the inside of her cheek in self-castigation, she grabbed her small son beneath his arms and lifted him to his chair. She couldn't resist burying her nose in his soft hair, inhaling the scent that was his alone. He was hers—a part of her. It didn't matter how or why that miracle had come to pass. What mattered most was Wade's health and happiness. Whatever it took, she'd ensure his well-being.

After playfully ruffling his hair with her hand, Abigail turned to retrieve a tin plate and cup from hooks on the wall beside the stove. All the china and crystal the Kingsleys had owned before the war had either been stolen or broken. Every single piece.

If her mother wasn't already dead, that knowledge would've killed her for certain.

Abigail filled a cup with spring water and placed it before her son to watch him take greedy gulps. What she'd give for a pint of milk to accompany the eggs . . .

No, don't think about that. It was a foolish waste of time to dwell on the impossible. The milk cows had vanished early in the war. What hadn't been taken by the Confederate Army was taken later by the invading one. Either way, her people at Elysium must do without.

Again.

Rosalie carried a steaming skillet to the table and carefully ladled the fluffy eggs onto Wade's tin plate. His smile made the hunger pangs in her own stomach more bearable. She slid a crude, hand-carved spoon across the table.

Wade grasped the spoon and started shoveling eggs into his mouth. His eyes glazed over and he hesitated after the third mouthful. "Mama, good."

"Yes, it's very good." Abigail's eyes stung, but she didn't want Wade to see her cry, so she busied herself near the pantry while he ate in typical two-year-old fashion with his wooden spoon. "I wonder what made that ornery old hen decide to start laying again," she mused aloud, casting a questioning glance at Rosalie.

"I dunno. You reckon she know'd she was gonna be stew if she didn't?"

Laughing, Abigail turned to smile at her son, who stared at the two women with wide, curious eyes. After a moment, he resumed eating while she prepared the cornmeal paste in a skillet, then divided the concoction between herself and Rosalie.

They sat together eating in silence for several minutes. "My, that was good," Abigail said, getting to her feet. Then she gathered her basket and bonnet from nails near the back door.

"I have to go to town, Rosalie." Rosalie's resigned expression indicated her understanding. The cupboard was bare. They could delay spending the last of their money no longer.

"All right, Miss Abigail. We'll be fine."

Abigail hugged her son and kissed his soft cheek, then she stepped outside, wondering all the while how they would ever make do with what little they had left. She slipped into a stride that matched the rhythm of her internal chant: *Anything for Wade. Anything for Wade.*

Pausing near the river road, she stepped into the trees and looked in both directions. Satisfied she was unobserved, she reached into a knothole in a sturdy pine, feeling around inside the sticky crevice until she found the soft leather pouch. After removing it, she glanced briefly at the insignia that had been burned into the leather.

U.S. Army.

Murmuring a brief prayer, she poured the three remaining coins into her palm, then stuffed the incriminating pouch back into its hiding place. Now that Natchez was undoubtedly crawling with Union soldiers, it would never do for Abigail to be seen with this pouch. The possible ramifications were unthinkable.

She'd do anything to protect Wade—anything at all.

Chapter Three

Mike ran as if the hounds of hell were hot on his trail. For all he knew, that could very well be true, considering.

Where the hell's a highway or street sign when I need one? He knew if he followed the Mississippi downstream, sooner or later he'd find Natchez.

A lot farther away than it should've been.

Crazy. His heart pounded relentlessly in his chest as he ran along a dirt road that followed the winding river. Some landmarks—large boulders, cliffs, and bends in the river,—looked exactly the same as he remembered. But all these familiar sights merely lent credence to this madness—not exactly what he'd had in mind.

What he wanted was to stumble around the next curve in the road to discover this had all been nothing but a bad dream. Maybe if he stopped and just flopped down on the ground and closed his eyes, he would waken later to learn that everything was fine.

That Barney was alive?

He stepped in a rut and fell face first in the red dirt. The skin on his knees scraped away right through his Levis.

Barney was dead—Mike had to face it. No more lies. No

more denials. His best friend, his partner, his sister's husband . . . was really dead.

He made no effort to stand. Why bother? He was in hell—he might as well be dead, too. *Shit.* It should've *been* him. Mike didn't have a wife or a baby on the way. All he'd ever had were Carrie and Barney.

Carrie was alone now, probably wondering where her husband and brother had disappeared to. By now, the department would be searching for them both. Barney's body—what was left of it—might eventually be discovered downstream.

Cringing, he squeezed his eyes shut. Dust filled his nostrils and coated his lips, but he didn't give a damn. He didn't give a damn about anything right now. At least . . . not about anything he could control.

He should be there for Carrie. The words informing her of her husband's death should come from her brother—the only family she had left. Now she had no one . . .

Except the baby.

Mike stiffened and lifted his face from the dirt road. He opened his eyes. Realization struck as if Home-Run Hank Aaron had stepped up to the plate and Mike's head was a perfect fast ball.

Carrie still had her baby. A bittersweet joy swept through Mike and tears burned his eyes. One watery renegade slid down his cheek and onto his hand, making a streak of red mud where the road dirt coated his flesh.

Carrie would have her baby.

He sighed. It wasn't the same, but that knowledge offered some consolation, as he knew it would for his sister.

Irritated at himself for sniffling, Mike struggled to his feet, wincing as his jeans clung to the raw flesh of both knees. Carrie'd be okay until he could figure out how to vacate this nightmare.

He took one step, then another. The sun was bright and hot overhead, baking into his bones, clearing his foggy mind. His sister was tough—she'd handle this.

Unless . . . she didn't have to.

Mike froze and swallowed hard. He dragged his shirtsleeve across his mouth, wiping away some of the road grime.

Ridiculous.

But what if the deal he'd made with the devil really worked? What if it hadn't been a nightmare, after all?

Was Barney alive right now in his time? Was it the day before the shooting—June nineteenth instead of the twentieth? *God, I'm confused as hell.*

Did his time and this time coexist? What the hell had happened? If this was really 1865, then it didn't matter if the calendar said the nineteenth or the twentieth.

Did it?

His bargain with the devil's pawn was obviously being enforced. Mike had to consider that possibility. Otherwise, how the hell could he explain his sudden appearance in 1865? And the fact that his reluctant hostess back at the mansion had told him the date was June nineteenth?

Maybe.

A horse and buggy came around the bend, forcing Mike to jump back from the road as it passed. A woman dressed in black drove the half-starved horse. An ebony veil covered her face; her body was completely concealed to the tip of her scarred shoes. Head bowed and shoulders stooped, she could've been any age from eighteen to eighty.

Mike stared at the horse—its ribs stuck out and its head drooped. The buggy itself looked like it had once been a show-piece. A huge rip marred the upholstery beside the driver and the nearest wheel wobbled precariously as it rolled by on the rutted road.

The Civil War. Reconstruction.

"Holy shit."

He'd fallen into his eighth-grade history book. Any minute now, Sister Bernadette would nudge him on the shoulder to wake him from an impromptu nap.

I should be so lucky.

The buggy continued its journey, vanishing beyond the next curve and a stand of pine. This was more proof, wasn't it? He was really stuck in the past, so that must mean Barney was alive. Now all Mike had to do was figure out how to prevent a murder that wouldn't take place for over a century.

"Great. That's just great." He shook his head in self-disgust. *Always the sucker, Faricy.* He'd been taken in by the devil, of all things. Carrie'd always claimed that used car salesmen wept with joy when they saw Mike coming. He was about as gullible as they came.

But then, the devil wasn't exactly a fair opponent.

"Talk about upping the odds and playing dirty."

There had to be a way. Closing his eyes, he grabbed his short hair with both fists and pulled, grimacing as he struggled for an answer.

"Damn." When he opened his eyes the answer was there, simple and indisputable. No problem—all he had to do was kill every possible ancestor of the gunman.

Kill? In cold blood? Mike's empty stomach lurched in protest and the flesh around his mouth tingled. His entire adult life had been dedicated to saving lives—preventing crime. Now, here he stood in an impossible situation, faced with the prospect of committing premeditated murder—possibly more than one.

There had to be another way. This answer came too fast, though it sure as hell wasn't what he'd call easy. Maybe he could come up with another plan, though that sure didn't seem likely under the circumstances.

"Perfect." Forcing his feet to move, Mike started walking again toward town. Three miles was a long way for a man who'd been through what he had in the last ten hours, especially without food or water.

Was Barney alive and trying to figure out where his partner had vanished to? There he went again. None of this made sense.

Gee, big surprise, Einstein.

Time travel and a deal with the devil. What the hell had he expected? Logic?

Fat chance.

It was 1865, so Barney and Carrie hadn't been born yet. He had to sort through this mess. What he did here and now—in the past—could very well change the course of history.

Talk about power.

A half-smile tugged at Mike's lips, making one parched corner crack and bleed a tiny bit. Ignoring the slight sting, he visualized his sister's husband searching for him. They'd be worried, but that couldn't be helped.

The smile faded. Mike *had* to prevent Barney's death—that was a given. Did it really matter what sacrifices he'd have to make beyond what he'd already endured?

Programming himself like a computer, Mike tried to convince his conscience that he was resigned to this. Of course, there was a prerequisite. His hopes plummeted. He had to know the identity of the gunman who had fired—or would fire—the fatal shot.

Mike had no idea.

Milton's gang was better populated than any neighborhood in suburban America. Though Mike knew many of the gang members, he couldn't be sure who had actually fired the shot that killed Barney.

No, he won't *kill Barney.* Mike forced those words into his brain, praying he could make them true. He had to think positively. The horrible events of that night would never happen—he'd see to that.

No matter what.

Milton was the key. Frank Milton, Mississippi's biggest crime boss hadn't been born yet. He wouldn't be for almost a century.

No . . . he'd *never* be born. Mike's heart pitched into overdrive. God, it was so simple, yet so impossible. All he had to do was make damned sure Frank Milton was never conceived. The only way to do that was to make sure his ancestor died before propagating the next generation.

Kill.

Again, it came back to that—a life for a life. *An eye for an eye?* It seemed pretty asinine to get biblical at this late date, but he was right. Dammit, for once in his life, he didn't want to be right.

Yeah, right. Mike almost laughed. He should laugh, now that he thought about it. Barney was alive and Mike was living one hell of an adventure. Why shouldn't he laugh?

Because he *couldn't* laugh, not with the nature of his mission. Not only did he have to find someone he didn't know, but he had to snuff out that person's life.

Sighing in frustration, he continued on his journey. In the century Mike had left behind, Frank Milton would live in Natchez. That was as good a place as any to begin.

As if I have a ton of alternatives.

Mike heard the sounds of civilization in the distance. He lifted his chin and looked beyond a limestone cliff, where the road made a sharp turn, then dropped out of sight. The town of Natchez, circa 1865, sprawled out before him.

He was not impressed.

However, he was intrigued.

Without slowing his pace, he continued into town, wondering if he'd find anything even remotely familiar. Hesitating outside a large building, Mike scratched his head. This was familiar.

Damned familiar.

He stepped off the boardwalk and into the street, backing up until he could see the upper floors of the brick structure. He'd seen this building before.

Turning around slowly, he looked across the road to see if any other sights triggered his memory. Yes, the entire block was familiar. In his time, it would be a stylish section the yuppies flocked to on weekends and evenings. They called it Old Town, or something equally stupid. He couldn't be sure. The only time he'd ever visited this area, other than driving through, was during an armed robbery in a fancy Creole restaurant. And the building he'd initially found familiar would one day be used as a popular Bed and Breakfast.

He had his bearings—sort of. He might be out of time, but he wasn't out of place. This *was* Natchez, after all—his hometown. He'd been born here, grown up here, seen his best friend die here, though that would never actually happen if Mike had anything to say about it. This was home, for all that was worth in 1865.

When no one knew him.

"Mike, Mike."

A chill chased itself down his spine and settled in his gut as

Mike turned slowly. The voice was hauntingly—*sickeningly*—familiar. It couldn't be.

As he completed a half-circle, he saw a man leaning against a post in front of the brick building. He was very old; a gray beard hung nearly to his belt. A hat rode low over his eyes and ragged clothing hung from his scrawny frame.

The old-timer couldn't possibly be the owner of the voice he'd heard.

"I see you made it." The man's lips moved behind the beard.

A stab of fear shot through Mike, making his stomach knot and his flesh turn clammy. He swallowed and nodded. He was helpless—that sing-songy voice beckoned to him and controlled his actions.

Again.

"You're off on your mission, eh?" The man pushed himself away from the post and took a step toward Mike, then paused to fold his arms across his chest. "I trust you have a plan in mind?"

Mike swallowed hard, but the persistent lump of terror and rage refused to budge from his throat. This guy was everywhere. There was no escaping him.

"What the hell do you want?" Mike asked from between clenched teeth.

"Mike, Mike." The demon shook his head and chuckled. "If not for me and our little . . . bargain, you wouldn't be here at all."

"No shit."

"And Barney'd be dead."

Those words pierced Mike's heart, then a surge of hope immediately succeeded the pain. "He's . . . alive?"

"In 1865?" The man made a patronizing sound with his undoubtedly forked tongue. "But you haven't done your job yet."

"I have to know. If I . . . *do* this thing, then Barney won't die?" Mike took a step toward him, though the last thing he wanted was to get too close. "How can I be sure? Why the hell should I trust *you?*"

"Do you have a choice?"

Damn. "You know the answer to that question."

"Just keep your end of the bargain, Mike. That's all you have to worry about." The demon sighed dramatically. "The rest, as they'll say, will be history. Now that was clever." The creep laughed out loud.

Mike was definitely not amused. "What about Carrie?" he asked, trying to ignore the maniac's laughter.

The slimeball shrugged as if none of this was more important than a stray dog on a Sunday afternoon. "Hey, don't push it. We made a deal. Besides, either way she'll have her kid. Isn't that just too . . . sickly sweet?" The creature's voice dripped pure acid, then he lifted the brim of his hat and probed Mike with his laser-like gaze. Flames, searing and red, appeared in their depths.

Mesmerized, Mike could only stare for several moments. "Why are you doing this?" he asked, his voice nothing more than a ragged whisper.

"It's my job." The demon's voice grew deeper. "I'm an evil bastard, literally, since I never knew or gave a damn who my worthless father was. My mother was a whore—she didn't care either as long as she had enough cheap wine to keep her in a constant stupor." His laughter was diabolical. "When I died and went to Hell, my assignment was in family relations. Perfect, don't you think?"

"Yeah, sure." Mike tried and failed to tear his gaze from those riveting red eyes. This creep was too damned powerful. "I'm sure you'll be happy to hear I think I've figured out how to do this."

"Yeah, I know." The monster took a step nearer. "You gotta *kill* someone to make this work. That's so . . . equitable. So . . . damned appropriate."

"You're one sick bastard." Mike drew a sharp breath, struggling for the strength to snatch his gaze from the maniac, but he couldn't. The ghoul wouldn't let him. "Who are you, anyway?"

"Me? Slick Dawson when I was alive." He shrugged. "Dead, I'm just Slick—apprentice devil. Y'know, if this had happened a couple months sooner, you might've been able to save Abe Lincoln's life. Nah, that wouldn't have worked, 'cuz Booth had already cut a deal with me. Even Hell has a Supremacy Clause, y'know."

Lincoln? How many tragedies throughout history had really occurred because of a pact with the devil, or one of his minions? But what difference did it make now? Mike's fate was sealed, just like Abe's.

"We made our bargain, so why don't you just leave me alone so I can do my job?" Except Mike didn't really want to do his job. The last thing in the world he wanted was to kill someone, especially someone who wasn't shooting back. This was the pits.

But to keep the Milton gang from ever existing, he had to make damned sure the entire family became extinct before then. Another disturbing bit of irony shot through Mike's thoughts. "Oh, this is just great—I'm the frigging Terminator."

The apprentice devil laughed—loud. He threw back his head and carried on until Mike thought he'd wake the dead. Of course, Slick Dawson was already dead.

God, this is sick.

Mike had at least a hundred questions he needed answers to, but one was most urgent. "What'll happen to me after . . . ?"

The laughter ceased, but a smirk remained behind the beard. "After you finish your mission? After you've made sure Frank Milton will never be born?"

"Yeah, then." Mike hated hearing it put into words.

"Then you're *mine.*"

The maniacally laughing figure slowly reduced in size. It was easily the most bizarre thing Mike had ever seen. One minute Slick had been a little old man, then he started getting smaller and smaller, shrinking until nothing remained, like something out of a cheap horror film. Mike watched in terror mingled with awe, then walked quickly to where the devil's pawn had stood a few moments ago.

Nothing.

With a vengeance, he ground his heel into the boardwalk where the creep had stood. He knew this was wasted effort, but couldn't resist the need to vent. At least Mike could pretend the evil beast was being pulverized beneath his high top.

Pretend.

As if that would do him any good.

Or save his lousy soul.

Abigail walked slowly toward town with the shopping basket slung over her arm, thankful she finally felt almost safe leaving Rosalie and Wade at home alone. The walk was too far for a two-year-old, but she still worried about leaving them. With the war finally behind them, maybe life could get back to normal.

No, things would never be the same. She knew that. The foolish war had turned the entire world topsy-turvy. Sighing, she glanced up at the cloudless sky. Nature had a lot of nerve creating a day this perfect while so many people suffered.

As if to punctuate her thoughts, her stomach rumbled audibly. *How embarrassing.* Though she was completely alone, Abigail felt her face flood with heat. Old habits were impossible to break. Years of training refused to abandon her, even when the thought of being a lady was the least important thing in the world.

Besides, she was hungry—*really* hungry.

Her measly breakfast had been insufficient at best. Her stomach rumbled again and she placed her hand across it, squaring her shoulders. Dwelling on her hunger wouldn't appease it. After all this time, experience had taught Abigail that keeping her mind off her empty belly was the only means of surviving this nightmare.

Someday, they'd have enough to eat again. Someday, now that the war was over.

Over. The war is over.

Abigail smiled. Suddenly, she truly believed the war was over. At first it had seemed as if the news must have been about some other nation—a distant land whose people had survived hell.

No. This was very real. Lee had surrendered—no more war.

A burning sensation started in her throat. God, the price they'd all paid for the never-to-be glory of the Confederacy had been too high. Relief and anger battled each other until relief won. Fretting over the past was pointless. She knew that well enough by now.

Both her parents were dead. Her brother'd been killed early in the war. All she had left was Elysium and her little boy. Thank God Rosalie had stayed on to help.

Rosalie was family—she wouldn't leave them. At least not until they were all safe and happy again. Then maybe she might want to see something of the world.

Someday.

Abigail's thoughts strayed to this morning's surprise—the one which had preceded Wade's discovery of the blessed eggs.

The man asleep on the floor.

Who was Mike Faricy? Why had he come to them? And what had made him so distraught?

Abigail shuddered at the memory of his deranged eyes—wide and frightened. They were hazel, with thick black lashes and heavy brows. Silently, she chastised herself for remembering such details. The pain she'd seen in his eyes overshadowed her other memories of him. What had caused it?

The war?

Yet he'd seemed unscathed by the perils of soldiering—at least, outwardly. Inside—in his soul—he bled buckets, she was sure.

She paused on the outskirts of town and stared in horror at the sea of people. Three months had passed since her last trip to town. The boardwalks and streets burgeoned with humanity. The world had gone mad. There was no other explanation.

"This is Natchez?"

Men in uniforms—blue uniforms—clearly outnumbered the citizens. This was insane.

Girding her resolve, Abigail lifted her chin and stepped onto the boardwalk. She had errands to run and run them she would.

As she made her way toward the dry goods, she took in the changing sights. The sound of hammers and saws filled the air and new construction was evident on nearly every block. Someone had money, but it surely wasn't the people of Natchez.

Throngs of newcomers hurried about. Ladies dressed in fashionable attire walked along on the arms of soldiers or men wearing coats of fine linen.

Surely no one honorable had money these days.

As she passed a young man selling newspapers, Abigail wished she could afford one, but pacified herself by reading the headlines as she passed.

Confederate States Never Left Union.

"Oh, my!" Abigail's heart constricted, though she had no idea how or why this information would affect her family. Even so, this was yet another example of how insane the world had become. Of course Mississippi had left the Union with the other Confederate States. Hadn't that been the cause of the war?

"That ain't real money. What kinda fool do you take me for?"

Abigail paused to stare toward the commotion. Another voice—a memorable one—answered, though she couldn't quite understand the words.

"By God, I oughta have you thrown in jail to rot."

Something drew Abigail nearer as she strained to hear the other man's words. His back was to her, yet she felt a tug of recognition. Her gaze traveled down his back until she saw the soft leather shoes.

It was him.

Her heart flip-flopped in her breast. Why should she care about Mr. Faricy? But *why* didn't matter—the fact was, she did. Moving closer, she strained to hear his words.

"That's perfectly good money for a lousy meal." He turned toward her and she knew from his expression that he immediately recognized her.

The restaurant owner grabbed Mr. Faricy by the arm. Abigail knew that was a mistake. Mr. Faricy's gaze darkened as he shifted it away from her and turned slowly to face the man again.

"Listen," he said slowly, enunciating every syllable. "That

slop you served was barely worth what it would've cost in my time, let alone this one. I paid the bill, now let me be on my way.''

The proprietor waved a paper bill under Mr. Faricy's nose. ''This ain't money, mister. Not *real* money anyway.''

His time? Abigail wondered briefly what he'd meant by that, then forced her thoughts back to the present. Mr. Faricy must have been trying to pay for his meal with worthless Confederate currency. Surely, he must realize the futility of such effort. Against her better judgment, she stepped nearer.

''It's real, you worthless—'' Seeming to think better of his words, Mr. Faricy fell silent. ''Look, it's all I have.'' He chuckled and held his upturned palms out in front of him. ''It's good money. Honest.''

''Nope.'' The big restaurant owner nodded toward another man leaning against the hitching post. ''Fetch Captain Fletcher. Tell him I got me a deadbeat for his jail.''

''No!'' Abigail said, rushing forward. *I must have lost my mind.* ''How much does he owe?'' Her mouth was obviously determined to ignore the voice of her conscience.

The proprietor turned his attention to her with obvious reluctance. He'd obviously enjoyed harassing Mike Faricy. ''I dunno . . .''

''I'll pay you if you'll tell me how much he owes.'' Abigail avoided Mr. Faricy's probing gaze, but she felt it. Why was she doing this? It wasn't as if she could afford to.

''Four dollars.''

''Four dollars?'' Abigail knew prices had skyrocketed, but that was ridiculous. ''I only have—''

''You don't have to do this.'' Mike Faricy's words stopped her, and he reached out to grab her wrist. ''Don't . . .''

Abigail forced herself to meet his gaze; the expression in his eyes tore at her, though it was far less maniacal now. He needed her help, yet he was too proud to accept it.

Dragging her gaze from his, she reached into her pocket and withdrew one of the coins. ''Here, take this *and* Mr. Faricy's money. Surely you can make do with that.''

The man looked skeptical as he turned the coin over in his

hand to give it a thorough inspection. "Well . . . I reckon it'll do." He looked up sharply and pointed a pudgy finger at his customer. "Don't *you* ever come in here again. Got it?"

"No problem, man."

The crowd that had gathered began to dissipate, obviously disappointed the argument hadn't erupted into an all-out fistfight. She felt Mr. Faricy's gaze on her again.

"Look at me," he ordered, his voice soft and unthreatening.

Slowly, she lifted her face until she peeked at him through veiled lashes. "I . . ."

"You didn't have to do that." He released a ragged sigh and dragged his fingers through his short dark hair. "I'll bet you couldn't afford it."

She brought her gaze up sharply to probe his—a mistake. His expression was gentle, searching. Disarming.

Oh, dear. Her body warmed beneath his gaze. "I—it doesn't matter now."

"I have to repay you."

"No, it—" She hesitated. It *was* necessary. She needed that money desperately. Now she barely had enough left to buy a little cornmeal.

Again.

And even that wouldn't last long. She looked away, then quickly back again. "Yes, I do need the money."

He shot her a sardonic smile that confused her even more. "All I have is what that man wouldn't take from me," he explained with a shrug. "Unless Visa will do."

"Pardon me?"

"Never mind." His laughter was bitter, with a sharp edge to it. "I'm strong—I can work."

His work wouldn't put food on the table. Abigail searched her mind. "Can you hunt?"

He laughed out loud and several people paused on the board-walk to stare.

"People are staring at us, Mr. Faricy," she whispered urgently.

"Is that bad?" he whispered back, then continued to chuckle.

"Abigail," a shrill feminine voice called, the sound of it sending rivulets of dread down Abigail's spine.

She knew the identity of the speaker without even looking, but she forced herself to lift her gaze. "Mrs. Barnes, how nice to see you," she lied. Of all the people she should meet here in Natchez today, why did it have to be Harriet Barnes, the pastor's wife?

The woman waited in silence, obviously expecting Abigail to introduce her to the stranger. "Oh, Mrs. Barnes, may I present Mr. Faricy?" She looked up at his eyes, half-expecting him to either laugh out loud or growl at any moment. He wore the characteristics of both emotions simultaneously. "Mr. Faricy, this is Mrs. Harriet Barnes—her husband is pastor at the Baptist Church."

"Baptist? I should've known." One corner of his mouth turned downward as his gaze swept the length of Harriet Barnes. "How do you do, ma'am?" He inclined his head slightly.

"Very well, sir. It's a pleasure to meet you, Mr. Faricy." The older woman shot Abigail a look lined with suspicion, then shook her head as if to banish such thoughts. "Have you been by the Yankee headquarters, Abigail?"

"No, I haven't." She frowned. "Is there some reason I should?"

"My dear, let me tell you," the woman continued as if given permission to share some great secret. "The pompous creatures have posted a list of properties that are to be auctioned for back taxes. Can you believe they actually expect us to pay taxes for the last four years?"

Abigail felt as if she'd fallen through a hole in the board-walk—a great roar began between her ears, deafening her to the woman's words for a few moments. Then she shook herself free of the madness and grabbed the woman's bony wrist. "Tell me, Mrs. Barnes . . ."

The woman obviously didn't need to be told what Abigail needed to hear. Her expression turned grim and she nodded slowly. "Elysium is listed, Abigail. I'm sorry, child. Lord knows you've had far more than your share of burdens to bear . . ."

Abigail brought her knuckles to her mouth and bit down hard. After a moment, she lowered her hand and drew a deep breath. "Thank you for telling me, Mrs. Barnes. I appreciate it."

Harriet patted Abigail's hand, then turned her attention to Mr. Faricy. "Pardon my interference, but considering Miss Kingsley's . . . circumstances, I feel it's my duty to look after her best interests. What business do you have with Abigail?"

"Circumstances?" Mr. Faricy stiffened and Abigail couldn't help noticing his fists clench and unclench at his sides. "I beg *your* pardon, but that's none of your damned business."

The woman's face turned crimson and her cheeks puffed out as if she were about to explode. She worked her jaw, trying to speak, but settled for a breathy "Harumph," then turned and walked away, her backside bumping people as she thundered down the boardwalk.

Though a part of her felt grateful for Mr. Faricy's interference, fear of public ridicule overshadowed that fleeting emotion. Abigail felt like crying. Her reputation was in shreds already— now what would people think? What would they say?

And how would that affect Wade?

A sinking sensation swept through her. "Oh, my Lord," she mumbled, then covered her mouth with her hand. "What have you done?"

"That's a damned good question, Miss Kingsley," he said quietly, staring across the street with an expression that told her he was looking much further. Searching for something. "What have I done?"

"I . . ." Abigail faltered, drawing a deep breath before rushing ahead. "I have to go find out how much the back taxes are on Elysium." She drew a fortifying breath and squared her shoulders.

"Elysium?" He turned to face her again. "Oh, your plantation." With a sigh, he shook his head. "I knew you couldn't afford to help me, but thanks for bailing me out. I *will* repay you."

"Of course you will." Hot tears burned her eyes, but she blinked them into submission. "Good luck to you, Mr. Faricy."

"Thanks, I'm sure going to need it."

He looked at her with a profound sadness that cleaved her heart in two. The man had no money, and she was certain he had no place to call home.

Well, it seemed they had something in common after all.

Chapter Four

Mike watched Abigail weave her way through the throng until she disappeared among the masses. Guilt, ugly and oppressive, churned around in his gut until it mutated into something he felt confident had its own genetic code.

Great—a new life form because of my stupidity.

He took a step in the direction she'd gone, then hesitated. What could he do to help her? The answer was swift and bitter—not what he wanted at all.

Not a damn thing.

Clenching and unclenching his fists, Mike tried to ignore his insane urge to rush after her. He was being ridiculous.

With a sigh, he raked his fingers through his hair. Now what? He had to begin his mission sooner or later. It could take him an entire lifetime to find Milton's ancestors.

He almost laughed. An entire lifetime? *Yeah, mine.* Whether it took him ten days or ten years to find Milton, it would *be* his lifetime, because once he succeeded, Slick would come to collect Mike's soul.

Payment for a job well done?

I sure as hell hope Satan gets his money's worth.

Slowly, Mike started toward the center of town. There had

to be records kept somewhere, even in 1865. The courthouse seemed as good a place as any to begin his search—his search for the man he would have to murder. No, not murder—assassinate.

Shrugging off the stabbing second, third, and fourth thoughts, he methodically surveyed his busy surroundings. Natchez hadn't changed much—correction, wouldn't change much. Though it would be slightly larger one day, it was busier now than in his time. In fact, except for the annual pilgrimage, when tourists arrived in droves to tour the antebellum mansions, he couldn't recall having ever seen so much activity in the sleepy town.

That was precisely why Natchez had made the perfect operating base for scum like Frank Milton. Who would have suspected a historic locale like Natchez of playing host to one of the South's biggest drug rings?

If not for the informant Mike and Barney'd busted last month, maybe no one.

Fishing boats came and went on a continuous basis, docking and departing without notice. Tourists drifted in and out of town with regularity. This was the ideal, low profile headquarters for Milton's creep show.

Or it would be. *No—never.* Why did everything have to remind him of Milton . . . and Barney?

Mike moved faster through the crowd until he reached what had to be 1865's version of downtown Natchez. At least a dozen people were crowded in front of a building across the street. He paused to stare, wondering what all the commotion was until something caught his attention.

The flag—the American flag—flapped in the breeze in front of a large stone structure. Was this the Yankee Headquarters the preacher's wife, Harriet What's-Her-Face, had mentioned?

A sudden need grew inside him, refusing to be ignored. Abigail Kingsley—was she here, too? He searched the crowd until he found her. His chest tightened and his heart slammed against his ribs when he saw her trying to maintain her position in the angry group.

This was just like a scene from *Gone With the Wind.* Great, like he needed his own personal Scarlett O'Hara to contend with.

But he owed her . . . or did he?

He looked up at the sky, trying to convince himself that he didn't owe her anything. After all, he hadn't asked her to bail him out of that mess with the restaurant owner. In fact, he distinctly remembered telling her not to.

He looked across the street again just in time to see a large man pushing his way past Abigail. She almost lost her balance. A woman as small as Abigail could be crushed in that mob. He'd seen the aftermath of a much larger riot following a rock concert in Jackson, where a fourteen-year-old girl had been trampled to death by overly enthusiastic fans.

Yes, he did owe her, and she needed help.

A protective surge coursed through him, and before Mike realized his intentions, he'd crossed the street and stood right behind her, hovering and protective. She obviously didn't realize he was there, but that didn't matter. In fact, maybe it was for the best. For now, he'd just stay close and make sure she didn't get trampled.

He shot a glance toward the soldiers standing guard outside the door, rifles resting against their shoulders as they stared straight ahead, seemingly oblivious to the crowd. The heavy man who'd almost knocked Abigail down was right in front of her, darting his own sidelong glances toward the sentries.

"Damned bluebellies," the man muttered just loud enough to be heard.

Mike swallowed hard. He should've paid closer attention in history class. If he had, then maybe he'd be able to remember exactly what Reconstruction had entailed in this part of Mississippi. Still, he didn't have to remember facts from history books to know that the man's comments wouldn't be well received by the occupying army. To their credit, the soldiers didn't react to the man's obvious attempt to goad them.

That was a relief. Mike wasn't exactly in the mood to witness a post-Civil War confrontation up close and *live*. Seeing Kevin Costner's horse shot out from under him on the big screen had been more than adequate.

Standing slightly behind Abigail, Mike looked beyond her at the notices posted outside the building. He squinted, trying to read the long list of properties scheduled for auction.

Then he realized something important. Here was the perfect opportunity to launch his investigation. This list would not only include property descriptions; it would also name the owners.

He was almost afraid to look. If he found a family named Milton, how would he handle it? Rush right out to the plantation and blow them all away?

Yeah, right.

His stomach lurched, partly in protest of the greasy lunch he'd consumed, but mostly in dread that he'd find what he was looking for. But he knew the longer he postponed the inevitable, the more difficult it would be. The repulsive image of Barney's dead body flashed through Mike's mind, an immediate catalyst to overshadow his reluctance.

"Damn."

Abigail half-turned toward him. Her eyes widened in surprise and recognition. If she knew he'd crossed the street to protect her, he suspected she'd be doubly surprised.

Hell, at the moment he wasn't entirely certain what he'd been thinking either. It was easy to convince himself that he'd walked across the street and into this mob just to read the names on the posted notices, but he knew that wasn't the entire truth. An irrational desire to protect her from harm had brought him here—a sense of duty to repay her for helping him out of his earlier predicament.

That was all—nothing more.

It didn't matter that her eyes were the bluest blue he'd ever seen, or that her hair smelled like his grandmother's sheets when she first brought them in from the fresh air and sunshine.

The pink that crept into her cheeks as she met his gaze was immaterial, too. His gaze drifted lower and he noted that the tops of her full breasts were no longer visible. *Bummer.* But his memory was still vivid. Devastating.

Lust shot through him—sudden and decisive. Raw sexual hunger pulsed through his veins, culminating in his groin like a gang protecting its turf. What was it about this woman that made him crave her like a heroin addict in detox looking for a fix? It wasn't like him to get the hots for a woman he was sure wouldn't give him so much as a second glance.

All his senses were raw—on edge—right now. His reactions to everything were sharpened by his recent nightmare—if only this living hell really was nothing but a bad dream.

Yeah, make a wish, Faricy. Just his luck—the one wish in his entire life to actually come true had to turn out like a bad episode of ''*Quantum Leap*,'' where Sam would discover he'd leaped . . . right into Rod Serling's body.

Witness Mike Faricy. A man from another time. A man who doesn't know what the hell he's doing in 1865. Consider, if you will, high noon in . . . The Twilight Zone.

Right. Now what he really needed was the chance to ask Sam Beckett about the possible side effects of quantum leaping. No fair. At least Sam had a handful of doctorates and a guy named Al with a computer link gizmo that told them everything about everybody. God, he could really use that kind of help about now.

But this was real life. Real time travel.

Real concern for Miss Kingsley, made worse by fatigue and anxiety. Or maybe he was transferring some of his concern for Carrie to this woman.

No. That didn't explain why his body skyrocketed to attention every time he saw her. Even while being threatened by an irate restaurant owner, seeing her had felt good. Right.

This is asinine, Faricy, he told himself, but instead of turning to walk away, he flashed what he suspected was his infamous Saturday-night-looking-for-a-woman smile.

Like a fool.

''Mr. Faricy,'' she said, lowering her gaze as the color in her cheeks intensified. ''What brings you over here?''

''I, uh . . .'' Mike scratched the back of his neck while he scanned his fried brain for a sensible answer to her very logical question. Finding none, he grinned again and shrugged. ''Nothing better to do.'' It was more question than statement.

Briefly, she met his gaze and nodded, then returned her

attention to the notices on the wall. "I've been trying to get close enough to read the posts."

His stomach lurched and twisted as guilt tried to regain dominance over the fragile thread of common sense he still possessed. He didn't need this crap. Why in blazes had he come here in the first place? But of course, all the events of the past twenty-four hours should have convinced him by now that he had shit for brains.

"Elysium, right?" he asked, shading his eyes in an effort to read the names of property owners owing back taxes. "Yeah, I think it's on there, but I can't quite make out the rest of—"

"I've waited here long enough," the heavy man in front of them said with a snarl, then gave a hard shove to his left, straight into Abigail.

"Hey!" Mike instinctively reached out and caught her before she lost her balance. "Watch what you're doing, slimeball."

"Slimeball? Who you callin' a slimeball?" The man towered over Mike and easily outweighed him by a hundred pounds.

Mike's steadying hands remained on Abigail's shoulders as he met the goon's rheumy gaze. "You. Who else fits that description around here?"

Uncertainty flickered across the man's fleshy face, then his cheeks reddened and his nostrils flared.

"What's a slimeball?"

"You are."

"Why, I oughta—"

"Stop this at once." Abigail squared her shoulders and shot Mike a pleading glance. "Please?"

Mike met her gaze, acknowledging her request by dropping his hands to his sides. "Sure, no problem."

"Still got men scratchin' at your door, eh?" the guy said, sweeping Abigail's full length with what could only be called an insulting glance. "You're a mite on the scrawny side now, but I reckon there's still a few who'd pay the price."

Something snapped inside Mike as he saw Abigail lower her gaze and redden beneath the man's slurs. That protective rush he'd thought to deny a minute ago exploded, demanding recognition.

"You dirty son of a bitch." Mike took a step closer. "I want you to turn your fat ass around and look straight ahead, and if you so much as look cross-eyed at Miss Kingsley again, I'll—"

"You'll *what?*" Instead of turning, the man took a menacing step, making a point of looking down at Mike as he spoke. "Well?"

Mike narrowed his gaze. "I'll rip your heart out and feed it to stray dogs," he said in his most intimidating voice—the one he usually reserved for juveniles caught playing senseless grown-up games with drugs and gangs.

Sometimes it worked.

Then again . . . sometimes it didn't.

The goon loomed nearer, but Abigail maneuvered herself between them. "I want you both to stop this right now." Her tone was urgent and pleading.

Mike didn't want to stop this—he wanted to beat the bastard bloody for insulting Abigail, though he knew that was unlikely, at best. This guy could sit on him and do more damage than Mike would be able to inflict with a black belt in karate.

Besides, it was obvious Abigail didn't want a scene, and people were beginning to pay more attention to them than to the notices on the wall. Seeing an opening, Mike lifted his gaze to meet his adversary's.

"Why don't you just go do what you came here to do?" he suggested. Much to his amazement, the bully merely grunted, then moved his massive form away from them.

He heard Abigail's soft release of breath and looked down to find her trembling. Without thinking, he put his hand on her shoulder again.

The expression that crossed her face was pain—pure pain, though he suspected it wasn't the physical kind. "Please, remove your hand," she whispered, then turned to face forward again.

Granting her request, he withdrew his hand, though he still felt her warmth on his palm. Mike frowned, reminding himself that these were different times. Women were censured for what was considered unladylike behavior here in this society—this time.

What did it matter that their entire world had fallen apart with the war? His gaze swept the crowd, noting the pride evident in the men and women who waited their turns to read the notices on the wall.

The ruffian had shoved his way beyond them all to read the posts for himself. With slumped shoulders and bowed head, he turned to walk away without a backward glance.

Mike knew without being told that the man's property must've been listed for delinquent taxes. Something almost like pity for the stranger roiled inside him. That was sure as hell unexpected, considering the way the man had treated Abigail just a moment ago.

With the giant's departure, the crowd moved in a more orderly fashion. Mike suddenly remembered his only sensible reason for being here—to read the names on the wall for himself. Was there a Milton among the men and women here now? Even the lowlife he'd almost come to blows with could be one.

He scanned the faces in the crowd—each one looking straight ahead at the ominous notices posted by their conquerors. Many of these people were about to lose their homes. They didn't care about Mike or his mission . . . or about Barney and Carrie.

For all Mike knew, the devil might have been at work here, too. In fact, that seemed damned likely. He winced, remembering the last time he'd seen the devil's flunky. How many disguises did Slick have? He could be here now, masquerading as a desperate Southerner about to lose his land.

I'm getting paranoid in my old age.

Mike swallowed the lump in his throat as the line inched forward, allowing Abigail to finally approach the wall to read the dreaded notices. He watched the proud lift of her chin as she stared in silence at the words.

Why did this woman affect him so deeply? With no effort whatsoever, she had him wanting to seduce her and be chivalrous at the same time. *Great—just great.* He was Ashley Wilkes and Rhett Butler rolled into one not-so-neat package.

Giving himself a silent and well-deserved ass-chewing, Mike stepped in behind her to read over her shoulder. The properties were listed alphabetically according to owner's last name. He scanned the names quickly.

Mason, Miller, Mitchell—no Milton.

A combination of disappointment and relief flooded him until Abigail's soft intake of breath made him look higher. *Kingsley—Elysium Plantation.*

''I'm sorry,'' he said, fighting the urge to touch her again.

She turned to face him and he felt as if she'd slapped him. The pain and fury in her eyes tore at him—reached right inside him with clawed fingers and yanked his conscience to the surface with a decisive twist.

''Sorry?'' she echoed, and her chin quivered slightly. Then she bit her lower lip and turned away.

Her unspoken accusation hovered in the air around Mike as she walked away. He just stood there, staring after her as she kept her back erect and her head held high, increasing the distance between them step by miserable step.

''Damn,'' he muttered as a couple stepped forward to take their turn at the wall.

Suddenly he saw the Viet Nam Memorial in Washington. The expressions on these faces was so similar to those who'd visited the wall—the pain, the loss. He had to get away from there.

''Pardon me.'' He started after Abigail again. After several steps, he paused.

What the hell was he going to do? He had no negotiable money to offer her. All his currency wouldn't even be minted for over a century. She was in trouble now, and just imagining what the army would say about that made him break out in a cold sweat. No, she didn't need more trouble.

She needed help.

Somehow, he had to pull off a miracle—more than one, actually. His self-confidence wasn't exactly at its peak in this strange place. This Natchez was so different from the one he knew. He felt lost.

Hell, he *was* lost.

Lost in time.

Leaning against the nearest building, he rubbed his gritty eyes with both fists. He was exhausted—physically and mentally. He needed a plan. Feeling sorry for himself wasn't doing any good.

A place to sleep for the night would be a great starting point, even though the day was still young. He let his head fall back against the building with a soft thump.

He was tired, hungry again . . . and homeless. Terrific combination. This was the pits. Whoever'd said life sucks must've known what Mike felt like at this moment.

A face flashed through his mind. Her face—the Kingsley woman. Just what he needed—a guilt reminder. He never should have allowed her to pay his restaurant bill. Hell, he should've known better than to try to spend money that couldn't even exist in this century.

One thing was clear—he needed money to support himself and to repay his debt to Abigail Kingsley. *That's right—get your priorities straight.* He drew a deep breath and raked his fingers through his hair. Food and shelter first.

A job. That's what he needed. But what kind of job could a twentieth-century vice detective land in 1865?

He chuckled softly to himself, then pushed away from the wall and shoved his hands into the pockets of his jeans. The keys to his apartment and his '68 Mustang jabbed his knuckles, mocking him by feeling so real and useful. They were nothing but worthless pieces of metal now—reminders of the life he'd left behind.

And the death.

A sense of purpose washed over him, and with it a sensation of calm he hadn't felt since before his journey through time and this virtual House of Horrors. He had to take this one step at a time, but first he needed a plan.

Remember those priorities, numb-nuts.

His money was no good here—*get that straight and don't*

forget it again—but he had other possessions. His stainless steel Smith & Wesson 5906—no, he'd need that. Eventually.

Ignoring the voice of his conscience, Mike looked down at his high-school class ring. It was gold—surely worth something even now. The raised letters and numbers around the red stone drew a scowl from him.

"Damn." Like his money, the ring bore a date. So much for that brilliant idea. He held his left hand out in front of him, tugging his cuff up to reveal his watch. A digital watch would be quite a marvel in this time.

A smile tugged at the corners of his mouth. Once the battery went dead it would be no good to whatever sucker he could convince to purchase it. In the meantime, it might mean the difference between feast and famine.

Well, snack and hungry, anyway.

Abigail increased her pace, leaving Natchez behind her within a few minutes. Her heart thudded in protest, but she pushed herself faster and faster until she was running down the rutted dirt road toward home.

Home.

For how long?

She couldn't escape reality by running from it. Elysium would be taken from her and sold to the highest bidder. Blinding tears scalded her eyes and she stumbled, falling to her knees in the red dirt. A sob tore from her throat and she bit the inside of her cheek to silence herself.

This would do no good. Her son and Rosalie needed her to be strong. She shuddered in protest. *I can't be strong anymore. I don't* want *to be.*

Oh, God. Why couldn't someone take care of *her* for a change? She was so tired of scraping and scrambling to put food in her son's mouth. Her own belly was so empty it rumbled and knotted in confirmation of their predicament.

Then she remembered the original reason she'd gone to town today. For food.

Panic forged to the surface as she shot her hand into her

pocket to confirm the little money she had left hadn't fallen to the ground in her earlier eagerness to flee Natchez. The smooth coin felt solid and comforting to her fingertips. She closed her eyes for a moment, then released a mournful sigh.

Regaining a semblance of control over her emotions, Abigail stood and turned toward town. She couldn't go home without food. That was that.

She glanced up once at the sun, estimating the time at midafternoon. It was still early enough for her to return to Natchez, purchase the cornmeal, and walk back to Elysium before nightfall.

Not that she had any choice. The cupboards were bare—there was nothing to feed her son or Rosalie. Or herself.

Memories tugged at the fringes of her mind as the hot Mississippi sun blazed down on her. It felt more like August than June. Her worn bonnet did little to protect her from the harsh rays, but what did it matter if she burned and freckled? No man would want her ever again. Not after—

"Stop it, Abigail," she ordered, lifting her chin a notch in self-defiance. She would not persecute herself again for something beyond her control. The past was over—nothing she did now could change that.

And she had Wade. That was something she didn't wish to change.

She forced her mind to more practical matters. The unpaid taxes on Elysium were over two hundred dollars. The amount due could just as well be two *thousand* dollars, for both figures were unattainable.

They would have to leave. There was no choice.

And go where?

Panic threatened her resolve again, but Abigail quickly quelled it. She would not allow herself the luxury of weeping again. Wade and Rosalie deserved more than that.

She had no other family left anywhere. What would she do? Where could they go?

Earlier memories invaded her thoughts. A man's face flashed through her mind, making her pulse quicken in terror. Her breath grew short and rapid as the familiar panic seeped through her. Though it was a face she hadn't seen for more than two years, its impact remained stalwart.

In her mind, she saw the document he'd left behind, staring up at her from the bureau beside her bed. A name—a place. She knew where and how to find him.

Oh, sweet Jesus, how can I do that?

He'd said he was rich—he'd flaunted that fact in her face. Now she desperately needed money.

And there was her son to consider. Wade. Remorse permeated her, a dreaded serpent twisting its way into her very soul as she reached the outskirts of town again.

What choice did she have? Those words played over and over in her mind as the man's face became clearer. Her throat threatened to close as she recalled that night—the terror.

She was suffocating, reliving her worst nightmare again and again. Leaning against a tree, Abigail pressed her hands over both ears and closed her eyes. She had to keep the images at bay for now. Later, alone in her bed, she would remember every minute detail—nothing could prevent that. But now . . . she must control herself and these thoughts.

"Miss Kingsley?"

Through her hands, the voice came to her muffled and distant, but when she opened her eyes, she found Mr. Faricy standing right in front of her. She stared at him for several moments, knowing his identity, yet unable to bring her panic under control enough to respond to his words.

"Miss Kingsley," he repeated. "Are you all right?"

Abigail swallowed hard and lowered her hands from her ears.

His gaze was gentle yet penetrating, riveting her with its intensity. Strangely, she had no desire to escape him—none at all.

"Mr. Faricy," she finally whispered, blinking rapidly to clear her vision. "I'm . . . sorry."

"No need." He cleared his throat and lowered his gaze for a moment. "Actually, I was on my way out to see you."

"See me?" She tilted her head to one side and frowned. It wasn't proper for Mr. Faricy to pay her so much attention, especially after spending the night under her roof, albeit without her knowledge or consent.

"Of course." He chuckled and shrugged. "I owe you some money—remember?"

Money. Did everything always have to return to that? Abigail sighed, feeling as if someone had struck her. "I know you don't have money, Mr. Faricy, so—"

"No, I don't have money," he agreed. "However, I did have something to trade for this." He looked over his shoulder, drawing her gaze along with his own.

Abigail gasped. How could something as large as a cow be standing only a few feet away without her noticing it before now?

"A cow," she said stupidly, then she shook her head and dragged her gaze back to his. "I don't understand."

He gave her a sheepish grin, then tugged on the beast's lead rope, holding it out in front of him. "It's yours. The cow *and* the fifty-pound sack of cornmeal on its back."

Stunned, Abigail could only stare. "I don't understand."

"You said that already. Besides, it's simple." He shrugged again. "I traded my watch for this cow, but I don't know how to milk it or take care of it. Hell, I've never been this close to a cow before in my entire life." He shot the animal a disdainful glance. "I'm not real crazy about the idea even now."

The beast gave him a derisive glance, then bellowed in protest. Mike's answering chuckle was infectious, and before Abigail could prevent it she found herself laughing along with him.

"See? She doesn't like me either." He stopped laughing and his expression softened. "So you have no choice but to take her off my hands." He glanced over his shoulder then back at her. "For both our sakes."

Abigail's heart swelled. "Just this morning I wished for a milk cow," she confessed without thinking, then felt her face flood with heat as she dragged her gaze from his. "What can I say, Mr. Faricy?"

"That you'll take this beast from me." He extended the lead rope again. "Please? I can't stand her and she doesn't like me. We've already established that fact. Besides, like I said earlier,

I don't know how to milk her. And just between us—I don't *want* to know how.''

Abigail looked down at the cow's udder, which appeared engorged even now. Wade could have fresh milk to drink. How could she reject this offer?

Then a nagging suspicion shot through her. What would he expect in return for such a generous gift?

"I . . ." Did it really matter? Wade needed nourishment. "This is too much. It wouldn't be proper for me to—"

"It's repayment of a loan, Miss Kingsley." His voice was steady and firm. "All I had of any value was my watch. This cow was for sale. Now it's yours. Case closed."

Tears stung her eyes, but she blinked them into submission. "Oh." She slowly shook her head and placed her hands on her flushed cheeks to cool them. "Sir, this cow is worth much more than the few coins I expended on your behalf this morning, I assure you."

He shook his head. "No, Miss Kingsley."

His voice was rough and smooth at the same time, rumbling around in her belly to tantalize and stimulate her senses.

"I got myself in trouble this morning," he continued. "You didn't have to, but you helped me out of a mess."

That was a true statement. Besides, she couldn't turn away an opportunity for fresh milk for her son. How could this man have known the cow would be more valuable to her than gold right now?

Unless he knew she had a child.

Her muscles tightened and her head pounded. For some insane reason, this man's opinion of her mattered. Ridiculous. Everyone in Adams County knew about Wade. What difference did it make if Mr. Faricy thought her a fallen woman when everyone who mattered already did?

Besides . . . fresh milk for Wade was too wondrous an opportunity for her to refuse. Her son came first. *Anything for Wade.*

"Very well, Mr. Faricy," she said, nodding matter-of-factly. "I thank you for your generous repayment."

She took the cow's lead in her hand and started to turn back toward Elysium, but something held her there, as if her feet were nailed to the earth. Who was this man? Where was he from? Where was he going?

"Miss Kingsley?"

The sound of his voice startled her from her musing. "Yes?" She turned to face him, then realized her error. There was something powerful about the man's eyes—something mesmerizing.

"I read the notice about your taxes," he said, looking down once at his unusual shoes, then back up and right into her eyes. He sighed and slapped his thigh with his hand. "Dammit, Miss Kingsley, neither one of us has that kind of money. I don't even think this cow would bring that much."

"You're correct, sir." She swallowed hard. Where was this conversation leading?

"I went back and read the fine print under the notice about your place." His gaze softened as did his voice. "The auction is only for the house and lands. Did you realize that?"

She shrugged. "That's everything. What furniture we have left is broken. Worthless." Why was he forcing her to relive this nightmare? When she first saw Elysium listed for sale, she'd nearly died right on the spot. "I don't understand your point, sir."

He shot her a crooked grin that made her heart suddenly do a flip-flop. What was it about this man that tugged at something deep in her core she'd thought long since dead and buried?

"My point, Miss Kingsley," he said steadily, "is that a place the size of your plantation must have other assets."

She shook her head and frowned. "The slaves were the only other asset I can think of, sir, and Mr. Lincoln freed them. They're gone now."

"No, not that." He made a sour face as if he had a bad taste in his mouth. "Slaves. I can't imagine . . ." He held his hand up when she opened her mouth to speak. "Never mind that now. I mean machinery and equipment."

Surprised, Abigail searched her mind. "Well, there are plows and tools of all types, of course. Is that what you mean?"

"Exactly!" Excitement danced in his eyes. "I don't know

why, Miss Kingsley, but I want to help you. Maybe it's because you helped me, or because I landed in your house."

"Landed?" Baffled, she furrowed her brow. "I don't understand what you mean."

"Neither do I, trust me." His laughter was cynical and the hard glint had returned to his eyes. "I don't understand any of this, but I do know that what little money you'd make from the sale of the equipment on your plantation might help you get a fresh start somewhere."

"Oh!" Abigail brought her hand to her mouth. Why hadn't she thought of this? "You're a genius, Mr. Faricy."

To her utter amazement, his cheeks reddened beneath the dark shadow of his whiskers.

"I wouldn't say that," he said quietly, "but it makes sense to get what you can out of the place before the IRS takes it."

"The . . . iyares?"

"Never mind." He chuckled again. "I was wondering . . ."

Lost in the midst of a mental inventory of the equipment remaining on the property, Abigail's enthusiasm waned. Most of it was badly damaged. "Wondering what, sir?" she asked morosely. How much money could she possibly hope to get for broken equipment?

"Well, I know it's probably considered rude of me to ask this, but that's my style." He sighed. "I need a job and a place to stay."

I should have known. He must have heard the stories in town, and obviously thought he could have his way with her in exchange for a few favors. When she didn't respond, he rushed ahead.

"I could help you inventory the equipment and repair some of it in exchange for room and board." Palms turned up, he held his hands out in front of him. "That's all I want or need right now. That, and enough free time to go into town almost every day."

Abigail was surprised. His suggestion wasn't nearly as unreasonable as she'd expected. In fact, it wasn't obscene at all. There were still cabins on the property where he could sleep— nothing improper about that.

Then his words suddenly penetrated her frazzled mind. "Town?" she echoed, wondering why anyone would want to go into that insanity so often. "Why?"

His face hardened and his eyes flashed suddenly with an almost feral light—anger, no doubt about it. Fortunately, it wasn't directed at her.

"I'm searching for someone." His words were clipped and grating. "Nothing for you to worry about."

He was certainly entitled to his privacy, too. Perhaps this situation would work out, after all. "Very well, Mr. Faricy." She nodded. "You'll repair the equipment and help me sell it in exchange for food and a place to sleep. Is that correct?"

"That's it."

She sighed. "There is one problem, though."

"What's that?"

"The only food we have right now is that cornmeal and the milk this cow gives."

His gaze softened again. "I see." He closed his eyes for a moment. "I knew you couldn't afford to help me out earlier. Why'd you do it?"

"I'm not sure," she said honestly. "I just couldn't stand by and not help, I suppose."

"You asked me earlier if I could hunt."

"Yes?" Fresh meat on the table would be marvelous.

"I can't, but I'm a fair fisherman."

Abigail couldn't prevent her smile. "Game has been scarce anyway, since the war."

"I'll bet there are fish in the river, though." His face fell and his voice sounded harsher than before. "Fish . . ."

Strange moan. He still seemed tormented, though she had no idea how or why. Did it matter? As long as he did his job and brought some food to their table, what difference did it make? His past was his business and hers was hers.

"Very well, Mr. Faricy. I think there's a cabin we can clean out for you."

"Cabin?"

She laughed at his shocked tone. "It won't be any less

comfortable than the floor you slept on last night, I assure you."

"Right."

She started to walk toward Elysium again, feeling younger than she had in months. Strange, considering she'd just learned they were about to lose their home. Still, for some reason she felt hopeful. She had decisions to make about their future, but for now, there'd be some food on the table, thanks to this cow . . . and Mr. Faricy.

"And thank God it won't be just cornmeal."

She watched him fall into step beside her, then he turned to glance back at the cow. Stumbling, he almost fell, though he continued to stare over his shoulder at the animal.

"Holy Mother of—"

The terror which suddenly sounded in his voice made icy and irrational shards of fear shoot through her, transforming her feet to immobile blocks of stone. "What is it, Mr. Faricy?"

He stood staring at the cow. Instinctively, she reached out to touch his arm, acutely aware of the warmth radiating through his jacket to her hand. The expression on his ashen face was one of consummate horror—she'd never forget it.

"What's wrong?" she repeated in a soft whisper.

He turned gradually and met her gaze. "Please . . . look at the cow's eyes."

The request was simple and ridiculous, but she wasn't about to question a man as frightened as he obviously was at this moment. "Very well." She obeyed.

"Red?"

"No, of course not. They're large and brown, just like every cow I've ever seen."

He released a ragged sigh. "Thank God."

She tightened her grip on his arm. "Mr. Faricy, what's wrong?" Was it safe to have someone this volatile around her son? Around her?

"It's nothing." His Adam's apple bobbed up and down in his throat. "Nothing at all. I'm sorry. Just forget it."

Warily, she turned toward home, leading the lumbering beast

behind them. Mr. Faricy would bear watching, she decided, and glanced askance at him again.

He seemed fine now, though after every few steps he looked over his shoulder at the cow. She couldn't imagine why he'd thought the cow's big brown eyes were red.

How strange.

Chapter Five

Oh, yeah, right—a possessed cow.

Mike needed a diversion. At home he could've flipped on a baseball game or plugged in Segal's latest video to get his mind off his troubles. What could he do here and now to occupy his thoughts? Something—*anything!*

A woman.

He shot a glance at his companion. She was drop-dead gorgeous—no makeup or artificial enhancements present or necessary. Twentieth-century women would pay a fortune for her secret.

As a matter of fact, he was paying for it himself—with pain. According to the Faricy School of Thought, unfulfilled lust was an unhealthy state for any man, and Mike had already passed serious and was racing toward the critical list. At this point he'd be considered high risk by most life insurance companies.

A droplet of perspiration trickled from behind her ear, then slipped slowly down the side of her neck. It paused over her pulse, teasing and begging to be wiped—or kissed—away.

Her blood thrummed through her veins, making the droplet dance and flicker in the sunlight, winking at him in silent invitation.

Get a grip, man.

He'd like to get a grip on something—on her. Losing himself in good old-fashioned, primitive sex was just what he needed right now. *Oh, that did it.* Just the thought of actually committing the act made his libido do a fair imitation of a shuttle launch.

"So, Mr. Faricy," she said suddenly, making Mike feel like a kid caught with his hand in the cookie jar. "Where do you call home?"

He dragged in a deep breath and struggled against his hormones for control. "Natchez." He immediately regretted his hasty answer.

"Natchez?" Without slowing her pace, she turned her head to stare at him. "We've never met, Mr. Faricy—I'm certain of it."

Yeah, I'd sure remember that. Mike gave her a sheepish grin and tried to convince himself he wasn't blushing, even though his face—among other regions—was on fire. "No, we haven't met." How was he going to get out of this mess?

"Well, I don't see how you could be from Natchez, then." Abigail continued to stare at him as they walked along the road. "I know all the local families."

C'mon, Einstein. Get yourself out of this one. "I, uh, meant I'm planning to live in Natchez from now on."

She furrowed her brow and lifted one corner of her mouth as if she wanted to believe him. Well, that was certainly better than the alternative.

"I see." She faced forward again. "So where did you live before?"

He had to think fast. His accent was regional, so where could he be from that wouldn't raise suspicion? It had to be a place he knew well in case she asked more questions, and he had a hunch she would.

"Jackson." He nodded, satisfied with his decision. "Born and raised."

"Oh, I've only been to Jackson once, and that was ever so long ago." She turned her head and flashed him a smile that revealed a dimple he hadn't noticed earlier. "Why did you decide to move to Natchez?"

Mike didn't like the direction this conversation was heading. He couldn't tell her the truth and he hated to lie. With a sigh, he dragged his fingers through his hair, wishing there was a hot shower in his future. *Fat chance.* He shot another covert glance at the nice way her breasts moved as she walked. On second thought, maybe a cold shower would be better. *An Arctic geyser might do the trick.*

Why was he moving to Natchez? He forced his thoughts and his gaze away from the buttons that closed the front of her dress . . . and speculation about the tempting flesh hidden behind them. "My family," he said—the truth in many ways.

"Oh, you have family in Natchez?" She immediately brightened.

"No." He ground his teeth together, searching his mind for some way to change the subject. "My family's dead, Miss Kingsley. I needed a fresh start."

A half-truth was better than a lie. His family hadn't been born yet, so they weren't *alive.* But the rest was a blatant lie.

He cringed. *Fresh start, my ass.* This was the end for Mike Faricy. Do his duty, then off he went to Hell—the *real* one—for eternity. Carrie'd have Barney and their baby, and Mike didn't rate anyway, with no wife or kids depending on him.

Or caring whether he lived or died.

"I'm sorry to hear that." Abigail's voice held genuine sympathy. "My family is gone now, too."

Did she live alone? There hadn't been anyone else around this morning. The odds were swinging over to his favor. *Easy, pal.* He allowed his gaze to make a lingering journey down her entire length—at least, what he could see of it through all that dress. She lifted her hand to mop perspiration from her forehead. For some inane reason, that simple movement made his loins explode with renewed need. What was it about this woman? Or was it his situation that made him burn?

Burn? Yeah, pun intended.

Still, picturing her living all alone in that big house sent all sorts of ideas ricocheting through his mind. Lusty thoughts. Sexy thoughts.

Hot and nasty thoughts.

With a Southern belle? A *nineteenth-century* Southern belle? *Sure.* She was probably as virginal as the day she'd been born. It wasn't as if she'd invite him to her boudoir, or whatever she called it. Hell, she didn't even plan to let him sleep in the house.

Then he remembered the man in town who'd commented about Abigail's reputation. His pulse catapulted and he snapped his head around to look at her—*really* look at her.

There was an undeniable sensuality about the way she moved, the way her hips swung from side to side with each step. Her hair was neatly tucked inside her bonnet now, but this morning, in his crazed state when he'd first seen her, all that dark hair had cascaded around her face and shoulders in a wild seductive abandon that had seemed almost deliberate. Could he be mistaken about her innocence?

The thought made him harden even more in anticipation. Could this Southern lady be as hot-blooded as that bum in town had hinted?

After all this, he needed a couple of lucky breaks. Indulging in some hardcore bumping and grinding would definitely rate up near the top of his list. An immediate and effective wave of guilt washed over him. Bumping and grinding was too crude for this woman. She had class.

They fell into companionable silence and Mike stole another glance at the cow. It looked right at him—no sign of red in its eyes now.

Releasing a long slow sigh, Mike turned to find Abigail staring at him again. Her blue eyes were wide and curious, filled with concern.

"Are you all right, Mr. Faricy?" she asked, never lowering her understandably wary gaze.

She thought he was crazy. Well, wasn't he? "Sure, I'm fine." Mike swallowed hard and tried to ignore the questions of self-doubt ricocheting through his mind.

His stomach growled. Great, he was hungry again. That

figured. And raw milk was all he had to look forward to. Then he caught sight of the river through the trees. He'd almost forgotten . . .

"Do you have a rod and reel I can borrow when we get back to your place?"

"A what?" She shook her head and lifted her shoulders. "I'm afraid I'm not familiar with—"

"A fishing pole," Mike interrupted, wondering what he'd use for bait. *Worms, what else?* Maybe he could even fashion a trout line, though the Big Muddy wasn't known for its trout. "Hooks?"

"Oh, my father was a consummate fisherman, Mr. Faricy." A smile lit her face. "So was my brother. You'll find what you need in the barn. I kept a few things hidden during the war . . . because of the soldiers. I even managed to catch a couple of fish myself once." She gave a nervous laugh. "I tried again several times, but the fish weren't as cooperative after that."

Despite her smile, Mike heard something in her voice—a telltale catch. "I'm sorry," he said quietly, knowing he didn't have to explain the reason for his remark.

"My brother was killed early in the war, and my father died . . . almost three years ago. Mama's been gone several years now." She laughed again—that high-pitched, forced sound—and her cheeks reddened. "It's all right. I've had time to get used to it. Besides, it isn't as if I'm all alone."

"You're not?" Mike mentally kicked himself for blurting out the words. "I mean . . . oh."

She reddened again. "Of course not. There's Rosalie—her people have been at Elysium for generations, so she's like family."

"A slave." Mike couldn't imagine owning people. The entire concept was so abstract he could barely grasp it. Had his ancestors owned slaves? No, only the rich planters had owned slaves. His heritage was blue collar—no doubt about it. Irish Catholic peasant stock, through and through.

Then another thought exploded through his mind. Were any of his ancestors in this area now? He and Carrie'd never bothered with family trees and the like after their parents died, and he wasn't sure when theirs had come over from Ireland. "Holy sh—"

"Rosalie is my friend, Mr. Faricy. We grew up together." Her lips were set in a thin line and an unmistakable challenge hardened her voice. "She stays with us now because she wishes to."

"Us?" Mike tilted his head to one side and stared at her. "I thought you said your family was all gone, Miss Kingsley." It was his turn to let suspicion sound in his voice.

"I did, but I meant my parents and brother, of course." She lowered her gaze and cleared her throat. "I have a son."

A son? Mike's mind churned with this new information. That answered his question regarding her innocence in a big hurry. She hardly looked old enough to have a child, yet he knew in this time period women married much younger than in his.

As if reading his mind, she lifted her gaze to meet his again. "Wade is two years old."

So young. Mike didn't like the sound of this. If she had a son, then did she also have a husband? It was beginning to look more and more as if "Miss" Kingsley might have a husband on his way home from the war at this very moment. He had to know. Should he come right out and ask, or would she volunteer the information?

Then he remembered the woman he'd seen driving the buggy earlier in the day. That memory combined in his mind with a parade of images from *Gone With the Wind.* Though he'd only seen the movie once, he remembered a scene with several female characters all dressed in black. Abigail wasn't wearing widow's weeds by any stretch of the imagination.

"I don't recall a family named Faricy around here," she said thoughtfully. "Hmm. And I know every family in the county."

Every family in the county. Every family in the county. Every family in the county. Those words played over in Mike's mind as his objective fought for renewed supremacy. If Abigail knew every family in the area . . .

"I had a friend," he began, grappling with his emotions as he spoke. He had to sound calm, cool, though he was anything but. His stomach burned and his sweat turned cold on his flesh. "I think he said he was from around here. His last name was . . . Milton. Do you know a family by that name?"

She stumbled and almost fell, but he reached out and caught her arm. All the color drained from her face and he heard her breath coming hard and fast.

"Miss Kingsley?" He moved his hand from her arm to her shoulder. "Are you okay?"

She blinked several times before turning to face him. Her expression was one of total shock. He'd seen it before, usually on the faces of crime victims—or their survivors.

"I'm fine, Mr. Faricy." She drew a ragged breath. "I merely had a catch in my side, but it's gone now."

The expression on her face hadn't been one of physical pain, but he let the matter drop. "You didn't answer my question." He had to ask, though he hated pressing when she obviously wasn't feeling well. Something had upset her. "Miss Kingsley."

Her lips pressed together and her expression grim, she looked behind them once at the cow, tightening her hold on the lead rope. "No, Mr. Faricy. There's no family by that name around Natchez."

"You're sure?"

"Positive." She started to walk again, jerking the rope to prod the cow into abandoning the patch of clover it had discovered. "We're almost there," she announced, obviously ready to change the subject again.

No family named Milton here. Now what, ace?

"Yeah," he agreed in a gravelly voice, forcing his disappointment—or was it relief?—into submission. Mike looked ahead of them at the now-familiar bend in the road, where pine trees towered over oak. He remembered from this morning that Elysium was just beyond the heavily wooded area.

It wouldn't be long before he met Abigail's son.

How long before he met her husband?

* * *

Milton. That dreaded name sliced through Abigail, threatening the thin veneer of sanity she'd managed to construct and maintain. How did he know that name? Dear God, *why?*

Surely it was a coincidence. Mr. Faricy couldn't possibly know *that* Milton. Could he? Was it possible someone had told this man to come to Elysium? Someone who'd visited the plantation before . . . ?

No, not that. Abigail pushed a stray tendril of hair back from her face, searching her mind for a way to avoid answering Mr. Faricy's other question. The one he hadn't vocalized.

Where is your husband?

It was a logical inquiry, considering she'd just announced she had a son. Avoiding the issue had been the right way to handle this, she decided. After all, it really wasn't any of Mr. Faricy's business.

Unless . . . *No.* Forcing such ludicrous thoughts away, she peeked at him from beneath veiled lashes. He was watching her, a look of curiosity on his handsome face. His expression was unthreatening, filled with concern. Not a trace of suspicion revealed itself. She was being overly suspicious.

Again, she was struck by his rugged good looks. He didn't possess the aristocratic air many of the young men in the area did—rather, *had*—before the war. Mr. Faricy's appeal went much deeper than merely his striking appearance. It was something more—something immeasurable which drew her to him.

His soul, perhaps?

She almost laughed at herself. What did she know of such matters? The sheltered heiress of a plantation, now in ruins, could hardly be considered worldly enough to ponder anything as significant as a man's soul.

She'd gone into seclusion after . . . that night. And the number of people she'd actually engaged in meaningful conversation since then could be counted on one hand.

After all, Abigail Kingsley wasn't received. Her mother must have rolled over in her grave with that knowledge. As if there were any social functions these days. Abigail hadn't appeared socially since before her father's death, right after Wade's fa—

Stop it!

A chill chased itself down her spine and her stomach lurched and knotted. Maybe someday she'd stop reliving that nightmare.

She looked down at her much-mended dress. *What must Mr. Faricy think of my appearance?*

She looked at him again. His thin jacket matched his denim trousers. The black garment he wore beneath the jacket had no buttons—like a sweater, but it wasn't. It stretched taut across his torso, displaying his physique in an appealing fashion.

The memory of how she'd ogled him this morning as he slept on her floor returned. Heat suffused her face, but she continued her perusal, permitting her gaze to follow the leather strap that crossed his chest until she saw the silver glint of his gun.

Suddenly she jerked her gaze away. She'd almost forgotten about the gun. It wasn't unusual for a man to carry a weapon, but there was something about the *way* he carried his that disturbed her. He had an air of self-confidence, even while in the throes of whatever nightmare ate at him.

Again, she wondered if he'd fought in the war. Did she dare ask? He carried himself like a soldier, though no portion of his clothing could be considered part of any uniform. A spy, perhaps?

That seemed more likely, though it hardly mattered now that the war was over. She peeked at him again, noting the way his jaw twitched as if something of great importance troubled him.

This man was going to live at Elysium, though not in the house, thank heavens. Still, it wasn't as if she could lock him out, should he choose to pay her a nocturnal visit.

Alarm tore through her. Her heart raced and her mouth went dry. What had she been thinking—inviting a *stranger* to stay at Elysium?

What choice did she have? Until she could ensure Wade's future, she must endure Mr. Faricy's presence. He needed a job and she needed the help. *So be it.*

Feeling somewhat calmer, she forced a smile to her lips,

hoping it didn't resemble a grimace. He still watched her, and when she smiled, he reciprocated with another of those boyish grins that washed away her worries—at least temporarily.

This man was nothing like that other one. For some insane reason, she felt certain Mike Faricy wouldn't harm her or her family. They would be safe in his company.

But why *do I trust him?*

No voice sounded in her mind to provide an easy answer. She *did* trust him, though common sense called her a fool. Did it matter why?

After all, he had repaid his debt. She glanced over her shoulder at the lumbering beast. *With interest.*

This was a business arrangement. Mr. Faricy would make the necessary repairs until the sale, and in the meantime, she must determine her family's future. Where would they go? What would they do?

As they turned to make their way toward the house, Abigail paused. Mr. Faricy took a few steps, then stopped and turned to look at her. She met his gaze and smiled wistfully.

"It won't be mine much longer."

He nodded in understanding and she felt a sudden, fierce bond with him. It rocked the foundations of her sense of reason. She had no genuine basis on which to place her trust in this man, let alone feel *close* to him.

Yet the feeling persisted, almost insolent in its clarity.

She continued to stare at the house as fragments of memory flooded her and brought tears to her eyes. Reality finally crashed down around her.

She was about to lose her home.

Her son's heritage.

"Oh, dear Lord." She bit her lower lip, then brought the knuckles of her free hand to her mouth in hopes of quelling the sob building deep inside her. The hunger, the senseless deaths, the indiscriminate violence all descended upon her with a force that rendered her frozen, unable to move forward or think clearly.

She was vaguely cognizant of the lead rope slipping through her fingers as silent sobs racked her body. The burning sensation in her constricted throat was almost unbearable. She couldn't breathe—the heat surrounded her, pressed down on her from all directions.

"Miss Kingsley?"

He was here beside her, and for some reason that felt good. Right. Almost as if he belonged with her at this desolate moment.

A small voice inside her tried to argue with that illogical thought, but it failed miserably. She needed someone to depend on right now—someone to help her carry the burden.

Was that person Mike Faricy? Could he help her endure all she must in order to ensure her family's future? *Would* he?

He was here, wasn't he? Didn't that mean something?

"I'm sorry," he said, then he reached out and touched her shoulder.

His touch was the catalyst her frazzled state required. Tears welled from her eyes and sobs tore from her throat. She no longer struggled against the onslaught—it was long overdue.

She could no more stop her tears than she could have stopped the war. Her knees quaked beneath her weight, and she was vaguely aware of strong arms enveloping her, pulling her against warmth . . . and hope.

He held her physically, but his embrace offered so much more. The feel of his arms around her dredged all the misery up from her soul and forced it into the open. Bitter, salty tears flowed in an endless stream—for her parents, her brother, Wade, Rosalie . . . and herself.

She had no concept of time as they stood there in the shady lane. Her tears slowly diminished to a trickle and the sobs eased, allowing her to breathe in a near-normal pattern. Reality crowded its way into her mind, forcing her to consider her situation.

Her proximity to this man.

Which inexorable moment her feelings changed, she wasn't certain. All she knew was that suddenly this man represented far more than merely someone to lean on.

He was a man—a strong, handsome one. A man who seemed as tormented inside as she, yet offered her a moment of comfort.

His tall lean body held hers close—much closer than she should've allowed—but she was loath to end his embrace. She was vaguely conscious of his gun pressing against her, but other matters refused to allow its presence to interfere. A strange and wonderful warmth grew deep in her belly, then spread through her veins like sorghum heated for candy.

She grew suddenly aware of the contrasts between her body and his—where soft met hard, she felt a maddening yearning for something more. Mercy, she knew she should pull away, but instead she permitted her cheek to remain in that small hollow beneath his shoulder which seemed to have been made just for her.

His musky male scent permeated her, made her ache inside for something she couldn't quite define. A slight movement— his lips against her bonnet?—prompted her to lift her face to meet his gaze with her own.

The expression smoldering in his eyes unhinged her.

He hooked his finger under her chin and lifted her face very slowly, simultaneously lowering his mouth toward hers. His lips brushed hers so softly she thought at first she might have imagined it.

A gush of liquid fire spurted through her veins, though his kiss was so gentle it almost mocked her physical response. He made no effort to increase the pressure of his lips, nor did he ease himself away. He growled deep in his throat and the vibration of it filtered through her, surrounded her with primitive need.

This was wrong—she hardly knew him. Yet the ability to stop the delicious proceedings was beyond her.

"Saints above—it's a cow!"

Abigail lurched away from his embrace, continuing to struggle against the onslaught of need which coursed through her as she sought the source of the voice. Rosalie. Had she seen them kissing?

"Two eggs, a cow, and—"

Rosalie stood a short distance away, staring at her mistress with a stunned expression on her face. "And the stranger,"

Rosalie finished, pinning her gaze on the man who stood behind Abigail. "What'd he come back here for?"

Relief swept through Abigail. Rosalie's attention had obviously been on the cow, who'd strayed a few yards away after receiving its unexpected freedom.

"Well?" Rosalie placed one fist on each bony hip and thrust out her lower lip. "I said—"

"I know, Rosalie," Abigail interrupted, searching her mind for a sensible explanation. "Mr. Faricy is going to work for us."

"Work?" The wrinkles in Rosalie's brow deepened. "What we gonna pay him with?"

"Food and a place to sleep," Mr. Faricy said, stepping forward to stand beside Abigail. "That's all I ask or need."

"I reckon Miss Abigail done told you we ain't got no food." Rosalie folded her arms in front of her. "And that reminds me. Where'd this cow come from?"

"Mr. Faricy was repaying a debt." Abigail knew her words would sound scandalous to her friend. They sounded bad enough to her, especially as the epilogue of that kiss. *Mercy.*

"What debt?"

Abigail noticed Wade's small hands clutching the folds of Rosalie's skirt. Her heart swelled with love at seeing her son, particularly poignant after learning they were about to lose their home.

"Miss Kingsley was kind enough to help me out of a pinch in town." Mr. Faricy shrugged and gave a self-deprecating laugh. "I ordered food, if you can call it that, without realizing I didn't have the right ki—I mean, enough money to pay for it."

"Oh?" It was clear Rosalie doubted both of them. "So Miss Abigail turned over *her* money to get you outta trouble?"

"That sizes it up. Yeah."

Abigail was acutely aware of the man standing at her side. What had come over her, allowing him to actually kiss her like that? She knew better, for heaven's sake. After the horrible experiences of these last years, the thought of having a man touch her at all should have revolted her.

But for some reason, this man's touch hadn't. In fact, her reaction to him had been quite the opposite.

Lord, give me strength.

"It's all right, Rosalie," she said with surprising steadiness. "As you can see, we now own a cow. I certainly couldn't have purchased it for the few coins I expended on Mr. Faricy's behalf."

"Well . . ." Rosalie's expression softened as she reached down to pull the boy around to her side. "Wade, do you see that cow?"

The child nodded. His eyes were large and round as he stared first at the cow, then at the man. "Who him?" He pointed his finger at Mr. Faricy, then blinked several times.

"Wade." Abigail rushed forward and took her son's hand in hers, then led him toward Mr. Faricy. "This is Mike Faricy. He's going to help us fix some of the broken things around here."

"Oh." Wade stared at the man, then tilted his head to one side. "Good."

Good? Abigail couldn't prevent the laugh that bubbled up from her chest. Rosalie stepped forward and chuckled along with her.

"There be plenty of broken stuff around here," Rosalie said with a sigh. "I reckon we could use the help. I sure hope you don't eat much, though."

"Rosalie!" Abigail couldn't quite bring herself to meet Mr. Faricy's gaze. She felt him looking at her and suspected she'd find a fire smoldering in his eyes again, and she wasn't at all prepared to face that just yet.

Convincing her small family that having a man around the place was a good thing was enough to contend with for the moment. And there was the very real problem of deciding where they would go once Elysium was sold.

Sadness returned to overshadow the brief moments of joy she'd known in Mr. Faricy's embrace.

"Which of the cabins is most liveable, Rosalie?" she asked, deciding to occupy her mind with other, safer, matters. "Do you know?"

"Yes'm, I know." Rosalie half-turned and pointed toward the cabin nearest the barn, on the far side of the house. "That one."

Closest to the house. Of course.

Abigail swallowed hard. Mike wasn't going to harm her. The gentleness of his kiss had told her she could trust him. Still, a small voice in her mind wouldn't let her forget another man—another night.

A man bent on ravishment.

Mike looked up at the sky. "If I'm going to try to catch some fish before dark, I'd better do it."

"Pish?" Wade echoed, then looked at Abigail with a curious expression.

"Mr. Faricy is going to catch fish for us to eat."

Mike laughed. "Mr. Faricy is going to *try* to catch fish for us to eat," he corrected. "Do you suppose we can convince your mother to just call me Mike? I'll bet that's easier for you to pronounce anyway."

Rosalie clicked her tongue. "That wouldn't be proper. No, sir."

Mike. It was improper, yet it seemed like the right thing to do. Abigail ignored Rosalie's remark. She was right, of course, but these were hard times. Something as trivial as how they addressed each other hardly seemed important anymore. "We'd be pleased to call you ... Mike, if you'll agree to call me Abigail."

"Abigail."

Her name sounded rich and musical on his lips. She liked it.

"'Tain't proper," Rosalie repeated, and clicked her tongue again.

"These aren't proper times, Rosalie." Surprised by her bravado, Abigail turned and saw the shocked expression on her friend's face. "I'm sorry, but it's true."

"Yes'm. I reckon that's so."

Rosalie sighed and Abigail knew she'd won this battle. The cow bellowed a mournful sound, reminding them all of her presence. "Oh, I almost forgot about the cow."

Rosalie looked at Mike. "You gonna milk her?" she asked, gesturing toward the animal.

Mike chuckled. "Not hardly. Fish and dogs are about the only animals I can handle, and I'm afraid even that's questionable."

"Harumph."

"Rosalie, Mike's job is to fix things, not milk cows." Abigail looked anxiously at Rosalie. "Do *you* know how to milk her?"

Rosalie sighed again. "I think so, but I ain't never actually done it."

"Oh." Abigail looked over her shoulder at Mike. The mischievous twinkle in his eyes was a wonderful thing to behold. It made her heart swell with a sudden joy that caught her by surprise. For a moment, all she could do was stare.

Then the cow mooed again.

"All right." She laughed and shot the beast a disparaging glance. "Wade, you come with us to learn how to milk the cow. I think . . . Mike can find the fishing pole in the barn. It isn't hidden anymore."

"Gotcha." As he turned to walk toward the seldom-used barn, there was a spring in his step which hadn't been evident earlier.

Could she be the cause of that spring?

Don't be ridiculous. Her face flashed with heat as Wade held his arms up for her to hold him. She lifted him to her hip and nestled her face against his soft hair, remembering against her will the night of his conception.

Self-loathing seeped through her.

Mike paused near the riverbank where trees crowded the sun for supremacy. Searching the soft dark earth, he tried to remember exactly how to identify a good place to dig for worms. Worms like it cool and damp. *X marks the spot.*

He leaned the crude fishing pole against a tree, grabbed the broken handle of the spade he'd found in the barn and jabbed the business end into the dirt. The soil was moist and he didn't have to dig very deep to find an abundance of squiggly worms.

A childhood memory tugged at the fringes of his mind. His

throat tightened and his pulse hammered inside his head. He and Carrie'd gone on a family picnic with their parents, to a park not far from this very spot.

The day had been warm and sunny—early spring, if he remembered correctly. Mike had spent the day digging worms with Dad and teasing Carrie mercilessly with the slimy creatures.

Ah, what fun.

He blinked his stinging eyes rapidly and cleared his throat. Jerking himself back to his task, Mike dumped a spadeful of worm-infested earth into the pail he'd found with the fishing pole.

He retrieved the pole then half slid, half walked down the embankment to the river. Swirling eddies of brown water scurried around a fallen tree. This looked like a good place to fish.

He dug his fingers into the damp earth in search of his first volunteer. Most of the worms had already found their way to the bottom of the pail where the cool soil would keep them from drying. He grabbed a dirt clod and flipped it over, revealing several squirming candidates.

"All right, who wants to be first?"

He chose a nice fat one. It had been years since he'd actually handled a worm with his bare hands, and he'd forgotten how slimy they really were. No wonder Carrie hadn't liked them.

With a grimace, he pierced it with the rusty barbed hook then dropped the line into the water. With any luck, there'd be fish for dinner.

And he didn't care what kind of fish, as long as there was plenty to go around.

His stomach rumbled again in anticipation. "Knock it off," he ordered, tired of the constant reminders.

He stared out across the wide river beyond the fallen tree. There was nothing to do but sit here and think.

Great—just what I need.

In self-defense, his thoughts immediately reverted to the only pleasant experience he'd had today. That kiss—that woman. What was it about Abigail Kingsley? He was drawn to her—

physically and emotionally. Was there some sort of psychic bond between them?

Well, that's really stupid, numb-nuts.

She was gorgeous—he sure couldn't deny that. He remembered how sweet her lips had tasted. God, what had made him kiss her? It didn't really matter now—he couldn't take it back.

Given the opportunity, he *wouldn't* take it back anyway.

That brief, chaste kiss had been sexier than the deepest, wettest, longest pseudo-tonsillectomy he'd ever experienced . . . and then some. Though he'd exploded inside with needs and urges so acute he could barely control them, he hadn't deepened the kiss, though he'd sensed she wouldn't have resisted.

Why?

"Damned if I know." Mike looked overhead at the blue sky visible beyond the trees. A few wispy clouds floated by and he knew twilight would come soon. "Come on, fish."

"Mike, Mike."

The familiar sing-songy voice paralyzed him. Mike's gut twisted and gnashed in protest as his gaze darted around, probing his surroundings for the speaker.

"Up here, Mike."

Mike very slowly tilted his head back until he was looking into the tree branches directly overhead. "Where the hell are you now? Or should I say *what* the hell are you?"

A low chuckle punctuated by a hiss drifted down from the dense foliage. Then he saw something—movement on a branch of the nearest tree.

A snake? Not very original, but certainly appropriate. Of course, he was hardly Adam and this sure wasn't the Garden of Eden.

"Garden of Eden? Oh, that's rich." The chuckle continued as the long snake wound its way around the lowest branch until its head dangled out in front of Mike.

Its eyes were red.

"Isn't this get-up sort of a . . . cliché?" Mike tried to drag his gaze away from those penetrating red eyes . . . but he couldn't. "At least the cow was more original."

Slick chuckled again. "That was pretty creative, wasn't it?" He dipped his triangular-shaped head lower and closer to Mike. "Scared you—didn't I?"

"Yeah, asshole. Happy?"

The snake's forked tongue slipped out to flutter near Mike's face. "Happy? I love watching people suffer, but I'm sure that's no surprise to you."

"You got that right."

Slick's eyes flared brighter, more hypnotic than before.

"What . . . what do you want now?" Mike asked in a strained whisper.

"Oh, I thought maybe you needed a little reminder." Riveting, bloodred flames appeared in the depths of his eyes. "What are you here for, Mike? To put the moves on Scarlett O'Hara? Or to prevent dear Barney's gruesome death?"

"God damn you," Mike whispered, tightening his grip on the cane fishing pole. "Why don't you just leave me alone? I'll get the job done. Abigail knows people around here—she can help me find Milton's ancestors."

"Hey, lighten up. I don't care if you want to dip your noodle while you're here. I just want to make sure you stay on task. Hmm?" Slick dropped from the tree and landed on the ground at Mike's side. "You haven't figured out her secret yet. Have you?"

Slick slithered his long, reptilian body along Mike's leg and up his torso. Mike didn't even breathe. As a rule he wasn't afraid of snakes, but this one had the devil inside him—not exactly a pleasant combination.

"Well, have you?" Slick repeated, flickering his tongue out again.

"Figured out . . . what?" Mike tensed. His nerves were wired for sound—hi-fi, stereo, and quad. "I don't know what you're talking about."

"Abigail, of course. Her secret?" Slick encircled Mike's mid-section, then brought his face back up to eye level. "Have you?"

"I still don't—"

The snake's body suddenly tightened around Mike, cutting off his air and his words.

"Think, Mike." Slick pinned Mike with his flaming red eyes. "Think, *dickweed.*"

"Damn ... you," Mike muttered with the little breath remaining in his lungs. He knew Slick wouldn't kill him— Mike hadn't done his job yet. A deal was a deal.

"You're smarter than I thought." Slick loosened his body, allowing Mike to draw in great gulps of air. "Now think about what I said."

"About ... Abigail?" Mike couldn't think straight. "I still don't get it. Sorry."

"Yeah, I bet you are." Slick shook his snake head—an almost comical sight.

But Mike wasn't laughing. "By the way, you don't look a thing like a boa constrictor."

"You're pissing me off, Mike." The snake's eyes almost came out of their sockets to rivet Mike's. "I don't recommend that. Of course, I suppose I should take my own advice. Lucifer's pissed off at me, too."

"Why?" *As if I really give a rat's ass.*

"Oh, nothing to do with you. I'm sure you're *real* sorry to hear that, too." Slick tilted his head to one side as if in deep thought. "Now that you mention it, though, he gave me this assignment right after I told him I could run Hell more efficiently than he does. He's too soft."

Mike laughed. It was a crazed sound, reminding him of a woman he and Barney'd arrested one night right after she took a carving knife to her abusive husband. He'd never forget that laughter—insane and hopeless.

Just like him.

"Hey, I guess that makes you my punishment." Slick chuckled again, then slithered away from Mike, lowering himself to the ground. "Just don't forget your job, Mike."

The snake coiled itself into a perfect, conical shape, then vanished in a puff of smoke. Mike stared at the empty place on the ground where the reptile had been a moment ago, then shook his head and forced himself back to the present.

"God, now he's bucking for David Copperfield's job."

He'd better get used to Slick's games. It looked as if the devil's apprentice intended to keep a close eye on Mike's progress. And what had Slick meant about Abigail's secret?

Mike looked down at the water just as his line gave a decisive jerk. This was what he needed, something basic and necessary . . . and edible.

He backed slowly away from the water, wrapping the fishing line around a spool on the side of the pole's handle. This was crude compared to the rod and reel he'd left in the future, but it was better than nothing.

Slowly, he eased the large fish out of the water. It was a beauty—its silver scales glistened in the filtered sunlight as it flopped and struggled to free itself.

With one hand, Mike dumped the worms onto the ground and bent down to fill the pail with river water. Then he cautiously gripped the squirming fish and looked at it.

A catfish.

Groaning, Mike reminded himself that he'd said it didn't matter what kind of fish he caught, as long as he caught plenty. This one was large enough to feed all of them, he decided, dropping it into the pail.

A bottom-feeder was better than nothing at all.

And at least its eyes weren't red.

Chapter Six

The ceiling. Abigail wondered how long she could stare at it without going blind. Maybe darkness would save her from such a fate.

Tugging the frayed quilt up to her chin, she rolled to her side to stare at the window. Moonlight streamed through the tattered lace curtains, throwing myriad shapes across her bedroom floor.

At least it wasn't the ceiling.

She closed her eyes, hoping sleep would lower its soothing hand. Considering all the work she'd done today, sleeping shouldn't be a problem. Cleaning out Mike's cabin had taken hours.

A smile tugged at her mouth and she allowed her eyes to flutter open again. A sudden flash of heat scorched her cheeks as she recalled the look on his face when she'd straightened from making up the straw tick in the cabin.

He'd been watching her. There was no doubt in her mind. What she couldn't understand was why that knowledge should please her.

She sighed. It didn't really matter why it pleased her, because it did. For some ridiculous reason, knowing that Mike found her attractive cheered her. Immensely.

"Oh, Abigail," she whispered, then flopped onto her back again. Why couldn't she sleep? Apparently exhaustion wasn't enough of a catalyst tonight.

It wasn't fear—she felt safe with Mike here. Somehow, she knew he meant them no harm, though his behavior continued to baffle her. And the fish he'd caught for their supper had been more than welcome—a rare treat. For the first time in many months, they'd all gone to bed without hunger pangs. Though catfish wasn't her favorite, tonight it had tasted divine.

After throwing back the quilt, she rose and padded barefoot to the partially open window. A gentle breeze wafted in from the river, making the curtain billow around her.

She pushed the curtain aside and stepped closer, gazing out at the moonlit grounds below. Elysium, its splendor tarnished by war, was no more.

A surge of sadness overtook Abigail, making her feel heavy and tired—much older than her years. The home she'd known and loved all her life no longer existed. This forlorn plantation would be sold and its new owners would undoubtedly call it something different.

Elysium. What had possessed her great-grandfather to give a plantation such a grandiose title?

Tears stung her eyes and she stepped closer to permit the breeze to bathe her in coolness. This place wasn't even a farm anymore, and she had absolutely no hope of saving it for her son. None at all.

She had to let it go. Elysium was a part of her idyllic childhood. That time, that plantation, *that girl* no longer existed. And never would again.

One tear slid down her cheek and she swiped it away furiously. She refused to cry any more. What good would that do, after all?

A movement in the darkness caught her attention. She leaned closer to the window and peered downward, where silver moonlight illuminated the grounds. What had she seen? An animal, perhaps?

She remembered the precious cow, then quickly assured

herself it was inside the barn, safe from predators. *I must be imagining things.*

Just as she convinced herself to return to bed, she saw it again. It was a tiny pinpoint of light, moving alongside the silhouette of a man.

It had to be Mike. Relief washed through her, then curiosity quickly replaced it. What sort of light did he carry? The way it moved back and forth convinced her the light originated from something held in his hand. How strange—what could it be? It was certainly far too small to be a lantern.

The rhythmic movement halted several feet from the dark shape of his cabin. As he stood there in the darkness, the moonlight seemed to define his features—or was it her memory filling in the missing details?

Abigail swallowed hard and brought her hand to the base of her throat, where she could feel her heartbeat thundering along at an alarming rate. That man unnerved her, yet it wasn't exactly a distasteful sensation. Far from it, in fact.

The small light in his hand suddenly lifted and he seemed to aim it toward her. Her gasp seized in her throat and her mouth went dry, though she knew the light couldn't possibly be bright enough to reach her.

Still, the suspicion that he was looking for her made her tremble. A tight spring of longing coiled inside her, low in her belly where it brought a sensation of painful pleasure—a sweet ache.

Suddenly she knew exactly what her body hungered for. "Oh, merciful heavens." She *wanted* Mike Faricy to kiss her, to touch her . . . and more.

Horrified, she struggled against the images and memories stubbornly mingling with the longing she now felt. Though the memories were vile, the fascination she felt for Mike wasn't. This didn't make sense, but no matter how hard she tried, Abigail couldn't thwart the obstinate yearning unfurling deep inside her.

She bit her lower lip. Her knees quaked and the room swayed. Pressing both hands against the sides of her head as if to obliterate the conflicting images, she turned and staggered to her bed.

Crawling beneath the quilt, she willed her breathing to slow and the trembling to cease. She couldn't want *that*. No, it was impossible.

That's why I can't sleep. Confusion made a restless bed partner. Her body craved things her mind recognized only as horror. Why?

Yet the quickening in her loins persisted each time she caught sight of Mike Faricy. Her stomach knotted in feeble protest. The thought of being with a man again in that way should be horrifying beyond words.

Unspeakable.

In the shadow of the rat-infested cabin, Mike stared through the darkness at the window where he thought he'd seen something—someone. Was that Abigail's room?

The penlight was worthless at this distance, but he aimed it toward the house anyway. The moon provided enough light to show the open window. Maybe all he'd seen were the curtains flapping in the wind.

Wind—empty air—was about the only thing whistling through his brain at this point. "Brilliant, Mike," he muttered, lowering the penlight and shoving it into his pocket.

An old television commercial popped into his mind. *This is your brain. This is your brain on drugs.*

No, Mike. This is your brain after selling your soul to the devil.

Raking his fingers through his hair, he turned and walked back into the cabin—his home away from home.

Correction—his home until death.

"Damn." Selling his soul to Slick had been so simple—he hadn't given it a second thought at the time. Anything to give Barney back to Carrie.

Even your . . . soul?

With a shudder, he closed the door behind him. There was no way to undo this deal, and he wouldn't even if he could.

Barney would live . . . and Mike was as good as dead. *So be it.*

He took off his jacket and hung it over the back of a chair, then slipped the holster off his shoulder and placed it on the table. Instinctively, he looked at his wrist, then remembered he no longer possessed a watch. He owned a cow instead.

Having stupidly—desperately—traded the watch for the cow, Mike still had no money. He pulled his wallet from his hip pocket and flipped through the worthless bills and credit cards, then suddenly remembered something else.

Something gold—at least gold-plated.

Suddenly feeling very old, Mike reached into his jacket's breast pocket and removed a small leather case. He opened it in the narrow column of moonlight shining through the lone window . . . and stared.

His gold detective's badge.

Even that would be worth something here and now. The thought of actually parting with it made his gut wrench and burn, but when the time came that he had to have money, he knew he wouldn't have much choice.

Disgusted, he shoved the case back into his pocket. But he wasn't going to do it until he absolutely had to.

He walked across the dirt floor and sat on the edge of the narrow bunk. Straw crunched under him and he looked down with a grimace. This wasn't exactly the Holiday Inn, but he was too damned tired to worry about it right now.

He kicked off his Reeboks and stretched out on top of the quilt, remembering when he'd walked into the cabin earlier in the evening and found Abigail bent over this bunk. With a groan, Mike felt his blood supply redirect itself. Good thing he was flat on his back.

That woman had more sex appeal than she had a right to, yet Mike knew she didn't realize it. And he recognized something else, too.

There was no husband here at Elysium. Abigail, Rosalie, and Wade were alone here . . . except for Mike. She hadn't offered any explanations either, so Mike had no idea if she had a husband on his way home from the war or not.

He mentally tallied the evidence. *Always the cop.*

She had a son, so there'd obviously been a man in her life—and in her bed—at some point. She didn't wear mourning garb—thank God.

For some reason, he sensed he was missing something, then he remembered Slick's taunting words down by the river.

You haven't figured out her secret yet, have you?

He sat upright in bed, wincing when his belt buckle pinched him right where it counted. Why hadn't he seen this explanation earlier? It all made sense now in a sick sort of way.

Abigail Kingsley was an unwed mother.

Mike shook his head and slowly eased his body back down to the straw mattress. What did this mean, exactly? If he was right, and all the evidence sure pointed in that direction, then how had she ended up in this situation?

Well, he knew *how*—maybe the question he needed to ask was *why*. In this day and age, women—ladies—didn't hop in the sack with just anyone.

His frustrated libido knew that only too well, though the thought had certainly crossed his mind more than once today.

Why did it matter to him? It wasn't as if he could help her, other than by repairing some farm equipment for her to sell and by catching a few fish.

That stupid snake slithered its way into his thoughts again, reminding Mike of something else Slick had mentioned.

Mike had a mission—he needed to remain focused. If he failed to prevent Milton's ancestor from being born, Barney would die.

"No." Mike's voice filled the small cabin and his body tightened with vivid, wresting memories. "No," he repeated, then sighed as resignation seeped through him.

He had to stop allowing himself to get sidetracked. Abigail Kingsley's life was her own business. Mike had more important matters to deal with.

Like fulfilling his bargain with the devil.

* * *

"He's doin' it again." Rosalie shook her head as she came in the back door with the morning's milk.

"Who's doing what?" Abigail smiled to herself as she mixed milk and cornmeal in a small bowl. After almost a week, Rosalie's comments regarding Mike Faricy were becoming part of the routine at Elysium. "What is it this time?"

"Runnin'." Rosalie sighed. "I ain't never seen nobody run for no reason, 'cept maybe younguns."

"Well, he's certainly not a child." Abigail tried not to think about how Mike had looked yesterday morning when she'd seen him strip off his shirt beneath the magnolia tree out by the well. Her insides warmed as she recalled the way his skin had glistened in the early morning light. Strange, but she'd never found sweat an attractive feature on a man before. "Did you ask him why he does it?"

"Ha! He said he needed the exercise to stay in shape— whatever that means."

"I see." Abigail's face flashed with heat. What was it about that man?

"Then, when I was in the barn this mornin' milkin', he come in singin'."

"What's so unusual about a man singing?" Abigail looked back over her shoulder as Rosalie poured the milk into a clean pail. "Hmm?"

"Well, it weren't the singin' that were strange," Rosalie continued, moving closer to look into the bowl. "We got more fish to go with that?"

"Of course." Abigail gave her friend a knowing smile. "Haven't we had some sort of fish every day since Mike came?"

With a sigh, Rosalie nodded. "He's a right fine fisherman— that's a fact. But I ain't never heard so many strange things out of a body in all my days."

And I've never spent so much time looking at anyone's body in all my days. Her face must've been crimson by now, she imagined. She dipped a piece of fish into the batter, then placed it gingerly in the hot oil. She knew Rosalie wouldn't be satisfied until she'd been allowed to speak her mind. "What was he singing this time?"

"A song. At least I think it was a song."

"What's so strange about a song?" Abigail knew this game of question and answer well, but it seemed to make her friend happy, so she was more than willing to oblige. "What did it sound like?"

"Strangest thing I ever heard," Rosalie said. "He was singin' about doin' somethin' in the road."

Abigail lifted her eyebrows and grinned at Rosalie. "You're right—that is strange." It wasn't the first unusual behavior they'd observed in Mike, and Abigail had the distinct feeling it wouldn't be the last. At least . . . she hoped not. "He earns his way around here, though."

"That he does." Rosalie gave a decisive nod, then returned to the milk, spreading a square of cheesecloth across the top. "We got more milk than we can use. I reckon I better start churnin'."

"Buttermilk would be heaven." Abigail sighed, remembering the smooth buttermilk her mother'd always kept hanging down the well where it would keep cool during the summer months. But they wouldn't be staying long enough to enjoy all the benefits of owning a cow.

Of course, Rosalie didn't know that.

Guilt pressed down on Abigail. She hadn't found the courage to inform her friend yet of their impending fate. This was their home—the only one either of them had ever known. Rosalie had a right to know.

"Rosalie?"

"Yes'm?"

Abigail turned the pieces of fish in the hot oil, then pivoted to face her friend. "I have something to tell you."

Rosalie's smooth, dark brow furrowed with worry. "Somethin' wrong?"

Nodding, Abigail blinked back the stinging tears and cleared her throat. "Yes."

"You ain't ailin', is—"

"No, nothing like that." Abigail took a step toward Rosalie, then gestured toward the table and chairs. "Sit down with me for a minute."

Rosalie nodded, then went to the table. Abigail glanced at the frying fish, then pulled out a chair and sat opposite her friend. "That day I went to town, when Mike came back with me?"

"Yes'm."

How would Rosalie take this news? "I learned while I was there that I owe back taxes on Elysium."

"Oh." Rosalie shook her head. "Well, you ain't got no more money, so they can't take what you don't got."

"That's true, Rosalie. They can't take what I don't have." She drew a deep breath, girding her resolve. "So, they'll take what we *do* have. They'll take Elysium."

"Oh, sweet Jesus." Rosalie closed her eyes, then held her head in her hands. When she looked up and met Abigail's gaze, her stunned expression had been replaced with calm reason. "There ain't no way we can raise enough money to pay?"

Abigail shook her head. "Mike realized that the tools and equipment weren't listed as part of the estate. He's going to try and fix some of the furniture, too."

"Why?"

Abigail stood and walked over to the stove. She moved the fish away from the heat, then transferred the flaky pieces to a cracked platter. Leaving the platter near the stove, she turned toward the table again, forcing a smile to her face.

"To sell," she finally answered. "See, we'll need all the money we can get to move somewhere for a fresh start."

"Where we gonna go?" Rosalie appeared skeptical. The wrinkles on her forehead deepened and her lower lip jutted out in a challenging expression. "What we gonna do?"

"I haven't decided." Renewed guilt permeated Abigail, intensified by the stab of fear which quickly followed. She'd argued with herself all week, and there really seemed only one course of action. All she had to do was muster the courage to see it through. "I'll let you know as soon as I have a plan."

"I'm goin' with you." Rosalie folded her arms across her

chest, her dark eyes glittering with unshed tears. "You hear that?"

"Yes." Abigail allowed herself a small sigh of relief. "It makes me very happy that you want to stay with us, but you don't have to. Do you understand that?"

"I know all about the Emancipation Proclamation, Miss Abigail." She waved her hand in the air and rolled her eyes. "I'm free, and that means I can do whatever I want. What I want is to go with you and your boy."

The burning sensation in Abigail's eyes intensified, and her throat felt full and tight. "Thank you," she mumbled, then reached across the table to capture Rosalie's hand with hers. Giving it a decisive squeeze, she nodded. "We'll be all right. Don't worry."

"I ain't worried."

Abigail knew it was a lie, and she loved her friend all the more for it. "Thank you."

"Ain't nothin' to thank me for." Rosalie gently extracted her hand, then pushed her chair away from the table and rose to her feet. "We're gonna do what we gotta do. I reckon that's all there is to it."

"That's right." Abigail bit her lower lip to still its quivering. She would do what she had to. That was that.

"I reckon I'd best fetch the menfolks for breakfast." Rosalie gave a low whistle. "I 'magine that boy's got hisself powerful dirty by now, out in that barn with Mr. Mike."

"I'm sure he has." *And loved every minute of it, no doubt.* "Yes, I'm afraid the fish will get cold if we don't eat soon." Abigail moved the platter to the table and watched her friend step out the back door.

Gripping the table edge, Abigail clenched her teeth tight and hard. She forcibly silenced the sobs which ripped at her insides. After a moment, she drew a deep breath, then reached into the pocket of her apron and removed the envelope.

She carefully slid the letter out and unfolded it to read her own words. This was her only choice.

A memory slashed through her mind, jeopardizing her

resolve. The horrifying image coalesced in her mind's eye—
oppressive and derisive.

The man's face was very near hers, hovering over her with
a victorious smile. His taunting words played over and over in
her mind.

You're mine now. You're mine now. You're mine now . . .

Her heart thundered, making her blood roar through her body
as she blinked, struggling to focus on the words before her.
This was her only alternative. She had no choice.

She dragged in a few shaky breaths, then read the words
she'd written a few days ago. Reality quelled her reluctance.
She *would* do this.

Quickly, she reread the letter and stumbled over the last
sentence. The words that could very well seal her fate leapt
off the page at her.

Your son and I await your reply.

"Oh, Lord."

With shaking fingers, she refolded the letter and slipped it
back into the envelope. When she turned it over, the man's
name stared back at her, along with his address in Denver.

After all this time, she couldn't be certain of the address. In
fact, it was possible he hadn't survived the war at all.

She permitted that thought to seep through her mind as
she considered the possibility. *Justice?* she wondered, then
immediately squelched such self-serving thoughts. His death
would do her no good now, though it might give her a moment
of satisfaction.

And relief.

No. Somehow she knew the vile man still lived. The hatred
seething deep within her surely would have quieted after all
this time if he were dead. That illogical thought in the wake
of her decision actually made sense, after a fashion.

"I *will* post this today."

She returned the letter to her pocket just as the back door
swung open. The sight of her son perched on Mike Faricy's
shoulders struck Abigail as so right it nearly paralyzed her.

Dumbstruck, her gaze met Mike's soft expression. There
was a twinkle in his hazel eyes this morning—an almost boyish

quality that warmed her heart and made her ache for something she was afraid to define.

"Good morning," he said, then reached up to lift Wade over his head and lowered the boy to the floor. "Hey, fish for breakfast. That's a switch."

Wade made a face and Abigail couldn't suppress her chuckle. They'd eaten fish three times a day since Mike's arrival. Though it was a welcome addition to their diets, some variety would have been appreciated.

"Pish," Wade muttered in disgust. "That sucks."

Abigail whirled around to stare down at her son in disbelief. "What did you say, Wade?"

"That sucks."

Abigail slowly lifted an incredulous gaze to Mike's reddening face. He gave her a sheepish grin and a shrug, then muttered an apology.

"What does that mean ... exactly?" she asked, knowing without any reservation that the words her son had muttered were unseemly, though she wasn't certain why.

Mike's eyes widened and he rubbed his whiskered jaw with his thumb and forefinger. The lovely ring he always wore winked at her from the third finger of his right hand. There were raised letters around the stone, though she'd never been able to read them clearly.

"Well, it means—sort of—uh ..." Mike grinned again. "It means he doesn't like something."

"I see." Abigail looked down at her son again, trying very hard not to smile. For some reason, having a man around to corrupt her son in masculine ways seemed a rare gift. She remembered her brother and father joking with her mother, and warm memories filled her heart.

Her own son had missed this. She pressed her hand against the pocket holding the envelope. "Next time, just say you don't like something, then. All right?"

Wade nodded. "No like."

"That's better." She ruffled his hair and conceded herself a smile at her son's impish expression. "But you *do* like fish, Wade," she insisted.

He wrinkled his face and scrunched up his nose, then Mike scooped him up off the floor and deposited a squealing Wade in a chair at the table.

"You *do* like fish, Wade." Mike smacked his lips in anticipation. "I caught it and your mom cooked it. How could you not like it?"

Rosalie came through the door holding something small and furry in her hands. "Look here what I found." She held out her hands to display a tiny kitten. "It was in the barn all by itself."

Abigail looked at the small creature in awe. "It looks like George Washington." She reached out a finger to stroke its soft head.

"That's what I thought, too, but—"

"George Washington?"

Both women turned toward Mike at the same time. Abigail gave him an indulgent smile. "We had a cat named George Washington when I was a little girl," she explained, enjoying good memories for a change.

"Oh." Mike shrugged. "Interesting name for a cat."

Abigail sighed. "I suppose." She straightened and walked over to the basin. "Did you two wash up before you came inside?"

"Yes, ma'am." Mike's exaggerated politeness produced a giggle from Wade. "We both did, at the well."

After washing her own hands, she placed the few dishes they still possessed on the table, then glanced at the kitten again. "He's so tiny."

Rosalie nodded. "I dunno how he got here neither. No sign of a mama cat around anywhere."

"Well, now I know what we'll do with all this extra milk," Abigail said decisively, then uncovered the pail and used a cup to skim cream off the top. She didn't have another bowl, so she placed the shallow tin cup on the floor.

"Why, sure." Rosalie put the kitten down in front of the cream, then took a step back.

The tiny kitten sniffed the air around it, then moved forward very slowly and dipped its head. Its face completely vanished inside the cup, and after a moment it lifted its head and licked its lips. Cream coated its nose and whiskers.

Abigail and Rosalie both laughed as the kitten sneezed and shoved its face back into the cup. "He's hungry," Rosalie stated the obvious.

"I can't imagine how he got here." Abigail straightened. "Wash up, Rosalie. I'm afraid the fish will be completely cold by now."

"It's not bad," Mike said from behind them.

Abigail turned and went to the table, taking a chair beside her son. "I'm sorry. We were distracted."

"Cat?" Wade's eyes were wide and curious as he looked over his shoulder at the small furry backside. "Cat?"

"Yes, Wade." Abigail touched her son's shoulder, urging him to turn back to his breakfast. She slid the cup of milk Rosalie had served him nearer. "I think you're already starting to fatten up now that you have this good milk to drink every day."

She glanced up and found Mike studying her with a thoughtful expression. They all ate in companionable silence for several minutes. Fish and milk—that was all they had, but it was like a feast compared to what they'd subsisted on before Mike's arrival.

"I'm going into town later," Mike announced, giving her a questioning glance. His face hardened and a muscle twitched in his cheek. "I told you when you hired me that I needed to go to town every day. I haven't been at all, but I really *have* to. Besides, a lot of your stuff's ready to sell now, so I thought I'd post a notice somewhere. Any suggestions where?"

"The post office." Abigail stiffened, remembering her own need to visit that establishment. "I have a letter to send anyway, so I'll show you where it is."

"Letter?" Rosalie shot Abigail a suspicious glance.

"Uh . . . I'm making plans for our future." Abigail cleared her throat, then quickly took a bite of fish and chewed furiously. When she swallowed and looked around the table, she found Mike and Rosalie both still staring at her. "What's wrong?"

"I just dunno who you be sendin' a letter to." Rosalie lifted her brows. "Hmm?"

Mike sighed and shrugged. "I'd be happy to mail your letter for you."

Fear made Abigail's skin prick. "No, no. That's all right." If this had to be done, she'd do it herself.

He looked at her curiously. "Well then, if you need to go to town, I'd appreciate it if you'd show me where to post the notice."

Abigail knew without a doubt that he was wondering the same thing as Rosalie. *Who in this world does the very isolated Abigail Kingsley know to send a letter to?*

They didn't need to know. Abigail's face burned as she forced herself to eat another piece of fish. She looked down at her son, surprised to find him staring at her, too.

"I don't believe this," she muttered, then felt something soft brush against her ankle. Remembering the kitten, she pushed her chair back and bent down to lift it.

Her mother would never have permitted anyone to sit at the table with an animal, but Abigail was pushed back far enough to prevent hair from landing in the food. Besides, she was finished eating.

The kitten's belly was engorged. As she held it close to her cheek, she heard a tiny belch escape. It felt good to know they finally had enough food to share. Only a week ago there would've been absolutely nothing to give the poor creature.

"I wonder where he came from." She held the kitten out in front of her face. "What shall we name you?"

Mike met her gaze from across the table. "Are you sure it's male?"

Abigail's face flooded with heat. "Well ..." Hesitantly, remembering how improper it was to have such a discussion with a gentleman, Abigail lifted the kitten's tail and took a quick peek. When she lowered the kitten, she found Rosalie's dark eyes wide with shock. "Oh, Rosalie," she said in an exasperated tone.

"Well, it ain't proper and you know it."

"Of course, you're right." Abigail pressed her lips into a thin line, then looked up to find Mike Faricy chuckling at them. "Mr. Faricy, this cat is indeed male."

"All right. Let's look at this logically." He leaned back in his chair and rubbed his chin thoughtfully. After a moment, he snapped his fingers. "I've got it."

"Got what?" Rosalie narrowed her gaze and lifted her brows in open curiosity.

"A name for the cat."

"Oh." Disinterestedly, Rosalie turned her attention back to her meal.

Abigail smiled, glancing down to see her son gulping milk from his cup. After a moment, he lowered it and displayed a milk moustache coating his upper lip.

"What name?" she asked, meeting Mike's twinkling gaze.

"I'm not so sure now. Let me think a minute." A wrinkle appeared across the bridge of his nose. "I had a friend with an orange and black cat when I was growing up. What did he call that cat?"

"I have no idea." Abigail glanced at her son's rapt expression as he watched Mike.

"Shadow? Inky? No, that's for an all black cat. What was that name?" Mike looked at Wade. "Do *you* know?"

"Nope." The child shook his head and giggled.

"This was a really great name for a cat of any color." He rubbed the back of his neck, then his expression suddenly hardened. The color in his face drained as if someone had pulled a cork. "What . . . color are his eyes?" he asked, staring long and hard at the small, purring kitten in Abigail's arms.

Remembering Mike's concern about the cow, Abigail didn't hesitate. She turned the kitten around and looked at its face. "Green."

Mike's relief was obvious. "Well, that other name won't do then . . . thank God." He shot her an apologetic glance. "He's male and he has a great appetite, as he's already demonstrated."

"That's true," Abigail said with a smile when her son looked up at her with a question in his eyes. Wade obviously thought the adults in the room were being silly.

"There's only one name for that cat."

"What is it?"

"Garfield . . . even if we don't have any lasagna."

Chapter Seven

The sun's heat was nearly unbearable. Mike glanced up, wishing for a few clouds. No such luck. Not even a wisp marred the clear sky.

"What I wouldn't give for a cold beer," he muttered without thinking, then remembered he wasn't alone. Glancing sideways at Abigail, Mike was rewarded with a shy smile.

Not what he needed at all.

What he needed was for her to act a little less appealing for a change. Instead, she gave him one of those melt-away smiles that should've sent him running in the opposite direction.

Then why didn't it?

I don't want to know, he decided, pushing the thoughts away and his gaze forward. He'd already wasted nearly a week of his time here. No more. Today he'd begin his search for Milton's ancestor in earnest.

That was that.

No more distractions.

That night flashed through his mind again. God, he'd been such a fool to let this much time pass without at least attempting to find his target. His gut wrenched and his blood pressure hit the red zone.

Who says stress is a bad thing?

Not for Mike Faricy. Not now. He needed stress to keep him in line—on task. Hell, maybe he even needed those occasional visits from Slick.

He winced. *Well . . . maybe not.*

Just remembering Barney spread out on that warehouse floor with his sightless eyes staring up at the ceiling was enough. Now all he had to do was *remain* focused until this nightmare came to an end.

Nightmare? Part of this adventure definitely qualified, but not all of it. He shot another glance at his silent companion, obviously as lost in thought as he. Walking down the road on a sunny day with a gorgeous woman at his side wasn't exactly his definition of a typical nightmare.

Angrily, he clenched his teeth and looked away. *Focus, Mike. Do it!* Still, what harm was there in an occasional peek?

His gaze followed his thoughts, right back to Abigail Kingsley's slightly upturned nose, her soft lips, the little wrinkle she always wore across the bridge of her nose when deep in thought. Her long, slender neck held her head at an almost haughty angle.

On her it seemed appropriate. Back in his youth a woman like Abigail would've been labeled a snob—a poor little rich girl. At least, for a while . . .

Not anymore. Her family had been near starving when he found them. *Found them?* That was a laugh. More like fallen through the roof . . . or over the rainbow.

Was there a *reason* Slick had sent Mike to Abigail? Or was his arrival in her house simple coincidence? That was where he'd started from, so that was where he'd arrived.

Logical.

Then he remembered Slick's taunting about Abigail's secret. Could there be more to this than Mike realized? Could she hold a key of some sort? Maybe she had valuable information and he'd been too busy panting after her to see it.

Fool. He reached up to wipe sweat from his eyes. Somehow, Slick Dawson didn't seem like the type to do something without a reason. That devil-in-training had to have a plan.

A plan Mike was too blinded to see.

He stared long and hard at Abigail's worried expression, thankful for the silence. If she talked to him, he might get sidetracked again. Right now, he needed to concentrate.

Add up the evidence, Detective, he silently chided. Was there more to this than logistics? Abigail's house, Mike's selection of hideouts, and his arrival in her house and time.

Coincidence?

Slick could have sent Mike to any period in history to stop Milton from being born. Why now? Here?

With her?

Abigail was more than merely a distraction. There was something about that woman that tugged at feelings he was ill-prepared to deal with. She made him crazy—not just horny-crazy. Abigail made him want to help her, reach out to her, vanquish her enemies and pave her future with security and happiness.

Get a grip, Mike. At least his hormones were something that didn't require emotions. He could deal with his libido—it didn't make his gut wrench or boggle his mind.

Fortunately, Abigail Kingsley had the sort of body necessary to distract him from those other pesky ideas. Thoughts of being her knight in shining armor were ridiculous. Foolish. Futile.

He was a dead man. There was no time for gallantry. Yes, sex was something he could handle—a diversion he could really benefit from at the moment.

Her tears, Wade's hunger, that damned helpless kitten this morning, were too much. Not now—not ever. Carrie and Barney'd been his family—he was finished now. Abigail's family would live and he was as good as dead already.

Then why did he want to share their challenges? Why did he want to help them? Why? What could he do for them anyway? He had to stop thinking about their future happiness and concentrate on his mission.

Abigail was one of those women that men like him—confirmed bachelors—avoided at all costs. She was vulnerable and needed help.

And she was beautiful.

Right now, he wasn't sure which was worse—wanting her physically or that other stuff—the emotions. But he knew the answer only too well. At least wanting her helped take his mind off things over which he had no control . . . like her future.

Those breasts . . .

His mind struggled to maintain control, but his body swelled and hardened with an ache that evolved beyond casual and straight toward desperate. He felt like a teenager on hormone overload, with one significant difference.

Mike knew what to do with the equipment nature'd given him. That was one hell of a lot more than he knew about taking care of Abigail and her son.

Milton. Slick. Barney. "Damn."

"I'm sorry, did you say something?"

Her voice washed over him, cool and refreshing in the sweltering heat. What he needed was a well-aimed pitcher of ice water. "Nothing important," he muttered, wishing he could discreetly adjust his clothing to accommodate his compressed body.

"I'm sorry if we've kept you from your business."

"Don't worry about it." Mike clenched his teeth and looked straight ahead, avoiding her smile. She wasn't helping him remain focused at all.

"Well, the post office is near where the tax notices were the other day," Abigail said.

Several moments of silence fell between them; then as they neared the edge of town, Mike stopped and stared after her, again adding up all the facts. He knew there was more—something he'd overlooked.

Abigail Kingsley was, as far as he could tell, an unmarried mother—not a big deal in his time, but in this time that spelled major complications. Based on what he'd overheard in town the other day, her reputation was ruined and she was about to lose her home.

His memory of the morning he'd awakened on her floor surfaced, bringing with it a string of images—flashes of Abigail's anger and fear. When she turned to face him, their gazes fused. Then he remembered . . .

Her words came to him as if she'd just spoken them.

"Don't make me use this," she'd pleaded, her voice betraying her fear. *"I promised God I'd never kill another man . . ."*

"Who'd you kill?" he asked steadily, wondering if that was the secret Slick had meant.

Her face blanched and she looked away. After a moment, she lifted her gaze and met his. Unshed tears sparkled in her blue eyes, making Mike feel like a real creep.

Still, he had to know.

"Who was it, Abigail?" *And what does that incident have to do with my mission—if anything?*

"I . . . I don't know what you're talking a—"

"Yes, you do," he insisted. "I remember now. You said you promised God you'd never kill another man." He sighed and shot her a crooked grin. "I guess I was about to be the 'other.' See, I don't generally forget things like that—especially since I was at the other end of your gun when you said it."

"I'm sure that isn't exactly what I said." She darted him a nervous glance and moistened her lips with her tongue. "You were distraught that day."

"I know what I heard."

"Well, if you're so positive, you certainly took your time to ask me about it."

He sighed. "I've been distracted." *By a pretty face . . . and a few other matters.*

Her chin quivered slightly and she bit her lower lip. "I think you're mistaken. I'm sure you must've heard incorrectly." After a moment, she nodded. "But if you insist . . ."

"I do." A wagon rumbled past and Mike realized they were practically in town now. "I guess it'll have to wait until later, but I'm not going to forget again."

"I'm sure you won't."

He saw relief etched plainly across her face. Whatever had provoked Abigail to take a human life must've been nothing short of catastrophe.

"The post office is a few blocks from here." She straightened the bow beneath her chin and overhauled her resolve in one breath, as plainly as if she'd stated her intentions.

"Let's get to it then." Mike took a few steps toward her, constantly fighting the urge to pull her into his arms and make stupid promises about taking care of her. Where the hell had that come from anyway? He could barely take care of himself, let alone Abigail and her son.

Besides, they were no concern of his. Where they? *No.* He had a mission—a death to cause and one to prevent. And it wasn't as if he'd be around long enough to do anyone much good anyway. They'd be all right without his help.

Wouldn't they?

"I have to stop at that dreadful place to find out when they're going to make us . . . leave." Her voice was quiet and thoughtful as they walked into the outskirts of Natchez.

"Yeah, I remember. The notice said the date would be announced. That'll let me know how much time I have to finish fixing stuff." Mike clenched his teeth, reminding himself that Abigail losing her plantation wasn't his fault.

With a sigh, he looked around at the town from a different— more sane?—perspective. Like his first visit to 1865 Natchez, he was struck with the realization of how much of it was like the town he knew, though very different at the same time.

A signpost on the next corner caught his attention. It almost mocked him with its familiarity. Although the words were the same, the sign and post were very different.

He and Abigail stood at the intersection of Monroe and Canal streets. He looked behind him from where they'd come. That meant the road they'd just walked along would one day be known as Cemetery Road. Maybe it already was, though there was no sign indicating that.

It felt good to have his bearings. Some of his old confidence surged to the surface, giving Mike the impetus he'd been missing.

He'd spent the last few days walking around stranded somewhere between horny and crazy. Actually, he'd wavered to the extremes on both ends, but now he was finally regaining his

self-control—that cool proficiency Detective Mike Faricy had
been known for.

As long as he could stop thinking so much about this woman
and her problems. *Sir Galahad,* fall *off your white steed.* He
drew a deep breath and forced himself to concentrate on his
mission.

Abigail had said she didn't know a family named Milton in
the area, but she'd been isolated from the mainstream. Natchez
was in a constant state of flux these days. Reconstruction had
drawn new families who had come out of desperation. Maybe
there were new families in Natchez she hadn't met.

He looked at her as she pulled an envelope from her pocket
and stared at it. Her jaw twitched as if she was clenching her
teeth.

That letter was obviously something of great significance.
She'd said it had to do with their future. Was this another clue?
Something he should heed?

Slick had him so full of questions it was a miracle he could
think straight at all. Mike looked across the street.

Abigail's letter was her business. He had his own to contend
with and he was late seeing to it.

A man walked by wearing a hat much like the one Barney'd
often worn—a combination of something Indiana Jones and
John Wayne would wear. The hat was even the same shade of
brown as Barney's.

That thirst for revenge he'd felt the night of his partner's
death shot through him anew. However, the blood lust that
sang through his veins now was far different from what he'd
felt when he first made his bargain with the devil. This was
more controlled—more deliberate.

More dangerous.

Mike was primed—ready to get on with life.

And death.

Abigail didn't want to relive that nightmare.

She swallowed hard and shoved the envelope back into her
pocket. More than one nightmare, actually. Her hand trembled

as she brought it to her chest and felt the violent beating of her heart.

She squeezed her eyes shut for just a moment, forcing the turbulent images from her mind. Today she must deal with matters which would wait no longer. The sale of Elysium and safeguarding her son's future.

Girding her resolve, she opened her eyes and cleared her throat. "The post office is this way."

"Great."

Mike fell into step beside her, making Abigail keenly conscious of him as a *man*. Under normal circumstances, before the war, she might have walked along these streets with her arm tucked discreetly in his.

But not now—not ever.

She paused outside the post office. Fighting the urge to jerk the letter from her pocket and tear it into tiny shreds, Abigail waited for her trembling to cease. She had to do this, she reminded herself again.

"You ready?" Mike asked, looking at her with a curious expression on his handsome face.

His rugged appearance and straightforward bearing unnerved her. "Yes, of course." She withdrew the envelope from her pocket along with her last coin. Soon, there would be none.

She stared down at the smooth circle, remembering how it had come into her possession in the first place. Tears of regret stung her eyes, but she quickly banished them and drew a deep, fortifying breath.

"Well," she said with a sigh.

"Well, what?" Mike looked at her with a question in his eyes. "That board over there looks like the place to post a notice. I'll take care of that. You going to mail that letter or not?"

With an emphatic nod, Abigail swept by him and into the post office, which had once doubled as a mercantile. A soldier behind the counter looked up; the sight of his blue uniform nearly cost her the smidgen of courage she'd managed to muster. Then she rationalized that the army would be running the post office for the time being, because during the war mail delivery in the Confederate States had become virtually nonexistent.

Thank heaven for small favors, she thought cynically, then squared her shoulders and stepped up to the counter.

"Yes, ma'am?" Judging from his boyish complexion, the soldier was considerably younger than Abigail.

"I have a letter." She held the envelope in her hand and stared at that name again, scrawled across the paper in her own hand. That terrible, dreaded name . . .

Despite her best efforts, her fingers shook as she proffered the letter to the soldier. *Please, take it quickly before I change my mind.*

When his fingers closed over the end of the envelope, renewed fear raced through her and she almost withdrew it. Then her refrain sounded through her mind, thrusting her reluctance into submission.

Anything for Wade. Anything for Wade. Anything for Wade.

She jerked her hand back when the soldier took the letter. It was gone—out of her hands. She would just have to accept it.

"Is this enough?" She placed the coin on the counter.

The soldier looked at the address on the envelope, then up at her. He had kind eyes—soft and brown. "Not quite, ma'am."

Relief mingled with regret as she reached again for the letter. "Oh, well then—"

"Ah, but that's all right." He leaned forward conspiratorially and whispered, "I'll make up the difference myself. It's the least we can do . . . considering."

Panic struck. Her skin turned cold despite the warm air around her. "Oh, no. Really, I insist, sir. That wouldn't be proper at a—"

"You sound just like my sister." His face fell and he lowered his gaze, then looked at her with naked grief. "She died last year. I wasn't even home when it happened."

"I—I'm sorry." Abigail's heart pounded like a drum, mimicking the maxim which had brought her to this moment in her life. *Anything for Wade.* "I'm grateful to you for your kindness, sir."

"Don't concern yourself about it," he insisted, again looking young and carefree. "It's my pleasure, ma'am. You have a nice day."

"Yes, thank you." She barely heard herself speak. "You too, sir."

Then she turned and walked from the dimness into the mocking sunlight. She glanced back over her shoulder once and watched the soldier take her letter to the back of the room, where he handed it to another man.

It was gone—now she *couldn't* take back the words which might very well seal her fate.

When she turned, she saw Mike Faricy leaning against a post, his hands shoved deep into his pockets. "You sure about this?" he asked, raising his eyebrows together. "I don't know what that letter was all about, or who it was to, but I don't think I've ever seen anyone as undecided about anything before."

Abigail bristled and lifted her chin. The deed was done—bemoaning it would do them no good at all.

Anything for Wade.

"You couldn't be more mistaken, sir."

He shook his head with a counterfeit smile. "Oooookay. Whatever you say."

"Did you post the notice?"

"Yep. As a matter of fact, one of your neighbors—Miller, I think it was—saw it and said he'd stop by in the morning to look at the plow and maybe some of the hand tools."

"That's good." Abigail felt better already. It was rumored that Mr. Miller had wisely left much of his money in gold during the war. Recalling the occasions when soldiers from both armies had visited—raided—Elysium these last few years, she considered where her neighbor could possibly have hidden his gold to protect it. "Very good."

Mike looked over his shoulder. "I wonder . . ."

"Excuse me?" Abigail walked toward him. "You wonder what?"

When he turned around, she saw mischief dancing in his hazel eyes—a pleasant and surprising sight. He smiled and she couldn't help but return it. "What is it?" she asked again.

He aimed his thumb back over his shoulder. "Is that State Street?"

Abigail tilted her head to one side and lifted her brows suspiciously. "I thought you'd never been to Natchez before the other day."

His cheeks turned sanguine and he shrugged. "I learn fast."

"I see." Somehow she knew he wasn't telling the truth, but it didn't really matter right now. "Well, you said you have business to tend to, and I really should go home now." *Where I can dwell on matters over which I have no control.* She shot a look toward the post office. *And those I can't undo.*

Mike looked disappointed. His face fell and her heart soared, then plummeted just as quickly. Her reactions to this man were utterly ridiculous. Besides, considering the letter she'd just mailed, she had no business thinking about other men. Ever.

Disappointment pervaded her. "Well, I'll see you back at the house, then."

"Wait!"

His voice carried an urgency which brought an absurd sense of elation to her heart. *Utter foolishness.* "What is it?"

"Don't you remember? You said you had to find out about the sale date."

"Of course." Abigail sighed. "Thank you for reminding me."

"Hmm. I have a feeling you don't really mean that, but you're welcome anyway." His voice was softer now.

"I can see to this myself, Mike." She wanted to do this quickly and go home. "I'll just check on the date, then go straight back to Elysium. Take your time. You've worked hard all week. I see nothing wrong with you taking the day off to take care of your own concerns."

Mike's eyes glittered in the sunlight; the greenish flecks intensified as he stared at her. Something pivotal tumbled around inside his mind—she knew it. What was it? Like the morning when she'd first found him asleep on her floor, he exuded something far more consequential than what was visible to the eye.

He was an enigma she doubted she'd ever unravel. After a

moment, she watched his gaze travel the length of her, then return to bore through her bodice to scorch the tender flesh within. Her breasts responded to his probing gaze by swelling and filling with a dull ache which made her feel hot and vulnerable.

Wanton.

No, I mustn't think about such things. She swallowed the hard lump of contrition lodged in her throat, then nodded. "I'll see you back at Elysium, then."

"Yes, ma'am," he said with a flourish, but the hard glint in his eyes remained.

"Good day."

Mike watched her maneuver through the crowd, his irrational anger increasing as she moved farther away. He wasn't angry with Abigail, though he certainly felt like directing it at her. His anger was all for himself.

"Damn." He straightened and turned to look at State Street, then glanced over his shoulder to see if Abigail was completely out of sight. She was.

The simple thought of that woman ignited his blood, but he had more important things to do with his time than lust after her as if she were a dog in heat. *Yeah, she's Lady and I'm the Tramp.*

And she deserved so much more than he could offer. He had no business thinking about her at all, let alone allowing himself to actually *care.*

Common sense tried to tell Mike that a considerable portion of his attraction to Abigail probably stemmed from his insane situation—his emotional state, or the fried state of his brain. *Take your pick.* It made no difference in the end.

The bottom line? He wanted a woman willing to relieve some of his tension, and Abigail Kingsley hadn't applied for the job.

Besides, her only qualifications were for the position of someone he could care about—a luxury he couldn't afford.

Or risk.

Quelling thoughts of Abigail, he faced State Street again and drew a mental map for himself. About a block over and toward the river should lead him straight to the infamous Natchez-Under-the-Hill section. The way this town was crawling with soldiers, chances were the seamier side of life in Natchez was flourishing.

His blood thickened and pooled in his groin, a coarse and unrelenting reminder of his unfulfilled physical needs. He took a few steps toward Under-the-Hill, then hesitated.

He couldn't do it. A prostitute wouldn't diminish the craving in his body—in his soul. What he wanted and needed was Abigail.

No.

Mike couldn't allow himself to think this way. Even though he could care about her—*did* care—Abigail deserved so much more than a man who would only use her body for a little distraction.

A man who would die very soon.

He had to think logically—emotions were something his mind couldn't handle right now. Hard, cold facts might help him think straight. That was the answer.

What if he caught something? That was logical. While it was true that AIDS wasn't a problem in 1865, other sexually transmitted diseases were. He didn't even know if penicillin had been invented yet.

Then he remembered his predestination. It didn't matter if he caught anything, because he'd be dead as soon as his job was finished anyway.

But what if you die before *that, numb-nuts?*

"Damn." Immobile, Mike stood a few feet from the board-walk. He racked his mind for answers to this latest dilemma, then he remembered something else.

He had no money.

That was a relief. At least now, he wouldn't have to talk himself into or out of anything. Hell, after his last experience in this town without money, he should've known better than to even consider trying to purchase anything—or anyone.

Still, curiosity demanded he at least walk through Natchez-

Under-the-Hill. In his time, all that remained of that notorious area was Silver Street. The river had eaten away—or would eat away—the rest.

Sure, why shouldn't he have a look? Only one reason. He glanced across the street at the courthouse, now occupied by the army brass. If there was anyplace in Natchez where he might learn of a family named Milton, it was there.

But his feet refused to budge in that direction. He was procrastinating, big time. Why?

Muttering to himself, Mike pivoted and jaywalked across the street, then marched up the steps of the imposing structure. He didn't stop until he'd reached the top, where he paused for only a moment to consider the consequences of what he was about to do.

No choice, Mike. With a deep breath, he walked through the huge archways and pushed on a heavy door. It didn't yield.

Locked.

Relief left a bitter aftertaste in its wake. "I don't believe this." He'd finally found the guts to face this, only to be foiled by a stupid locked door.

He looked around and saw the notice near the entrance. They were closed and would reopen in two hours. That gave him just enough time for a little sightseeing.

His libido nudged him in that direction again, but he quickly reminded himself he had no money and no inclination for a prostitute. He'd never paid for sex in his life, but he'd sure as hell seen his share of twentieth-century hookers.

None of them had looked like Abigail Kingsley.

That woman was driving him batty.

Doggedly, he ran down the steps and headed toward State Street. Something nagged at him—a thought not fully formed. What was it?

As he neared Silver, his pace quickened. He wanted to do something *rotten*. The urge struck him and spurred him down the hill, lower and lower until he stood at the top of Silver Street.

Its reputation had failed to do the area justice; it was an EPA nightmare.

The filth that spread out before him was nothing like he'd expected. Trash lined the streets, as did inebriated bodies in a variety of colors. Shouting resounded from almost every building as Mike walked cautiously down the hill.

He'd wanted rotten—he'd sure found it.

Mike tried not to breathe through his nose as he explored history. The stench was deadly.

What a contrast to his nightly ritual of rinsing out his only pair of socks and briefs and hanging them up to dry. *I sure hope they last as long as I do.*

With a grimace, he worked his way down the hill to Middle Street, noting the gradual but definite change as he neared the river. *This neighborhood sure went to hell.* Where Silver Street had been crowded with merrymakers, Middle Street boasted a quieter, and Mike suspected, more dangerous clientele.

Then reality struck. He *knew* what subconscious thought had driven him to the sleazy riverfront. Milton. The Milton he'd known would've been right at home owning this entire area.

What about his ancestors? What better place for Mike to begin his search?

"Well, I'll be," a sultry voice called from an open doorway.

Mike knew he shouldn't stop to fraternize with the natives, but male instinct made him disobey common sense. *Why change at this late date?*

She was gorgeous, with skin the color of molasses and startling green eyes. Her reddish brown hair fell to her waist in tight ringlets. When she smiled, even white teeth bore a sharp contrast to most of the other gap-toothed inhabitants of the slum area. And she was clean—nothing less than a miracle, considering her surroundings.

"Where you from, handsome?" she called, leaning forward so the loose bodice of her dress gaped open to reveal the slightest hint of her barely concealed nipples.

Mike's mind screamed "No," but his body shouted "Yes, yes, yes!"

Wouldn't a wild romp in the sack with a hot-blooded woman help take his mind off Abigail? No, that was impossible.

Logic, Mike. He knew his brain wouldn't respond to anything less than cold, hard logic and even that was doubtful at best.

I'm broke—that's logical.

For once in his life, Mike was thankful for poverty. That might save him from himself, but not from Slick.

He sighed in resignation, but took a step closer despite himself. A little polite conversation wouldn't hurt, and it was probably even free.

"What's your name?" he asked, allowing his gaze to feast on the flesh she seemed eager to display.

He was on fire. Though another woman had started the blaze, this one definitely had the necessary fire-fighting equipment.

And then some.

"Honey," she whispered, allowing her tongue to slip between her lips and run slowly from side to side.

"Honey," Mike repeated, already regretting his decision to come down here. Why torture himself? He wasn't interested in anyone but Abigail, and besides, this woman would expect payment for her services. "Well, I'll be seeing you. Have a nice—"

"Wait!" She reached out and grabbed his elbow and looked into his eyes with a near-frantic expression. "I need help, sir."

That figures. Mike released a mournful sigh and shot her a crooked grin. "What is it—your pimp giving you a hard time about tricks?"

Her smooth brow furrowed and she shook her head. "I dunno what you're talkin' about, but I really need your help."

"With what?"

She moved closer, brushing his jacket with her breasts. Mike's temperature skyrocketed, despite his best efforts to maintain self-control. "I asked you what you needed help with."

"My . . . uncle."

Honey's eyes were soft and liquid—sincere. Genuine fear and worry marred her lovely face.

"He'll beat me," she whispered.

Mike's natural male instincts seemed to have a mind of their own, refusing to listen to the one telling them to back off and give this woman a wide berth. "Why?" *Uncle, my ass. Once a vice cop . . .*

"He owns this place." She directed a hurried glanced over her shoulder, then faced him again. "He said if I don't get me some business today, he'll hurt me bad."

Every muscle in his body lurched and twitched. If there was one thing in this world Mike hated, it was injustice. This, in a word, stank. Some things never changed. "I know it's a radical concept, but why don't you just leave?"

Honey shook her head. "He'd hunt me down and kill me. Besides, I don't got no place else to go." Her lips suddenly curved into a bewitching smile. "Don't you *want* to do it with me?"

Want to? Mike was so hard he could barely breathe. He felt like a sausage crammed into a casing and double-sealed with shrink wrap. But, unfortunately, this woman wasn't the one he wanted.

This was all Abigail's fault.

Yeah, right. Mike shook his head and chuckled at this bit of irony. Relieving his sexual urges with this very willing prostitute might help him handle finding Milton a little better.

She pressed herself closer and wiggled against him. Her breasts were lavish and tempting, and she smelled like some sort of tropical flower. It was an intoxicating scent, fueling him like a powerful drug.

Powerful drug . . .

Oh, crap. He placed his hands on her shoulders and gently but firmly pushed her away. "No sale, doll."

"What's wrong?" she taunted. "Ain't you *man* enough for Honey?"

Mike's desire waned in light of more practical matters. He wasn't about to fall victim to whatever sick game they played in this place. Was this one of the infamous opium dens prevalent in the nineteenth century? Strange, he'd thought they were all in San Francisco.

Think again, Faricy.

"Honey, I'm man enough, but I have no money. Got it?"

She gave him the once over and shook her head very slowly,

her mouth pressed into a thin line of disbelief. "You look rich to me."

"Looks can be deceiving. I don't have a single cent. Thanks anyway." He turned and started walking. The only way to handle this was to leave.

"Uncle Milton's gonna beat me bloody."

Mike froze, then turned very slowly to face her again. His blood ran cold; numbness tingled around his lips. *Milton.*

Her hands covered her face and she cried, shoulders heaving with great racking sobs. *Damn.* He wanted to walk away. Hell, he *should* walk away. But these tears were legit.

"Uncle . . . Milton?" Mike took a step nearer. "Is he a white man or Afri—er, black?" His mouth went dry and sweat burst from every pore on his body.

She looked up at him with tears streaming. "He claims he's white, but he ain't *all* white." She wiped her eyes with the backs of her hands and took a step nearer. "You change your mind, sugar? You gonna let Honey pleasure you?"

He had to get a look at this man. But even then, how could he know for certain? "Is Milton his first or last name?"

The expression on her face made him wonder if she'd even understood his simple question. Instead of answering, she took a step closer and reached for his hand, but Mike grabbed her shoulders to pull her roughly against him. "Answer me."

She bared her teeth and sucked her breath through them in an animalistic hiss. "You like to play rough? Honey knows some—"

"*Answer me, dammit!*" Mike didn't intend to harm her, but his insides were filled with fury and fear. He had to do right by Barney and Carrie. This might be his big chance and he couldn't blow it. He'd already given up too damned much to risk losing now. "Answer me," he repeated quietly, hoping he hadn't frightened her to the point where she'd be unable to talk.

A wicked gleam danced in her eyes, then she lowered her lashes to peer at him. "I ain't sure. It's his only name as far as I can tell."

The woman was far from frightened, and obviously used to

playing hardball. "I have no money," he repeated, then caught a glimpse of something glittering on his finger. Without hesitation, he whipped his right hand out in front of her to display his graduation ring. "Will this cover your price, Honey? It's gold."

She touched his hand and turned it so sunlight reflected off the stone. "It's queer-looking, but I reckon it'll do." She turned his hand over and brought it to her lips, tracing his palm with the tip of her tongue. "You like that?"

"Yeah." He drew a deep shuddering breath. At this moment sex was way down on his list of priorities. "Let's *do* it."

Mike's heart sounded louder and louder, beat by beat, nudging him closer and closer to destiny.

To fate.

To death.

Chapter Eight

Abigail stood on the road in front of the house, staring at the only home she'd ever known. Before summer's end, it would be hers no longer.

"It isn't fair," she whispered, feeling a cruel knot form in the pit of her stomach—cold and hard, like a stone. That's how she felt right now.

Cold as stone.

Dead . . . like that soldier.

She brought her knuckles to her mouth and bit down hard, swallowing the burning sensation in her throat and commanding her tears to remain unshed. Nothing in this lifetime could ever make her forget that awful night. She suspected even death couldn't provide respite from that eternal nightmare.

Nightmare? Yes, it had been a nightmare from beginning to end. But if not for that night of terror and death, she wouldn't have the most precious gift of her life.

Wade. That lone thought drove the coldness away, though she knew it was never far. The slightest impetus would bring the chill racing back to torment her.

She drew a deep breath, then closed her eyes as she slowly released it. When she opened her eyes, Abigail knew she couldn't face Rosalie and Wade just yet. She needed time to be alone, to consider everything that had happened today.

Like the letter.

The coldness threatened to reappear, but she shook her head and pressed her fist against her abdomen, willing the sensation to pass.

Where could she go? There had to be someplace where she could rest for a while before facing Rosalie and Wade. If she slipped through the house to her room, they'd know. Then she'd have to pretend again.

I can't. I just can't. Not yet. Her gaze swept the surrounding countryside, surveying the dilapidated cabins, the empty smokehouse, the barn.

Then she remembered one clean cabin where she could hide for a while.

A sensation of calm washed through her, urging her to pivot in the direction of Mike's cabin. Surely he wouldn't return for hours and all she required was a little privacy. A trifle of time to gather her thoughts before facing Rosalie's questions and her son's needs.

Time for herself?

She almost laughed. How long had it been since she'd thought of herself as something or someone more than the woman responsible for her son, Elysium, and Rosalie? How long?

Oh, but she knew the answer only too well. The date was one she'd never forget no matter how desperately she tried.

Abigail hurried her pace until she came to the cabin, small and square, built directly against the ground with a stone chimney at one end and a small window beside the door.

Anticipating blessed privacy, her heart flipped over in her chest, but guilt immediately followed to chase away her moment of peace. Rosalie would be waiting for her. Abigail shouldn't shirk her responsibilities, nor should she enter someone else's home—albeit temporary—uninvited.

Yet she knew she'd be more capable of handling Wade and Rosalie after a smattering of time to sort through her jumbled thoughts. What was wrong with her taking a rest after her long walk?

After mailing that dreadful letter?

A quaking sensation in her middle reminded her of the possible consequences of her actions. "I can't believe I sent it."

What would his reaction be when he opened her letter? Would he deny his own son? Possibly. She knew all too well what heinous acts that man was capable of.

Anything for Wade.

Drawing a deep shuddering breath, Abigail pushed open the cabin door and stepped inside. The cool dimness enveloped her and triggered a shiver from a corner inside herself she rarely visited anymore.

After a moment, her eyes adjusted to the diminished light. She sighed and walked toward the chair, but her gaze was drawn to the bed. She felt so tired. So heavy.

A short nap might refresh her and restore her spirits. Soon she'd be able to resume the facade, but not now. Not yet.

Her decision made, she walked to the clean straw tick and paused. Mike had slept in this bed. A strange, comforting warmth chased away her earlier chill as she lowered herself to the smooth surface.

Serenity—foreign and unexplainable—descended over her as she stretched out on the bed and closed her weary eyes. Mike. She smelled his singular scent and it brought her peace mingled with something totally contrary to that benign sensation.

There was something about that man.

The same sickly sweet odor Mike had noticed in Honey's hair permeated the interior of the shabby building. Other hookers occupied the hallway in various stages of undress. A few open doors revealed couples in the midst of getting their cheap thrills, oblivious—or indifferent—to being observed.

Milton's ancestor might be here in this hell-hole.

Mike's gut coiled into a hard knot of readiness. At this moment, he could do the deed and take Milton out. What he remained uncertain of was how he would verify the identity of his victim. All he had to go on was a name and a face from the future.

"This way." Honey held his hand and led him down an adjoining hallway where most of the doors were closed. Yellowed, peeling paper covered the walls; stains and scars marked the wood flooring, which creaked and groaned beneath Mike's weight.

A thin film of smoke crept from beneath one closed door to mingle with the cloying moldy stench of the old building. Mike knew the peculiar odor and its insidious future all too well.

So what? He had to concentrate on finding Milton. It wasn't as if he had any jurisdiction here anyway, even though he had a badge that boasted otherwise. Besides, these people weren't about to listen to reason.

"In here." Honey pushed open a door at the end of the hall and gave Mike's hand a tug. When he stopped and refused to budge, she frowned. "What's the matter?"

He looked beyond her toward the bed—a bare, stained mattress hanging haphazardly on a rusted iron frame. "Don't you think we'd better let your Uncle Milton know you have a customer?" Mike smiled, though he knew it probably more closely resembled a grimace. "I'd kind of like to meet this guy anyway."

"Why?" Honey's brow furrowed and she dropped Mike's hand. "Why you want him?"

Think fast, Mike. A shudder bolted down his spine, but he denounced it, ignoring his anxiety. He gave a cynical laugh. "Why not? I'm not afraid of him." *But he'd better be petrified of me.*

"Why you wanna see *him,* sugar?" Honey's lower lip protruded and she narrowed her sultry green eyes to small slits of candid suspicion. "Did you come in here to let me pleasure you or not?"

Without hesitation, she reached up and slipped her thumbs beneath the gaping neckline of her dress, then slid the garment down until it pooled near her bare feet on the filthy floor. "Take a good, long look at Honey."

And he did.

He didn't want to, but his gaze fixed itself to the base of her throat where her pulse thudded against smooth skin. Then he followed the line of her collarbone downward to where the two halves almost met.

From that point, he looked lower still until the lush curves beckoned him. The flesh over her breasts was taut and glistening, the color varying from brown sugar to mahogany where her nipples gathered to a tempting pucker.

Damn.

"You like?" she asked, taking a step toward him to wrap her arms around his neck. Her lips were slightly parted and moist—inviting.

Mike's blood pulsed through him at a dire pace, left no extremity untouched, and pooled to near bursting between his legs. "I want to see Milton," he repeated, his voice hoarse. He swallowed hard. It didn't help.

Honey reached down and took his hand in hers, boldly bringing it up to cover her breast. She felt soft and warm to the touch—hot. Her nipple, hardening and begging for his mouth, pierced an illusory hole through his palm.

Instinctively, Mike's hand closed over her breast, kneading the pliant flesh until she moaned and dropped her hand away. She reached between them and ran her fingers along the hard ridge at the front of his jeans.

"Oh, you're a big one," she murmured, rubbing the length of him through the fabric. "Big and hard. Honey likes 'em that way."

Mike clenched his teeth, commanding himself to resist this professional seductress. He had to find this man named Milton. Nothing was more important than that, especially not a romp in a bug-infested bed with a possibly diseased prostitute.

He dropped his hand from her breast and jerked hers away from his overzealous erection. "I want to see your Uncle Milton."

She took a step back, holding out her hand. "Gimme the ring first."

Mike grimaced. "Some things never change." He wrenched the ring from his finger and slapped it into her outstretched hand. "Now, take me to your Uncle Milton." *And I'll bet he's no Uncle Miltie.*

She examined the ring, then slid it onto her thumb before pulling her dress up to cover her breasts. "I can't figure out why you don't want what you paid for."

"Don't worry about it. What do you care as long as you got paid?" Mike wanted this over with. While she straightened her dress, he instinctively checked to ensure his weapon was present and accounted for. Four bullets—if all went well, he'd only need one.

She pushed past him and walked back toward the front of the building. Mike followed her, listening to all the strange sounds along the way, keenly aware that within the next few minutes, his time in this would might come to an abrupt halt.

The death of Milton's ancestor meant Mike's death as well. *Gee, that'll make Slick real happy.* Big surprise—that thought brought Mike no pleasure whatsoever. He had to concentrate on the main purpose of all this—Barney and Carrie. And their baby.

And all the kids who might not die from drug overdoses if Frank Milton were never born.

Honey paused outside a door at the end of the hall and lifted her hand to knock, but Mike reached out and stopped her. He shook his head very slowly. "No," he whispered. "Is he in here?"

Honey nodded and took a step back, looking down at her hand to admire Mike's ring.

Mike turned away, no longer caring about Honey or the ring, if he ever had. The man behind this door was far more significant.

Banishing thoughts of Honey—*and* Abigail Kingsley—Mike turned to face the door. He drew a deep breath and lifted his hand to knock.

"Who the hell is it?" an angry voice growled. "Go away. I'm busy."

Mike tensed and stepped to one side of the door frame. He reached for his weapon and the doorknob simultaneously, checking once to make sure Honey was out of the line of fire, just in case.

Instinct took command, making every muscle in his body tense to alertness. Knees slightly bent with his hand fastened over the familiar smoothness of his service revolver, Mike flung open the door and swung himself into the room with his gun drawn and aimed.

Adrenaline surged through him, conversant with this routine from years of experience. Mike's gaze encompassed the room in one expert sweep, ensuring the only person present was the white-suited obese man seated behind the small desk.

This was no Colonel Sanders.

The man's jaw went slack and his cigar hung from his mouth at a bizarre angle as he stared at the intruder, money clutched in both pudgy hands. After a moment, he clamped his mouth shut around the cigar, puffing several times and sending up a cloud of pungent smoke.

He dropped his hands to the desk and covered the bills. Good. That would keep the pimp's hands busy. Mike held Milton's gaze with his, allowing himself a leisurely inspection of fleshly jowls and beady eyes.

Finally, the man reached up slowly and removed the cigar from his mouth. "Who the hell are you?" he asked with a thick Southern drawl.

"A customer checking out the facility." Mike banished all emotion from his voice—a feat of gargantuan proportions. "Just make sure you keep your hands on top of the desk where I can see them."

"Fine." The man complied. "I repeat—who the hell are you and why are you in my office waving that damned pistol in my face?"

"I need to find out who *you* are."

"Why?"

Mike hesitated. The man's skin had a slight pigmentation suggesting the possibility of mixed race. That didn't help at all, because Frank Milton had been—would be—blond and blue-eyed. Or maybe it did help . . .

"What's your name?" Mike asked carefully, not straightening from his crouch or lowering his weapon. "Your *full* name."

"Milton P. Snodgrass." The man carefully enunciated each syllable. "Now, *again,* what the devil are you doing in my office with that gun?"

Devil? Mike's hopes plummeted as suspicion coiled through his subconscious. "Snodgrass?"

"That's what I said, dammit. Now what in tarnation is the meanin' of this? If you're a thief, you're a piss-poor one." The man's face reddened and he leaned forward to glower at Mike. "One of my girls fail to give you your money's worth? Is that it? We got a money-back guarantee here, but you don't need that gun to collect it."

Mike shook his head, searching for the words necessary to get himself out of this mess and away from this man with his hundred questions. "No, nothing like that. I thought you were someone else. Sorry."

"Yeah, well . . . ?"

Mike pointed his weapon toward the ceiling to indicate his intentions, then he lowered it and slid it into its holster. "Sorry for the intrusion."

"Well then get the hell outta my office before I call one of them soldiers."

Mike backed out through the door and pulled it shut. With a sigh, he closed his eyes and leaned against the wall, allowing his head to hit with a soft thud.

"Mike, Mike."

An appropriately perverse epilogue to this scenario, the familiar voice speared right through him. He groaned. Of course, he should've known Slick would be lurking nearby to witness this fiasco. "Oh, God."

"Not hardly."

Mike opened his eyes and looked in the direction of the voice, but saw only Honey leaning against the opposite wall.

"Where is he?" Mike asked, realizing how stupid he sounded.

"Right here, boy genius." Honey's mouth moved. That

slimy used car salesman's voice came from between her lush lips.

"Man, you just get sicker and sicker with these disguises."

"Yeah, and I'm getting one helluva kick out of this one, too." Slick sighed and ran a hand over Honey's voluptuous breast. "Too bad you didn't take Honey up on her offer. I was sorta looking forward to revealing myself to you at just . . . the right moment."

"Like I said—really sick." Mike pushed himself away from the wall and took a few steps toward the door, but he hesitated, pivoting to stare at Honey—rather, at Slick. "*Is* there a Honey, or are you going to disappear again with some cheap theatrical gimmick?"

"Oh, I'm just borrowing Honey's bod for a while. First thing I did was give her a nice, long bath." Slick looked down at Honey's breasts, cupping both of them and squeezing them into greater prominence. "These are magnificent, don't you think?"

"For some reason they looked a lot better to me earlier." Thank God there was no one else in the hallway to overhear their ridiculous conversation. Mike couldn't imagine what someone might think, hearing Slick's voice coming from Honey's body. "Why don't you leave the poor girl alone?"

"Yeah, I suppose it's just as well. I can't quite figure out a way to pork myself. What a waste." Slick's diabolical laughter filled the narrow hallway. "You think you came in here on a wild goose chase, huh?"

"Yeah, I suppose you had something to do with this, too."

Slick's gaze narrowed and Honey's green eyes underwent an instantaneous transformation. Piercing, hypnotic red held Mike in place with brain-numbing power.

"Mike, I think you're beginning to figure out that old Slick doesn't do anything without a reason." He laughed again. "At least I hope you are . . . for Barney and Carrie's sake."

"You son of a—"

"Time for me to vacate this luscious bod. Remember, listen and pay attention to everything. You might get lucky when you least expect it." Slick sighed and gave Honey's breasts another squeeze. ''It's been nice, Honey. Gotta go—someone's coming.''

Mike took a step toward him—or her—but a pair of voices from the adjoining hallway distracted him. Instinctively, he stiffened and slipped his hand inside his jacket to rest near the butt on his gun.

Heavy footsteps came closer and closer. Apprehensive, Mike pressed himself against the wall.

''Where'd they say Lieutenant Denny was heading when he was last seen?'' one voice asked.

''Some plantation a few miles north of town,'' another man answered. ''For a while, we though he'd been killed at Vicksburg, but his body was never found.''

The footsteps stopped and Mike strained to hear the words, never moving his hand away from his weapon. Who were they? Why did overhearing their conversation suddenly seem so urgent?

Then he remembered Slick and shot Honey a probing glance. She looked up at the soldiers and he swore there were dollar signs in her eyes. The real Honey had definitely returned. What Mike couldn't be certain of was at which point in this comedy of errors Slick had taken control of Honey.

Terrifying thought.

''Which plantation?'' the first voice asked, jerking Mike back to the present.

Then another voice sounded in his mind—a taunting, singsongy voice. *Listen and pay attention to everything. You might get lucky . . .*

''Slick.'' Mike barely whispered the word and his heart hammered against the wall of his chest. The red-eyed monster had been trying to give Mike a hint for some reason.

Pay attention, Mike, he reminded himself when the sound of a boot scraping against the wood floor reached him. Slick's words held him paralyzed, waiting for the men to continue their discussion.

''It had a really bizarre name. Utopia, or something like that.''

The other man chuckled. ''You gotta be kidding.''

"No, it wasn't Utopia, but something real similar."

Silence.

Mike frowned—his brain had slipped into neutral, but he forced it back into gear, trying to sort through the jumbled messages until they made some sense. Hell, nothing made sense anymore.

"E-ly—Elysium—that's it."

Elysium?

"These Rebs sure were proud of their plantations. Can you imagine naming a cotton farm something like Elysium?"

Elysium.

Their laughter was loud and rough. "So Denny was on a mission behind enemy lines when he disappeared?" one man asked.

"Yeah, he was with Milton's scouting expedition just after the Vicksburg campaign."

No!

"Oh, yeah. I remember that incident now." The footsteps paused again near the intersection of the hallways. "Denny'd been reported missing after a small skirmish. Somehow, he ended up here. Milton said . . ."

Milton.

"That's right." The sound of a match striking wood filled the silence.

"I don't understand why we're going to so much trouble over one missing lieutenant."

"You don't have to understand, Brown. Denny's daddy owns a huge shipping company. Andrew Johnson says find the man's son, so we're gonna find his son."

Damn.

"Or at least find out what happened to him."

A derisive chuckle punctuated the other man's comment. "Hell, you and I both know Denny's dead. He *must* be dead—he has to be." The man's voice roughened. "All I can say is his daddy must be one powerful son of a bitch."

"Waste of time, if you ask me."

Mike remained pressed against the wall as the men walked

by. They paused to stare at him for a moment, but all he could do was swallow. He didn't trust himself to speak.

The taller soldier shook his head slowly. "Must be one of those poor bastards who came home with only half his wits."

"Hello." Honey stepped out in front of the soldiers, swishing her skirts around her bare ankles. "You come to see me?"

"We're leaving now," the tallest soldier said, turning away from Mike. "What's your name? I'll ask for you next time I'm down this way."

"Honey."

"Hmm. Honey. I won't forget that."

"Promise?" At his nod, Honey stepped aside and let the soldiers pass.

Mike continued to stare as the blue-clad officers turned the corner, leaving behind only lingering pipe smoke and the thundering between his ears. His gut coiled and wrenched, threatening to spill this morning's fish on the floor.

Elysium was the key—had been all along.

"Holy shit." Mike's whispered words sounded more like an injured animal's last breath—the death rattle.

Old Slick never does anything without a reason . . .

Mike jerked his gaze around to where Honey still leaned against the opposite wall, admiring his ring. No sign of Slick now.

Raking his fingers through his hair, Mike pushed away from the wall and let his hand fall away from the butt of his gun. His fingers felt numb—his *brain* felt numb.

Instead of solving riddles, his adventure had merely provided more questions demanding answers. But now he had some idea where to look. He'd been there all along.

There had to be a reason for Slick to have sent Mike to this particular point in time. What?

Damn.

Mike swallowed hard, clenching and unclenching his fists to restore circulation. For a few hellish moments, his heart must've stopped.

Just like that night.

Like Barney.

His constricting throat nearly gagged him as he took a few staggering steps toward Honey. He didn't know why. All he knew for certain was that he had to solve this mystery soon. It hurt too damned much to continue like this.

Was Honey another key? Or simply a vehicle for one of Slick's depraved games? She didn't look up, even when he stopped in front of her.

Breathing seemed to take every ounce of strength Mike could muster as he maintained his balance. The pounding in his head did a fair imitation of the last rock concert he'd attended, reverberating through his bones, making the blood in his veins quiver like gelatin. The New Madrid Fault had nothing on this.

Elysium.

A man had disappeared there during the war—Denny. Who the hell was Denny and what did he have to do with Milton?

Major Milton. Imagine that.

And Abigail had denied knowing anyone by that name.

Realization unfolded inside him like internal chemical warfare. Mike stiffened—every muscle in his body tightened. His heart hit the gas pedal and sent his pulse into overdrive.

Elysium was only part of the picture. Like a combination lock, other factors were required to open the mechanism.

Other factors like Abigail Kingsley.

"Well, it's about time."

Mike looked up at the sound of Slick's voice. A sneer transformed Honey's face into a hideous mask of evil. The devil's flunky had set Mike up big time.

"I want to know where to find Milton. Tell me, damn you." Mike clenched his teeth and waited, though he knew Slick had no intention of making this mission easier. After a few moments, he took a step closer, not caring that his chest pressed against Honey's breasts. "You're enjoying this, aren't you?"

"Smart, Mike. You're making progress. For what it's worth, we're both already damned, but go ahead and say it if it makes you feel better."

Slick laughed, then consumed Mike with his cutting gaze. Honey's green eyes slowly gave way to the red flames of Hell. "This is your mission, Ace—you find your own answers. I'll leave you with a few more hints, though. It keeps me . . . entertained.'' The junior-devil's voice sounded like FDR announcing the bombing of Pearl Harbor. Doom. Peril.

Mike stared, transfixed, as the flames seized control of his mind and implanted Slick's message. *Abigail. Elysium. Lies. Secrets.*

As Slick's eyes slowly lost their feral glow, Mike came out of their spell. The hints he'd been promised had done nothing but plant more questions—more doubts.

Dizziness gripped him, threatening to send him crashing to the floor as the redness vanished completely and Honey became herself again.

"Oh, you changed your mind," she said, pressing herself more firmly against him.

"No." Mike jerked himself free, staggering to the opposite wall. He let his cheek rest against the peeling paper for a few moments. "Abigail," he whispered in supplication.

"Who's Abigail?" Honey's voice came from right beside him. "She your woman?"

Mike slowly shook his head and forced himself upright. Drawing a deep breath, he looked at Honey. "Where's the door? Get me out of here."

Honey sighed and clicked her tongue. "Suit yourself." She walked ahead of him, then stopped where two hallways intersected. "There." She pointed down the shortest of the two passages. "And don't come back 'til you got money. Honey'll cost more next time."

"Not in this lifetime." Mike squared his shoulders and walked purposefully out the front door. Outside, he paused.

Abigail. Elysium. Lies. Secrets.

Slick's words reverberated through Mike's mind as he turned and walked up the hill. Reaching the edge of town, he turned onto Cemetery Road and broke into a run.

A dead run.

Anger fueled him—charged his muscles and made him fly along the red dirt road.

Abigail. Elysium. Lies. Secrets.

His endorphins kicked in, but rather than calm him, his body's chemicals made him burn.

Burn for revenge.

Burn for justice.

He had to find a release. Somehow there had to be a way to break this consuming madness before it broke him.

Images flashed through his mind as his arms pumped at his sides, alternating with his long strides. Carrie's face when she'd announced her pregnancy. Barney's neck—a pulpy mass. His first encounter with Slick . . .

Abigail. Elysium. Lies. Secrets.

Abigail had answers.

And, by God, he'd have his answers today.

Dark, sinister clouds gathered, darkening the sky to slate. Mike looked up, slowing his pace as he neared Elysium. Lightning sizzled across the sky; thunder shattered the quiet countryside.

The perfect ambiance for his mood.

His rage was a palpable entity, feeding off his physical form to torment and control him. *A frigging vampire.* He was crazy with the need to vent his fury, preferably where it would do the most good.

By fulfilling his destiny.

The clouds burst open, releasing a deluge. Raindrops pelted his face and neck, soaking through his denim jacket within seconds.

He plodded to a sloshy stop in front of the plantation and stared through the veil of rain at the house—his time portal. The wind whipped the rain with even more ferocity, stinging his bare skin until it felt like raw meat.

The air temperature cooled rapidly as he glanced upward again. Like any good Mississippian, Mike knew when to take shelter.

And he was late.

He squinted through the rain, buttoned his jacket to protect his gun as much as possible, then started toward the cabin. Red clay ran in rivulets at his feet as the torrent continued and lightning struck the ground somewhere close by.

Too close.

Though the storm had cooled his body considerably, his mood remained volatile—on edge. The yearning to break something and wreak havoc on anything and everything in his path remained just beneath the surface, momentarily suppressed in deference to his need to seek refuge from Mother Nature.

A gust of wind that could've delivered both him and the cabin to Oz, slammed into his back. Except Mike's wicked old witch was a man named Milton.

Ding-dong, the witch ain't dead. Yet.

The gale propelled him through the cabin door and sent him halfway across the dirt floor before he managed to stop against the edge of the primitive table. Staggering, he turned back to slam the door against the storm, then returned to the table. Gasping great mouthfuls of air, he gripped the splintered wood for support until he regained his strength.

He blinked several times, then peeled off his soaked jacket and hung it over the back of the chair. His holster and T-shirt soon followed. Though he didn't relish the thought of walking barefoot on the dirt floor, the condition of his shoes left him no alternative. He removed his sodden shoes and socks, then placed them on the table to dry.

A lull in the weather seemed unlikely, at best. It was just as well—a few hours to devise a plan might help him control the rage that continually warred with his sense of reason for jurisdiction.

Maybe.

Lightning struck close again, making the ground rumble and shake beneath his bare feet. "Damn, that was cl—"

A startled cry from the corner knifed through him and he jerked his head around to stare in disbelief.

At Abigail Kingsley.

In his bed.

Chapter Nine

"I—I must've dozed off," Abigail stammered, swinging her legs to the floor and straightening her skirt. How unseemly to be caught sleeping in a man's bed. Her cheeks flashed with heat. "I'll go now. Forgive me." She had to get out of there—quickly.

Simultaneously, she pushed to her feet and lifted her gaze. A mistake. The smidgen of light the stormy sky provided was insufficient, yet like that morning when she'd first seen Mike Faricy, the expression smoldering in his eyes was as vivid and memorable as if they'd been standing in full sunlight.

Memorable . . . and terrifying.

The madman had returned.

She swallowed the hard lump of trepidation in her throat and moistened her parched lips, but couldn't drag her gaze from his no matter how she tried. He held her captive with that negligible effort, rendering her immobile—helpless.

No, not helpless.

Abigail would never be helpless again. There had to be something she could do to escape. The small cabin had only one door—she aimed her gaze toward it longingly.

"Don't even think it," he warned, his voice harsh and grating.

His words commanded her to look at him again. Unable to speak, she simply stared, wondering what he intended, though terrified to even consider the possibilities.

Yet she had to ask herself if what she perceived from deep inside herself was solely terror. No, she knew there was something more flourishing from a dark corner of her soul—something all-powerful.

She also sensed—God help her—where this man was concerned, her own emotions were more of a threat than he was. He'd intrigued her from that first morning, and now she was at his mercy.

Or lack of . . .

"Why'd you lie to me, Abigail?"

The discordant timbre of his voice crept inside her, evoking a perniciously pleasurable ache deep in her belly. Why did he affect her so? What was it about this one, unconventional man?

"Lie?" The sound of her own voice startled her at first. After a moment, she shook her head and held her hands outstretched at her sides. "I don't understand. I haven't li—"

"Shut up!"

Three strides—she numbly counted them. That was all it took to bring him directly before her, magnificent in his fierceness.

She should've feared him, yet fright failed to describe the inexorable sensations that spiraled through her. Her mind reeled against this insanity, but her feet refused to move.

A predator—he looked at her as if he could eat her in one bite. The muscles in his neck were taut and his left cheek twitched ever so slightly. What had become of the mocking rogue she'd left in town? The man who'd taken a moment to name a kitten just this morning?

Wind struck the cabin with such force the door blasted open, banging against the inside wall as rain lashed across the small room. The open door reminded her she should run. Spurred to action, she bolted toward the gateway to freedom.

The wind collided with her as she burst across the threshold. Rain slashed at her eyes and the gale snatched her breath.

Before she could venture farther, Mike's sinewy arms snaked around her waist and dragged her back inside. Abigail could only scream futilely into the deafening tempest—no one would hear her cries or come to her aid.

No one at all.

His body heat permeated her flesh through layers of soaked fabric. With a hard jerk, he melded her against his torso, dragged her completely inside, and kicked the door shut.

Imprisoning her with one solid arm, he lowered the bar and secured the door against the wind . . . and against any possibility of assistance.

"Let me go!" She kicked his shins, painfully aware of her vulnerability. Her earlier lack of fear had been foolish.

With a guttural growl, he carried her to the bunk and dropped her like a sack of cornmeal. Abigail sprang upward immediately, but his strong hands gripped her shoulders and pressed her back against the clean straw tick.

"I'm going to have some answers." His lips barely moved as he spoke, though every syllable was unquestionably distinct. "Why the hell did you lie to me?"

She shook her head. Her throat worked but no sound came forth. Why did he think she'd lied? What could she know that could possibly be so important to him?

No answers thrust themselves to the forefront of her frantic mind. She couldn't think clearly, though she had to try. She needed to breathe—her heart thundered, echoing the turbulent storm.

But she *had* to breathe, endure and live . . . no matter the consequences. Even if he forced her to relive that other horrible night.

Anything for Wade.

Her son needed her. She had to regain control of herself for Wade. Surely she could reason with this man who'd shown her family such kindness these past few days. She forced a shuddering breath into her starved lungs, then whispered, "Please, don't hurt me."

Though she'd thought the words feeble in light of her predicament, their impact was evident straightaway in his expression. Fury gave way to confusion in his eyes, though desperation remained.

"You lied to me." Pain flashed across his features. "You knew . . ."

Tears stung her eyes and spilled down her cheeks to pool in her ears. She remained his prisoner.

"You knew," he repeated.

She shook her head in denial and confusion, realizing her error immediately when the glint of anger returned to his eyes. Now she knew he was beyond caring about the truth—so lost in his own misery he couldn't see what his actions did to her.

His pain, confusion, and anger touched her somewhere beyond fear. A strange, almost nurturing, need grew within her. Since that first morning, her struggle against the irrational urge to help this man had been constant. She had no idea why she wanted to reach out to Mike, especially when he held her captive on his bed.

He released her shoulders and braced himself with one arm, then brought his free hand to her cheek, gently brushing away her tears with his callused fingertips. Lightning flashed, and in its brief light she saw his Adam's apple working in his throat.

The additional light was fleeting, though in its wake she saw him more clearly. There was a hunger in his eyes—a fierce, questioning need he obviously expected *her* to answer.

Answer . . . or fulfill?

Apprehension merged with the other undefinable emotion— the one she feared even more than this man in all his fury. Something leapt between them in that breadth of a second. She couldn't define it, though its significance was indisputable.

He brushed the backs of his fingers along her cheekbone, gently stroking the soft flesh of her earlobe. A shiver skittered down her spine, but not of fear.

It was a quiver of longing—a dulcet, unbridled need she was ill-prepared to face. She closed her eyes for a moment to savor the contrast of his rough fingers against her skin. An exquisite spasm raced through her, leaving behind a slow burn and a million silent questions.

Why did he make her feel this way? The fear she'd felt earlier—where had it fled? Why didn't she fear him now, after he'd forced her to his bed? How could she endure his touch at all after what she'd suffered at another's hands?

And how could a gesture as simple as the stroke of his fingertips against her ear feel so extraordinary? So wonderful?

He came closer, covering her wet, shivering body with his. The welcome warmth soothed her tremors while creating a quaking of a different sort.

A decidedly more dangerous variety.

"Mike . . ." His name left her lips as her eyes fluttered open and his bare chest pressed against her fully clothed one. The paroxysms low in her belly intensified, becoming almost unbearable as he lowered his mouth to hers.

She should have stopped him, but couldn't. Her body craved his touch, his kisses, and more . . .

Soft and undemanding, he slanted his mouth across hers. He lowered his weight to his elbows and cupped her face with both hands.

A moan slipped from some dark place deep inside her. Outside, thunder boomed and lightning sizzled through the sky, though she knew the powerful longing surging through her body undoubtedly rivaled the storm.

His tongue sought entrance to her mouth, stroking the seam of her lips until she tremulously parted them. *What madness is this?* she wondered, then lost her ability to think clearly as his tongue explored and tantalized at leisure.

His gentle yet thorough possession left her shuddering beneath him. A gravelly sound rumbled from inside him, overflowing into her mouth, lush and full of promise.

Her breasts tingled, savoring the feel of his heated flesh pressing intimately against them through her clothing. Abigail's head swam. She should fight and scream, but she couldn't.

She didn't want to.

Whimpering, she locked her hands behind his neck and invited him to deepen his intoxicating kiss. His hair was soft against her fingertips, enticing her to bury them in the short strands.

Something moved at her side—his hand. He shifted it to cup her breast. Immediate shock yielded to a staggering swell of hunger. Like a clock wound too tightly, her insides clenched and waited for the impetus that would release the tension and set her free.

Her nipples tightened and strained against her bodice as he kneaded her flesh. Renewed panic threatened to overshadow desire, but for only a fleeting moment. Before she could fully form the thoughts necessary to resist his seduction, his thumb brushed against her.

Surely, this was magic.

She should stop this before it was too late, but she didn't know what to protest—which wild and unexplainable action— his hand caressing her breast or his tongue thrusting into her startled and vulnerable mouth.

Like an artist, he initiated a masterpiece of desire deep within her. She moaned as he intensified his kiss, boundlessly exploring her mouth with his tongue. Instinctively, her hips thrust upward, meeting his body with an intimacy that took her breath away.

The long hard ridge at the front of his rough jeans made the coil of longing tighten even more. She wanted this intimacy, and she wanted it with this man.

Raging deep inside her, the excruciating memories of another man, another night, demanded recognition. Desire for *this* man battled the waves of panic which threatened to overtake the delicious sensations sweeping through her now.

She didn't *want* to remember, yet she must.

Heaven help her.

Mike hadn't planned to touch her. Hell, finding her in his cabin—on his *bed*—had been the farthest thing from his mind when he'd rushed in from the storm.

The softness of her breast filled his hand and made him burn to taste her more completely.

Totally.

He should hate her—she'd lied to him. But at this moment all he cared about was making her want him as desperately as he wanted her. Later, once they'd both reached their fill of each other, he could interrogate her. Right now his body didn't give a damn about lies or secrets.

So the Southern belle really was a hot-blooded woman. In confirmation, her throaty moan filled his mouth like good whiskey, smooth and robust.

His hand found the hard nub of her nipple through her dress and he knew this wouldn't be enough—not nearly enough. He wanted all of her, naked and quaking for him. The macho role had never been his style, but Abigail Kingsley brought out something primitive and reckless from inside him. Neanderthal Man had nothing on Mike Faricy.

Her lips were sweet; there should've been a law against a woman tasting so good. It wasn't fair to men like him—desperate and hurting. Hungry.

He could blot out all the pain for a while in her arms. No doubt about it. The thought of burying himself within her made him burn. But it was more than lust that drove him. He wanted her sweetness, her sensitivity, the fierce devotion she gave her son. He wanted it all—her body, her mind, her soul . . .

Every day he'd spent with her had made his desire to touch her, possess her, love her more insistent.

And now she was in his arms, returning his kiss with a wild abandon that stripped away his final threads of resistance and left him ready to take her all the way.

And beyond.

Her arms were wrapped around his neck, holding his head as if she feared he might move away. The only thing he planned to move away for was to get rid of some unnecessary clothing.

His fumbling fingers found the buttons at the front of her dress and quickly opened them. Blood trumpeted through his veins in anticipation of touching and tasting her. Since the morning he'd first seen her, Mike had thought of her breasts— full and tempting, despite her inadequate diet. His dreams had been filled with images of her body, her smile, the sound of her laughter.

He dragged his mouth from hers and they both gulped air into their lungs. Eager to see her face, he looked down and found her staring up at him, her blue eyes glazed with passion and filled with questions.

Groaning, he kissed her flushed cheek while his hand pushed aside her open dress to reveal bare skin—hot and inviting. It didn't take him long to fill his hand with her breasts. Her rigid nipple teased and beckoned as he covered it, then rolled the tempting peak between his thumb and forefinger.

He was crazy with wanting her—he was crazy, period. But it didn't really matter. Nothing he could do would change his situation or the nature of his mission.

Weren't the condemned always given a last request? Abigail Kingsley would be his last meal. He intended to be with her in every sense of the word until the sun set, then rose again in the morning.

This was his payback—his perk.

And so much more.

His salvation?

As he explored her breast, Abigail's enthusiastic mouth never stopped wandering from his cheek to his temple and back, while seductive little whimpers sounded in her throat. Every breath, every brush of her lips against his skin, sent riot guns exploding through his body.

He'd never wanted a woman with such desperation. For some insane reason, she had become a lifeline to him. He had to taste her, touch her, make love to her . . .

Now.

Abigail. Elysium. Lies. Secrets.

He ground his teeth in an effort to obliterate those taunting words from his mind. Why now? *Please, not now.* But Slick's voice played over and over in Mike's mind, resurrecting his anger. Was it only his memory, or was Slick really here, filling Mike's head with his taunts?

Abigail. Elysium. Lies. Secrets.

No, stop, he silently pleaded, forcing his attention away from the voice and back to her—so fine and tempting. With Abigail, maybe he could push his living hell to the back of his mind. For a while.

Something more drove him now. It was almost as if he'd lost control of his actions. Was it Slick?

Mike strived for command, wondering if it was Slick or himself ruling his actions now. Lust, all-consuming, melded with other reckless emotions to drive him.

No longer gentle, he sought her mouth again with his and plundered it. She met his thrusting tongue, stroking and matching his movements.

Mike was on fire.

A situation he could remedy.

A small voice in the back of his mind cautioned him to proceed slowly with this woman, but he couldn't. Something—Slick?—compelled Mike to take what he wanted, regardless of the consequences. The voice of reason—his conscience—where the hell had it gone?

He lifted himself slightly and lowered his mouth to her long, slender neck. The white column of her throat made a perfect path to lead him downward to regions as yet unexplored. She shifted slightly, altering the pressure of her pelvis against his groin in the best and worst possible ways.

She tasted even sweeter here, at the base of her throat where her pulse thrummed against his questing lips. He cupped her breast fully in his hand, then brushed his lips across the upper curve, savoring the smoothness of her pearly flesh. With his tongue, he traced tiny circles around her nipple, postponing the moment when he would draw the puckered tip into his mouth and take them one step closer to ending his misery.

She was gentle, loving and good. He didn't want to hurt her; he just *wanted* her.

Abigail. Elysium. Lies. Secrets, Slick taunted again. *Abigail lied . . . she wants you.*

Why couldn't that creep leave him alone? Anger and lust whipped together throughout his body, fueling his craving for this woman to an ominous, powerful state. Hate and passion mated with desperation to create something new and absolute. He lost control—there were no more limitations.

She'd lied to him—this woman who moaned when he touched her.

Abigail. Elysium. Lies. Secrets.

She was no better than Honey. Abigail even had an illegitimate child. This was no innocent virgin bucking against him.

Determined, Mike reached downward and pulled her skirt up between them, searching for an end to his madness. He had to have her—he'd die if he couldn't thrust himself inside this woman.

Abigail. Elysium. Lies. Secrets.

Leave me alone!

There was only one explanation, he decided before the voice had a chance to fill his brain again. He'd lost his mind—control had fallen into other hands.

Evil hands.

His breath came in loud, ragged pants as he continued his search for a way to rid her of the ridiculous underwear. They seemed to have no beginning and no end, and her arching and writhing beneath him offered no assistance.

She mumbled something, but he was too lost to grasp her words. Momentarily abandoning his search, Mike concentrated again on her breasts. He cupped them both in his hands and looked at them, milky and round with rose-tipped nipples.

He brushed his thumbs across both peaks, watching the buds grow beneath his touch. Unable to resist a moment longer, he lowered his mouth to her. *So sweet . . .*

She moaned and again murmured something unintelligible as he kissed his way from one succulent breast to the other. Her thrashing became more pronounced as she pressed herself against his mouth.

Abigail. Elysium. Lies. Secrets.

That voice—Slick's—stole every shred of gentleness from Mike, leaving him only with an overly aggressive way of touching and kissing her. She should be punished for lying to him.

He was harder and more uncomfortable than at anytime in his life, even adolescence. He reached between them and released a few more buttons. He needed relief—had to have it.

This hot-blooded woman was the key to his relief. As a matter of fact, she was the key to a lot of things he needed. He pushed his hand lower, nearly exploding on the spot when he felt her warmth. The farther he eased his hand, the hotter she felt and the more volatile his state of arousal became.

He inched his hand along her smooth, flat abdomen until he found crisp, curling hair. She pressed upward against his hand and he heard her gasp mingle with more broken, unintelligible words.

Yes, she wanted him as desperately as he wanted her. So why didn't she help him get rid of all these damned clothes?

Frustrated, he lifted himself away from her, dragged in a rasping breath, and stared down into her face. "You gotta help me get rid of—"

Brimming with tears, her eyes were huge and round in her flushed face. Her nostrils were slightly flared, and her chin quivered until she bit her lower lip with straight white teeth.

The expression on her face was one of confusion . . . and pure terror.

Stunned, Mike eased his hand away from her and swallowed hard. The throbbing between his legs protested—*loudly*—but he'd be damned before he'd have sex with a woman who was afraid of him.

Of course, he was already damned.

"Abigail," he whispered, but she continued to stare upward in paralyzed silence. What the hell had he done?

"Oh, God." Suddenly, he knew. Her twisting and squirming hadn't been the movements of a woman writhing in ecstasy.

Abigail had been trying to escape.

He remembered her mumbling and her words returned to haunt him, as clearly as if he'd heard them correctly in the first place. *Please, don't hurt me.*

What had come over him? *You horny bastard.*

Slick.

Mike's gut twisted and burned as he lifted himself away from her. Trying not to let his gaze linger on her lovely breasts, he reached down to gently pull the front of her dress together. She made no move to help him close the buttons, so he sat upright, ignoring the painful protest of his body at being compressed even more in this position.

After a few minutes, he had her clothing straightened, but she showed no sign of coming out of her trance.

What if she never came out of this? What about her son?

Filled with self-loathing, Mike stood and looked around the cabin. No matter what Abigail may have done in the past, one thing was clearly evident. She was *not* the experienced, hot-blooded woman he'd convinced himself she was. Far from it, in fact.

Realization struck him full force.

"Oh, God." He groaned and ran both hands over his sweaty face, then turned to look down at her again. She stared silently upward at the beamed ceiling, oblivious to his presence.

He should've figured this out before now. What an ass he'd been. There was only way a woman like Abigail Kingsley could've ended up pregnant.

Bile rose in his throat and he shook his head. Her tears had dried, leaving white streaks on her cheeks. She didn't even blink, her breathing shallow and barely evident.

He knew. Raking his hand through his hair, Mike cringed in self-directed malice.

Unable to look at her stricken face another second, he crossed the room and leaned his forehead against the stone hearth. Regret was every bit as difficult to live with as hate.

Just what he needed—another challenge.

A rustling sound crept into his subconscious, rallying him from his recriminations. Tiredly, he pushed himself away from the hearth and turned toward the bed.

Abigail stood beside his bed, her beautiful hair hanging in disarray around her face. Her blue eyes were huge and her gaze darted from the door to him, then back again.

He opened his mouth to speak—to beg her forgiveness—but only silence filled the cabin. Suddenly, she bolted for the door and fumbled with the board, glancing frantically over her shoulder every few moments.

Mike took a step toward her, planning only to help with the door, but her gasp of fear stayed him. After he took a step backward, she turned again to her task, and finally the door swung open.

"Abigail," he said softly. She stood in the open doorway with her back to him. "I'm—"

Without turning to face him, she pressed her hands over both ears and ran out the door. And away from him.

"—sorry," he finished morosely, dropping his hands to dangle at his sides.

How could he have been such a fool? The evidence was overwhelming. Even a rookie should've seen all the signs. There was no doubt in his mind.

Abigail Kingsley had been raped.

And, damn him, he'd almost repeated that crime.

"What a wuss."

Mike's head snapped around in search of that dreaded voice, but he found nothing in the now silent cabin. The storm had long since passed, unnoticed by him in his Slick-fueled lust. *Jerk.*

"Wuss."

Again, he couldn't find the source. "Where are you?" he asked, surveying the room as he traveled the few short steps to the table and his discarded shirt.

He pulled the T-shirt on over his head. "Come on out here and face me like a man, you son of a bitch."

"Even dead, I'm more of a man than you, Mike. Of course, technically, I'm not a man at all anymore."

Mike snorted derisively. "No shit. What was your first clue?"

A movement in the corner caught Mike's attention. After a moment, a dark shape appeared on the dirt floor and scurried into the center of the room.

Frowning, Mike wished he wasn't barefoot. The earth floor somehow felt dirtier now, knowing Slick was down there playing one of his warped games. "What are you this time?"

"You said something earlier about a rat's ass. Remember?" The shape came nearer. "I decided to bring more than its ass."

The shape moved into a path of sunlight in the center of the room. "What do you think?" Slick asked with a chuckle. "I could be a movie star in this get-up."

"Same thing I always think. You're a sick bastard." Mike

glanced toward the open door, then faced his nemesis again. "This is all your fault."

Slick sighed and inched closer. His yellow eyes glowed in the dimly lit cabin. A long, pointed rat's face seemed the perfect complement to Slick's personality.

"You had her right there, Mike." The rat shook his head. "With that boner you're sporting, another couple of seconds and *bam!*"

"Get out of here and leave me alone." Mike felt lower than he ever had. He'd almost committed rape, for God's sake. "Why do you keep butting in? Just let me do this *my* way and leave her out of it."

"No can do." Slick eased himself closer to Mike, then suddenly—magically—the rat was on the table. Those rodent eyes changed from yellow to orange, then red, with hypnotic rings encircling the rims.

"Damn."

"That's right. Damnation is yours, sayeth *moi.*" Slick punctuated his assertion with a wheezing chuckle. "Let's get this show on the road, Mike. I'm sick of this gig—time to move on to a new phase."

Mike clenched his teeth. "What I wouldn't give for a truckload of D-Con about now."

"Yeah, I'll bet."

"I'm doing the best I can, but you keep interfering." Mike clenched his fists at his sides, struggling without success to wrench his gaze from Slick's. "If you hadn't dragged me into that nineteenth-century version of a crackhouse this afternoon, I could've gone back and checked on—"

"Mike, Mike." The vermilion in Slick's eyes intensified. "Remember, Slick doesn't do a thing without a reason. You learned things in there with Honey. If you'd been more of a sport, you might have learned a few little tricks along the way. But *no.* You had to play good cop."

Mike didn't feel the least bit respectable right now. He'd hurt Abigail. How could he have misjudged her reactions so badly? At first, she'd definitely been receptive to his kisses and caresses. It was later, when things had turned more serious, that she must've started resisting . . . and he'd ignored her. *Please, don't hurt me.*

"You could've had both women today," Slick taunted. Blood red flames leapt in his eyes as he raised up on his hind quarters to hold Mike's stare. "You can stop being such a good boy now, Mike. It won't help you anyway. Why not enjoy some of life's guilty pleasures, hmm? Before it's too . . . late?"

Mike drew a deep breath and commanded himself not to respond to Slick's bait. "What did you mean about Abigail telling lies and keeping secrets?"

"You heard the soldiers."

"Dammit, just *tell* me!" Frustration wrapped itself around and through Mike as surely as a prison cell. He hated himself— hated this rodent-devil even more. "Just tell me where to find Milton's ancestor so I can get this nightmare over with."

"Mike, Mike." Slick pulled his gums back to reveal hideous rat teeth, jagged and yellow. "I can't just *tell* you—it'd take all the fun out of the game."

"I'm not having fun." Mike's voice fell to a ragged whisper. "I want this over with before someone else gets hurt."

"You realize what you're saying?" Slick tilted his head to one side. "When your job's done—"

"Yeah, I know. I'm dead meat."

"That about sums it up."

"What difference does it make?" Mike asked, shoving his fists into his pockets. "I'm going to be miserable no matter what, so just let me finish my job."

"In a hurry to get to Hell, eh?" Slick's laughter was maniacal. "Things would be much . . . hotter down there if I were in charge."

"Well, you're not, so can we get this over with?" Mike's chest constricted and he couldn't breathe for several seconds. "Soon?"

"Good. That blood lust is after you again." Slick nodded in obvious satisfaction. "I can tell."

"What of it?" Mike realized he'd probably get farther if he played along. "I want to kill Milton's ancestor. That's why I'm here, so let's just do it."

Slick gave another melodramatic sigh. "It isn't that simple."

"Why the hell not?" Mike noticed the flame in Slick's eyes flicker slightly, almost as if someone had blasted him with a fire extinguisher. *Wouldn't that be nice?*

"Watch it, dickweed."

"Stop reading my mind—I asked you a question." Mike was foolishly unafraid of Slick at the moment. The devil's pawn wanted this mission to be successful, so he wasn't going to take Mike to Hell until the job was done. Now, in light of what had almost happened with Abigail, that's all Mike wanted. "Let's finish this."

"No can do." Slick lowered himself to the table's surface. "It's against the rules for me to tell you the answers. All I can do is drop hints."

Mike barked a derisive laugh. "Gimme a break. Devils play by *rules?*"

"Yeah, ain't it the shits?"

"What about Abigail? There's no way she could be expected to know the names of every soldier who came here during the war. You really had me going for a while." Mike felt his gut clench again. "Is she going to be okay?"

"Who cares?" Slick turned, releasing Mike's gaze in the process.

"*I* do."

Slick pivoted again—his red eyes seemed to leave their sockets, thwarting Mike's moment of rebellion. "Watch it, wuss," he warned. "Remember everything you learned in town today. Hmm? Sometimes our enemies are a lot closer than we think."

Then Slick spun in a circle—faster and faster until he was nothing but a blur on the rough surface. A whirring sound filled the cabin, then the spinning rat vanished.

Mike blinked several times, then turned toward the empty bunk.

What had happened to Abigail this afternoon in his arms? And why had he allowed things to go so far? He'd never done anything this vile before. Why'd he have to start at this late date?

Slick's voice invaded Mike's thoughts again. *Remember everything you learned in town today. Sometimes our enemies are a lot closer than we think.*

"Are you my enemy, Abigail?" he whispered.

Chapter Ten

Abigail slowly opened her eyes and looked around. Shadowy memories of bare flesh, warm hungry lips, and fear slipped insidiously into her thoughts. She bolted upright and blinked, taking in her surroundings in one frantic sweep of the room.

Her room.

"How did I get here?" Her voice cracked and her hand went instinctively—protectively—to her bodice. All the tiny buttons were neatly done, leaving no part of her exposed.

On wobbly legs, she pushed to her feet and walked to the window. The sun slowly settled beyond the storm-swollen river, bathing the rain-washed countryside in pinks and oranges. The beauty of the scene mocked her feelings of despondency.

She bit her lower lip, trying to remember exactly what had happened. Her face flooded with the fervor of recollection. Oh, she remembered most of it well enough, but not how she'd ended up here in her room. She pressed her hand against her breast. And fully clothed.

Had he . . . ?

No. Her memory slowly filled in the missing pieces. She had herself to blame for this. For a while she'd responded to him as if she'd *wanted* him to do those things to her body.

Heaven help me.

Nothing less than a miracle had saved her. She had no way of knowing why Mike had stopped—all that really mattered was that he had.

He'd touched her in ways and places that made her burn inside even now, though she silently thanked God for sparing her the ultimate violation. Her conflicting emotions released other images—memories of something she hoped never to endure again.

Still, despite her fears, she knew her experience with Mike was far different from that other time. That other man.

Fortunately, she hadn't been observed entering the house. Rosalie would have seen immediately that something was amiss, and Abigail couldn't imagine how she could possibly have explained.

Scalding tears stung her eyes and she dragged in a weepy breath. What horrible thing had she done in her life to deserve this?

Again?

Had she done something to give Mike the impression that she wanted *that?* Her heart sank. Of course she had. She'd been asleep on his bed, of all things, when he walked through the door. What man wouldn't have assumed the same thing?

Mike's kisses had evoked an undeniable response, and it certainly hadn't been one of resistance. She'd responded like a willing, eager woman.

Her insides turned quivery and her face felt downright feverish as she recalled more of what had transpired between them. Her nipple hardened beneath her palm, making her gasp and drop her guilty hand away.

How could she compare what had happened this afternoon with Mike to that other man—that other time? It had been so different, until—

"Mercy!" She brought her hand to her mouth to silence herself. Pressing her fingers against trembling lips, Abigail remembered the way Mike had made her feel. She had wanted him to touch her—no point in denying it.

Then she remembered the moment when things had changed.

Like a pendulum, her passion had swung from fervent desire to terror. A shudder swept through her. *Don't hurt me.*

Then, in her mind, he'd become that other man. Trembling started in her core and spread unrelentingly throughout her body and her very soul. *That* man hadn't cared about her innocence or her fears. He'd taken her brutally, without preamble.

Even Mike hadn't stopped when she'd begged him to. How did that make him different from that other man? Because he *had* eventually stopped. That made him infinitely different.

Her only defense against Mike—and against herself—had been to die inside. There and then, she'd turned inside herself like a turtle ducking inside its shell. The memory of that dark place—that safe place—terrified her now. What if she'd been unable to find her way back?

A shudder of horror swept through her. What would happen to Wade if—

No! All was well, after all. What point was there in dwelling on it?

Still, she should never have let things go as far as they had. For that matter, she should never had gone to Mike's cabin at all.

What had she been thinking? What had made her behave so foolishly?

The letter.

Her heart sank and she closed her eyes against reality. That letter had driven her to Mike's cabin . . . and into his arms?

If Mike Faricy's touch sent her into such a state, how did she ever expect to deal with—

A knock at the door made her jump. Her eyes flew open and she whirled around just in time to see Rosalie rushing into the room.

"Miss Abigail, I'm sure glad to find you awake."

"Rosalie, I'm sorry I haven't been down to help this afternoon, but—"

"Never you mind that." Rosalie shook her head. "That ain't important."

Abigail noticed the crease marring her friend's normally smooth, dark brow. "What is it? What's wrong?"

"Soldiers, Miss Abigail. Downstairs."

Abigail's heart sprinted away with her self-control, but she quickly reestablished command. "Soldiers," she echoed, then moistened her lips with her tongue. "What do they want?" Were the soldiers here to make them leave Elysium already?

"They asked for the master, but I told 'em he was dead."

"I see." Abigail straightened and smoothed her skirt. Drawing a deep breath, she crossed the room to the mirror and coiled her hair into a knot, then secured it with the large comb Rosalie handed to her.

Her lips were still red and swollen from Mike's kisses. Was it only her imagination or did her eyes look different, too?

"I wish we knew what they want here. Them Yankees done took enough from us already," Rosalie said quietly. "And they ain't done takin' yet."

Take? Yes, they took . . . and they'll take again if we let them. Again, that wretched memory stirred from the dark place where Abigail had buried it. She squeezed her eyes shut, praying for the images of that night to relinquish their perpetual hold on her.

"You all right, Miss Abigail?"

Anything for Wade. Abigail opened her eyes and nodded. "I'll just have to go downstairs and speak to them. Won't I?"

Rosalie stared over Abigail's shoulder, meeting her gaze in the warped looking glass. "Yes'm. And I'll go with you."

Abigail turned and gave Rosalie a quick hug. "I know you will, but keeping Wade occupied and safe is more important."

"He's with Mr. Mike out to the barn."

Mike. The mere mention of the man's name sent her heart soaring; perspiration coated her palms. "That's good," she said quietly, hoping her voice didn't betray her true emotions. She took one last glance in the mirror to make certain her clothing was all in place. For some reason, she felt exposed and vulnerable. As if the world knew where—and how—she'd spent her afternoon.

"All right, then." Abigail squared her shoulders and walked to the door. "Let's find out what they want." She glanced back over her shoulder.

Rosalie nodded and their gazes locked for a few seconds. Abigail knew in that whisper of time that their thoughts were congruent. The same memories that tore at Abigail also haunted Rosalie.

Bracing herself, Abigail turned and stepped through the open door. Worrying wouldn't change things. She must face this without buckling under to her inner fears. Somewhere inside, she knew the strength she'd summoned earlier to enable her to post that dreaded letter remained. The past was over— nothing could change that.

Pausing at the top of the curved staircase, Abigail looked down into the great hall—the same room where she'd first seen Mike Faricy. A surge of joy swept through her. *Joy?* Where had that come from?

That strange and unusual man had brought long absent happiness to everyone at Elysium. She knew now that he'd misunderstood her intentions after finding her in his cabin.

On his bed.

Heat flooded her cheeks as she drew a deep breath to quash thoughts of Mike and the afternoon past. Evening was upon them now.

And soldiers.

She felt, rather than heard, Rosalie's comforting presence behind her on the stairs. *Thank you.* Abigail's gaze swept the span of the great hall.

Clenching her fists at her sides, she continued to search for the soldiers. As she reached the bottom step, she saw them standing near the French doors with their backs to her. Their blue uniforms summoned memories, but she forcefully doused them.

Anything for Wade.

Whatever their mission, she could handle it. After all, she'd already seen soldiers at their worst, and the war was over now. Surely peace should bring with it at least a modicum of decency.

Even to Yankees.

Abigail lifted her chin and drew a deep breath. Her upbringing wouldn't fail her now. Mustering years of training at her mother's insistent hand, she started toward the soldiers with a forced smile on her face.

"Good evening, gentlemen," she said in a smooth drawl, holding her breath as they turned to face her. "What brings you to Elysium?"

Hats in hands, both men stared at her in silence for a few heart-stopping moments. She wished they'd speak and end her speculation. For all she knew, they could order her family to vacate the premises this very night.

"Good evening, ma'am," the taller man said, inclining his head very slightly. "I presume you must be Miss Kingsley."

"I am, sir. And you are . . . ?"

"My apologies for the intrusion, ma'am. I'm Major Thiel and this is Lieutenant Brown."

She turned to look directly at the smaller man for the first time. *Heavens.* Her insides twisted as she recalled him taking that wretched letter from her hands today. Though he'd treated her with kindness and respect, he was a reminder of something she'd rather forget.

"Oh, I remember you from the post office." Lieutenant Brown flashed her the same boyish grin he'd worn earlier today.

Abigail acknowledged the smaller man with a stiff nod and a tight smile. Not only did she have unwelcome visitors, but one of them was a walking reminder of the terrible duty she'd performed today. "Yes, I remember," she said with far more aplomb than she felt.

"You two have met?" The major's surprise made his voice loud enough to create an echo.

"I . . . I posted a letter today." Wasn't it enough that she'd been forced to correspond with the one man she hated above all others? Now this, too?

Surely these soldiers hadn't come to evict them. Where would they go? Her letter needed time to reach Denver first. Why hadn't she thought to ask how long it would take? "What brings you gentlemen to Elysium this evening?" She forced her voice to sound calm.

"We're investigating the disappearance of a soldier last seen in this area," Major Thiel explained.

Abigail didn't like his eyes. They were small and dark, closely set, and filled with suspicion. "I see."

"He was with an advance scouting party on assignment near here." The major's eyes glittered and he stared at her as if expecting something. *"Very* near here. His name was Denny— Lieutenant Denny."

Abigail went cold inside. Her head swam and she could've sworn the floor buckled beneath her for an instant. Why did so many bad memories have to surface in one day? This couldn't be happening. "Denny," she said stupidly, praying Rosalie would follow her lead. "What does all this have to do with us here at Elysium, sir?"

"Well, probably nothing, ma'am," the Lieutenant said steadily. "However, Denny's commanding officer reported that his company was visiting this plantation the day Lieutenant Denny disappeared."

Icy fingers of dread slithered down her spine. *Denny's commanding officer* . . . She knew all too well the identity of that horrible man. What was she going to do? Somehow, these soldiers knew something. Mentally, she paused, then drew a long, shuddering breath. "I don't recall, sir."

One corner of Major Thiel's mouth turned upward and he shook his head. "Well, then maybe you remember a scouting party. I imagine they would've been among the first Union soldiers you saw in this area during the war."

The man didn't believe her. Skepticism etched itself plainly across his face. Abigail chewed the inside of her lower lip and searched her mind frantically for something—anything—that sounded plausible.

"I'm sorry, Major." She clasped her hands in front of her while continuing to meet his gaze. "I don't remember exactly when the first soldiers *visited* us here. And I certainly didn't make a habit of asking their names. As I'm sure you're aware, soldiers from both armies came uninvited. They . . . took things which did not belong to them."

The major's smirk became more pronounced. "Hmm, I'll bet."

Whistling sounded from the back of the house, followed by

Wade's high-pitched giggle. *Mike.* Relief blended with trepidation, making her breath quicken and her stomach lurch. Seeing him again after . . .

Embarrassment heated her face and she avoided the Major's gaze, drawing comfort from the sound of Mike's approaching footsteps.

"I don't smell any fish coo—" Mike's words ceased as if sliced away with a knife as he pushed through the swinging door from the kitchen.

He stopped in midstep, obviously as surprised as she was about their visitors. "Well, if it isn't Rambo and John Wayne."

The three men stared at each other in silence as Mike lifted Wade from his shoulders and placed him on the floor.

"Me milk cow," Wade announced, running to Abigail and burying his face in her skirt.

"That's good, Wade." Abigail reached down and placed a protective hand on her son's blond head, then turned her attention back to the soldiers. "Was there anything else, gentlemen?"

Major Thiel turned purposefully in Mike's direction. "You look familiar. Who are you?"

Mike's eyes narrowed, glittering in open suspicion. "Who's asking?"

"I am." The major's face reddened and the veins on his neck bulged.

"Mike Faricy."

Abigail watched the silent exchange, realizing the men were playing out some ancient ritual, as basic and primitive as a pair of bantam roosters circling and scratching in the barnyard. What she couldn't determine was why.

The young officer turned to face his superior, an eager expression in his youthful eyes. "By God, he's the man we saw in the whorehouse Under-the-Hill this afternoon."

"Mercy!" The sound of her own voice startled Abigail.

Rosalie's sharp intake of breath drew a precise analogy with Abigail's thoughts.

Lieutenant Brown had the decency to blush when he looked at her. "Sorry, ma'am."

Abigail tried to meet Mike's gaze, but couldn't. Was it shame, shock, or desire that made her stare directly at his feet?

"Of course. I remember now." Major Thiel turned to look at Abigail. "Does this man . . . *live* here, Miss Kingsley?"

Scorn filled the man's voice, mocking Abigail's efforts to face him with at least a smidgen of confidence. "Yes, Mr. Faricy works for us." She could've kicked herself for that. Why did she feel compelled to explain Mike's presence? It was none of the Army's business.

"Work?" Cynicism filled the Major's chuckle.

"Yeah, *work.*" Mike's voice held a menacing edge and he took a step closer. "What do you want here, *Major?* State your business."

"We're investigating the disappearance of a soldier in this area."

"There haven't been any soldiers at Elysium since I got here. Until now." Mike shrugged and cast a covert glance at Abigail. She seemed all right, though he couldn't help noticing how pale she looked.

My fault.

Mike wanted to hit something, preferably something that would bleed.

Profusely.

He remembered the conversation he'd overheard in town between these two men. He'd never forget it, especially since Slick's colorful taunts had punctuated the event.

Abigail. Elysium. Lies. Secrets.

With difficulty, he ignored the voice in his head and folded his arms across his chest.

"Enlighten us. What makes you think this is the place to look for a soldier who couldn't find his way home? And, for what it's worth, you never did mention *your* name."

"Thiel. Major Thiel." The man took a step closer, his dark eyes never wavering from their intense scrutiny of Mike. "This is Lieutenant Brown, and the man we're looking for vanished after being at *this* plantation in '62. Satisfied?"

Yeah, and Daddy Warbucks is some shipping magnate.

Mike's foggy memory slowly unfolded itself. "Hmm. Satisfied? I'm not sure yet. Give me a couple of minutes."

"Take your time." Thiel's gray eyes reflected a hard glint of anger.

God, why couldn't the jerk's name have been Milton? With any luck, when he found Milton, maybe Mike wouldn't like him any more than he did this tin soldier. That could simplify his mission. Maybe.

Though nothing could soften the memory of the shitty things Mike had done—and almost done—to Abigail this afternoon.

Shaking his head to free his thoughts, Mike summoned his detective persona. "I can't imagine why you're looking for someone who disappeared *during* a war—bear with me, this is an important point—three years ago. Hmm? Color me skeptical, but that just doesn't jive, Major."

"Jive?" the major repeated.

"Make sense." Mike shook his head, trying to ignore Wade's questioning gaze. *Poor kid.* "This whole thing doesn't make sense."

Thiel's eyes bulged and his face darkened. If Mike didn't know better, he'd have searched the good major for a stash of Angel Dust.

"It's none of your concern, Faricy." Thiel took another step forward. "This is official United States Army business."

"I see." *And was Milton here on official business, too?* "Sorry, but I still don't get it, Thiel. The war's over and this soldier is probably dead like thousands of other poor bastards."

"Probably, but we've been ordered to investigate."

Mike rubbed his chin thoughtfully, struggling against rage and confusion. Why had Abigail lied to him? *Had* she lied to him? Was Slick playing more of his sick mind games? No surprise if that proved true.

"So, investigate already. Nobody's stopping you." Mike issued a blatant challenge with his gaze. He knew from the way Thiel's eyes continued to bulge that the message had been received and understood.

Waiting for the man to regain enough self-control to carry on a sensible conversation, Mike ventured another glance at

Abigail. Her blue eyes were large and round; faint smudges marred the translucent skin beneath them. She looked tired and frightened.

Correction—make that terrified.

He'd caused this. Damn Slick Dawson for planting those seeds of doubt. Still, how could Mike forget what he'd overheard in the whorehouse? That a Major Milton had led a scouting party here—to Elysium.

Mike's pulse leapt and every muscle in his body tightened. If he gnashed his teeth any harder they'd shatter.

Thiel gave a dramatic sigh. "Faricy, were you living here in '62?"

Mike laughed quietly. *Maybe in 1962.* "Nope."

"Then stay the hell out of this."

Thiel turned to face Abigail again. Mike clenched his fists, denying himself the pleasure of punching in the soldier's smug face. The gratification of feeling flesh and bone crunch beneath his fist would be immediate and awesome about now.

"*Miss* Kingsley," Thiel continued, casting a suggestive glance at Wade. "You're absolutely certain you don't remember Lieutenant Denny?"

Mike watched Abigail's lashes flutter to veil her eyes, but not before he saw the unmistakable expression in their blue depths. She was lying.

Abigail. Elysium. Lies. Secrets.

And Milton.

Mike's gut twisted and burned as he watched her and waited for her to answer the inquisition.

"Miss Abigail done told y'all she don't know nothin' about *nothin'.*" Rosalie stepped forward to stand beside her mistress.

"Well, how about *you?*" Thiel turned his attention from Abigail to Rosalie. "Were you here then?"

"I was born here." Rosalie pushed out her lower lip and lifted her chin. "This be my home."

"Then do you remember the man?"

"No, sir." Rosalie's mettle was admirable. "Plenty soldiers come through here from both armies. How come you 'spects us to remember one man?"

Bravo.

"Because I asked you to. Because it's incredibly ... important." Thiel took a menacing step toward Rosalie. "If you can't offer anything helpful, then remain silent."

Abigail jerked her eyes open and her head erect. "You will *not* speak to Rosalie in such a manner. I think we've answered enough questions, sir."

Mike lifted a speculative brow when Lieutenant Brown shot him a questioning glance. Obviously, they both expected some reaction from the good major.

"You heard the lady," Mike said, waiting for Thiel to blow.

Ramming his hat onto his head, Major Thiel loomed large and threatening over Abigail. Mike didn't like it—not one bit. A protective surge swept through him, making him want to throw the soldiers out the door by force. In fact, nothing— almost nothing—would give him greater pleasure at this moment.

"I have a suggestion for you, *Miss* Kingsley," Thiel said slowly. "Try to jog your memory. I feel secrets lurking within these walls. And I damned well intend to uncover them *all.*"

Thiel pivoted on his heel and walked to the French doors. Without turning to face her again, he added, "I'll see you at the sale, Miss Kingsley."

Without another word, the major opened the door and stepped out, leaving it open behind him. Lieutenant Brown's face reddened and he mumbled an apology before turning to follow his commanding officer.

Abigail stared at the door until the lieutenant pulled it shut behind him, then she covered her face with her hands. Her shoulders gave a great shudder and Mike knew she was crying.

This mess was ripping him apart inside—bone by bone, nerve by nerve. Part of him wanted to gather Abigail in his arms and comfort her, but another unrelenting voice from deep in his gut wouldn't let him forget her deceit.

Rosalie put her arms around her mistress and, with Wade clutching his mother's skirt, the threesome turned toward the stairs. Mike watched their ascent, wishing ... Abigail needed him almost as much as he needed her, and not merely in the physical sense.

Much as he hated to admit it, he felt a link with this woman—an unbreakable bond.

He heard a door upstairs slam and knew it was her room. A gut-wrenching feeling coursed through him. He felt shut out—locked out of their lives.

And he hated it.

He took several long strides to the piano and brought his hands crashing down on the keys. A cacophony of discordant sounds came from the broken instrument, reminding Mike of that horrible night and the music he'd heard just before Slick walked through the door.

"Why, Abigail?"

The horses plodded along in the quagmire that passed for a road. "So you saw the Kingsley woman in town earlier, Brown?"

Henry Brown bobbed his head, then realized the major wouldn't be able to see the gesture in the thickening darkness. "Yes, sir."

"Tell me everything you remember."

"There isn't much to tell—she was just mailing a letter, sir."

Major Thiel continued to face forward, his back erect, creating an impressive silhouette against the glittering river. "To whom?"

"I don't know, sir." Henry tried to remember the name that had been written in her neat hand across the envelope. "I don't know who the letter was addressed to, but I do remember *where*."

Thiel's head snapped around. "Where?"

"Denver, in the Colorado Territory, sir." Henry wondered if he should tell the major everything. For some reason, he didn't want to, but he was the kind of soldier who placed duty above all else. This was duty. "Sir?"

Thiel grunted, obviously deep in thought.

"I sent the letter with one of the men, sir."

Thiel turned to face Brown, making the leather of his saddle squeak in protest. "Go on. Explain."

Henry sighed, wishing he could take back his words. He felt almost protective of Miss Kingsley. If only she didn't remind him of his dead sister . . .

"Lieutenant, I'm waiting."

"Yes, sir." Henry slapped at a mosquito drilling the side of his neck. "Sergeant Leeson left today for Fort Riley. I figured Miss Kingsley's letter would get to Denver a lot faster if he took it partway."

"Hmm." Thiel fell silent and faced forward.

"I'm sorry I can't remember the name, sir."

"Mark my words, Brown. That woman bears watching." The major slapped his forearm. "The mosquitoes in this godforsaken place are as large as crows."

"Yes, sir."

"She was lying," Thiel continued. "I can't imagine why, but I know she was and I *must* find the truth. Instincts, Brown. That's the mark of a good soldier. Trust your gut."

"Yes, sir." *Another lecture.*

"Elysium—I still can't believe that name—is scheduled for sale next month."

"Oh." Henry felt a sinking sensation. "I wonder where they'll go."

"Exactly my point."

"I don't follow, sir." Henry rubbed the back of his neck, suddenly wishing he'd volunteered to go west *with* Sergeant Leeson.

"The woman is lying and right now she's desperate. She's hiding something, and she's about to lose her home. Desperate people do desperate things. We'll have to be watching for any signs."

"Signs?"

Thiel gave a derisive chuckle. "Think about it, Brown."

"I'm trying, sir." *He's mad.*

Thiel sighed and muttered something under his breath. "The *man*, Brown. Who is he and why is he there?"

Henry shrugged. "They said he worked there."

"And what is he being paid with?" Thiel snorted in open contempt. "The woman has a child, but no husband. Faricy is working for her, yet she has no way to *pay* him."

Henry's face flooded with heat. If Major Thiel weren't his commanding office, he'd reach over and knock the zealot off his horse. "Miss Kingsley doesn't seem like that kind of—"

"You've got one helluva lot to learn, Brown."

"Yes, sir." *You dirty son of a bitch.*

"The Kingsley woman is obviously whoring with Faricy. Why else would he be there . . . *working* for her?"

Henry swallowed the lump in his throat. "I can't believe that, sir, though she is an attractive woman."

"And that's all she has."

Henry had no idea why that should matter, or how it affected the investigation, but he wasn't about to question Major Thiel further. If his commanding officer volunteered more information, there wasn't anything Henry could do to prevent that. However, at this point Henry had heard far more than he wished to.

"If you remember anything more about that letter—Denver, you said?"

"Yes, sir."

"If you remember anything more about that letter to Denver, I want you to come to me immediately."

"Yes, sir."

Thiel sighed. "I just have a feeling about that woman. She knows something about Denny. Did you see the way she reacted?"

Henry clenched his teeth together. "No, sir." Why was Thiel so adamant about this? It made no sense.

"Well, you should have. She was lying."

"I still don't understand what she has to do with anything, sir." For that matter, he still didn't understand why they were wasting so much time searching for one missing soldier. Henry released a long sigh, knowing he took a risk by questioning a superior officer's judgment. "We both know Denny must've been killed in the war, sir."

"I have to make absolutely sure." Thiel's head bobbed in the darkness. "But there's a great deal of difference between a soldier dying in an act of war, and a soldier being murdered."

"Murdered?" Henry furrowed his brow and studied the shape of the major's profile in the darkness. "What makes you think Denny was murdered, sir?"

Thiel chuckled again. "Murder? Did I say that? It doesn't matter. Denny disappeared somewhere near Elysium, and that woman is lying. Why?"

"I don't know, sir."

"Neither do I, Brown, but I sure as hell intend to find out why."

Chapter Eleven

Blood.

The overpowering stench of it besieged him; the feel of it turned gummy on his hands. Copious and dark, it poured from Barney's neck and drenched Mike.

Sightless eyes returned his stare.

Dead eyes.

Milton. He had to stop Milton. Mike couldn't—wouldn't—forget that. His obsession was omnipotent.

Again, he felt the dogged pull toward destiny. Toward death. It was close—he could feel it, taste it, almost touch it.

Slick's face flashed through his mind, the way the son of a bitch had looked the night Mike's world had come to an unnatural end. Then as an old man, a cow, a snake, a prostitute . . . and a rat. Each version was more devious, more menacing, than the last.

The images slowly changed as flames appeared and engulfed Mike in a vivid red inferno, surging and growing until it was everything.

The only thing.

The greedy torrent consumed him. His flesh curled into thousands of blackened strips, eaten away, burning and sizzling, until he became one with the fire.

But there was no death—no respite from the unforgiving holocaust. The pain, blinding and searing, continued unabated. Forever.

Eternal damnation.

Something—a sound—wrenched him from Hell's clutches. He bolted upright in bed, wondering whose unholy screams filled the night.

The hideous sound shattered the air around him yet again . . . and he knew it was his own horrified wail.

He drew in great, ragged breaths and threw off the tattered quilt, swinging his bare feet to the floor. Sweat dripped from his brow and into his eyes, blinding him even more than the darkness.

Mike raked his fingers through his sweat-damp hair again and again—first one hand, then the other. Somehow, this perpetual nightmare had to end. He couldn't take much more.

Little by little, he was losing what remained of his sanity. The thoughts Slick had been planting in Mike's mind, trying to understand Abigail, and searching for Milton . . .

Damn. He forced another deep breath into his starved lungs, then released it ever so slowly. Control gradually returned, mercifully obliterating the vicious images fostered by his nightmare.

Thank God.

Yes, thank God.

Mike had never been an outwardly religious man, though the Church had dominated his childhood. Raised a Catholic and educated in parochial schools, Mike knew his scripture, despite the fact that religion hadn't played a major role in his life for many years.

And he regretted that now. Too late. Too damned late.

"Oh, God." Mike's raw, burning throat constricted and he felt a stinging sensation behind his eyes. He was too old and tough to start crying now. Besides, tears wouldn't change a thing.

Then another desperate thought crept into his mind. No, this wasn't new. It had been there all along—suppressed—waiting for him to stop being an idiot and recognize it. Even though he saw it now, that didn't mean it would do any good.

Could prayer help him? Wasn't it worth a shot? What did he have to lose, after all? Did he even remember how to pray?

Could he pray now for deliverance from evil? Did God listen to men who'd already sold their souls?

"Mike, Mike."

Growling in rage, Mike leapt to his feet and rushed to the table. He gripped it with both hands and flung it onto its side, surveying the darkness for glowing eyes of any species. No telling what form Slick had assumed this time.

"Come out, you coward," Mike muttered into the black night, clenching his fists at his sides as he slowly turned, never ceasing his vigilant search.

"Mike, Mike." A red glow began in the corner, enlarging until it was the height of a grown man. "Right here, Einstein. Happy now?"

Mike swallowed hard and focused on the emerging shape. Slick was . . . Slick. The used car salesman's persona had returned.

"Run out of disguises?" His throat felt as if he'd been drinking acid.

Slick's laughter filled the cabin. "Oh, you're good. I'm going to miss our little . . . talks once you've taken up residence in your new home."

"Yeah, I'll bet." Much as he hated to admit it, Mike needed answers and Slick had them. Whether or not the asshole could ever be convinced to part with any truly useful information remained to be seen.

"I wouldn't hold my breath."

"Don't worry, I won't." Mike turned his back on Slick— probably not a wise move—and returned to bed. He suddenly felt very old. Tired.

Lost.

"Why didn't you drag the truth out of that Southern belle bimbo?" Slick's voice sounded from right behind Mike as he threw himself down on the bed.

"Shut up and go away." Mike kept his face pressed against the mattress. If he didn't look at Slick, he wouldn't see those devil-eyes.

"That's what you think, asshole."

"Leave me alone."

"We've played this gig before. It didn't work then and it won't work now. Give it a rest."

Mike sighed and pressed his hands over his ears. "Go away. I'm not going to look at you or listen to you anymore."

Mike increased the pressure of his hands over his ears, but Slick's words bypassed his auditory nerves and sent the sinister messages directly to Mike's scrambled brain. There was no escaping Slick's evil.

"Abigail has lots of secrets, Mike."

Mike squeezed his eyes shut against a sudden glow. Everything around him turned red, pressing and penetrating as if a giant crushing swell had appeared from nowhere. The scarlet wave forced him lower, into depths where the pressure would surely pulverize him. It was warm. Hot. Scalding.

"No, stop!"

"Then look at me," Slick demanded. *"Look,* you righteous bastard."

Mike leapt to his feet and threw himself at Slick, clutching at his enemy's neck, squeezing with all his might. Those damnable red eyes locked with his, displaying no evidence of succumbing to the brutal pressure on Slick's windpipe.

The glow emitted by Slick's body illuminated the room, making every despicable detail of his face visible. "I'm already dead." Slick's voice sounded, though his lips didn't move.

Mike tightened his grip, clenching his teeth against an onslaught of pain that began in his gut and spread throughout his body. His head felt as if it would burst as the pressure built from within.

"Let me go, Mike."

"No!"

A lightning-like jolt seared Mike's body, throwing him across the room and against the far wall. He struck with a dull thud, then slid slowly to the floor, still upright with his head resting against the wall.

He felt numb, but at least the pain and pressure had passed. His throat was so dry he could scarcely breathe, let alone swallow. It felt burned, as did his skin and eyes.

Why did he continue to fight Slick?

The red shape appeared in front of Mike, drawing his gaze upward to those eyes—red-ringed with fury.

"Good question. Why do you fight me? I'm sure you realize there's only one outcome." His laughter was low and hauntingly evil. "Give it a rest. Don't defy me again, Mike."

Though he couldn't free his gaze from Slick's spell, Mike summoned his voice. "Why?" he croaked, wincing as his raw throat again protested the use of his vocal chords. "You *need* me."

Slick's eyes flared even brighter, more penetrating. "Don't push me. I guarantee you'll regret it."

Mike snorted, but made no comment. Those eyes imprisoned him, with flames leaping where pupils should have been.

"I gave you more hints today than you deserved." Slick's voice expanded, taking on an unholy hollow sound that filled the cabin. "But you didn't use them. Just for that, you've been punished."

Mike flinched, then slowly straightened his shaky legs until he stood erect again, though his back was still pressed against the mud-chinked wall. "Every minute of this is punishment. What's one more nightmare?"

Again, Slick laughed, making the cabin shudder in protest. "You really thought that was only a nightmare? I thought you were smarter than that."

"Nightma—" Comprehension hit Mike with the force of a thousand bullets. "Holy shit."

"Nothing holy about it." Slick's eyes grew larger and brighter. "I took you on a little trip while you thought you were sleeping. Your throat a little sore, Mike? Your skin looks like you've been sprawled out on Waikiki Beach for at least a week without your sunscreen. How about that? Hell's a beach."

Mike tried to close his eyes, but they wouldn't cooperate.

Bile rose in his throat, but he forced it back down. "You mean that was . . . Hell?"

"The real thing. For your entertainment—a little preview of coming attractions." Slick's maniacal laughter filled the room.

Speechless, Mike stared straight ahead, wondering how he could have agreed to this so easily. *Easy, numb-nuts.* Like most humans, he'd thought of himself as immortal. The *physical* consequences of his actions had never been a consideration for any decision he'd made in his whole damned life.

And now this.

What a fool.

"Yeah, but if you were that smart, Barney'd be dead."

"Thanks for reminding me." Mike shook his head slowly and tried to swallow. At least now he knew *why* his throat was so raw.

"Breathing fire does that to a person." Slick folded his arms across his chest, but the brightness of his eyes never wavered.

"Oh, God."

"Give it up, Mike."

"No." Something—a stubborn surge of determination—pushed Mike away from the wall, though he grunted in protest. "I'm not going to give up."

"You gave up the day you met me. You just curled up and agreed to die—no fight at all." Slick snapped his fingers and took a step closer. "Next time I give you hints, you'd better act on them."

"Or . . . ?" Mike was really asking for it, but what did he have to lose?

"Hmm. Good question. What *do* you have to lose?"

"You've already taken it all."

Slick shook his head. "Nope. Wrong. Buzz. You lose again."

Mike frowned. "I don't—"

"You don't *have* to understand, Mike. When will you get that through your head?" Slick grew larger and brighter as he moved closer, looming over Mike. "Why did you sell your soul? Do you remember *why?*"

"How the hell could I forget that, you son of a bitch?" Mike tried again to close his eyes, but he couldn't. They burned like his throat. "I did it for Barney . . . and Carrie." *My sister.*

"Bingo. Give the man a cigar."

"Cut the crap."

"So ask yourself again what you have to lose, Mike. Something you really want . . ."

A tightening began in the pit of Mike's gut. "No. You wouldn't."

"Think again."

"If you don't give me what you promised, then you don't get my soul."

"Not true. That's the beauty of this scenario." Slick laughed again, sending chills racing through Mike. "I've given you every opportunity to get on with this, but you're resistant."

"No, I—"

"Yes, you *are.*" Slick's voice grew louder and less human with each syllable. "Now start using that brain you've got. I know it's there, because I've been inside it. If you defy me again, I have the option of calling this game and sending you to Hell for lack of effort. Got it?"

"That's not fair." God, that sounded lame. "You can't let Barney die. You . . . promised." His voice fell to a despondent whisper.

"Promised?" Slick laughed again. "All I promised was to send you back in time so you could prevent Barney's death, bucko. Well, *I've* lived up to my part of the bargain. You're a cop. Remember the intent of the law?"

Simple. So simple. Win or lose, Slick would take all. "I see."

"Good. It's about time." Slick moved away, gradually releasing Mike from his spell.

The air around Mike cooled immediately as Slick reduced in size. "I'll pay more attention to your hints from now on." *God, Carrie. What have I done?*

"That's progress. You're learning."

"Yeah. Bully for me."

"What did you learn in town today?"

Mike brought his hand to the back of his neck and rubbed

the tendons at the base of his skull. His head felt as if it would explode with very little provocation.

"Well?" Slick came closer again. Ominous. Threatening.

"I learned that Abigail lied to me." Mike felt as if he'd been kicked in the gut. "She lied to me . . ."

"Right. But hey—if you want to dip your noodle while you're at it, I don't care. Just don't forget she lied to you, and make sure you pay *real* close attention to everything she does."

Mike resisted the urge to argue. "Sure."

"Ah, I think I liked you better when there was a *little* fight left in you." Slick chuckled and moved across the room again, stopping in front of the fireplace. The red glow emanating from him continued to fill the room with its unearthly light. "Don't forget about that nightmare either. Next time, it'll be much worse, Mike. More real. More painful."

Mike didn't respond. He simply stared in silence as Slick slowly dissipated into a cloud of noxious red smoke. The stench was unforgettable—burning flesh—human flesh. Gradually, the thin trail drifted up the chimney until nothing remained.

Nothing but hate and evil.

And fear.

Mike took a few steps closer to the hearth, wishing he had one of those fast-lighting fire logs and a disposable lighter. Strange thought. Fire certainly couldn't hurt Slick.

"Ho, ho, ho."

The fiendish sound echoed down the chimney, making Mike take several backward steps until his calves came against the edge of his bunk. His body gave a great shudder of exhaustion just before he collapsed into bed.

Now he felt cold instead of hot. Cold and lost.

Abigail. Elysium. Lies. Secrets.

And Milton . . .

Morning came too slowly, Abigail decided as she threw back the quilt and stood. The first rays of sunshine were barely visible by the time she crossed the room and opened the curtains.

She hadn't slept well in weeks—not since Major Thiel's

visit to Elysium. Though he hadn't returned, she couldn't help
but wonder if—no, when—he would.

Her gaze wandered across the countryside as the sky unfolded
before her eyes, slowly illuminating the world for a new day.
Would today be any better than yesterday?

Dawn gave promise of summer warmth. The weed-choked
fields which had once boasted acres and acres of cotton, mocked
the sunshine and reminded Abigail of her family's predicament.

And the waiting.

How much longer would it be before she received a response
to her letter? Or would she? Again, she had to face the possibility that her son's father—how she hated giving that title to
him—wanted nothing to do with either of them.

One part of her wanted to sing out in relief that she might
never have to face that despicable man again, while another
more practical side wondered what would become of them if
he failed to respond. The sale of Elysium was less than two
weeks away.

They were about to lose their home.

She went to her bed and reached behind it to retrieve the
worn silk purse from its hiding place. The nail protruding from
the back of her headboard seemed a godsend for this purpose.
Surely no one would ever find her precious cache there.

Carefully, she opened the purse and poured the coins onto
her bed. The equipment Mike had repaired and sold had brought
some money, but would it be enough to start a new life?

And where would they go?

West.

The answer struck with such certainty, it stunned her. She
sat on the edge of her bed with the coins clutched in her hand.
West.

But Denver was west.

Her stomach knotted and she squeezed her eyes shut. When
she reopened them, she spread her hand flat and stared at the
coins. This was their future.

If she had more money, she could forget about Denver and
the letter and the man. Forever. But this paltry sum wasn't

enough to allow her that luxury, though it might very well have to be.

Biting her lower lip, she reached her decision. If she didn't receive a response to her letter by the sale date, she would move her family west—as far as this money would take them.

How she wished she could make it multiply right here in the palm of her hand, but such whimsy wouldn't feed and clothe Wade, let alone keep a roof over his head. She had to be realistic.

Closing her eyes again, she remembered his agonizing cries as a hungry infant. Watching her tiny baby nurse frantically for her meager milk had been heartbreaking. The guilt of being unable to feed her own child returned to twist itself through her heart like a knife.

Wincing, Abigail opened her eyes, then forced herself to look at the money again. She couldn't let Wade be hungry again.

Anything for Wade.

This trifling sum wasn't enough. If Wade's father offered to support his son, she had no choice but to allow it—regardless of the price she might have to pay.

And what if that price was her son? What if Wade's father wanted to raise his son . . . without Abigail?

"God, not that." She could endure anything but that.

Then she heard Wade's hungry cries again in her mind, and she knew that wasn't true. Even if it meant losing her son, she'd never allow him to go hungry again.

Dear Lord, please.

She drew a deep breath and cleared her throat, then resolutely stuffed the coins back into the purse and rehung it behind her bed. Satisfied the money was safely hidden, she crossed the room to stare out the window again.

Morning brought renewal. It was past time for that. Way past time.

Her gaze traveled along the river road toward the family cemetery—the one place they'd kept free of weeds. Her throat constricted as memories assaulted her.

As if she had no control over the direction of her gaze, one corner of the small fenced area commanded her attention. All the graves were marked with fine headstones, bearing names and dates.

Almost all.

One unmarked grave occupied that small corner, where the branches of a tall willow brushed the ground when the wind whistled through. A graphic picture of that dark night thrust itself to her mind. Abigail remembered being there beside Rosalie, frantically digging and clawing at the ground with her bare hands.

One unmarked grave . . .

Perspiration coated her face and neck, dripping between her breasts as the memories assailed her. The sheer terror of that night had mellowed somewhat over the years. No matter how justified, taking a human life had been the most difficult thing she'd ever done. Tears of remorse stung her eyes, but she blinked rapidly, banishing them to another place and time, when she might permit herself such indulgence. But not now.

Who'd you kill, Abigail?

Mike's words returned to haunt her, but she shook her head and drew a deep breath. He'd said he wouldn't forget again, but he obviously had. In fact, he'd barely spoken to her at all since that day.

That afternoon she'd spent in his arms.

A shiver swept through her and she rubbed her arms to warm herself, though the day already promised typical July heat. After a moment, genuine warmth began deep inside her and spread throughout her body as she remembered Mike—remembered his kisses, his touch, his hand on her breast . . .

The now familiar coil of longing tightened in her belly, banishing thoughts of cemeteries and death.

"Enough of this." She threw her hands up in despair and turned to her selection of dresses. All three of them hung from hooks near the mirror. Once upon a time, she'd owned a wardrobe overflowing with fine gowns, shimmering silks frothy with lace. Alas, crazed soldiers had thrown those garments across their saddles. Now, this meager collection of mended work dresses served her quite well.

What would I do with lace and ruffles now, for heaven's sake?

She must turn her attention to more practical matters. The future. It was time for her to make definite plans, since each day's passing made it less likely her letter would be answered.

Abigail swallowed the lump in her throat, forbidding herself to take joy in this knowledge. After all, her reasons for posting the letter in the first place still existed.

The need to feed her son.

Regardless of the consequences, she had to face the future. Resolutely, she pressed her lips together and vowed to take some definitive steps before it was too late.

Today.

She'd have to go to town, of course, to make arrangements— that much she knew. After that, she had no idea how to proceed. How did a woman plan to move her family west? Was it too late in the season to begin such a journey?

Answers—she needed them now.

Maybe Mike could help her with the preparations. Surely he knew something about such matters.

If he would only speak to her.

Look at her.

Touch her? *No!*

Yet even as she denounced it, Abigail couldn't deny the nights she'd lain awake thinking of Mike's magical touch. A reckless impulse raced through her and she reached for the least practical, but by far the nicest, of her dresses. Several yards of yellow sprigged muslin, faded but still pretty, made something she would have worn to a summer picnic or church social in days gone by. In its present condition, it wouldn't have been considered suitable for gardening.

Now it seemed rather grand.

An unexpected emotion blossomed inside her as she pulled the dress over her head and twisted around to fasten the back and tie the sash at her hip.

Hope.

What was wrong with her? Her heart flip-flopped, then raced out of control as she turned to peer at her reflection in the mirror. The yellow fabric brought welcome color to her cheeks. Her blue eyes held a certain sparkle this morning that had been missing for months.

Years.

A quiet knock at the door jerked Abigail from her reverie. "Yes?" She turned to face the door as it swung open.

Rosalie poked her head in the room and grinned in open delight. "My, don't you look pretty this mornin'?"

Abigail blushed, suddenly besieged with guilt for her irrational behavior. "Thank you, Rosalie." She reached for the bow at her side. "I was just trying it on, but I think I'd better save this and wear the—"

"No, you ain't either." Rosalie closed the door behind her and took a few steps toward Abigail. "There's somethin' I need to talk to you about."

Fear—unwarranted but real—shot through Abigail. "What? Is something wrong?" *Something else?*

"No, no. Nothin's wrong." Rosalie lowered her dark lashes for a moment, then lifted her gaze to stare directly into Abigail's eyes. "I wanna talk to you about . . . Mr. Mike."

Heat suffused Abigail's cheeks as she lowered her guilty gaze for a mere second. Then she cleared her throat and lifted her chin, hoping her discomfiture over Mike Faricy wasn't as obvious as she feared.

"What about Mike?"

Rosalie sighed and pursed her lips together. "He's a right fine man—a mite queer—but good."

Abigail furrowed her brow, wondering where this peculiar conversation was leading. "I agree on both counts, though he does seem determined to hide the fact that he can be nice." A smile tugged at the corners of her mouth.

"Yeah, he does pretend he's mean sometimes. Don't he?" Rosalie laughed softly. "Well, I been wonderin'—since we gotta leave here anyways—why he couldn't go with us." Her voice grew quieter as she spoke. "I know we're both strong and could probably do this without a man, but neither one of us can catch a fish to save our lives. We might get powerful hungry again without fish. An', Miss Abigail?"

"Hmm?" Abigail waited for Rosalie to finish, realizing these same thoughts had lurked in the shadows of her own mind.

"Somethin' like bein' able to catch a fish might come in right handy."

She knew Rosalie was remembering the hunger. A knot formed in Abigail's stomach as she remembered, too. She couldn't put her son through that again. He deserved much more from life than what she could give.

His father had money, or so he'd boasted.

Anything for Wade.

And if that beast of a man didn't respond to her plea for help?

Mike's craggy features flashed into her thoughts. His presence had contributed much more than the desperately needed fish on their table. That man had brought them all security and . . . hope.

There was that thought again. *Hope.*

"I . . . I don't know, Rosalie." Abigail feared this foreign sensation. Hope was something she'd lost with her innocence. Did she dare risk believing in it again? "Mike may have other plans."

Rosalie scoffed and rolled her eyes dramatically. "You tell me what other plans that man could have. It's as plain as can be he ain't got no family." Rosalie's eyes glittered with unshed tears. "We be all he has, Miss Abigail."

Abigail nodded slowly in agreement, reaching for her brush and running it through her hair. Rosalie stepped behind her and peered over her shoulder at the cracked mirror. The expression in Rosalie's dark eyes was imploring, but there was something more.

Hope.

"Oh, Rosalie." Abigail bit her lower lip and dropped her hairbrush, then turned to wrap her arms around her friend's shoulders. "What if he says no?"

The fear of leaving Elysium pierced Abigail's armor, shattering the false front she'd worn all this time. If Mike would only agree to accompany them to their new home, then she might be able to find the strength to make this work.

"Ask him." Rosalie hugged Abigail, then pushed her at arm's length to meet her gaze. *"Ask."*

Such a simple word. Abigail drew in a shaky breath and nodded her head. "I will."

"When?"

Abigail allowed herself a small smile of resignation as she met her friend's gaze and recognized the renowned stubbornness of Rosalie's mother. "Today."

"I reckon that'll do." Apparently satisfied, Rosalie turned toward the door. "I like that man."

Abigail smiled again. "So do I."

And, heaven help her, she meant it.

Chapter Twelve

More than a little uncomfortable, Mike looked across the kitchen table at Abigail. He tried to stare right through her, wishing he could do more than merely pretend he didn't see her smiling face, or notice how pretty she looked in the yellow flowered dress. He'd never seen this one before, but he knew she couldn't have anything brand new. This must be something she'd been saving for a special occasion.

Such as?

And why had Rosalie insisted on taking Wade outside for a walk at this particular moment? Suspicion trickled through Mike. He wasn't a man who'd ever claimed to know women and their mysterious ways. He'd never had problems deciphering his sister, Carrie—an exception, he was sure. To him, most women seemed as if they'd been born on another planet.

Something was up.

He hadn't seen much of Abigail since that day in his cabin, because he'd spent the past few weeks haunting Natchez, searching frantically for any evidence of Milton's ancestor. Unsuccessfully. He'd visited every cemetery and government office.

Nothing.

There was no record of anyone named Milton in this area. Yet. That would change, though, unless Mike succeeded in his mission. He had one more place to investigate—a place he'd avoided since falling through the looking glass.

Saint Mary's.

The mere thought of going inside his family's church set his gut on fire. Somehow, he expected his ancestors to be there. Watching.

Passing judgment.

Deservedly so.

And all the hints Slick had been bent on providing had suddenly stopped. In fact, Mike hadn't seen his tormentor since that memorable visit to Hell. Undoubtedly, a temporary reprieve.

Mike's gaze dropped to his hand, spread out on the table before him. The dark hairs on the back of his hand mingled with flakes of dead skin. He was almost finished peeling now. The burn he'd suffered as a result of Slick's warped mind had been a humdinger. He hadn't bothered trying to explain his lobster imitation to his hostess. How could he?

I forgot my Coppertone during a visit to the South of Hades? Yeah, right.

And there was that damned guilt, as if he didn't have enough problems. Every time he looked at Abigail, he remembered that afternoon in his cabin and ended up hating himself for what he'd almost done to her.

A lump formed in his throat at the memory, and his heart slipped into fifth gear. While part of him struggled with guilt, guilt and more guilt, his libido was determined to relive the experience from a more self-serving perspective.

Good thing the table covered everything below his waist.

"The sale is going to happen very soon now." Abigail cleared her throat and lowered her gaze. Her hands with their bloodless knuckles were clenched in front of her on the table, mere inches from his. "I . . . I realize you probably have other plans, but it's time for me to make arrangements for us to leave."

Ah, I'm being evicted. They all were, but he was the one

being left behind. Abigail couldn't leave him—what about Slick's insistence that she and this plantation were the keys to his success?

"Mike, I . . ."

Her chin quivered and her eyes sparkled dangerously—Mike recognized the signs. He could handle almost anything but tears right now. Since the afternoon he'd almost committed the vilest of crimes, Mike's vow to avoid her as much as possible, and not to speak to her at all, had been very effective. Why was she doing this to him? And why now?

Why the pretty yellow dress?

Damn. Time was running out—he had to speak before it was too late.

"Where are you going?" There, he'd broken his silence and the earth hadn't opened up to swallow him. Yet.

Her eyes widened as she straightened, dropping her hands to her lap. "I—er, west, I think."

That counted him out. How did Slick expect Mike to keep a close eye on everything Abigail did if she wasn't here?

And how was *he* going to get by without Abigail's beautiful face to look at every morning? Without Wade's little-boy curiosity and laughter? Rosalie's good-natured banter?

He didn't like this—not one iota. He had no right to the feelings coursing through him at this moment. No right at all. Besides, he wouldn't be around long enough to do any of them a bit of good.

His throat felt full and he cleared it noisily. "I, uh . . . west. Hmm. That's a lot of places." A smile of remembrance tugged at his lips, but he suspected it more closely resembled a grimace. He could tell her a lot about the future of the western United States.

But she was leaving him.

Pain lanced through him at the thought of being without Abigail and her family. Until this moment, he hadn't realized how crazy he was about them. "Any idea where?"

"Maybe." Abigail squirmed and it was obviously her turn to feel uncomfortable. "Possibly Denver, but I can't be sure until . . ."

"Until what?" *Make sure you pay* real *close attention to everything she does.* What the hell had Slick meant by that?

"That letter—the one I posted several weeks ago," she said so softly he barely heard.

"Oh, yeah. I remember." The day things had started to change for the worse. The day Slick's games had turned really ugly. The day Mike had almost raped Abigail. *Bastard.*

His gut wrenched and he rubbed both hands over his face. There had to be an important point to all this. "So, you're moving to Denver." He dropped his hands to the table. "When?"

"I . . . I'm not *sure* it will be Denver." Her face turned crimson against the yellow dress—not a flattering combination, though she was still the most beautiful woman he'd ever seen. "It depends on a lot of things."

"Oh, yeah. Your letter." He remembered their trip to the post office vividly . . . as well as everything that had happened afterward.

Why had that particular day been the turning point for this mess? Slick never did anything without a reason. Did Abigail's letter have anything to do with this? No, it couldn't. Denver was a long way from Natchez. "I remember you didn't want to mail it at all."

"No, I didn't." She drew a deep breath, then released it very slowly. "It's been weeks since I sent it, and now time's running out. I have to make plans to move my family." She shrugged as if it didn't really matter—an obvious lie.

"Where?"

"West . . . just west."

"That's a lot of territory."

"I don't know exactly where. Do you have any suggestions?"

Mike leaned back in his chair and chuckled. "Denver's nice, but the Broncos are about as consistent as Mississippi weather."

"Pardon?"

"Never mind."

"I—we were wondering if you have any plans?" She fidgeted with the ruffle on her sleeve and averted her gaze. "Do you?"

She looked up at him and Mike suddenly felt the urge to run. Fast and sure—away from the conflicting emotions raging through him. He shouldn't—couldn't—feel these things.

He had no right.

None at all.

"I don't know," he muttered, wishing she hadn't looked at him. His gaze fastened with hers as surely as it had with Slick's during his visits of torture. No red there, though—thank God. Her eyes were so blue, so soft. Moist. *Please, don't let her cry now.* That would be the death of him. "Abigail . . . ?"

"Hmm?"

Her tongue slipped between her lips to moisten them, sending a jolt of desire through Mike's body. *Abigail. Elysium. Lies. Secrets.*

No, not now. He wouldn't think about Slick's warnings now, though Mike had to know her intentions—monitor everything—until he found Milton.

Then he could release her from his nightmare. Set them *both* free.

Her, to build a future for her son.

Him to burn in Hell for eternity.

Fair deal? Definitely not, but it didn't matter, because it was a *done* deal.

"Do you have enough money?" he asked, watching her for any reactions Slick might consider significant. "Enough to go wherever it is you're planning to go?"

"I'm not sure." She sighed and spread her hands out on the table before her, palms down. "I was hoping you could help me make the arrangements."

"Arrangements?" Mike furrowed his brow and stiffened. Somehow, he'd lost the thread of their conversation. "I'm sorry. What arrangements?"

"For our journey." She lowered her gaze, but continued to speak. "And we—Rosalie and I—were wondering if you could accompany us. Be our guide."

There it was, out in the open. Stunned, he could only stare

at her while she kept her hands pressed flat against the table.
Make sure you pay real *close attention to everything she does.*
Despite his best efforts, Slick's voice filled Mike's mind.

All right. Mike was paying attention. Now what? Leave
Natchez with Abigail and her family? How could he do that
with Milton's ancestor still alive? Besides, Mike wouldn't be
around long once his mission ended.

There was a one-way ticket to Hell with his name on it—
guaranteed delivery.

"I . . . I can't." The words almost gagged him. A huge chunk
of him was willing to go anywhere with Abigail, but that was
a part of Mike better left buried. "I have to stay . . . to finish . . .
something."

She closed her eyes for a moment, then looked at him as if
her fate were sealed. The combination of fear and bravery that
filled her expression tore at him. Asking him to go with them
must've taken more courage than Mike had ever known. Who
the hell was he to tell her no?

"I understand." Her voice was quiet and steady. "Well,
good luck to you then."

You couldn't possibly understand. "Are you throwing me
out now?" Cynicism lent a harsh edge to his voice. "Or do
you want me to stick around and catch fish until you're ready
to leave?"

Abigail nodded without hesitation. "Stay. Please." She met
his gaze again. "I . . . I want you to."

Something amazing filled her gaze and seeped into him.
This woman was dangerous—to him, to his mission. Mike
swallowed hard, but the urge to take her into his arms and
promise her the impossible remained.

Fool.

"I'll stay." His voice sounded strange, as if it came from a
great distance. Lost in a void.

Lost in time.

"There isn't really anything else for me to fix, though. Is
there?" Stupid question—he already knew the answer.

She shook her head very slowly, never breaking eye contact.
"But I really do need some help making the arrangements."

"Ah, for your trip." Perfect. This woman he was supposed to watch was going to leave, and she wanted *him* to help her do it. *The story of my life.* "What do you need?"

She stared at him in silence for several seconds, then moistened her lips again before she spoke. "We'll need a wagon, I suppose. I don't know if we should have horses or oxen. And should we go partway on the train or by boat?" She sighed and shook her head. "How far can we go with the money we have?"

Mike clenched his teeth, wishing he knew more about this time in history. He had no idea how to plan a cross-country trip in 1865. It wasn't as if she could phone her friendly neighborhood travel agent.

AAA, where are you?

"What makes you think I'd know the first thing about this?" His remark sounded sarcastic, though he hadn't intended it to. Softer, he added, "I'm not sure. I've never made that kind of trip." No lie there.

"I see." She stiffened. "I just assumed, being a man and all, that you'd know more about such matters."

Women from his time would've cringed at hearing such arbitrary crap. He was a man, so he had all the answers. *Yeah, don't I wish.* If being male made him so smart, then what answer could he give Abigail? Sighing, he knew there was only one answer—the truth. "I'm sorry, but I don't."

"I apologize for bothering you."

She pushed her chair away and stood, turning quickly toward the door, though she made no effort to leave. Without thinking, Mike followed her and rested his palms on her shoulders. She felt so small and vulnerable beneath his touch.

Renewed shame raged inside him as he remembered that afternoon in his cabin, and the look of pure terror on her beautiful face. He felt sick—his insides twisted into a knot. The last thing he wanted was to frighten her again, but he couldn't bring himself to remove his hands.

"Abigail, I didn't mean I don't *want* to help you. I just don't have the answers you need." He tightened his grip, absently massaging her tense muscles. Warmth ebbed from her into his hands. It felt so good—so right—to touch her.

To want her.

To need her.

God, help me.

The short time he had left didn't allow for these feelings. Why now? Even rage and guilt couldn't mollify the steadily increasing sense of well-being he felt with his hands on Abigail Kingsley.

The woman he'd been looking for all his life?

No, it's too late for me.

No room remained in his life for gentleness now. No latitude for clemency or warmth, and if he permitted himself to want too much, even for a moment, he'd risk everything.

He wanted to kiss her fears away, but he couldn't. If he took her, as he so desperately wanted, who would pick up the pieces after he was gone?

Rosalie? Perhaps. But the selfishness of indulging himself with this strong yet vulnerable woman was too much for him to deal with now. She deserved better.

She deserved forever.

Pain penetrated his defenses, threatening his stoic front as they stood there, suspended in time. She made no effort to pull away as he moved his hands in circles, massaging the tenseness from her shoulders while his own body tensed in ways he felt certain would intrigue medical science.

And his heart shattered into a million splintered, broken bits. He had no right—none at all.

The trembling of her delectable body could have been brought about by fear, but he knew somehow that wasn't the case. Not now. At least, not yet.

A shiver rippled through her, and he felt her blood racing just beneath the surface of her skin, through layers of clothing, pulsing against his palms. She withstood his touch, still and quivering, and all he wanted was to pull her closer, to reassure her. To breathe tender, soothing words, caress her until she relaxed and turned toward him.

Ready.

Unafraid.

Like willing prey.

Abigail felt like a snared rabbit—one who'd deliberately placed itself in the trap. Frantic, she searched her mind for the wherewithal to move away from Mike's touch. His simple gesture of placing his hands on her shoulders didn't warrant this response. Yet the innocence of the moment only served to intensify her reaction, rather than diminish it.

Why? Why did this man affect her so? No man should have such power over a woman, and especially not over her. She was stronger than that. She had to be.

But his hands rotating against her shoulders made her blood heat and pool low in her belly. Her insides clenched and she warmed from somewhere deep inside herself, that place she'd tried to keep guarded.

Protected.

This man wasn't safe. Hadn't that afternoon in his cabin taught her anything? But Rosalie's words returned to haunt her, contradicting everything Abigail's memory tried to provide.

I like that man.

Abigail more than liked Mike Faricy. She caught her breath as emotions fought valiantly to evolve into words. No, she couldn't. She wasn't thinking clearly with his hands on her.

Oh, but it would be so simple to turn in his embrace until she faced him, her lips mere inches from his. She felt his breath on the back of her neck and something—his lips?—brushed the top of her head, sending tremors racing through her.

She was weak, weak, weak. How she ached to feel his mouth cover hers again, to claim her as his own.

Mercy.

It was good he'd rejected her impetuous invitation to accompany them when they left Elysium. Yes, good. For the best.

Then why did the thought of never seeing him again make her feel as if someone had reached inside her and plucked a vital part from her?

His hands slid lower to the softer flesh of her upper arms. Quaking began in her knees as the seconds ticked by. How long had they stood here like this?

"Abigail."

His breath was a caress against the back of her neck as he gently urged her to turn. Powerless, she shifted with the slight pressure on her arms until she fully faced him, so close the tips of her breasts brushed against his hard chest.

Her knees felt weak, as if they might give with the slightest stress. He eased his hands around to her back and pulled her closer until he held her—*really* held her—in his arms.

The warmth of his embrace unhinged her. Abigail buried her face against the solidness of his shoulder and inhaled his musky male scent. All the reasons she shouldn't want this man fled as strange and insistent emotions swelled within her.

He was strength, comfort, reassurance and so much more . . .

She was lost.

"Abigail," he whispered again.

His husky voice sent shivers skittering down her spine. "Hmm?" She felt so warm, so safe.

So wanted.

He brought one hand up to the back of her neck and gently stroked the fine hairs which always slipped from her bun. Delicious tingling waves pulsed through her as he cupped the back of her head with his hand.

Kiss me. Please, kiss me.

She wanted this—wanted him. He wasn't the man who'd hurt her—who'd raped her. Strange, but now she could think the word, almost as if she'd finally given herself permission to accept what had happened and move on with her life.

With love.

Love? Did she love Mike? Could this strange yet wondrous feeling be love? She lifted her face to meet his gaze.

Terrifying.

Undeniable.

The feeling took root and grew in her heart. His hazel eyes were moist and expressive as he met her gaze. That haunted appearance remained, but there was something more now, waiting to be revealed.

"Mike."

Very slowly, he lowered his mouth to hers, barely brushing her lips in a kiss so soft she thought she might die from both its exquisiteness and the want of more. Much more.

No fear coursed through her now. She knew only desire at this moment. All her fears and doubts fled, banished by a sweet ache in her heart and soul. He moved his mouth away and she moaned in protest.

Then he kissed her again.

Lingeringly, he enticed her response with all the mastery at his beck and call. He kissed her cheek as her eyes fluttered closed, then he kissed the side of her neck until she thought she might scream for him to take her lips.

She pressed herself against him and he covered her mouth with his, wondrously silencing her whimper of surrender as he tightened his arms around her. Aware of every hollow and bulge of his tall, lean body, Abigail melded against him, savoring every delicious point of contact.

Her body swelled and softened, flowing counter to his hardness. It was such a vital, breathtaking sensation, she moaned into his mouth, sinking even more fully against him.

She wished their clothes were gone, that every inch of his tall body was bared to her touch, to her hungry lips. She wanted to see him, touch him, taste him.

All of him.

Such thoughts had never filled her mind before, at least not in such explicit detail. Her young girl's fantasies of years gone by had been nothing like this powerful need. These womanly appetites.

Strange that she felt no self-reproach at such thoughts now. What had changed? Why was this different than the other time in the cabin?

A tremor raced through her as he brought his hand to the underside of her breast as if to test its weight. His thumb brushed against its hardening peak.

He moaned and deepened their kiss, his tongue stroking hers

and drawing it inward to mate with his. She was as close to him as possible, pressing and rubbing her pelvis wantonly against the long solid ridge at the front of his trousers.

A desperate hot need flowed through her veins like warm cane syrup, making her think and do things she'd never thought herself capable of. Molten longing filled her; inside, she grew tighter and tighter with each stroke of his tongue in her mouth, each pass of his thumb against the peak of her breast.

Suddenly—incitingly—he brought his hands behind her and cupped her buttocks to lift her upward. Against him.

Hard.

Gasping, she broke away from his kiss to stare into his eyes. The hard glint of desire in his hazel eyes penetrated her defenses. He asked a silent question.

One she couldn't answer. Not yet.

Though her loins pulsed with life, acutely aware of him throbbing against her in return, she wasn't ready. Where soft met hard, she felt an unbearable ache for more. A void inside her cried out for this man, for all he had to offer.

Everything.

She was a woman now, no longer the young girl who'd fallen victim to cruelty and violence. Was she truly ready to forget that night?

That man?

"Miss Abigail!" The voice came from outside.

Quickly, Mike set her away from him, reaching out to steady her when she swayed. She drew a deep breath and he dropped his hand to his side just as the back door burst open.

"Miss Abigail!"

Rosalie rushed toward her, then stopped to look suspiciously from Abigail to Mike, then back again. A huge smile split Rosalie's dark face as Wade followed her to stand next to Mike.

Was the unruly desire which still coursed through Abigail so obvious? Did Rosalie know?

Lord, have mercy.

"Miss Abigail," Rosalie repeated, clearing her throat and plastering a solemn expression on her face. "Lookee here what I got. Mr. Miller brung it on his way from town."

Before Abigail could ask what their neighbor had delivered, Rosalie pulled a long smudged envelope from the pocket of her apron.

"A letter," Rosalie announced with pride as she extended the wrinkled object to Abigail. "Here, take it. Mr. Miller brung it. He said it come all the way from the Colorado Territory."

Abigail's breath froze in her throat as she reached out to take the dreaded letter. Trembling, she gripped the corner of the envelope and slowly brought it close enough for her to read.

She felt Mike's gaze on her, watching and wondering, but she couldn't bear to look at him now. Not with this letter in her hand.

Miss Abigail Kingsley, she read. Then she forced her glance to the upper left hand corner of the envelope, where a name leapt off the paper.

Paralyzing her.

It didn't matter that she'd expected this—that she'd *asked* for it. None of that mattered now. How could she have done this? Why had she done this?

Anything for Wade.

The skin around her mouth tingled and she thought for a moment she might faint. Unable to breathe, she brought her hand to her throat and clutched at the neckline of her dress.

"Miss Abigail?" Rosalie reached out and grabbed her arm. "You all right?"

"Fine." Abigail forced air into her lungs and managed to avoid Mike's probing gaze as she turned toward the kitchen door. Without looking back, she said, "I'm going to my room for a while."

"Miss Abigail?" Rosalie's worried voice followed Abigail's retreat.

She had to get away from them to read the letter. The thought of having their curious gazes on her as she read that man's words sickened her.

"Let her go, Rosalie," Mike said quietly, his husky voice filled with compassion and something more. Empathy?

Hesitating for a moment at the doorway, Abigail knew why

Mike's touch hadn't sent her into that dark, safe place she'd discovered the last time. It was really very simple, though the timing had classic irony.

Heaven help her, but she loved Mike Faricy.

Why now? After all she'd suffered and survived, why did she have to find this now?

Chapter Thirteen

Mike stared after Abigail as the door swung closed behind her. What the hell had happened to her? One minute she'd been in his arms, eager and pliant, and the next it was if the world were coming to an end.

In many ways that was true. The world as she knew it— this plantation—was coming to an end.

His world was a lost cause. His own personal Armageddon.

Still, he shouldn't have touched her, though her response to him had been different today. Very different. The eagerness she'd shown had been far more than mere curiosity. She'd reacted as a woman—an eager, loving woman.

His woman?

Yeah, right.

However, one thing he was sure of—she hadn't fled the room in fear of him this time.

Thank God.

Maybe, in some small way, he'd helped her overcome the understandable fear rape victims often suffered. If that proved true, he might be able to forgive himself for the afternoon in his cabin.

Maybe.

Raking his fingers through his hair, he forced his thoughts away from the way she'd felt in his arms, pressing her softness against his hardness, welcoming his kiss with everything she had to give. But how could any man ignore this insistent throbbing between his legs?

How? Simple. Because he had to. More urgent matters—though that seemed more than a little difficult to believe—demanded his attention.

That damned letter.

What was it?

"I dunno what got into Miss Abigail."

Rosalie's voice penetrated Mike's soul-searching. "Hmm?" He turned to her, grinning down at Wade before meeting Rosalie's dark gaze. "Do you know who the letter was from?"

"No, sir." Rosalie folded her arms across her chest and shook her head. "I can't read much. I only know it come from a place called Denver. Mr. Miller told me that's in the Rocky Mountains. I wonder how big them mountains are."

"Very." Absently, Mike rubbed his chin, wondering if he'd get the knack of shaving with a straight razor before he died, or if it would be a direct cause of death. Abigail hadn't seemed to mind the places he'd missed shaving, or the nicks.

He looked again toward the door, remembering how difficult it had been for her to mail that letter in the first place. Who could it have been to? And from? What on earth could have such power over her?

"Must be a pretty place," Rosalie said reverently. "Reckon Miss Abigail's plannin' to take us there?"

Jarred back to the present—or the past—Mike grunted. "Yeah, I think so." *Why?* What—or who—was in Denver?

Of course it was a who. Mike should've realized that right away. She'd written a letter to a person, and that person had obviously responded.

And she hadn't seemed a bit pleased about that. Why? It always came back to that. Why Denver?

Or why *not* Denver?

Anyone could see Abigail didn't really want to go, nor had

she really wanted a reply to her letter. Then why had she sent it? Another mystery—just what he needed.

But it was none of his business. After all, he had no right to concern himself with Abigail's plans. No rights toward her at all . . .

"I think I might like to see really big mountains someday, with snow on them. It's snowed a little here a few times, but it never did last long," Rosalie said slowly, then turned to face Mike. "I sure wish I knew why Miss Abigail was so upset." She met his gaze and arched an accusing brow.

"Whoa. Hold on a minute, Rosalie." Mike held both hands out in front of him. Suddenly, he felt like he had in tenth grade when Sally Olsen's father had caught them in a lip-lock on her front porch. "I didn't do any—er, it isn't my fault." Uncertain, he looked toward the door again. "At least I don't think it is."

"You was kissin' her," Rosalie stated rather than asked.

"How did you—"

A knowing grin spread across the woman's face. "'Cuz you just told me."

"Very funny." Mike flashed Rosalie a grin. "So we were kissing."

Rosalie's shrewd smile lit her entire face. "I think it's right fine, Mr. Mike. Right fine, indeed."

"You do?" Surprise filled his voice—not exactly a self-assured, macho response. Of course, when it came to Abigail, he didn't feel the least bit confident. Far from it, in fact. He narrowed his gaze suspiciously. "Why?"

"Oh, never you mind. You just go right ahead and kiss her again when you gets the chance."

Wade giggled and Mike looked at him suspiciously. Was the kid in on this, too? Mike's face flooded with heat. "Rosalie . . ."

"Hmm?"

The woman's satisfied smirk was encouraging, yet inflicted guilt at the same time. Was she thinking what he thought she was? That he and Abigail might—

"No." The sound of his own voice startled him and his heart swelled to lodge in his throat. He couldn't allow this. Lord, if Rosalie thought his future was with Abigail, what did Abigail think?

The yellow dress. Rosalie taking Wade for a walk. The evidence was overwhelming—stacked up right under his nonobservant nose.

Some detective.

Abigail had . . . set her cap for him. Was that the right term? Hot to trot? No, that sure as hell didn't suit her. This was asinine. Just because she'd put on a pretty dress and managed to find him alone didn't mean she was chasing him.

Did it?

Then a more logical thought presented itself as he turned his suspicious glance on Rosalie. A matchmaker. Perfect, just perfect. Now how was he supposed to convince Rosalie to lay off her Dolly Levi imitation?

He was far from an eligible bachelor.

"Rosalie, I can't . . . *mean* anything to Abigail." He took a step closer and something soft brushed against his ankle. When he looked down to investigate, he saw Garfield and leaned over to scoop the kitten into his arms. "Abigail has a future ahead of her and I . . . I can't be a part of it."

He couldn't look at Rosalie as he said the words, because he hadn't realized how painful they were to *him* until he'd heard them spoken aloud. He couldn't be a part of Abigail's future. It wasn't that he didn't want to be.

Make sure you pay real close attention to everything she does.

How could he not pay attention to everything Abigail did, especially when she'd invited him along for the ride? A ride he couldn't accept.

Damn.

"She needs your help." Again, Rosalie's voice sliced into Mike's thoughts. "She's been carryin' a heavy load and it's past time she got some help. And them soldiers botherin' her again after . . ."

Mike blinked, forcing his attention on Rosalie's words. Soldiers. Milton. It always came back to Milton. Even if Milton had visited Elysium, there was really no reason for Abigail to have known his name. He'd probably been another nameless soldier to her. Did Rosalie know the truth?

"Do you know why the soldiers were here, Rosalie?" he asked, hating himself for doubting Abigail again—still.

"Nope." She stiffened and looked at her bare feet for a moment. "Them's times best forgotten. Right now, I just wanna find the best way to help Miss Abigail."

Yes, Abigail had asked him for help. But what could he do? He couldn't go with them, though that's exactly what he wanted to do. There was no reason he couldn't at least *try* to help them here before they left.

They're leaving me.

His gut twisted in protest. There was nothing he could do to change things. Abigail and her family had a future—he didn't.

Simple.

Garfield latched onto Mike's T-shirt, crawled over his shoulder and down his back. "Ouch." He tried to pry the tenacious kitten off, but the pesky fur-ball had other ideas.

Wade squealed with laughter when Rosalie reached for the cat and it meowed politely and allowed her to lift it from Mike's back. She placed the vicious beast on the floor while Mike rubbed his shoulder.

"That cat has a thirst for blood."

Rosalie sighed. "I hope you can find a way to help Miss Abigail."

"You don't give up easily, *do* you?" Mike gave her a wan smile. "I'll do what I can, but I can't be part of her future." He swallowed hard and realized Wade was looking up at him expectantly.

"I see," Rosalie said tightly.

"No, Rosalie. I don't think you do." Mike half-turned toward the back door, wishing for escape . . . from a lot of things. "I *have* no future."

* * *

Abigail sat on the edge of her bed, still clutching the letter. Again, she stared down at the dramatic, masculine scrawl and her stomach lurched.

Why now? Why not a week or two ago, before she'd discovered her feelings for Mike?

Her hands shook as she blinked back her scalding tears and turned the envelope over to look at the wax seal—an ostentatious letter "M." She had to read the contents. After all, her family had very little time left before they'd be forced from their home.

And Mike wouldn't accompany them. Despite that kiss? Despite the new feelings she had for him? He'd touched her again—intimately—and this time she hadn't withdrawn in fear.

She'd wanted that kiss to go on forever. In Mike's embrace she'd felt wanted, safe, needed.

But he didn't really want her—not enough to go with them. Not enough to save her from whatever future this letter might inflict upon her.

She brought one hand to her mouth and pressed her fingertips to trembling lips. If only Mike could have said something—anything—to give her hope.

Tilting her head back, she looked up at the ceiling and swallowed again. This foolishness would do her no good and certainly wouldn't provide food and shelter for her son.

Anything for Wade.

Resigned, she looked at the letter again, then lifted the corner of the seal with her thumbnail. There was only one way to find out what words the wretched man had written. Only one way to end this miserable speculation once and for all.

Fueled by desperation, Abigail ripped open the envelope and unfolded the single page, gasping in surprise when another page fluttered from the folds to her lap. Distracted, she set the letter aside and retrieved the page, holding it up before her eyes.

"Mercy."

A letter of credit.

Her heart fluttered, then thudded into a steady *boom, boom, boom* as she placed it neatly in her lap and reached again for the discarded letter. The words blurred, but she squinted to clear her vision.

July third, 1865, she read.

My Dearest Abigail . . .

The words purloined her breath and made her gag, but she forced herself to resume.

> *You can't imagine my surprise and pleasure at hearing from you after all these years, and to learn I have a son has brought Mother and I great joy. We look forward to meeting you both. Therefore, I'm enclosing a letter of credit to expedite your arrival. Part of the money will be advanced to you prior to your departure, and a larger share at our bank in St. Louis. Mother is planning our wedding to take place here at the Landmark Hotel. I hope you approve. Devotedly, Casper.*

Numb, her hands fell to her lap with the letter, covering the other page. He made it sound so simple. And he didn't seem even a little skeptical regarding Wade's parentage. A woman he met once during the war—a woman he raped—wrote to inform him he has a child, and the man didn't question it at all? Not that it would make a bit of difference in the end.

No tears filled her eyes now—only a feeling of emptiness remained in her heart.

Now she remembered why she'd been desperate enough to write a letter to the man who'd raped her—who'd left her with his child. She'd burned the papers he left behind, but not before reading them. For some reason, even in the aftermath of his brutal attack, she'd felt compelled to know his name. His crime, his name, his face were burned into her memory for eternity.

Even after almost three years, the recollection of how she'd felt after that man forced her to receive his seed, had the power to make her feel soiled. Filthy. Marked.

Dead.

Closing her eyes, she remembered the wet, sticky feeling

between her legs after he'd finished with her and left her here in this bed. Her stomach roiled and burned as she recalled staggering to her feet afterward, only to feel *him* trickling down her inner thigh with her virgin's blood.

She'd washed herself over and over again that night before dressing and leaving her room to visit her dying father. He never knew what his daughter'd suffered . . . and, mercifully, his death had prevented him from seeing her belly swell with child.

That night had seemed as if it would never end. Opening her eyes, she remembered the other man returning to the house after the others had left. She remembered what he'd wanted— his share, he'd called it—and she remembered her father's gun . . .

A sob tore from her throat and she clutched at her collar, pulling it slightly away as she dragged in a shaky breath. She couldn't undo the past. That man was dead and buried.

She looked at the letter again. *This* man—Wade's father— had money. A roof to put over her son's head. Food to help Wade grow up strong and healthy.

Casper Milton even had a mother. How strange. Somehow, she couldn't imagine that monster with anything as human as a mother. But that also meant her son would have a grand- mother. And there was a family business for Wade to inherit one day—something to replace Elysium.

Clutching the letters in her hand, Abigail stood and removed the drawstring purse from behind her bed. Carefully, she folded the letter of credit with the letter and stuffed them inside with the meager coins she'd saved.

Staring at the purse, a niggling thought prodded and taunted. Couldn't she simply take the money she would be advanced in St. Louis and disappear? Take Wade and Rosalie somewhere to begin a new life? But how long would those funds last? What about Wade's future? His education?

Anything for Wade.

At what cost?

Did it matter?

The answer was swift and sure. No, it didn't matter at all.

Her son's future came first. Wade would have everything money could buy, and he'd always have his mother's love.

And his mother would have him.

She walked stonily to the window to look outside. The morning had seemed so fresh and bright earlier, but now there was a dismal heaviness in the air. Oppressive.

Smothering.

What choice did she have? Mike didn't want them—*doesn't want me*—and they had to leave Elysium. Sulking wouldn't change things.

Squaring her shoulders, Abigail lifted her chin and turned back to the bed. After retrieving the purse again, she removed half the money, then carefully rehung the purse behind her bed.

By train or boat—undoubtedly this would be enough for either. If the train couldn't take them the entire way, then she would buy a wagon and drive it across the prairie herself.

And when they reached Denver, she'd have to face the man who'd attacked her. And she would stand up before God and his mother and become his bride.

And when night came, she would share his bed . . . as his wife.

Terror ripped through her and she brought her knuckles to her mouth to bite down hard. That dark, safe place she'd inadvertently found with Mike in his cabin could be hers again. She knew it was there, waiting to shelter her from reliving the torture again and again.

Anything for Wade.

She had no choice. It was within her power to ensure her son would never go hungry again. What mother could pass up such an opportunity?

Regardless of the price.

Mike walked slowly back to his cabin, mentally kicking himself for kissing Abigail again. He'd probably given her the impression he might change his mind about going with them.

Don't I wish.

That woman had really crawled under his skin, invaded his

dreams ... and touched his heart. He slowed his pace and turned in a half-circle to look toward the river. Heat waves were already rising from the barren fields to blur his view.

He had to stop thinking about Abigail. Her beautiful face, lush lips, firm breasts ...

"Damn."

That strong yet vulnerable way she had of dealing with life tugged at his heart, made him burn inside to help her in any way he could. He'd never met a woman more deserving. Nor had he ever known anyone he wanted to help as much, despite the doubts which continued to plague him.

What did Milton have to do with her? With Elysium? Maybe nothing. Wasn't it possible Slick had planted these doubts simply to torture Mike?

Yeah, more than possible.

Abigail was sexy, smart and strong—everything he'd ever wanted in a woman and then some. Why now, when it was too damned late for him?

Not to mention more than a hundred years too soon.

Wincing, he turned toward the cabin and kicked the door open, vaguely aware of Garfield slipping inside before the door swung closed. "Cat, you've got a lot of nerve following me around after claw—"

"Mike, Mike."

"Shit."

"Nice to see you, too."

Mike waited patiently for his eyes to adjust to the dimness, amazed to find Slick as himself, sitting casually at the table. "What do you want?"

"Sit down." Slick dropped Mike's wallet, shoulder holster, gun, and badge on the table in front of him. "Should you be walking around without these? You might need something."

"Smart ass." Mike kicked the other chair away from the table, then straddled it, staring morosely at his personal belongings. "What are you doing with my stuff?"

Slick flipped open Mike's wallet and pulled out a handful of cards. "Driver's license—don't need that here, do you?" He tossed it onto the table, then pulled an assortment of other cards out to follow suit. "Ah, a library card. I'm sure you used that a lot."

Mike simply glared, knowing to protest would be wasted effort. One by one, credit cards and membership cards fell to the table. He didn't even blink.

"Ah, what do we have here?" Slick slowly removed a clear plastic case from the back of Mike's wallet. "Pictures."

"Gimme that." Mike lunged for the photographs, but Slick stilled him with a penetrating glance. Frustrated, Mike resumed his position in the chair.

"This must be Mom and Dad." Slick removed the old photograph from its protective covering. "Hmm. Let's see. You were how old when they died?"

Mike cleared the lump in his throat, but didn't answer. Slick was baiting him and he didn't even want to know why. All he knew was that he couldn't let the asshole realize how important those pictures were to him. If he could help it.

"You can't help it."

"Bastard."

"Yep." Slick dropped the photo of Mike's parents to the table and removed the other one. "Oh, isn't this sweet?"

Yes, it was sweet. Mike knew the faces in that photograph as well as he knew his own—Carrie and Barney on their wedding day, smiling under a shade tree on the lawn at Saint Mary's.

That photo soon joined the growing pile on the table, followed by Mike's wallet falling with a dull thud. Then Slick flipped open the leather case that held Mike's gold badge.

"My, my." Slick clicked his tongue and turned the case just enough to allow Mike a painful glimpse. "This will melt fast where you're going. Won't be needing that either."

"I guess not." Mike released a long, slow sigh. "Cut to the chase. What do you want?"

"Oh, that's right. You know I never do anything without a reason." Slick laughed low in his throat, dropping the badge to the pile, too. Then he lifted Mike's gun and the only remaining magazine. "How many bullets do you have left?"

"Enough." Every nerve in Mike's body sizzled, on edge. "All I need is to *find* Milton's ancestor."

Slick shook his head. "You're not doing a very good job of it."

Mike bolted up from the chair and walked over to the fireplace. Slowly, he turned to face Slick, remembering how sorry he was the last time he'd turned his back on the son of a bitch.

"Satan will be sorry someday."

Mike shook his head in total confusion. "What are you talking about now?"

"Sorry for not promoting me."

Rolling his eyes, Mike ran his fingers through his hair. "Who cares?"

"I do. And you should." Slick stared at Mike's personal belongings, then placed the gun off to one side with the holster and magazine. "You'll be needing those things, but the rest of this is disposable."

Mike swallowed hard, clenching his fists at his sides as he wondered what Slick was up to now. The creep held one finger out in front of himself and stared at it. Red light shot from Slick's eyes to his finger, igniting a flame just like a disposable lighter.

"Cute trick," Mike said, trying hard not to think about his visit to Hell. About the fire, the pain, the terror . . .

Slick pulled a dollar bill from the stack and held it in the flame until it ignited, curling away and falling in a pile of ashes. Then the demon reached again, allowing his hand to hover over one of the precious photos. Mike held his breath.

"Do you remember the reason you're here?"

"Yeah, I remember." Mike waited as Slick kept his hand poised over the discarded photographs while his other hand and its burning finger remained ready to reduce what remained of Mike's family to nothing more than charred paper.

"Then why aren't you doing what I told you to?" Slick closed his burning finger within his palm, extinguishing the blaze as he shot to his feet. "Why, Mike?"

"I . . . I am." Mike shook his head. "I've been to town

almost every day searching. There's no one named Milton around here.''

''No kidding, boy genius.'' Slick took a few steps closer and his eyes gradually reddened with each step. ''Listen to yourself. What did you just say?''

''There's no one named Milton—'' Stunned, Mike blinked once, then was captured by Slick's burning gaze. ''—around here.''

''Bingo. Nobody ever said Milton's ancestor had to be here in Natchez, Mike. Nobody.'' Slick laughed again as he came closer, grew larger, brighter with each step. His eyes glowed, pinning Mike with their feral, wicked brilliance. ''Of course, that doesn't mean he isn't here either. What do I have to do, draw you a map?''

''Map?'' Mike didn't even struggle to free himself from Slick's power. He knew by now how wasted such efforts were.

''Milton ain't here, dickweed. Got it?''

Not here. The words took several seconds to penetrate Mike's hypnotized mind. ''Not here,'' he repeated aloud. ''Then, why am *I* here?''

''Nope. You have to do some of this for yourself. I'm in enough trouble with the boss as it is.''

Slick's eyes burned and Mike saw his own image reflected in the red pupils. Flames surrounded his reflection, engulfing and devouring him as they would in Hell one day soon. Too soon.

''Or not soon enough.''

''Stop reading my mind and tell me where.'' Mike's voice sounded strange as he tried to drag his gaze from Slick's. *No, don't try,* he reminded himself. Fighting was useless. He needed his strength to find Milton's ancestor. ''Where will I find him?''

''Soon, Mike.'' Slick laughed, the sound echoing through the small cabin until it shook in protest. ''Just do as you're told. Pay attention to the Southern belle bimbo. Watch her real close now, or you might miss something important.''

''Abigail.'' Mike's throat tightened and felt full. He cared about her and it hurt. He had no right—no future. Nothing to offer her.

"You're getting soft, Mike." Slick loomed closer, bigger, brighter. "Remember Barney . . . and Carrie. Their baby."

Milton had to be here. Why else would Slick have—

Sizzling heat jolted through Mike's body and sent him hurtling against the hearth. Even during this purely physical torture, Slick didn't release Mike from his spell. Those devil eyes continued to hold Mike prisoner.

"Milton isn't here. How many times do I have to tell you before you'll get it through that thick skull of yours?"

Mike staggered, pushing himself away from the hearth. Pain lanced through his elbow, but he straightened his arm in spite of it. "No more. I heard you."

"Good." Slick backed away slowly as Garfield darted across the room between them. "Hmm."

Mike wondered briefly what Slick was thinking, but knew better than to ask.

"You'll like Denver."

"How the hell would you know?" Mike shook his head in disbelief.

"I grew up in Denver, smartass."

Gradually, Slick changed from solid mass to vapor, then simply melded with his surroundings and vanished.

No longer surprised by Slick's theatrics, Mike took a step toward his belongings on the table and gingerly lifted the photographs and slid them into their plastic covering. With dangerous, unnatural calm, he placed all his belongings in his wallet where they belonged.

He felt strange—sort of frozen inside. All these weeks he'd been searching . . . Why? What was Slick up to now?

The worn brown leather which encased his detective's badge beckoned to him. He turned it over and stared down at the table. Even that really no longer mattered. He'd been so damned proud to receive his last promotion.

Funny how death and destruction could make a man see what was really important in life. And what wasn't.

Still, it held some meaning to him. He remembered Carrie's pride when she'd seen the gold badge for the first time, and his eyes stung. Clearing his throat, he reached down and grabbed the case, bringing it close to his face to read the numbers and letters.

He and Barney'd been promoted the same year. *Barney.* Mike closed his eyes for a moment, then looked at the badge again. His sister and brother-in-law would wonder what had happened to him one day, assuming he would ever exist. Wouldn't they?

Was there a way to let them know?

Suddenly, he knew what he had to do.

Even if Milton wasn't in Natchez, Mike had to visit there one more time.

He picked up his gun and stared at it.

Soon, but not yet.

Chapter Fourteen

A silent sentinel, Saint Mary's steeple thrust upward into the night sky. Mike stood for a long time staring at it from across the street, praying for the guts to go inside. He had to do this.

Then, maybe, he could commit murder and still die in peace. Not much to ask.

"In the words of Saint *Nike,* just do it." Woodenly, he walked across the deserted street, pushed the heavy paneled door open and went inside. He paused and dipped his fingers in the holy water and crossed himself.

God, how long had it been?

Years—years in the past—years to come. He didn't want to know. He felt enough like a thief stealing into the church as it was, without reminding himself how far he'd fallen from his family's faith.

A fall from grace?

A helluva lot farther than that.

The huge crucifix hanging over the altar drew his attention, implanting a hideous thought—a fear, really—into his mind.

Would Slick dare follow him in here?

His heart thundered as he turned to look over his shoulder

in search of anything or anyone who could be playing host to that demon from Hell. Surely not in here. Not now.

Please.

"Good evening, my son."

The voice startled Mike and made him jump as he jerked his head in its direction. A priest stood in the center aisle, his black robe draped around him. Visions of *The Exorcist* flashed through Mike's mind, and he cringed in self-recrimination and horror.

"Good evening, Father," he whispered, searching deep inside himself for strength.

"Welcome. I'm Father McBride. I don't believe I've seen you in the congregation before."

Mike nodded and swallowed, wondering how he should begin. *Forgive me, Father, for I have sinned?* Somehow, that fell a little short of the truth. *Forgive me, Father, but I sold my soul to Satan.*

No. Mike saw no reason to inflict others with his own misery. He had another reason for being here—another need of the Church.

"What can I do for you?" The priest took a step closer. "Are you on your way home? In need of a place to lay your head? A warm meal? Confession?"

Confession. Yes, that's what Mike needed, but he couldn't very well—

Why couldn't he?

This was *the* church—*his* church. He'd been baptized right here in this very sanctuary. *Confession is good for the soul.*

Even the souls of the damned?

"C-confession." He swallowed the lump in his throat and ignored the insistent voice of his conscience that told him what he was about to do was wrong. He'd made enough sacrifices. He needed this.

For himself.

He was going to die and burn in Hell. Wasn't that punishment enough for anything he may have already done or would do?

"I'm afraid anonymity will be impossible now." The priest

shrugged and flashed Mike a gentle smile. "Perhaps you'd like to come back in the—"

"No. It has to be now and I don't care about anonymity. In fact, can we do this right here? Right now?" Mike's gaze was drawn back to the crucifix. "In front of Him?"

The man seemed thoughtful for several moments as he contemplated Mike's request. Something passed between them. It was obvious this priest knew—sensed—Mike's urgency.

"As you wish." Father McBride conducted him up the aisle toward the altar, turning to face Mike at the front pew. "Shall we sit here? It's unconventional, but if this is your wish . . ."

Mike nodded, noting the man barely reached his shoulder as they stood there facing each other in the empty church. Candles flickered and danced from the altar, triggering a long lost memory.

Grandmother had brought Mike and Carrie here after their parents' funeral. *Candles.* The vivid memory slashed through his mind, and he saw himself in this church, watching the flames through his tears as their grandmother placed two candles on the altar for Patrick and Mary.

So here he was again. He felt nervous, like a kid caught doing something really rotten and forced to tell all in front of God and everybody. That wasn't far from the truth, though he sure wasn't a kid anymore and he hadn't been caught. Yet.

"What troubles you?" Father McBride finally asked.

The man's soothing voice gave Mike courage. He drew a deep breath and nodded, as much to himself as to the priest. "I . . . I'm not from here, Father."

"Oh?"

"I mean, I'm from here, but . . ." How could Mike tell him he was from the future? No one would believe him. Well, Mike wouldn't tell him—he'd show him. "Here."

Mike reached into his hip pocket and withdrew his wallet, opening it to remove his driver's license. "See? Here's my picture, and right there in that corner's my birthdate."

Indulgently, the man took the plastic card, turning it over in his hand to examine it. He stared long and hard at the photo.

Father McBride's eyes widened, and Mike knew the priest had read his birthdate.

"This is . . . interesting, but I'm afraid I don't understand." He looked at the card again. "Michael Patrick Faricy. That's a good Irish name."

"Yeah, it's Irish." Mike wasn't so sure about the good part, though. "It's simple, Father." *Yeah, simple.* "I'm . . . from the future."

Shock registered in the man's soft brown eyes, then a twinkle began and he smiled. "A joke. I see." He laughed quietly and held the license out for Mike to take.

"No joke, Father." Mike took his driver's license and slipped it back into his wallet, not that he'd need it anytime soon. Or ever. He reached into his front pocket and found a nickel. "Look at the date on this. It was made in 1995. See?"

The man took the coin and turned it over in his hand, then he shook his head in disbelief. "I see it, but I'm not sure what this means. How can I believe you're from the future? Such a thing is impossible."

Not if you sell your soul . . . Mike struggled for words, dug deep into his mind and tried to dredge up anything that might convince Father McBride he was telling the truth.

Did it matter? Couldn't this priest fulfill Mike's wishes—grant absolution—whether he believed him or not?

With a sigh, Mike resigned himself. So be it. "I have a letter here for someone. I know you don't believe me, Father, but it's very important that this letter be kept here at Saint Mary's for . . . a long time."

"Will this person know to come here for the letter?"

Mike shook his head. "No. I'd like Saint Mary's to notify him . . . when the time comes." He reached into his breast pocket, flinching when his hand brushed against smooth metal, and removed an envelope. He'd been fortunate to find one among the few items Abigail kept in the small office at Elysium.

"Very well." Father McBride took the letter from Mike and read the name written neatly across the front. "Patrick Faricy. A relative of yours?"

Mike felt as if he'd been kicked in the gut. "My father."

He pointed to the words printed beneath his father's name.
"Read this."

"Deliver in March, 1964." The priest pressed his lips
together and exhaled slowly through his nose. "My son, this
is im—"

"No, it *isn't* impossible." Mike's desperation sounded in
his voice, but he didn't care. He had to make Father McBride
understand. "My parents will be killed in a car crash in April
of that year unless Father Perez—he'll be the priest here then—
delivers this letter. Warning them."

"Ah, you're one of those who claims to be able to see the
future."

"No, Father. I don't *see* the future, I've *been* there." How
could Mike make this man understand? "A priest from this
very church performed their funeral service, baptized me and
my sister. Will baptize her . . . baby."

"You need rest." Father McBride placed his hand on Mike's
shoulder. "Tell me, did you receive an injury in the war?"

"Father, please!" Mike closed his eyes, drew a deep breath,
and released it very slowly. Then he remembered something
else and reached again for his wallet. "Look at this picture."
He removed Carrie and Barney's wedding picture. "It was
taken right here on the front lawn at Saint Mary's."

The priest looked long and hard at the photo. "Yes, this is
Saint Mary's. I recognize the front steps. But what is this?"
He held the photograph out and pointed to a shiny yellow car
parked in front of the church. "It's extraordinary."

"A car, Father." Mike allowed himself a tired smile. "An
automobile."

"And these colors are . . . incredible. If it didn't look so
real, I'd think this was a painting. Well, it must be." He rubbed
his thumb over a corner of the picture. "This is definitely not
paint, though." He met Mike's gaze, his brow furrowed in
open bewilderment. "I don't understand. How can you be from
the future? Tell me how this is possible."

"It isn't possible, Father. It just *is*." Mike shrugged. "It's
one of those things we can't explain, but we just have to
accept."

"Like communion . . . or death." The priest nodded know-
ingly.

Death? If Mike had simply accepted Barney's death, none
of this would be happening. He wouldn't be back in time with
the opportunity to prevent not only Barney Sloane's premature
death, but Patrick and Mary Faricy's as well.

Of course, he also wouldn't be doomed to eternal damnation.

"Sort of like that. Yes, Father." Mike smiled again, though
he felt more like crying.

His parents would live to raise Carrie and maybe even other
children, but Mike would never see them again. He'd never
feel his mother's cool hand against his cheek, or hear his father's
deep chuckle.

He'd never see Carrie roll her eyes at him and tell him
he was hopeless. Barney would never slap Mike on the back
again and call him brother. And he'd never see his niece or
nephew . . .

But they would *live*. All Mike had to do was kill a man,
then join him in Hell to ensure that. No problem.

Life sucks sometimes.

"I don't know why, but I believe you. Who am I to question
a miracle?" Father McBride handed the picture back to Mike.
"This is very bizarre, but if you say you're from the future,
then you are. And I will have this letter stored with instructions
about its delivery." His expression grew solemn. "I'll be very
specific about when it is to be delivered."

"Thank you, Father." Mike started to rise, but something
stayed him. He wasn't ready to leave, but it was more than
that. There was something more he had to do—something he
hadn't considered before now. What was it?

Then he remembered.

A cold sweat popped out on his forehead as he reached into
his breast pocket and removed his badge. "One more thing,
Father, if you don't mind."

"Yes?"

"This." He extended the brown leather case to the priest.
"I need to leave this here for someone, too."

"For your father?"

Mike shook his head. "For my brother-in-law. For Barney."

He couldn't breathe. His throat clogged with tears. Hot and stinging, they filled his eyes and spilled over, running down his cheeks and dripping off the end of his nose and chin.

No sound came from his anguish—only tears. The priest bowed his head and prayed quietly while Mike wept, but that only made matters worse. Mike was being drawn inside out, twisted and crushed beneath the onslaught of grief and misery that poured from him.

He had no idea how long he sat there bawling. All he knew was that he couldn't have stopped the torrent of tears any more than he could change his situation.

"Natchez Police Department." Father McBride's voice jerked him back.

Mike wiped his tears with his jacket sleeve and sniffled loudly. "I'm sorry, Father. I haven't cried like that since—"

"It's good to let go of what hurts in here." The priest touched his own chest with his hand while holding Mike's badge in the other. "Tell me about this beautiful golden medal."

"It's beautiful, all right." At one time, Mike had thought his gold badge the most beautiful sight in all the world. Until the first time his gaze had feasted on Abigail Kingsley.

God, how he loved her. Yes, loved her. Why couldn't they have met in a different time and place?

"What is it?" Father McBride asked.

Mike forced a weak smile of remembrance. "In my time, I was a detective for the Natchez Police Department."

"An officer of the law. A good man, then. I knew you were a good man."

And it was obvious to Mike that Father McBride was more than a little relieved to have what he considered confirmation of Mike's integrity.

"And who did you say this should be given to?"

"Barney Sloane." Mike cleared his throat. "If you have something to write with, I'll leave you all the information."

"Here." Father McBride handed Mike a piece of paper and something that looked like a lump of coal.

"I fear that's the best I have at the moment. The war has left us without many things."

Mike nodded and scratched Barney's name, address, and the date the badge should be delivered on the paper as neatly as possible. As he stared at his dark scrawl, another thought made his heart leap into his throat.

Couldn't he warn Barney about that night?

Nervously, he glanced around the sanctuary, wondering again if Slick could have followed him in here. Was it possible that Slick *couldn't* come in here, to this holy place?

Mike's hand shook as he looked at the paper again, then hastily scratched a message he prayed his brother-in-law would be able to read more than a hundred and thirty years in the future.

More importantly, would Barney Reckless Sloane heed this bizarre warning?

Mike squeezed his eyes shut and knew the answer, though he had to at least try. *Barney, for once in your life, use your head. For Carrie ...*

Once finished, he passed the items to Father McBride, who read the message and lifted only one brow this time, then neatly tucked the note inside the case with the badge.

If only Mike could be certain that Barney would receive and consider this warning. Then, maybe, Mike could forget about his mission.

Forget about killing an innocent man.

But he couldn't. There were no guarantees that Barney would ever see the note, or that it would be legible by then. No guarantees at all.

There was only one way to ensure Barney's future.

Resigned, Mike started to stand again, but Father McBride's hand on his arm stopped him.

"I haven't heard your confession, Michael Patrick."

Something warm started deep inside Mike—warm and comforting. No one had called him Michael Patrick in years—not since his grandmother. This church was familiar and reassuring—a part of him belonged here.

"Confession." Mike simply stared in awkward silence.

Should he tell the rest of the truth? He swallowed hard and his chest hurt when he tried to breathe. If he told Father McBride about his deal with the devil, would Slick seek revenge?

Did it matter?

Mike closed his eyes for a moment. He was going to Hell regardless of what he might do or say here and now. Besides, Father McBride seemed open-minded enough to handle the rest of Mike's story.

"Are you sure you're ready for this, Father?"

"I'm ready, my son."

"Forgive me, Father, for I have sinned . . ."

Abigail didn't want to admit it, but she was waiting for Mike. She'd watched him walk away from Elysium hours ago, long before darkness had settled over the plantation. From her room, she could see the river road which separated the fields from the Mississippi, but would the almost moonless night permit her to see his return?

If he returned at all?

Despite her decision, she hadn't mustered the courage to venture into town today to purchase their passage. Tomorrow would have to be soon enough.

Her stomach tightened as she recalled Mike's refusal to accompany them when they left Elysium. But it didn't matter now, because she was going to Denver, after all.

To be married.

She drew a long, shuddering breath and stood before the open window. Though the evening breeze wafted around her, bathing her in softness, she felt stifled and reckless.

Trapped.

Soon, she really would be trapped, in marriage to a monster.

Without deliberation, she went to the door and down the stairs. She had to get out of the house for a while. No one was around to see her state of undress, or to pass judgment on her tattered nightgown.

Mike was gone.

Her heart constricted as she slipped through the kitchen and

out the back door. Sounds of nature filled the night. Bullfrogs
sang from the riverbank in the distance and a mockingbird
answered from the grove of trees on the south side of the house.
An owl hooted, low and ominous in the night air.

Before the war, such a calm, dark night would've frightened
Abigail, but not anymore. She'd experienced too many real
terrors to fear noises in the dark now.

The moon was nothing more than a silver sliver in the black
sky. A blanket of stars canopied the earth, serene in its sim-
plicity.

She felt better here in the fresh air beneath the starry sky
and drew a deep, appreciative breath as she walked barefoot
across the dew-kissed grass. The impetuous urge to run through
the darkness was ridiculous, of course, but she couldn't resist.

Her feet flew across the lawn and around the edge of the
house. She didn't know where she was going, only that she
wanted to run. Her hair whipped free of its nightly braid and
billowed around her shoulders and out behind her as she ran
blindly toward the road.

Was she running toward something or away? She didn't
know or care. She craved freedom—she yearned for it. Perhaps
it was knowing she would soon lose it that made it all the more
precious.

Near the road, she stepped on something sharp and cried
out, crumpling to her knees to examine her injury. She felt,
rather than saw, the warm stickiness oozing from the wound,
and she used the hem of her gown to dab at the blood.

Though not serious, her injury was enough to temper her
urge to run any farther. Besides, she was behaving childishly.

As if she really could escape destiny.

Assuming her foot had stopped bleeding, Abigail stood and
placed her weight on her heel to spare herself additional pain.

"Hurt yourself?"

She started as the familiar voice came from right behind her.
After a moment, fear yielded to relief and Abigail nearly
shouted with joy as she turned toward him. She didn't need
sunlight to illuminate his features. Every detail of his face was
etched into her memory.

"Mike," she whispered, not certain if it was surprise at his return, fear of being alone with him, or something far more dangerous which made her heart thunder and her breath come in short gasps.

"Is it bad?" He took a step in the darkness, then stopped in front of her. "Your foot?"

"No, I'm fine. It's just a scrape." She looked down, wondering why he'd returned, but afraid to ask. "I'd better go back to the house now. I . . . I thought you were gone."

"I was, but I came back." He fell silent for a few moments, then sighed. "For some reason I couldn't stay in the cabin tonight."

Just as she had been unable to remain in her room. The heat of embarrassment flooded her face. Did he suspect her feelings?

"Abigail?"

His voice paralyzed her, held her in a spell so powerful, she knew it was beyond her ability to sever the bond. "Yes?"

He took another step and stood mere inches away. He was so close she smelled his captivating scent and thought, for a moment, she even heard the steady drumming of his heart.

"Are you going to Denver?"

The question surprised her. For a moment, she stood suspended in time, unable to speak. "I—yes."

He sighed. "When?"

"Right away. Soon." She lifted her gaze to look into his face, wishing suddenly for a full moon to bathe him in a silver glow so she could see his eyes, his expression. Did it sadden him that she was leaving? "Soon," she repeated.

"I've decided to help you get ready for your trip." He cleared his throat. "We'll go to town and make the arrangements. Together."

Together? His voice sounded strange, tight, with a huskiness she couldn't define. "All right," she said, amazed by how calm she sounded. "I thought I'd do that tomorrow." Oh, how she wished he really could help her, but that was impossible. No one could. If only—

"God help me, Abigail," he whispered into the night.

She stared at him in silence, wondering. The raspy intensity of his whisper crawled inside her, provoking those urges she'd sought to deny. Passions only Mike Faricy had ever roused within her resurfaced with a vengeance. She felt suddenly warm, expectant.

"I want you."

His words were so simple. So profound. They were everything she'd ever dreamed and feared, all rolled into three powerful little syllables. *I want you.*

Despite her naïveté, she didn't need anyone to explain what he meant. He wanted her the same way she'd wanted him this morning in the kitchen—the way she *still* wanted him.

Now.

"I . . ." What could she say? Her heart pounded louder and louder in her chest until she thought surely he must hear it, too. Did he know what she felt?

Thought?

Wanted?

"Mike."

He took another half-step and looked down at her, his breath warm against her face. "Do you understand, Abigail?" His voice was quiet and intense, barely discernible yet undeniable.

She swallowed hard and felt her insides clench in anticipation. Her future was with a man who'd raped her, who hadn't cared about her feelings or her innocence. He hadn't cared about anything or anyone but himself.

But this man cared. She knew it, feared it, cherished it.

"I . . . I think so," she whispered, not backing away even when he moved closer. "You—"

"Want you." He bent closer, so close she could taste him without actually touching him.

"Want me," she echoed, unable to move.

"I want you like I've never wanted any woman, Abigail Kingsley."

His voice grew more intense with each utterance, and she was powerless to do anything more than stare in silence.

"I want you more than I want food." He drew a deep breath. "Air. Water."

He inched his face closer and she could see his eyes glittering in the darkness.

She was going to die. His proximity squeezed the air from her and made her blood sing through her body at an alarming pace. Though the night was cooling rapidly, her flesh felt hot, tight and tingly beneath her loose cotton gown.

"I want you to touch me in ways and places that only you can." He captured her hand and pressed it to his chest. "Here."

She felt his heart hammering against her palm, through flesh and bone, echoing the frantic rhythm of her own.

"Here," he repeated so softly she thought for a moment she must've been mistaken. "Touch my heart, Abigail. My soul. Make me feel alive . . . for a little while." Then suddenly, he released her hand, but made no effort to move away.

"Mike." Indecision slashed through her. For this one night, couldn't she pretend? Would he show her the meaning of the feelings he'd evoked in her earlier? In his cabin the other day, before she'd become frightened?

She was about to give her entire life to a man who'd abused her in the worst possible way. Could Mike Faricy make her forget that . . . for even a little while?

They stood facing each other beneath the stars, and Abigail wondered if these feelings were the sort of things poets thought of when they penned beautiful, heartrending words. She felt so strange, as if she and Mike were no longer of this world. They were with the stars, suspended apart from pain and reality.

Safe.

His breathing grew louder and mingled with her own as the seconds ticked by. Though he hadn't touched her again, she felt him, a power emanating from him and into her. That ever-present, invisible bond spanned the distance between them, drawing her to him unlike anything she'd ever known or even dreamed.

She could almost see it—this magical force which drew her to him. Her insides ached and throbbed, empty and weeping for him. "Mike." His name was barely more than a strangled whisper, torn from her lips by desperation and a need so raw and fierce she thought she might die from it.

Then he touched her.

The tips of his fingers drifted along her arm, inciting her desires, making her burn. He wanted her—she wanted him.

A shiver of anticipation pulsed through her body as she flicked her tongue across suddenly parched lips to moisten them. She was acutely aware of every brush of his fingers against her arm, through the worn cotton fabric, almost as if he reached inside her to touch the magic she hadn't known existed before now.

Before him.

"I want you," he murmured, his lips so close they brushed against hers as he spoke. "I want you."

Tears stung her eyes, but they were tears of joy, and of resignation. She knew now what she should've known the first moment she saw him asleep on her floor.

This man was the one meant for her, though she could have him for only a short while.

Not forever, but for now . . .

Chapter Fifteen

Mike brushed away the wild mane of hair that fell about Abigail's face as she came toward him. Never in his life had he known a need as fierce as the one that summoned him now. The yearning to possess her was far more than mere physical lust.

This was love—pure and simple.

And terrifying.

God help him, he *needed* her to return his love, to want him as desperately as he wanted her. Could she? Or would her incredible passion again dissolve into terror in his arms?

He wasn't sure he could bear that now. Not again. His insides were raw, vulnerable, like an open wound. Confessing to Father McBride had nearly done him in, and now—miraculously—Abigail was in his arms.

She alone was either the balm to soothe his pain, or the weapon that could destroy him. Far too much power rested in her unsuspecting heart. It was unfair, he knew, but at this moment he was beyond caring about fairness. He needed her, wanted her, loved her. Nothing else mattered.

Maybe for just a little while, he wouldn't let anything else matter. Not Barney, not Slick, not even Carrie and her baby.

Willing and pliant, Abigail came toward him and he encircled her with his arms. The insistence between his legs combined with the surge of love in his heart and nearly destroyed him on the spot.

He was as good as nuked.

"Abigail."

Then she kissed him, and took his thrusting tongue and returned parry for parry. Her body melded against his and set his loins ablaze. *Loins, hell.* He was a semi-automatic, loaded and ready to fire.

But he couldn't risk frightening her again. She was still vulnerable. He knew making love to Abigail would be the most spectacular experience of his life, but it was also a huge responsibility. There was no other way—Abigail would leave his arms as a satisfied and happy woman.

And most of all . . . unafraid.

He intended to leave her with a memory she would never forget, even after he was feeding the flames of Hell.

Reveling in each tiny moan, every tremor that swept through her slender body, he kissed her thoroughly. She threw her arms around his neck and deepened their kiss of her own accord, nearly sending Mike beyond the point of no return.

But he wouldn't allow that. Just in case she couldn't follow through with this, he had to make sure *he* could stop. For Abigail, he would become Superman, John Wayne, *and* Alan Alda.

His exploring hands massaged her back, dipping low enough to confirm that all she wore was the thin white nightgown. *Jesus.* He hadn't realized . . .

She sagged against him as if unable to support her own weight, reminding Mike where they were. Reluctantly, he broke the kiss, but didn't venture far from her luscious lips.

He could take her right here on the ground beneath the stars, but she deserved better. Comfort might help her overcome the ghosts that haunted her. Tonight, he wouldn't allow her frightening memories to come between them.

But where could they go? Not his cabin. He didn't want to

take her there, where he'd almost committed one of the worst of crimes. No, definitely not there.

And there was always Slick to worry about.

"Where—"

"Shhh." She pressed her fingertip to his lips. "Come with me."

She slipped her hand into his and shifted from his embrace. After a few steps, he realized she was limping and he put his hand on her shoulder. She stopped and turned toward him, releasing a tiny gasp when he eased his arms around her and gathered her against him.

Though he couldn't see her clearly in the darkness, he sensed the question in her eyes. "I want to carry you," he said carefully. "Just tell me where."

Her nod was barely discernable. "The west wing."

The last thing in the world Mike was certain of at this point was the difference between east, west, north and south, but he started walking toward the house with her in his arms. She relaxed in his embrace, resting her head against his shoulder in a place that seemed shaped just for her.

It felt so good, so *right,* to hold her in his arms, to carry her to bed. Reminded of their intentions, Mike's body pulsated and hardened even more. His erection rubbed against his jeans with every agonizing step, reminding him release was near.

Maybe.

If she hesitated at all, he would stop. He had no choice. It was crucial that he make this memorable for her—a memory she could cherish after he was gone.

Dead.

No, he wouldn't think about that now. Clenching his teeth, he banished thoughts of Slick, death and Hell. In that order.

He went to the French doors, remembering for a moment the first time he'd entered this house. Swallowing the lump in his throat, he eased her down the length of his body, wincing as her softness pressed against him right where it hurt the most and felt the best.

This woman had no concept of her incredible power over him.

"Shhh." She took his hand and escorted him inside. "Up the other stairs."

He remembered the other half of the twin staircases that wound their way up to the second and third floors of the huge mansion. When they reached the bottom step, he lifted her into his arms again and started up the winding staircase.

Guilt nudged at him, telling him that what he was about to do was wrong, that he had no right to take advantage of her this way. He paused on the landing. "Are you sure?" he whispered, praying he knew her answer. "Very sure?"

"Yes." She pressed her lips to the base of his throat. "Very sure."

Shivers raced along his nerves and his blood trumpeted through his veins. This was like something from a movie, walking up a long staircase with a beautiful woman in his arms.

Then he remembered the scene from *Gone With the Wind* when Rhett had carried Scarlett up the stairs to make love to her. Except he wasn't Rhett Butler and this beautiful woman was much more generous and giving than Scarlett O'Hara could ever have been. A smile tugged at the corners of his mouth when he reached the top step. He could see the movie marquee flashing the title.

Dirty Harry Meets Scarlett O'Hara.

"That way." She pointed toward the front of the house.

Though he felt her tremble, he sensed—hoped—it was from anticipation rather than fear. So far, she'd displayed no outward signs of reluctance or fear.

And they were so close now.

He quickened his pace, then stopped in front of a closed door at the end of the hall. Abigail reached down to open the door.

With a creak and a groan, the door swung open and Mike stepped into the room. The dusty air told him no one had ventured in there for a long time. Whose—

"This was my parents' room," Abigail explained as if reading his thoughts. "Tonight . . . it's ours."

He squelched the urge to ask her again if she was sure. She'd given her answer and now it was time . . .

Past time.

Mike eased her to the floor and stood with his hands on her shoulders. Her unique, mesmerizing scent drifted up from her loose hair to fill his nostrils, and made his body nearly explode.

Spontaneous combustion was a definite possibility.

He was thankful he'd taken his jacket and gun to the cabin before finding Abigail out by the road. The restlessness that had driven him back outside after his return from Saint Mary's was nothing less than a miracle. If he'd stayed in his cabin, he would've missed this . . .

She brought her hands up to cup his face. They felt cool and soft against his heated skin. Her fingertips traced a line from his jaw to his mouth, then gently stroked the contour of his lips. Lips that wanted nothing more than to taste every delicious curve, every hollow, every soft inch of her.

He swallowed hard when she stepped closer and captured his mouth with hers. Instinctively, his arms went around her and pulled her hard against him.

Her lips were soft and sweet, like apple pie fresh from the oven, only better. She parted her lips, inviting him inside to taste and explore.

And he did.

God help him, but he was lost, taking advantage of her when he should have walked away. He had no right.

Then why did this feel so damned *right?*

How could this really be wrong?

Sweet. That one word described and explained so much. In the midst of his agony, he'd found this bit of heaven. Goodness in the midst of evil.

And he clung to the sweetness.

Their mouths became feverish, searching, claiming, devouring each other until Mike thought he'd die from the sheer want of her. This woman had more innate sexual expertise than the most skilled lover he'd ever been with.

And then some.

Her hands explored him, rubbing his back, then pulling his T-shirt from his waistband. Her small whimpers of pleasure filled his mouth, fanning the flames that already scorched him to the core.

Abigail's movements became jerky and eager; her hands trembled as she eased his T-shirt upward until he broke their kiss to yank it over his head. Then she found his chest and traced small circles around his nipples with her tongue.

He was hot and hard—desperate.

With a groan, he reached for the tiny buttons at the front of her nightgown, easing it back off her shoulders while she continued her torture. He'd never known his nipples could be so sensitive. Then she nipped him with her teeth and he growled, allowing her gown to fall to the floor at her feet in a pool of white cotton.

Stark against the dark floor, the white fabric screamed *innocence*. He tensed, wondering if he could really go through with this. Then she lifted her head to look at him and he knew his own conscience lacked the power to halt these proceedings.

Only Abigail could stop him now.

Would she?

As if in answer, she reached for his belt buckle, unfastening it, then releasing the snap of his jeans. "Your turn," she whispered, a tremor in her voice.

Swallowing hard, he reached for her hands and stopped her fumbling, stimulating, fingers. "Abigail, if we go any farther, I'm afraid I won't be able to stop."

She stepped closer, pressing her bare breasts against his chest. "I don't . . . want you to stop."

God, what he would give for a little light—just enough to let him see the expression in her eyes. His gaze dipped lower to her breasts, their shape barely visible in the darkness.

Maybe he couldn't see her, but he sure *felt* her.

Her nipples were hard, tempting nubs against his chest. He held her waist, amazed at how tiny she was. His large hands nearly encircled her, reminding him of her hardship and hunger during the war. This woman was so brave, so strong.

And tonight, she was his.

He slid his hands over her smooth skin, savoring the gentle slope of hip to waist and back again. Then he brought his hands around and filled them with her magnificent breasts. Her thrusting hips punctuated the gasp that left her lips.

He wanted to taste her—all of her.

His gaze swept the dark room, finding large white-draped shapes in various corners. Instinct chose the largest shape as the bed and he pulled her into his arms to carry her the short distance.

She trembled again and he kissed her mouth, relishing every inch of her warm, bare skin against his hands. God, how he wanted her, loved her.

Slowly, he eased her down to the bed, dropping to his knees beside her, never breaking their kiss. With one free hand, he found her breast again and cupped it, brushing her nipple with his thumb until her moan filled his mouth and vibrated through him.

This was everything he'd imagined it would be . . . and more.

Pulling his mouth from hers, he kissed the long column of her throat and found her pulse throbbing at its base. Lingeringly, he rested his lips there until she pressed her breast against his hand.

Lush despite her meager diet, her breasts had beckoned to him since that first morning. He had to taste her. He kissed his way lower, then returned the torture she'd inflicted on him by tracing warm, wet circles around her passion-swollen nipples.

Gripping the back of his head with her hand, she pulled him against her, offering herself to him.

Then he closed his mouth over her nipple and knew heaven. He found her other breast with his hand and cupped them both into greater prominence, sharing himself equally between them.

She pressed herself more fully against him, panting and raking the back of his neck with her nails. Her soft moans and growls communicated her pleasure, reassured him that he hadn't frightened her, that she wanted him as desperately as he wanted her.

The hot, unrelenting throbbing between his legs reminded him of his cumbersome jeans. He reached down to lower his zipper, then backed away to remove the final barriers between her skin and his. He stood and stepped from his jeans and

briefs, wondering if this was the moment her desire might shift
to terror.

God, just shoot me instead.

In the darkness, he saw her reach out to him, holding her
arms up to welcome him into bed. Unable to resist her silent
plea, he went to her, sliding his long body against her softer
one, wondering if the feel of his expectant—impossible-to-
hide—erection against her hip would frighten her away.

She turned toward him and met his lips with her own, hot
and seeking. Mike knew in that moment that she wouldn't stop
him now. This time she was going with him all the way.

Unafraid.

Abigail relished Mike's flavor, hot and compelling against
her mouth. Better than the most expensive delicacy her father'd
ever brought home from one of his trips. Mike's kiss was
deep, wet, wild and she welcomed it, wondering what amazing
discovery she would make next in this man's arms.

She felt no fear—only curiosity and desire as his lips left
hers to venture down her throat again. She ached against his
chest and she was eager for him to repeat the attention he'd
given them earlier.

Naked and wanting, she felt each brush of his lips, each flick
of his tongue against her as he moved closer. She felt strange,
removed from her body, yet keenly aware of every pulsing
need which swept through her.

Her insides quivered and she felt empty, deep in her core
where she knew Mike would soon fill her. She knew it, but no
longer feared it. Her woman's flesh craved this joining.

His tongue was like a branding iron imparting his insignia
as he laved her breast, then finally drew her nipple into his
mouth again. She moaned and clasped her hands behind his
head to hold him to her, savoring each stroke of his tongue,
each tug against her breast.

She tingled all over and grew suddenly conscious of his male
body. He was naked and hot, pressed intimately against her
hip. The urge to touch him was overwhelming, and she inched

her hand between them until she found his hot, pulsating member.

A scorching flush swept up her body as she closed her hand around him, savoring the petal-like skin and the vital, pulsing promise. This was Mike . . . and she wanted him more than anything.

All of him.

She wanted him to show her the meaning of the hunger he'd created inside her with his touch, his kisses, his warmth. Only he could assuage the ache deep in her body, her soul, and her heart. Only Mike . . .

Her body wept for him as he abandoned her to the night air and kissed his way down her belly. Instinctively, she tightened her grip on him, but he winced and slipped from her grasp, lowering himself between her thighs.

What madness was this? Gooseflesh erupted as he kissed the curve of her hip and slipped his hands beneath her buttocks to hold her. She wanted to break away, to pull him back to her breast, to touch him again.

But he held her firmly in his hands, tilting her pelvis as he kissed lower. A quiver dawned in the depths of her belly and spread relentlessly throughout her body as he kissed her inner thighs and eased them farther apart.

She tensed, wondering his intentions, then gasped when his mouth covered her and sought her very core. Never in her wildest dreams could she have imagined anything this wicked.

This wonderful.

Blistering liquid filled her body as he brought her higher and higher toward the unknown. She knew—sensed—this was part of a journey, though she couldn't begin to fathom her destination.

All she knew was pleasure—delicious, wanton pleasure.

He'd awakened in her something she'd never known existed. Desire—a dormant and powerful emotion she'd never been unaware of until now.

Until Mike.

A raging fever consumed her body as she heard a strange

animal sound and realized vaguely it was her own guttural growl of pleasure. This was primitive, animalistic, savage.

Miraculous.

She buried her fingers in his hair and held him to her as she climbed toward the summit—a place she had to find or die. Everything culminated around his possession, his mouth on her most intimate regions.

He pushed her, his tongue claimed her, his hands held her captive against his merciless mouth. Her head thrashed from side to side and her hips arched upward, wanton and demanding.

Then she burst—shattered into a million brilliant particles of herself. Wave after wave of convulsive gratification swept through her, carrying her away on a sensual voyage from which she prayed never to return.

She'd had no idea . . .

Then he was kissing her thigh again and easing himself upward, laving her navel with his tongue and cupping her breasts with his work-roughened hands. Every inch of her felt so sensitive she wanted to shout from the merest touch of his lips, his fingers.

But she didn't. She knew there was more.

And she knew he would give it to her—all of it.

He touched her face, his fingers long, coarse and titillating against her skin. She tried to see his eyes and couldn't, though she envisioned their haunted hazel depths in her memory. It was enough, for now.

His mouth covered hers again and she tasted herself on his lips, strange but not unpleasant. She made a faint whimpering sound as he covered her with his full length, stroking her tongue with his.

Then she grew aware of his hardness against the swollen, empty folds of her womanhood. A moment's hesitation filled her as a dark memory threatened to interfere, but she squelched it. Banished it.

Forever?

His deep thrust filled her and she gasped in shock as his

mouth left hers. He froze over her, his breath coming in ragged gasps as they lay joined in the most intimate way a man and woman could be.

Wet and hot, her body closed around his engorged manhood. A sigh left her lips as he withdrew, then filled her again. And again.

She felt so complete, so wanted . . .

His next thrust was more powerful, more demanding as he reached for her legs and wrapped them around his waist, bringing him even deeper into her body. She couldn't get enough of him, couldn't get close enough, couldn't let this end without answers to all her questions.

His body acknowledged her silent plea, pressing into her again, showing her that she could not only take all he could give, but that she could want even more. She wrapped her arms around him; the muscles of his back were hot, rigid cords beneath her hands.

His movements increased, each stroke driving her deeper and deeper into this madness. She fell into a pit of darkness, a place of pleasure and sensation, where thoughts ceased to exist. Where memories bowed to the more powerful forces of the present.

Her body convulsed beneath and around him, drawing him inward and answering him thrust for thrust. Each time he withdrew and returned, she found a higher plateau of pleasure. A more delicious level of madness.

Trembling and shaking, she watched the darkness around them dissolve into radiant hues. Then the colors blurred and she surrendered to the urgency as the explosions came again and again.

On fire, her body swallowed him, urged him to fill her, to take her higher and higher into this unknown world, this place of carnal indulgence. She was broken yet whole, filled with this man as he sent her to the summit again; he seemed determined to keep her there, suspended in time and space.

He pushed deep, sure and powerfully into her. His earlier tenderness had vanished and she was glad. She was mindless, ready for every thrust, ready to revisit the oblivion he'd shown her. And she did, until she lost the ability to determine when she left the peak and when she returned. The convulsive waves blended together into one, long, exquisite sensation.

She exploded again as he buried himself inside her and tensed, filled her, branded her, with his hot, pulsing seed. Welcoming his completion, she held him with her body, her arms, her legs, stroking his back and shoulders as he strained against her and emptied himself into her.

Made her his.

He showered her face with tiny kisses and eased himself from her body, rolling onto his side. Gathering her against him, Mike rolled her to her hip. She felt him pressed against her backside and she cherished the tender kisses he sprinkled across her shoulder.

Her throat felt full and tight as she struggled to stop the tears. The need to tell him what was in her heart nearly destroyed her, but she bit her lip to silence the words.

Tomorrow would be soon enough to deal with truth.

He cupped her breast with his hand and held it. A contented sigh left his lips and ruffled her hair. A smile tugged at the corners of her mouth as she felt his body relax against her. Still holding her breast, he slept.

She squeezed her eyes shut against a flood of regret—not for being here with Mike, but for the future that awaited her. How could she allow another man—especially *that* man—to touch her now?

Would Mike change his mind after this? Would he accompany them when they left Elysium? Would the prospect of being without her tear him apart inside like she was being torn right now?

The warmth of his breath stirred her senses and the coil of longing tightened within her again. Her nipple grew against his slack hand and she held her breath, combatting the onslaught of renewed desire.

How could she want him again so soon?

She turned her head to look over her shoulder, seeing only his silhouette in the darkness, his head nestled against her shoulder. It felt so right to be here with him, naked and unashamed.

"I love you," she whispered, then turned back to bury her face in the dusty sheet.

Her tears fell in secret silence.

Chapter Sixteen

Sunlight streamed through the window, illuminating billions of displaced dust particles. Mike blinked several times, trying to recall where he was.

Then he felt the warm, female body pressed against him and he remembered. A torrent of memories washed over him, stirred his senses . . . and renewed his guilt. *Damn.*

Yet how could he regret anything as wonderful as what he'd shared with Abigail? She squirmed, pressing her round bottom against him.

That did it. He was definitely awake now.

This was a lot more critical than his usual morning hard-on. She stirred again and he tensed, suddenly conscious of her soft breast filling his hand.

The urge to see her in the early morning light swept through him, inflaming his already aroused state. If she shared his mood, he saw no reason not to make love to her again. After last night . . .

Mike eased away from her and she followed his retreat until she was flat on her back at his side, wrinkling her nose and moaning in protest. He should feel guilty for waking her, but he knew she'd want him to before Rosalie discovered their absence.

Watching her come fully awake was an amazing experience, unlike anything he'd never felt before. This was the sort of stuff married couples probably took for granted. The early morning intimacy tugged at something deep inside him—something he'd thought nonexistent in Mike Faricy.

Something vulnerable as hell.

But he wouldn't trade this moment for anything—her warm body beside his, her almost comical expression as she struggled against sleep.

Smiling, he kissed her cheek and pulled the lobe of her ear into his mouth as he brushed her hardening nipple with his thumb. She moaned and stirred, and he sought her mouth with his, kissing her deeply. Hungrily.

Definitely awake, she returned his kiss, wrapping her arms around his shoulders and her leg around his. The crisp curls at the juncture of her thighs rubbed against him, teasing. Asking. Promising.

He pulled back to look at her face, shocked by the transformation. His Southern belle looked up at him like a sexy tigress, hungry for her mate. Her blue eyes glittered with a feral light as her tongue slipped between her lips, leaving behind a silken sheen. Long, dark curls cascaded around her face and shoulders, surrounding her like an open fan.

"Morning," he said huskily.

Her slow, sexy smile nearly unhinged him. "Morning." Her voice sounded sultry and sleepy.

Allowing his eager gaze its fill, Mike looked down at her perfect breasts, rising and falling rhythmically with her breathing. Her nipples were swollen and rosy, tempting.

Unable to resist, he lowered his lips to her breast and drew its peak into his mouth, savoring her immediate reaction as she curled and arched against him. Her fingers splayed across the back of his neck, holding him to her as he suckled deeply.

Her soft moan prompted him to further explorations as he stroked the side of her rib cage and found the gentle curve of her hip. Caressing her breasts with his tongue, he lowered his hand to the dark curls where he knew bliss awaited them both.

When he pressed against her mound with his palm, she lifted herself against him, turning his blood to molten lava.

"Oh, God." Groaning, he inched his hand lower until he found the soft folds which had received him last night. He nearly exploded from the memories themselves, but the feel of her pushed him beyond the point of no return.

She was hot, wet and ready. She closed around him—a preview of what he had to look forward to. He had to have her.

Now.

He swung himself between her legs and nudged them farther apart with his knee. Her immediate response was even more than he'd hoped for as she opened to him and wrapped her legs around his waist to welcome him home.

Hot and tight, she milked him, drew him deeper until he feared he would lose it all too soon. Carefully, he held himself frozen until his throbbing eased enough that he knew he could prolong their lovemaking.

Her internal tremors massaged and held him, creating an almost electrical sensation as he withdrew and returned. He recognized her response and knew she felt it, too. He'd never experienced this with another woman—this unconditional surrender to instinct. To love. Even in his aroused state, he knew that made all the difference.

She met and matched him thrust for thrust, grinding her pelvis against his, taking everything and giving even more in return. The sudden need to see her face compelled him to look down. Dark lashes fanned against her flushed cheeks and her nostrils were slightly flared with her heavy breathing. A bewitching smile played about her lips and she bared her teeth in an expression of savage sexuality that sent him tumbling over the edge.

This woman was everything he'd known she would be . . . and so much more.

He pressed his forehead against hers and moved faster, harder, deeper, taking her with him into a vortex of raw, uninhibited pleasure. The rippling sensations deep inside her pulled at him, growing more insistent with each stroke until he could hold himself back no longer.

She clung to him, cried out his name and something unintelligible, as he reached his climax. He gnashed his teeth to silence the shout that threatened to burst free as he spilled himself into her. Her legs held him fast and her body closed around his in a sexual vise that took and gave in turn.

Fulfilled, their bodies fell still and quiet. Lifting his face, he watched her again. Her eyes fluttered open, though she continued to hold him deep inside her as they pulsed in mutual completion. God, it had never been like this before. This was the kind of sex men dreamed of all their lives, but he doubted many actually found it.

But this was about much more than sex, and that's what terrified him. The expression in her eyes told him more than any words could.

Euphoria gave way reluctantly to reality. What the hell was he going to do?

It wasn't as if he could marry her, though it stunned him to realize that's exactly what he wanted. Nothing would give him more pleasure or satisfaction than to propose to her with his body inside hers.

But he couldn't. *Until death do us part* . . .

Suddenly, he felt cold and wretched. Guilty.

Shit. How could he explain this to her? It was unfair for him to have taken her love, knowing he couldn't stay with her. What if . . . ?

"Oh, God," he muttered, realizing safe sex and contraception were virtually unheard of in this time. He'd always been so careful about such things, so he was confident he hadn't infected Abigail with anything. *Thank God for that.*

But condoms had been used for something other than disease prevention long before the HIV epidemic. Lord knew he and Abigail had done everything right to make a baby, last night and this morning. He swallowed hard and eased himself away from her and rolled onto his side, shifting his gaze from her trusting, questioning blue eyes.

Creep.

Right now he hated himself, but it wasn't the first time for that, and he was positive it wouldn't be the last. With what he had left to accomplish in his life, self-hatred was a given.

She deserved something from him. What could he say? Do? *Thanks, it was great?* No.

"Abigail . . ." He wrapped a tendril of her hair around his index finger, mentally kicking himself. Still, if he could undo what they'd shared, would he?

The answer came fast and sure. *No.* After he'd returned from town last night, to find her in the moonlight, to feel her welcoming arms, nothing on earth short of her resistance could've prevented this. Nothing.

She reached out to touch his face and he winced inwardly as his gut burned and twisted. *Guilt is a real pain in the ass.*

He captured her hand in his and kissed her palm, drawing a deep breath to steady his nerves. What should he say? What *could* he say?

Dare he tell her he loved her? Wouldn't that bind her to him in some invisible but powerful way? He knew it would, because of the kind of woman she was.

"Mike."

Her whisper prompted him to look at her expression; what he found there was the most beautiful, wondrous thing he'd ever seen. Her heart was in her eyes, overflowing with love, offering him so much more than he deserved.

His throat tightened and his eyes burned. God, how he loved her. He wanted to say the words, but he couldn't. It wasn't fair to her—to either of them.

Well, dammit, he had to say *something.* "You're beautiful." He brought his fingertips to her cheek, tracing the delicate lines of her face. "Beautiful," he repeated, choking back the other words that screamed for release.

She blushed and smiled, lowering her gaze for a moment, searching his again for answers he couldn't give. Silence stretched between them, and her natural, open smile gradually transformed to one obviously strained. Forced.

"I think we'd better get dressed before Rosalie wonders

where we've disappeared to," she said quietly, pulling away to sit on the edge of the bed.

Seeing her tremble, he ached to pull her back against him and say the words he knew she wanted to hear, that he ached to share. *I love you, Abigail Kingsley.*

But he'd taken enough. What right did he have to take her future from her, too? Saying the words would shackle her to a condemned man, because he knew she would be devoted to him even after he was burning in Hell.

God help him—he couldn't do that to her.

"Where are my jeans?" He rolled to a sitting position and found his briefs and jeans on the floor beside the bed. She sat motionless as he dressed, her dark hair offering a stark contrast with her smooth, pale back and shoulders. He closed his zipper but it separated from the bottom up. "That figures." His only pair of jeans . . .

She stood and moved a few feet to where her nightgown had fallen last night when he'd slipped it from her shoulders. She pulled the gown over her head, letting it fall around her as she turned to face him, covering her gorgeous body from his roving scrutiny.

"What's wrong?" Her voice sounded strained and distant as she walked around the edge of the bed and looked down at his broken zipper.

When she looked up, Mike knew her thoughts mirrored his own. She was remembering . . . and wanting.

"My, uh, zipper's broken." Hell, he wasn't even sure zippers had been invented yet.

"I've never even seen one of these, so I can't mend it." Suddenly, she was all business as she crossed the room and pulled a sheet off a trunk near the window. "There are a few things here that belonged to my brother and father."

"Oh, I couldn't—"

"What choice do you have?" Her expression and stance issued a challenge.

"I have no choice—as usual." Mike would give anything to have her look at him with love again, but it was better this way. At least, in the long run, he knew it would be.

She turned around and dug through the trunk, then pulled out something gray and stood staring at the fabric clutched in her hands. "His uniform." Her words were barely audible.

Mike crossed the room and stood before Abigail to look at the Confederate uniform. "I . . . I couldn't take that," he said quietly, sensing this was something precious to her. "Your brother's?"

She nodded and pressed the gray wool into his hands. "Here. There are trousers and a tunic. Take them."

"I—"

"Then borrow them," she insisted, turning away from the trunk and walking to the door. "When you can, I'll let you know . . ."

Stunned, Mike looked up at her as she reached for the doorknob. "Where to send them," he finished, nearly choking on the words. She was going to leave him, after all. *Fool, of course she is.* What alternative had he offered her? Absolutely none.

She nodded and opened the door. "I'll see you at breakfast."

Then she was gone.

Mike felt an actual physical pain at the separation as the door closed quietly behind her—searing through his chest and into his heart. He loved her and she loved him, but that didn't make a damned bit of difference.

He was a dead man—a doomed man. A man with no future and nothing to offer.

Drawing a deep breath, he placed the uniform on the bed while he slipped from his useless jeans and into the gray wool. The trousers were loose, but the length was good. Her brother must've been a large man.

He'd been a soldier.

The significance of the uniform suddenly struck Mike and he slipped on the jacket—she'd called it a tunic—and walked back to the trunk to peer inside. A gold sash with heavy fringe caught his attention, as well as a hat which obviously went with the uniform.

What compelled him to put on the sash and hat was a mystery to him, but he did, then crossed the room to the cracked mirror in the corner. The transformation was incredible. He looked like a man who belonged in this time, rather than one who'd been displaced from over a century in the future.

Had he been born in this century, his life would have been very different. He could've stayed with Abigail and made her his wife. This uniform could have been his, and he never would have known Barney Sloane. Never would've seen his best friend's dead body in a pool of blood.

Never would have sold his soul to Slick.

Scowling at his reflection, Mike jerked off the hat and sash, then turned away from the nonexistent man in the mirror. He was too damned old to play soldier anyway. He placed the items back in the trunk, slipped off the tunic and folded it, replacing everything but the pants, which he had no choice but to wear.

She'll let me know where to send them . . .

He jerked his T-shirt, socks and shoes on, then raked his fingers through his hair as he surveyed the room. He'd never forget last night or this room. This was one memory even Slick couldn't take from him.

Though Abigail was leaving him, he'd have his memories to keep him company.

And Hell to keep him warm.

Numb with denial, Abigail dressed and hurried down the stairs from her own room, wondering if her empty bed had been discovered. Rosalie and Wade were probably out at the barn milking the cow by now.

She patted the knot of hair at her nape and took a deep breath as she reached the bottom step. Her gaze was inexorably drawn across the great hall to the other flight of stairs. The west wing.

And Mike.

Was he still there or had he found his way back to his cabin? Rosalie would wonder if she came in and found Mike coming down the stairs from that wing.

Abigail almost laughed at herself for such foolishness. Did it matter what anyone thought? Her entire world was coming to an end. Not only was she losing her home and the man she loved, but she was selling herself in marriage to the monster who'd raped her.

The pain of realization sliced through her, to her heart and soul. Her husband would expect—demand—his conjugal rights. "Oh, Lord."

Anything for Wade.

Anything? After Mike? How would she go through with this? How could she let anyone else touch her that way? Ever?

Her heart hammered and swelled as she remembered Mike's touch, his kisses, his gentleness. He'd shown her the way loving *should* be between a man and a woman. At least, between them.

When she'd looked into his eyes this morning, she'd seen something there. Something wonderful and terrifying. For a moment, she'd thought it might be the same mysterious emotion which filled her own heart.

Love. Oh, yes. She loved him more than her own life, but that would do her no good if he didn't share her feelings. Though he'd loved her gently and thoroughly, it had been only physical for him.

But for her, it was something she could hold close in her heart—something to chase away the fears when she faced the weeks ahead.

When she would be forced to share such intimacy with another man.

She closed her eyes and felt the room sway. How could she go through with marrying Wade's father after last night? And this morning?

Because Mike didn't want them. He still hadn't offered to go with them, let alone asked her to become his wife.

His wife.

The thought brought a surge of joy which immediately dissolved into grief. If only . . .

A knock on the seldom-used front door snatched her from her reverie. She opened her eyes, squared her shoulders and crossed the broad expanse of flooring. The hinges squeaked as she swung open the door to reveal her uninvited guest.

Major Thiel.

"Good morning, Miss Kingsley," he said slowly, removing

his hat as he spoke. "I wonder if I might have a word with you."

"I—I'm afraid it's awfully early for callers." She searched frantically for an excuse to make the man leave her in peace. Soon, she'd be gone from Elysium and Natchez for good.

"I apologize for the hour, but this is a matter of the utmost urgency. May I?"

"Very well." Abigail stepped aside reluctantly, to allow the man into her home. At least, for now, this house remained hers. "What is the nature of your business, Major?"

He turned to face her the moment she closed the door, the expression in his eyes knowing and insolent. "I understand you've received some correspondence, Miss Kingsley."

Abigail couldn't have heard correctly. Her mind reeled as if he'd reached out and struck her. "I . . . I beg your pardon, sir?" Her mouth was dreadfully dry and her face felt numb.

"Oh, I believe you heard me." He took a step closer, his tall frame blocking her view. "You received a letter yesterday—*I* know who and where it came from."

Fear and outrage blended to form a dangerous emotion she couldn't quite define. "That letter is my personal business, sir."

He arched a brow and hovered over her. "Tell me about it, Miss Kingsley. I need to know what was in the letter. I'm afraid I must insist. It's crucial to me—to my mission."

She stiffened, summoning the indignance which should have been her natural reaction to this affront. "Don't you already *know*, Major?" she taunted, wondering from where this sudden and imprudent brazenness had come. "If you know who sent the letter, then why didn't you just open it and read it?"

Shock registered in his eyes; one corner of his mouth quirked at an odd angle. "Ah, I might have if Lieutenant Brown hadn't taken it upon himself to ask your neighbor to deliver it."

Abigail remained silent, swallowing the lump in her throat as she waited for what she knew would come next. If this man truly knew who had written the letter . . .

"Fortunately for the lieutenant, he had the good sense to

record the name of the person who sent the letter.'' Thiel leaned closer. ''Tell me how well you know the man, Miss Kingsley.''

A roaring sound began in her ears as she struggled to maintain her dignity. What she wanted was to burst into tears, to run from the room, to throw herself into the safe haven of Mike's arms.

It was a luxury she couldn't afford—an option unavailable to her.

''Tell me, Miss Kingsley,'' Thiel repeated, sneering as he leaned even closer. ''I knew you were lying to me the other night, and now . . . *now* I have proof.''

She drew a sharp breath and closed her eyes for just a moment. ''Major, you're taking our home from us. Isn't that enough?'' Her voice fell to a ragged whisper as she reopened her eyes. She was so tired.

''This is part of an official investigation. I must learn Denny's fate. It's critical!'' He straightened, no longer hovering over her, but still very close.

Too close—still blocking her view and her escape. She felt trapped.

''Miss Kingsley, as I explained the other evening, Lieutenant Denny's commanding officer believed he may have returned to this house the night he disappeared.''

Steely cords of trepidation shot through her body as she stood paralyzed, staring helplessly at this man. Her accuser.

Her executioner?

''I don't see what my letter has to do with any of this, Major,'' she argued, clutching her hands together in front of her. If only he'd go away and leave her alone. ''I can't help you with your investigation, because I don't know anything.'' The lie fell with difficulty from her lips. She hated it—hated herself.

Hated him.

''What is that man to you? Why would he write a letter to *you,* of all people, a woman he met during the war under less than ideal circumstances?'' Thiel took a menacing step closer. ''Were you lovers, Miss Kingsley?''

''No!'' Abigail pressed her hands over her ears. Lovers. The

mere thought of that man and that night made her feel sick and
weak with terror. "Noooo." Tears filled her eyes and ran down
her cheeks.

"Yes," he hissed. "I can see by your reaction that I was
right."

"No." Abigail squeezed her eyes shut, then wiped away her
tears. Drawing a deep breath, she rallied the little strength
remaining to her and met the major's indicting gaze. "We were
never . . . *never* lovers." Her voice assumed a modicum of the
fierceness she felt with those words. Anything but lovers. Mike
Faricy was the only lover she'd ever had.

The only genuine lover she would ever have.

"No?" Thiel looked at her through hooded eyes; his voice
dripped with sarcasm. "Well, what other reason would he have
for writing to you? Perhaps, if you can explain that little mystery
to me, I'll leave you and your little bastard alone. Fair enough?"

He knew about Wade. Abigail sniffled and knew what she
had to do. "He's my . . . my betrothed. We're to be married."
Heaven, help me.

"Married?" Thiel rubbed his chin with his thumb and forefinger and stared toward the window, then looked back at her.
"Yet you deny he was your lover."

Fury consumed her and she stared at the major, knowing
every bit of her rage was openly displayed. "Never. Now I've
told you the truth. Will you leave my home? It is still mine
until the sale, I presume."

"So it is." Thiel put his hat back on his head and stood
straight and tall as he surveyed her. "Mark my words, Miss
Kingsley. I'll get to the bottom of this, and I don't care what
it takes."

"I've told you the truth, as you asked. Please leave us in
peace, Major." Abigail prayed her fear didn't show in her
voice. "I'm going to Denver to marry Casper Milton, and that's
all there is to it. He asked and I . . . I've accepted." *More than
adequate punishment for my sins.*

"We'll see." Thiel stepped around her, jerked open the door
and stormed out of the house without another word. Abigail
feared this wouldn't be the last she'd hear from Major Thiel.

Turning to make her way to the kitchen, she looked up and gasped.

"Mike."

The expression in his eyes was wild, like that morning when she'd first found him. His mouth was set in a grim line; his jaw twitched several times while she stared at him. "Mike," she repeated, but he didn't even blink in acknowledgement.

How long had he been standing there on the stairs? Suddenly, she realized what he must've overheard—what made him look at her that way. He knew that last night she'd slept with him, while engaged to another man.

She swallowed hard and looked down at the floor, unable to meet his accusing glare. Of all the people in the world who might judge her, this man was the only one whose opinion mattered.

"Abigail?"

The ragged edge to his voice sliced through her and incited her guilt to an unbearable level. He hated her, and he had every reason to, but she forced herself to look at him.

What she found was more heartbreaking than all the fury and hatred he could have directed at her. His eyes held a penetrating chill—an icy apathy which stung and destroyed any hopes she might have harbored.

Hopes that he might come to her today and declare his love. Hopes that he might ask her to be his wife. Hopes that they might have a future together, far away from Elysium and her grievous memories.

"Abigail," he repeated. "Do you still need an escort to Denver?"

Confused, she furrowed her brow and nodded. "Yes, that would help." What she really wanted was for him to stop her from going—stop her from marrying that contemptible beast of a man.

"Consider the job filled." His words were clipped and harsh—almost a snarl. His eyes held no emotion, but the madness she'd seen before remained.

"I . . . I thought you didn't want to leave Natchez." Why

had she said that? She should be overjoyed that he'd decided to go with them. Maybe . . .

"Changed my mind."

"I—I'm glad." She took a step toward him and saw the glint of something in his eyes—emotion, albeit fleeting. He looked away and the moment was lost. She had no way of knowing what he'd been thinking at that moment. For some reason, she *wanted* to know.

"Fine. Just tell me how much money you have to spend, and when you want to leave. I'll arrange it."

"Very well." Scalding tears burned behind her eyes, their pressure almost intolerable. "The day before the sale."

"No problem."

He stepped off the last step and stood there looking down at his feet. After several agonizing moments, he looked up at her—his face hard and unforgiving, his eyes stark and cold. One corner of his mouth turned downward in a sneer. "You almost had me fooled," he whispered.

Then he left her with only her misery for company.

Chapter Seventeen

Amazing, but the wood and mud cabin looked almost inviting when Mike returned to Elysium after making their travel arrangements. The last thing in the world he wanted right now was to see Abigail.

No, that was a crappy lie and he knew it. He wanted to see her, touch her, taste her. Every day. All day.

Forever.

How much of her conversation with Thiel had he missed? Did it matter what they'd said before he arrived to hear the words that had almost killed him? He'd never forget Abigail's voice or the words.

I'm going to Denver to marry Casper Milton, and that's all there is to it. He asked and I . . . I've accepted.

Nothing else mattered. Anything they may have said before that was irrelevant. Besides, Mike didn't give a damn.

Not anymore.

He had a job to do and now he knew the end was near. There was no doubt in his mind that this Casper Milton was the ancestor of Frank Milton, the drug king.

Mike had to kill a man named Casper.

And he didn't give a damn if Casper turned out to be a

friendly ghost or not. For all Mike knew, the Milton family's legacy of crime may have already begun. The money he'd spent for Abigail today and what remained in his pocket might very well have been obtained through illegal means.

Blood money.

Mike hadn't asked Abigail any questions after she went to the bank with the letter of credit. He knew where—who—it had come from. It had to have been inside that letter. That damned letter.

If he had it all to do over again, he wouldn't have let her mail it. *The hell I wouldn't.* That letter and Abigail were directly responsible for him finding Milton. After all, Slick Dawson never did anything without a reason.

Now Mike knew why Slick had sent him to Elysium. To Abigail.

He kicked open the cabin door and went inside, never pausing to consider what—or who—might be waiting for him. Stupid move.

"Mike, Mike."

"Ah, *shit.*"

"Nice to see you, too." Slick's chuckle filled the cabin as the door slammed shut behind Mike of its own volition.

"Where are you? *What* are you?" Mike scoured the cabin with his gaze, but found no sign of Slick Dawson. The creep had come to gloat, no doubt.

"Damn straight." The voice came from nowhere and everywhere. "Sit down."

"What do you want?" Mike knew better than to argue with Slick, so he went to the table and straddled one of the two chairs. Still no sign of Slick. "Go ahead—get it over with."

"Patience, Mike. We have all the time in the world." The voice sounded louder, filling the cabin.

Mike heard a strange sound and looked over his shoulder. The board used to lock the door slid into place, apparently by itself. Of course, he knew better. What was the bastard up to this time?

"Watch it, boy genius."

Mike shook his head and gave a derisive chuckle. "Cut to the chase, Slick."

A foul stench filled the cabin and Mike searched for its source. "Christ, what is that?"

"Watch your language around me. I'm easily offended."

Mike tried not to breathe, then finally opted for taking small breaths through his mouth, to spare his olfactory senses. Then, suddenly, he recognized the odor. "A skunk, Slick? Gimme a break."

The black and white creature took shape and appeared on the other chair. "For your sniffing pleasure." Slick chuckled again, sitting up on his rear haunches like an animated character. "Disney would've loved this. Think I could've gotten a role in *Bambi?*"

Mike shook his head and tried unsuccessfully not to think about the ever-increasing stench. "Could you turn off the stink for a while?"

"Maybe."

It could have been Mike's imagination, but the odor seemed to lessen somewhat. Either that, or he was getting used to it. Lovely thought.

"Tell me what you've learned since our last . . . chat." Slick folded his front skunk legs across his chest and stared at Mike through small dark eyes. "Hmm? I have it on good authority it's been considerable."

Did Slick know about last night? About Abigail?

"I know everything about you, Mike." Slick sighed and shook his head—an unbelievable sight. "I even know when you take a leak, and that you prefer that tree out behind the cabin instead of the outhouse. Can't say I blame you there. And I know where you spent the—"

"That outhouse doesn't smell as bad as you do right now." Mike didn't want to discuss Abigail with this jerk. The wound was too fresh. Too deep.

"Give it a rest, copper."

Mike chuckled and covered his face with both hands. "Copper? Just when were you born, Slick?" Why had he asked such a question? Because he'd ask anything to distract Slick from discussing Abigail.

"Doesn't matter."

"Suit yourself." Mike shrugged and looked at the skunk—Slick—again. "Like you said, it doesn't matter."

"1866."

Interesting. Slick had risen to the bait. "How can you be here if you haven't been born yet?"

"Stupid question, Einstein." Slick laughed, pointing his nose at the ceiling. "You're here, aren't you?"

"Oh, yeah." Mike ran his fingers through his hair. "I guess time is sort of irrelevant to you."

"Got that right. Sometimes you amaze me, Mike. I've picked up bits of history from the days of Neanderthal man and I've even seen what would've been your future. You might say, I never go out of style." He looked at Mike and his eyes gleamed with an odd light. A red light.

"Damn."

"Gotcha again."

"What do you want?"

"Your soul, of course."

Silence filled the cabin for several minutes. "You already have that, you bastard." Mike's voice was barely more than a rasping whisper.

"Yeah, ain't it sweet?"

Slick's eyes grew redder, more mesmerizing with each second that passed. "So, tell me," he taunted. "How was she?"

"Go to hell."

"Been there—done that." Slick leapt onto the table, his red gaze boring into Mike's. "How was she? Worth the wait?"

"Shut up."

"Hot and tight, Mike? Hmm? Did you like it?" Slick barked a sickening sound. "Did *she* like it?"

Mike swallowed hard, wishing for the strength to free his gaze from Slick's. "What do you want?" he repeated, refusing to answer Slick's perverted questions.

"I told you. Your soul."

"And I told you, asshole, you already have that."

Slick chuckled. "Yep, but it's getting close to collection time, bucko." His eyes flared brighter and the inevitable flames appeared in his pupils. "Soon, Mike. Soon."

Distract him—have to. "So you were born in 1866."

The flames diminished somewhat, though Slick's eyes remained crimson. "What's it to you?"

"Just curious." Mike struggled for words, scrambling for anything to change the course of Slick's interrogation. "That must mean your folks are alive now."

"So what? I already told you my mother was a whore, and I don't know whose cock did the deed." The flames leapt again. "Drop it, Mike. You have more important things to think about."

"Sure." He'd reached something deep inside Slick. Amazing, but Mike had seen it with his own eyes. Still, it wouldn't do him any good in the end.

"That's right, Mike. No good at all." Slick took a step closer and bared his skunk teeth. "Now you know where you're going to find Milton. It's about time."

Mike nodded, unable to argue with that bit of sick logic. "I'm going to do the job, so why don't you leave me alone now?"

"Because I don't want to." Slick's voice grew louder and more evil with each syllable. "I like my job, Mike. I get a kick out of watching you squirm. I should've followed you into that church."

"Shit."

"See? I do know everything you do. I was right there when you crossed the street and walked inside."

Mike couldn't even blink. "Then why *didn't* you follow me? What stopped you?"

Slick lifted his furry shoulders and shook his head. "Why bother? It won't do you any good. You can confess until . . ." He gave a morbid laugh. ". . . Hell freezes over."

"Smartass." Mike ignored the burning sensation in his gut. "I'm going to Denver to do the job, so buzz off."

"I have to keep a close eye on you—boss's orders."

"Why?"

"Oh, let's just say I'm on probation right now." Slick laughed loud and sat back on his hind quarters again, though he never broke the eye contact which held Mike prisoner. "I keep pissing off the big guy."

"Yeah, I'll bet."

"Just remember, Mike."

"Remember what?" The flames left Slick's eyes and shot toward Mike, but he couldn't even flinch out of their way as they surrounded him. "What?"

"Hell, Mike. Remember *Hell,* because it's waiting for you."

"How could I forget that?" Mike wished his sarcasm was justified, but the truth was too painful to allow such shallowness.

The need to bait Slick further possessed Mike, though he had no idea what he could possibly gain from such perilous activity. "1866, hmm? Tell me about your mother, Slick."

"Drop it, dickweed."

"Why? Why don't you want to talk about her, Slick?" Mike knew this was a dangerous game, and that he was really reaching to test Slick this way. It didn't matter, though. This was more than just Mike Faricy looking for a way out of a tight spot. He knew better than to hope for anything like that.

This was nothing less than his sick, perverted thirst for revenge. "Tell me about your mother."

"You're asking for it big time. Tell *me* about Abigail, Mike." Slick's voice took on that sing-song quality he'd used the night he bargained for Mike's soul and Barney's life. "Hmm? Was she good? Did she let you do it to her fast and hard? Or was it slow and deep?"

Mike didn't answer. The memory of his lovemaking with Abigail was too precious, too painful, to let Slick destroy it. Of course, she'd already done a pretty fair job of that without Slick's twisted brand of help.

"Did she go down on you?" Slick inched closer, his eyes brighter than ever, the flames swirling around them. "No, probably not. Too bad, because it's probably the last time you'll get to dip your noodle."

"Jealous, Slick?" Where had that come from? Mike could've kicked himself. He knew he'd pushed the son of a bitch too far this time. So why stop now? "Wonder how many men had your mother. Which one of a thousand was lucky enough to be your old man?" Mike hated himself; he was no better than Slick.

The flames swirled and flared, enveloping Mike, devouring the room, though they never actually touched him. Hotter and hotter they burned, threatening to consume him at any moment. Slick's rage was palpable, feeding the flames as they tormented Mike with lusty intent.

Then, slowly, the blaze diminished until it vanished as Slick dropped to all fours and turned around, lifting his tail. "Eat this, dickweed."

Abigail stood at the ship's railing to watch as the paddle-wheeler chugged its way northward. Wade's hand tucked into her own gave her strength and helped to ease the pain in her heart.

Elysium was lost. She'd never see the big white house again after this. Swallowing the lump in her throat, she waited until the ship had rounded the bend she knew would bring them near the plantation.

One last time, she ached to see the house on the knoll in the distance, reigning proudly over the fields. Any minute now . . .

She felt another's presence and peered from the corner of her eye at Rosalie, who also stared at the passing countryside. In silence, they watched together. Even Wade seemed reverent as the house appeared through the trees in the distance.

A lone tear trickled from the corner of Abigail's eye, but she ignored it, determined not to dwell on the past any longer. Though the most painful part of her past awaited her in Denver, and would dominate her future.

Give me strength, she prayed as the house and fields vanished forever from her sight.

Rosalie sighed, marking the passage for them all. "Well," she said, "I wonder how big them mountains really is. Don't you, Wade?"

"Yes." Wade's eyes were round and eager, taking in his surroundings as only a child could. "Big."

"Very big," a strong, masculine voice answered, making Abigail's heart stop for a few fleeting seconds. "I've seen them myself."

"You have?" Rosalie turned her attention to Mike. "Why didn't you tell me that before?"

"You didn't ask."

"Well, I never . . ." Rosalie chuckled and shook her head. "You is right, though, Mr. Mike. I never did ask outright."

"Thanks for helping me with that little . . . problem."

"Whooee!" Rosalie waved her hand in front of her nose. "It took some doin', but at least you smell better now." Laughing, she glanced from Mike to Abigail, then sobered as she took Wade's hand in hers. "C'mon, Wade. Let's go see what's on the other side."

Abigail didn't argue when Wade skipped away clutching Rosalie's hand, though the last thing she wanted right now was to be alone with Mike. He was so different from the man whose arms had held her only a few days ago.

His mocking, knowing gaze raked her. "So you're going to get married." The words sounded caustic. Insolent. Accusing. "You still haven't told me anything about the lucky groom."

This was the first time he'd mentioned her impending marriage. Abigail swallowed the lump in her throat and half-turned away from him, unable to meet his gaze while discussing her future husband. "No, and I don't intend to."

"Why?" His tone was taunting and hateful. "Afraid I might tell him . . . about us?"

Abigail lowered her gaze, unable to defend herself. If only she could blurt out the truth and free herself from further torment. But Mike hated her. He'd made that painfully evident since Major Thiel's last visit. Mike wouldn't believe her if she told him how she truly felt.

That she loved him and wanted only him . . .

Mike's ridicule would be the end of her, and she had Wade to think about. Her son's future was at stake. Regardless of what happened to her, Wade would have his father's money, his name, and even a grandmother.

Anything for Wade.

All she had to do was endure what she must—something she'd been doing since that night. Perhaps that dark, safe place she'd found once before would be her salvation. Frightening as that possibility was, it paled to insignificance when compared to the prospect of Casper Milton violating her again.

And again.

And again.

For the rest of her life.

She choked back the sob which tore with sharp talons at her insides. If only she could make Mike understand *why* she was doing this.

If only he would offer her some alternative.

But it was too late for nonsense. Mike had rejected her and she had to move forward. So be it.

Anything for Wade.

Conversation might save her. "You've made the arrangements for the rest of our journey?" She knew the answer. He'd stoically given her their entire itinerary days ago.

"Yep. All done." His smile was tight and cynical. "All you have to do is cash in your letter of credit." Sarcasm tinged his voice like acid.

She met his gaze and he arched an inquisitive brow.

"What a pity there's no train," she said.

"Yeah, a pity." Mike sighed and shoved his hands deep into the pockets of the gray wool slacks. His hair had grown considerably since they'd first met, giving him a youthful quality he'd lacked before. "Wade brought Garfield. You know that, don't you?"

Abigail nodded and allowed herself a small smile. "Yes. He begged and I couldn't refuse."

"At least he left the cow." Expressionless, Mike looked out across the water, then turned his gaze sharply in her direction when she dared to rest hers on his handsome profile. "It was good between us."

His voice was scarcely more than a whisper, yet served to

close the distance between them. Abigail's body flashed with the sudden and unexpected heat of desire and her heart broke all over again with the agony of despair.

She couldn't lie to him. "Yes."

His gaze held hers and, for a few moments, the harshness left his hazel eyes. His despondency tore at her, begging her to reach out to him.

But she didn't.

She couldn't.

Her future belonged to another. Heaven help her.

The glint of anger, the rage, returned to his eyes and his emotions were fully shuttered again. "If only you hadn't lied to me," he muttered, shaking his head. "But hell, life's full of those."

Abigail frowned, trying to follow the direction of his bizarre words. "Full of what?"

"If only's." Mike smiled, but it wasn't a pleasant expression by any means.

Abigail turned to look over the rail, gripping it with both hands as she watched the swirling brown foam of the Mississippi. "Yes. If only . . ."

He stood beside her at the rail, resting his hand mere inches from hers. The urge to reach out to him, to touch him, surged through her. Her fingers actually tingled at the prospect of feeling his warm skin beneath them again.

Fool, she chided herself.

"I'm really looking forward to meeting this man of your dreams." Mike half-turned toward her, though his hand remained on the rail. "I can hardly wait, as a matter of fact."

The bitterness in his tone was unmistakable. Did he care for her? Was this jealousy talking?

Dare she hope?

What else could it be? A thirst for revenge? In search of an answer, she turned her head and lifted her gaze to meet his. Sadness mingled with pain in his eyes and caught her by surprise. Before she could stop herself, she gasped.

"Guess I'm busted." He turned and walked away, leaving her alone with her despair and total bafflement.

He does care.

That knowledge brought a rush of gladness to her heart, then truth intervened and it was as if someone had knocked her off her feet. She fell quickly and surely to the bottom again.

It didn't matter if Mike cared. It was too late for them.

She watched him maneuver his way through the crowd on deck and her heart felt as if someone were tightening a vise around it. Even wearing that unusual jacket of his with the dark shirt and her brother's gray trousers, he was easily the most handsome man she'd ever known.

Yet his physical appeal went far beyond mere appearance. He was far from perfect; his face bore the scars of combat. What battles had he fought in his life? Whose joys and trials had touched him and made him who and what he was?

And what—who—exactly was he?

She knew nothing about Mike Faricy. Nothing at all.

Yet it didn't matter, because she loved him.

Her blessing and her hell.

A covered wagon.

Laura Ingalls Wilder would've been proud—Mike wasn't impressed.

He couldn't believe his eyes, though he'd expected this. Hell, he'd *arranged* for the monstrosity.

Not only a covered wagon, but a pair of oxen to sweeten the deal. He didn't know the first thing about oxen, horses, or cows.

Though he had learned to milk a cow. Eventually.

And he would learn everything he had to know about oxen before this trip was over. Before his life was over . . .

Before Milton's ancestor was dead.

Swallowing hard, Mike watched Abigail moving around the wagon, climbing inside with bundled objects, then jumping back to the ground. She was preparing for their journey.

And her wedding?

Except, if all went as planned, there would be no wedding for Abigail Kingsley and Casper Milton. Mike's gut wrenched

as he imagined how stricken she would be with her husband-
to-be and Mike both gone.

Then again, maybe he was giving himself too much value.

By completing his mission, was he robbing her of the future
she deserved? Christ, he was planning to kill the man she
intended to marry.

Not just planning to—*going* to.

The wind whipped across the prairie on the outskirts of St.
Louis, Missouri, a far different place from the city Mike had
visited a time or two in his life. In his time.

His past—the future—seemed so distant now it was almost
as if it had never existed. But all he had to do was close his
eyes and picture Barney . . .

Why was Abigail marrying a man she barely knew? Mike
had struggled with this question and was determined to have
some answers, though in the end it wouldn't matter.

It was a long way across the prairie and halfway across
Colorado—or was it Colorado Territory now? A lot of time
between now and their destination to talk.

Or not.

He couldn't force her to talk. Besides, there would be no
privacy, he reminded himself as Wade scampered around the
end of the wagon, chasing Garfield. Close quarters with Abigail
and no privacy.

A living hell.

But he had to get to Denver and so did she. At least, she
thought she did.

He didn't like playing the role of Terminator. Not only would
he end Milton's existence, but he'd have to end Abigail's plans
for the future. But Barney's life depended on this. Not to
mention all of Frank Milton's other victims.

God, why Milton? A woman like Abigail could have almost
any man. Was it because her reputation was in shreds? He
couldn't help but remember that day in town when her pastor's
wife had accosted her. The open suspicion in the woman's eyes
had been undeniable.

Mike sure as hell hadn't been any help in restoring Abigail's
reputation.

Was Abigail so desperate for a husband that she'd marry anyone who offered? And why had Milton offered?

I'm going to Denver to marry Casper Milton, and that's all there is to it. He asked and I . . . I've accepted.

Milton had asked Abigail to marry him, out of the blue, for no apparent reason. It didn't make sense. If Mike asked her, would she tell him the truth?

There was only one way to find out, but now wasn't the time.

"Are you ready?" he asked, walking toward the wagon. "The water barrels are full and I think I know how to handle these two creatures."

Abigail avoided his gaze as she pushed her hair away from her face and looked toward Wade. "Time to get in the wagon, Wade," she called against the unrelenting wind.

The child ran over and, with his mother's assistance, climbed into the back of the wagon. Rosalie scooped up the cat and dropped the animal in beside Wade before joining them.

"I never thought I'd see the day," she mumbled.

"You and me both." Mike was certain their feelings had completely separate meanings and origins. "Let's hit the road."

Nodding, Abigail went to the front of the wagon and lifted her skirt enough to expose her foot. Thank God she was no longer barefoot. At least he'd been able to convince her to buy shoes for the three of them.

Instinctively, he reached for her waist and helped her into the wagon, painfully aware of her stiffening beneath his touch. Once she'd been pliant in his arms.

The memory of her expression the morning after they'd made love, tore at him, shredding what was left of his heart. Why did love have to hurt so damned much?

Simple. Because of Slick.

She glanced at him from over her shoulder once, then quickly shuttered her eyes from his probing gaze. Mike nodded once, then walked around to the other side of the wagon. Swinging himself up onto the hard bench seat, he gathered the reins and released the brake as the merchant had shown him.

"I sure as hell hope I know what I'm doing."

He glanced sideways at Abigail, surprised to find the barest hint of a smile playing at the corner of her mouth as she tied her bonnet strings beneath her chin. When she turned to face him, the smile had vanished.

"So do I," she said simply, then turned to face forward again.

Stunned, Mike stared at her profile, proud and alert as she looked forward, toward her future.

Toward Milton.

Rage rippled through him as he jerked himself around and flicked the reins and clicked his tongue. He was supposed to say something to the oxen—haw, hee or something equally profound—but he couldn't remember which so he didn't bother.

As the countryside engulfed the wagon, Mike found himself casting several overt glances toward the woman at his side. Each time he did, renewed pain slashed through him. Why did he keep torturing himself?

In the end, he'd have revenge by preventing her marriage. That should satisfy him, but it didn't. All it did was make him feel even lower.

Because of him, Abigail would be left alone with a child to raise in a strange city. *Damn.*

But she'd betrayed him. Hadn't she?

He cast another covert glance at her. *Did she betray me?*

He remembered asking her about anyone named Milton back when he'd first arrived at Elysium, and she'd denied knowing anyone by that name. But he'd specifically asked about anyone by that name in Natchez.

Not Denver.

If anyone was guilty of betrayal, it was Mike Faricy, Devil's messenger.

Staring straight ahead at the oxen's hindquarters, Mike decided this sojourn across America was deserved punishment for his sins. He'd made love to Abigail without offering her anything in return. Hell, he hadn't even told her he loved her.

And he was going to deprive her of the security she wanted so desperately for her son.

Enough, dammit. There was nothing he could do but deliver her to Denver, then take care of his own business. That was that.

He looked around at the changing landscape. A sea of grass encircled the wagon as they ventured farther into the prairie, reminding Mike how vulnerable they were, thanks to his inexperience. All he knew was to point the oxen west and follow the deep ruts in the grass left by previous wagons. There was no wagon train to join this late in the summer, and John Wayne hadn't been born yet.

"Well, I guess this must be the right direction." Abigail shaded her eyes and looked into the distance. "I hope."

She didn't look at him, but the sound of her voice raised his hopes. At least she wasn't ignoring him anymore. It was a long way across Kansas. They'd have to talk.

Hell, he *wanted* to talk.

He wanted a lot more than that, but he'd settle for the sound of her voice, a few kind words, and maybe a smile here and there.

"We're going west. That's all I know." Mike stared straight ahead, but felt her lingering gaze.

"Then I guess that means you know where you're going."

Her choice of words robbed him of his moment's peace, as surely as if she'd deliberately intended to. "Yeah," he croaked.

To Hell.

Chapter Eighteen

"How longer, Mama?"

Wade's words sliced through Abigail—again. How many times had he asked that same question, and how many times could she lie to him?

"Not much." She touched his sun-browned face, startling against his light hair. "I'm sure it won't be too much longer."

And that was the lie.

She had no idea how much longer it would take them to reach Denver. The really frightening part was that she knew Mike didn't either. They were out in the middle of an endless sea of grass—a perfect circle.

Grass spread out in every direction for as far as she could see, without a tree in sight. The starkness of the landscape was beautiful in a way, though frightening as well. Since everything looked the same day after day, for all she knew they could have been traveling the same circle all these weeks.

She heard Mike returning from the creek and watched him hitch the team. Their noon break was over and it was time to go again.

Their journey would end . . . eventually.

Then her misery would really begin.

Battling a surge of panic, she allowed herself a moment to gather her composure, then passed Wade to Rosalie in the back of the wagon. Resignedly, Abigail took her place in front with Mike.

"I'm sorry," he muttered, gathering the reins as he climbed up beside her.

"Sorry?" She shaded her eyes as she turned to watch him. His jaw was set in hard lines and a twitch began just below his ear.

"I think we're lost."

Finally, he'd said the words. "I know, but it isn't your fault."

"We have to get to Denver." He rubbed his eyes with his thumb and forefinger. "We have to . . ."

Abigail's heart fluttered and her head ached. It was true, they had to reach Denver, unless Mike himself put a halt to those plans. Only he had the power to change the future. Didn't he realize that?

All he had to do was take her in his arms and commit himself to her . . . and to Wade. Though she knew he didn't have money, he was strong and intelligent. Together, they could take care of Wade.

If only . . . *No.* She could not afford herself the luxury of dwelling on what wasn't meant to be, regardless of how desperately she might want it. Her future was set.

She was trapped.

"We're still heading in the right direction," she said quietly as the wagon inched forward. "The sun shows us the way every day."

Mike nodded and leaned forward to rest his elbows on his knees. When he looked at her, she saw the despair in his eyes. And something else.

Guilt.

"It isn't your fault." Without a wagon train to lead them, it was a miracle they'd made it this far. Wherever *this* was. "Just keep heading west. That's all we can do."

"And follow this sort of road." He nodded and released a ragged sigh. "Thanks."

"For what?"

"Not blaming me . . . not hating me." A tight smile lifted one corner of his mouth. "This would be one helluva lot simpler with something to follow. God, what I wouldn't give for a sign telling me the way to I-70."

"What?"

"Never mind."

He shot her a crooked grin reminiscent of the man who'd made love to her weeks ago. The man she'd fallen in love with . . .

"I never was much of a Boy Scout, I'm afraid."

Mike had never talked much about himself, and Abigail listened eagerly to his words. Who was this man? And why did she love him so much it hurt?

"Boy Scout?" Anything to keep him talking about himself.

He laughed quietly. "It's a club for boys, but I wasn't much for camping and stuff like that. I was always more interested in catching bad guys." His voice faded away, then he cleared his throat. "Being a hero . . ."

She felt his pain and wanted to help, but she had no idea what troubled him. What ghosts ate at him and gave him that haunted expression?

He faced forward again, shielding his expression from her. How could she hate him? Far from it, in fact. She adored him. She'd do almost anything to ease his pain, to banish whatever it was that bothered him. If only she could take him in her arms . . . The mere thought of touching him again made her melt inside.

Touch him.

Her hand followed her thoughts and she reached out to cover the back of his hand with hers. A fierce longing swept through her, far more powerful than mere desire.

Nurturing. She wanted to take care of Mike, similar to, yet different from the way she cared for Wade. It was a strange and wonderful feeling that mingled with her physical needs to form something precious in her heart.

Physically, they'd all suffered during their journey, but no one more than Mike. His hands had bled and blistered from driving the team without gloves, and she'd longed to ease his discomfort, though there was nothing either of them could do. Besides, now his hands were calloused and toughened to their task.

She made no effort to remove her hand, marveling at the way the bones and muscles hidden by his tanned skin rippled beneath her touch. Then he looked at her. She felt his gaze and her face flooded with heat, though she knew her blush wouldn't be apparent because of her sunburn.

He didn't withdraw, nor did he encourage her boldness. Feeling somewhat inspired, she allowed herself the extravagance of remembering the way it had felt to have his mouth and hands caressing every inch of her.

Her body warmed and softened from the inside out as she stroked the back of his hand with the tips of her fingers. A reckless thrill swept through her, and she traced the curve of his wrist around to the softer skin on the inside, hearing and taking satisfaction from his sharp intake of breath.

"Abigail," he said softly. "Do you know what you're doing?"

She turned to meet his gaze. "Yes," she answered, and meant it. She knew, hoped, prayed he shared her feelings. Her needs. Her desires. "I know."

She saw his Adam's apple bob up and down in his throat and he turned away for a moment, then looked at her again. The expression smoldering in his hazel eyes could not be denied.

He still wanted her.

Heaven help her.

Mike must think her a horrible, brazen hussy. Maybe she was. All she knew was that all too soon she'd belong to another man. A monster.

Now she was with Mike in the wilderness, and they wanted each other in the worst and best ways. Besides, she loved him with all her heart. If they could be together again before it was too late, was that such an evil thing?

It was wrong by the laws of God and man—she knew that. But that didn't matter anymore, though once, such things had seemed so important.

Promise filled his gaze, then something hard obliterated the softness which had been so welcome but fleeting.

"What's the matter?" he asked. His voice had a hard edge as he turned to face forward again. "Can't wait until your wedding?"

Gasping, she snatched her hand away and looked down at her lap. What had possessed her to actually touch him? To want him?

To love him?

She felt him watching her again, but she didn't dare look, fearing what she might find. Was he mocking her? Hating her?

"Shit." His curse shattered the silence and she knew the answer.

He hated himself. Why?

Before she could summon the courage to ask him, the relentless sun suddenly vanished behind a cloud. After weeks of harsh, blistering heat, the momentary reprieve stunned Abigail from her misery. She glanced up and saw more clouds gathering to completely cover the sky; the air immediately cooled.

"That's a welcome sight," he said without looking at her.

Mike seemed as relieved as she that something had broken the tension between them. If he wanted to pretend she'd never touched him, that was fine with her, though she knew she'd be unable to follow his example.

She'd never forget the unrelenting throb of desire, or the distress of rejection. Never.

"Is it gonna rain?" Rosalie's dark head thrust out from the back of the wagon. "Praise be."

Abigail nodded, trying not to notice the way Rosalie's gaze strayed from Mike, then back to her. *Forget it, Rosalie. He doesn't want me.*

Mike looked up at the darkening sky and she followed the direction of his gaze. Lightning sizzled and thunder shook the countryside.

"Looks like we're in for it." He pulled the reins hard and turned the wagon northward. "That looks like a bluff in the distance, though I won't believe it until I see it. See those dark things? I'm hoping they're trees. I know trees attract lightning, but—''

"They do?"

"Yeah, but there might be something other than wide open spaces there, too."

Abigail squinted and looked at the horizon. It was true— the landscape was finally changing. Mike clicked his tongue and flicked the reins until the oxen quickened their sluggish pace as much as possible, which wasn't much.

The wind started to blow, whipping dust into their faces. Rosalie and Wade ducked their heads inside the wagon again, and Abigail clung to the bench seat with both hands as they bounced across the prairie toward the dark smudges on the horizon.

They really were trees. Surely she'd been mistaken. She reached up to rub her eyes, then gripped the seat again when the wagon lurched again.

As they drew closer to the dark area, the clouds turned a sickly shade of greenish gray and began to churn overhead. A chill raced through her perspiration-soaked body.

Mike steered the wagon along a path where other wagons had obviously preceded them. It led downward from the trees until she saw something glistening in front of them.

"A river?" She looked questioningly at Mike, who merely grunted in response.

He stopped the wagon and set the brake, then leapt to the ground. She had no idea what he was doing, but for some reason she trusted him.

He returned a moment later. "Abigail. Rosalie," he shouted over the rising wind. "Grab half the rations and follow me."

Confused, but recognizing the need to hurry, Abigail obeyed his unusual request. Even the opinionated Rosalie didn't question his authority as they each took as much as they could carry and followed him.

He led them back up the bluff along the road from where they'd just come, to a small cave. No, not a cave. It was more of a hollowed out area in a wall of earth—a dugout. Her heart surged with love and relief as she returned to the wagon with him for another armload of food, dividing everything exactly in half.

In the cave, Mike started a small fire near the entrance and made certain the bags of flour and cornmeal were near the back of the cave where they would remain dry. The storm seemed to be waiting, building to something unholy.

Mike grabbed her hand and led her outside and turned to face her. "I'm taking the wagon across the river now."

"What?" She shook her head. He was leaving them here alone. "Why? Wait here with us until the storm—"

"No." He closed his eyes for a moment, then opened them again, his expression unreadable. "I have to, Abigail. If this storm is as bad as it looks, the river will rise and we won't be able to take the wagon across."

She shook her head again. "I still don't understand."

"Listen!" His voice was fierce. "I can carry the three of you across one at a time, if necessary, but I can't carry that wagon across. This is obviously a ford. I have to get the wagon across before the river rises."

The sky suddenly burst open and rain came down in a solid sheet. Abigail gasped for breath and Mike steered her back inside the cave.

Without another word, he turned and left her standing there.

Panic struck her full force and her heart thundered in her ears. What if he never came back? What if he left them here in the wilderness—alone?

No, Mike wouldn't do that.

But she still couldn't let him go alone. Without pausing to think, she rushed to Rosalie. "You and Wade stay here until we come back for you. There's enough food and water for several days, but we won't be that long."

Rosalie's expression was solemn. The cave wasn't high enough for them to stand upright, so they faced each other at a half-crouch. The darker woman merely nodded, placing her hand on the shoulder of the boy at her side.

Struggling against rising panic, Abigail bent to hug Wade. Reluctantly, she released him and darted from the cave and into the driving rain. She half-ran, half-slid down the path

toward the river, unable to see more than a few feet in front
of her.

She almost ran into the back of the wagon at the bottom of
the hill. It was inching slowly into the river's edge when she
managed to pull herself into the back. Thankfully, the wind
and rain shrouded any noise she might have made.

Panting for air, she wrung water from her skirt and crept
toward the front of the wagon, knowing better than to allow
Mike to see her. Then something solid struck the side of the
wagon and a queer sensation gripped her.

It took her a moment to recognize what had happened, then
she realized how impetuous following Mike had been.

Heaven, help us.

The wagon was floating.

Mike held onto the reins as if they were a lifeline. At this
moment, they were. The water had come out of nowhere, striking the wagon bed with a vengeance and nearly tipping it in
the process.

It was all he could do to keep his seat. He braced both feet
against the lip of the wagon, every muscle in his body tensed
to an unbearable level. He had to get this thing across the river.

Through the blinding rain, he could barely see the oxen in
front of him. They were swimming, their noses pointed skyward
as they struggled toward the riverbank. He had no idea how
far away that was now. When they'd started across, it hadn't
seemed far, but with the rain coming down like this, the distance
could have doubled by now.

I sure as hell hope I'm doing the right thing.

What sort of instinct had possessed him? Hell, he must be
possessed by the spirit of John Wayne at the height of his
career. How else could he have known to do this? And, more
importantly, was he right?

Too late now for second thoughts.

The wagon lurched and something thudded underneath. For
a moment, Mike thought it was going to break apart right on

the spot. Then he looked toward the oxen again and realized their bodies were out of the water.

"Hot damn," he whispered against the howling wind. He was going to kiss those ugly beasts.

Well, maybe not.

This bank of the river was similar to the other, with a wall of earth separating the water from the prairie. Mike couldn't see well enough to drive the team up the narrow road, so he leapt down and went to the front, leading the beasts until they were sheltered somewhat from the storm and on high ground.

The earthen wall shielded the wagon and the team from the wind, but the rain continued to pelt them mercilessly. There wasn't a thing he could do for the oxen, but he could sure get himself out of the storm for a while.

After setting the brake, Mike leapt down and ran to the back of the wagon and climbed inside, shaking water from himself like a sheepdog. That was undoubtedly the most thorough bath he'd received since leaving Elysium. He was squeaky clean and freezing cold.

Trying not to get the bedding wet, Mike removed his denim jacket, shoulder holster, and T-shirt, draping them across the back of the wagon bed where they might dry at least partially. His shoes and socks soon followed.

In his time, he knew the gray slacks would have had a label saying "Dry Clean Only," but now all he knew was they were saturated. Hopefully, they wouldn't shrink and force him to travel cross-country with no pants.

Not exactly a fitting image for a cop with a mission.

Shrugging, he unbuttoned the fly and raised up on his knees to inch the wet wool downward, then he sat and peeled the pants completely off and spread them out with his other discarded clothing.

The storm had made the afternoon as dark as dusk and cooler than any he could remember since his quantum leap, but at least the wagon bed was relatively dry. He stretched and reached for a blanket, turning toward the front of the wagon.

Lightning flashed and flickered for several seconds, illumi-

nating the inside of his canvas-covered home away from home.
Then he saw her. "Abigail?"

She sat on her haunches near the front of the wagon, her
eyes round and frightened as she stared at him. He inched
toward her.

"What the hell are you doing here?" Fury mingled with
relief as he reached for her shoulders. Shudders racked her
body through her sodden clothing. He sighed. "Like it or not,
you've got to get out of these wet clothes."

She didn't protest when he reached for the buttons at the
front of her dress. As each button slipped through the wet
fabric, Mike's desire grew. By the time he eased her dress from
her shoulders, his breathing was coming in ragged gasps.

He knew how to keep her warm.

How to keep them both warm.

God, help me.

She peeled the wet dress from her body and let it fall around
her, then she sat back to kick it free of her bare feet. Mike
took the garment and placed it with his at the back of the
wagon. Then he rested his hands on her shoulders, feeling her
tremble from cold . . . and something more?

Then he reminded himself that he should be angry with her.
With difficulty, he summoned his sternest voice—one he might
have used with a kid caught shoplifting.

"Why didn't you stay with Wade and Rosalie?"

"I—I . . ."

She shuddered again and he knew there was no turning back.
It didn't matter *why* she'd followed him. All that mattered was
that they were here together in the waning storm, separated by
a swollen river from the only two humans within a hundred
miles.

This woman who'd taken all he could give and asked for
more. Who'd touched something deep inside him—something
he'd thought dead.

He loved her, though he knew he shouldn't. He should hate
her. The mere thought of hating Abigail Kingsley was ludicrous.

He adored her.

Wanted her.

Needed her.

"Abigail." He reached for the clinging fabric of her slip and eased it over her head, then tossed it aside. A convulsive spasm gripped her and he gathered her against him to soothe and warm. "You're freezing."

She nodded against his shoulder and he held her even tighter, while he worked his fingers through her long braid of wet hair until it fell free and wild. Her skin was cold and clammy beneath his fingers as he massaged her back, acutely conscious of her nipples pressed against his bare chest.

She'd touched him earlier, before the storm. Did that mean she wanted him to make love to her again? The thought of stopping now made him feel physically ill, but he knew he would if she wanted him to. But at this point, that seemed unlikely.

Uncertain whether that knowledge frightened or pleased him, he cupped her chin in his hand and lifted her face to meet his gaze. The storm rumbled from a distance now and the sun broke through the clouds overhead, filling the wagon with light and welcome warmth.

"Abigail?" He gazed into her eyes and she smiled up at him, taking his breath away with her open desire.

She nodded, seeming to understand his unspoken question. Mike's heart slammed into his ribs as he covered her mouth with his, gently seeking and receiving her undeniable response.

With a whimper, she moved against him, wearing nothing but her Victorian underwear. His briefs did little to shield his eager anatomy from her softness.

While resignation had played a major role the first time they'd made love, today it was desperation which drove Mike. He didn't have much time left. Soon, he'd be taken from her to fulfill his destiny.

She was soft and sweet, taking and giving, as he separated her lips with his tongue to taste and explore. He couldn't get close enough to her, though she was molded against him now, returning his kiss with wild abandon.

His blood roared through his veins, setting every nerve-ending ablaze with the fires of passion. Her hands were everywhere, stroking and kneading his flesh as he kissed her forever, though he knew it would end far too soon.

She eased her hands inside the waistband of his briefs and pushed downward until his erection sprang free, enthusiastic, ready. They were still on their knees facing each other and Abigail reached between them with both hands to encircle him.

Mike jerked and broke their kiss, looking down into the fathomless depths of her eyes to assure himself of her intentions. The tigress had returned, but there was something more.

Love.

His heart soared, then plummeted back to earth like a Gemini capsule on reentry. Abigail loved him as he loved her. He'd hoped so before, but now he was sure.

She tightened her grip and he nearly exploded from the pleasure she inflicted. Knowing she cared made his passion soar to new heights—life-threatening at this level.

Growling in complete surrender, he reached for her breasts, watching her head roll backward as she bit her lower lip. He pulled back to watch her, then dipped his head to flick his tongue against her tawny nipple.

Her hands worked the length of him until Mike knew he could take no more. Easing her hands away, he pressed her to the bedroll in the wagon, then knelt above her to stare in wonder. She didn't even flinch as he peeled her wet underwear off and tossed it aside to reveal every luscious inch of her.

She reached out to him and he shifted against her with an eagerness which terrified him. He wanted her desperately, but what frightened him was the fact that he *needed* her even more than he wanted her.

"Abigail," he murmured, kissing his way down the side of her neck to the curve of her shoulder. "I want you."

"I want you, too." Her voice was low and sultry, inciting his already overblown desire to a dangerous level as she reached for him again.

Pulling away, he knew better than to let her touch him again just now. Eager to taste her, he covered her nipple with his mouth and drew it inward until she moaned and pressed herself upward. No woman had ever tasted sweeter.

Then he found her mouth again and rolled onto his back, pulling her with him to cover him. The feel of her soft curves melding against the hard planes and angles of his body was incredible. They fitted so well together, as if made for each other.

No, he couldn't allow himself to think about that. They both wanted this physical joining, and that was all they could ever have together. It would have to be enough.

She broke their kiss and lifted herself up to gaze down into his eyes. Her dark hair formed a damp veil around them, enclosing them in a make-believe cocoon of love and warmth. A bewitching smile spread across her face as she eased her leg over him until she straddled him.

He gasped as she inched her body along his torso, creating a tremor of longing he knew only she could fulfill. Her breasts, so perfect and round, beckoned to him. He reached out to hold them, brushing her nipples with his thumbs, reveling in her moan of pleasure.

All sense of reason fled, vaporized by the fire that erupted between them. Her skin no longer felt cold as he urged her forward until her breasts were mere inches from his face.

Unable to resist, he locked his mouth over her breast, flicking his tongue against the swollen bud, then drawing it inward hard. Her moans evolved into small cries of pleasure, urging him to share himself equally with her other breast.

Blind to everything but passion, Mike let himself go, allowed the pain and torment to leave him for a while. It wasn't difficult with this passionate woman to distract him.

To his amazement, she eased her bottom downward as he enjoyed her breasts, and he knew her intentions. The mere thought of being buried deep inside her again made him nearly explode instantaneously.

Her eagerness merely fueled his already volatile state.

Then he felt her warm, moist folds teasing the tip of his erection and his control broke. He couldn't wait any longer for her to take him inside.

Releasing her breasts, he gripped her hips and lifted her up slightly, poised above him.

Their gazes locked and he saw that she wanted this as desperately as he did. There was no turning back.

A wicked smile flitted across her face and he knew he'd created the world's most irresistible monster.

Chapter Nineteen

Abigail felt empty inside, and the need to fill herself with all this man had to offer was overwhelming. She wanted him inside her more than anything.

And she wanted it now.

Her breasts tingled from his delicious assault, but it wasn't enough. The core of her shouted for him. Nothing short of his full possession would suffice.

Straightening, she reached behind her and found his bulging member. He was hard and smooth as an iron rod, hot and heavy, throbbing with life.

And he was hers . . . at least for now.

He groaned as she lowered herself closer, teasing his round tip with her body, wondering how to proceed. She'd never done anything like this, and had only a vague idea of her body's aptitude for such an endeavor. But at this point she was more than willing to experiment.

Seeming to sense the reason for her hesitation, Mike pressed her hips downward with gentle pressure. She closed her eyes as he slowly filled her until she could scarcely breathe.

Her body stretched unbelievably to accommodate his. This

felt so right. So good. Then he thrust himself upward, hard, making her gasp in shock at the depth of their union.

Weak with desire, she leaned slightly forward with her feet tucked behind, on her knees with him beneath her. Inside her.

Her woman's body instinctively tightened around his large male one as he began to move. She wanted that total abandonment, that wild ecstasy again and again.

Only with Mike.

Always with Mike.

Rhythmically, exquisitely, he pressed himself upward and into her, then withdrew. Rivulets of pleasure undulated deep inside her as she contracted around him, tried to hold him inside and not let him go again. But each time he withdrew only meant his return would be that much better, harder, deeper.

"Don't stop." Was that her voice?"

He didn't answer—he didn't have to. She knew he wouldn't end this until they'd both found the magic he'd shown her before. She also sensed that this journey was even farther into that special place than he'd taken her the first time.

His momentum snatched her breath; heat enveloped them. She was on fire. Every plunge reached a threshold within her no one had ever crossed.

Behind her eyelids everything flashed white, then a mosaic of brightly colored lights exploded. Her body contorted around his as a liquid inferno purged her and she found journey's end—the goal she'd so desperately sought.

She heard Mike's grunt as he propelled himself deeply into her again and filled her with a torrid surge. Time and space were suspended as she dug her nails into his shoulders and sobbed his name.

And something more.

She slumped against him, vaguely aware of the way his arms tightened around her, of his breath in her hair, of the tiny kisses he placed on the side of her head and face. The ache of love was so great in her heart she could barely keep the words to herself.

Then a terrifying thought swept through her and she lifted

her face to look into his eyes. Had she spoken the words aloud?
She moistened her lips and watched him for any reaction.

He looked at her with sadness mingled with something more.
Was it pity? Heavens, *had* she said the words? Had she blurted
out her love for him in the afterglow of passion?

She didn't want his pity; she wanted his love. Seconds ticked
by in silence as she stared at him with his body still joined
with hers. She waited for him to say the words.

He reached up to touch the side of her face with his hand,
the expression—pleading, desperate—in his hazel eyes so profound it made her breath catch in her throat.

"Don't love me, Abigail," he whispered.

She felt as if he'd driven a knife through her heart. With a
whimper, she jerked away from him and lunged for her clothing,
tugging her slip over her head. Tears scalded her eyes and she
didn't even try to prevent their escape. They flowed freely
down her face as she tugged on her pantalettes and tied the
drawstring at her waist.

This had been their last chance. She knew this time her hurt
went too deep. If he couldn't commit himself to her now, he
never would.

He'd taken her love, but he refused to return it.

Though she'd seen something there, in his eyes. She looked
at him with her dress clutched in her hands. He was watching
her, that helpless, pleading expression still filling his eyes.

"What is it, Mike?" she whispered, suddenly frightened for
him. Forgetting her broken heart, she scooted on her knees to
his side and touched his face. "What's wrong?"

The look on his face held more pain than any human should
have to endure. She saw guilt, distress . . . and love. He *did*
love her. She was certain of it.

Then why did he refuse to acknowledge it?

He'd asked her not to love him. Well, that was something
she couldn't change. She *did* love him, and even if he refused
to accept it, he was going to know it.

"I love you, Mike Faricy," she whispered fiercely as tears
continued to slip down her cheeks and drip off the end of her

nose. ''I don't know why you refuse to admit it, but I know you love me too.''

Surprise flickered across his face, then he closed his eyes for a moment as if to shutter his emotions. When he looked at her again, the coldness had returned. ''No, Abigail,'' he said quietly. ''I don't—*can't*—love anyone. Not anymore. It hurts too damn much.''

Without another word, she crawled to the back of the wagon and climbed out, pulling her dress over her head and closing the buttons. She paused with her dress only half-closed, remembering Mike's words.

His expression.

The look of resignation that had crossed his face frightened her. Then she remembered *why* it should frighten her. She'd seen that look of defeat before, on her brother's face the last time he'd come home from the war.

Just before he died.

She brought her knuckle to her mouth and bit down hard to silence her sob. Mike Faricy had looked like a man about to face his executioner.

Mike's gut was on fire.

After tugging on his pants, he looked out the back of the wagon at Abigail. Her back erect, she stood perfectly still. Hating himself almost as much as their situation, Mike climbed down from the wagon and walked toward her.

He cleared his throat noisily, but she didn't acknowledge his presence. She simply stood as if frozen, staring into the distance, beyond the river and to the west. Toward Denver.

Toward her husband-to-be.

He felt as if she'd taken a knife and stabbed him through the heart. A sense of rejection and betrayal slashed through him. True, their lovemaking this afternoon had been stupid and reckless.

But it had also been fan-damn-tastic.

''Shit.'' He scrunched his bare toes under his feet in the mud

and avoided the stare he felt directed at him. The mission ahead
of him suddenly weighed even heavier on his shoulders.

She walked down the hill toward the roaring river. Cursing
himself, Mike followed, wishing he'd taken a moment to put
on his shoes. Hell, everyone else was barefoot half the time—
why not him, too?

"Abigail." He shouldn't talk to her. Every time he did, it
seemed to make their predicament much worse. She didn't even
look back as she approached the water and stopped near its
edge.

Uprooted trees bobbed along like toothpicks on the violent
current. The full impact of what they'd narrowly escaped struck
Mike anew. If only she'd stayed with Rosalie and Wade like
he'd asked her to . . .

Then he would've missed hearing her say she loved him.

"God." He raked his fingers through his hair and looked
across the swollen river, following the direction of her gaze.
There on the opposite bank stood Rosalie holding Wade's hand.
They were both waving and smiling.

He watched Abigail lift her hand and return their gesture,
and he followed her example. After all, it wasn't Rosalie or
Wade's fault he'd taken something he had no right to—again.

Mike looked at Abigail's profile and saw her forced smile.
He also saw tears streaming down her cheeks and dripping
from her chin, unheeded.

His fault.

After waving once more, he turned and made his way back
up the hill to the wagon. He trusted Abigail knew better than
to go into the water, and he needed a few minutes to get his
act together.

Christ, he was more of a fool than he'd ever imagined possible. Shaking his head in self-disgust, Mike climbed into the
back of the wagon, jerked his T-shirt on, and tucked it into his
waistband. All he had to do was get them to Denver . . . and
kill Milton.

Case closed.

"Mike, Mike."

Wincing, Mike sat down and pulled on his socks without

even looking around for the source of that all-too-familiar voice. He didn't want to know—didn't even want to acknowledge Slick's presence.

"So how was she this time?"

Mike tied his Reeboks and covered his face with both hands. "What do you want now?"

Slick's evil chuckle surrounded Mike and filled the back of the wagon with sinister intent. "I'm just checking up on you, as usual."

"I thought, just maybe, you'd decided to leave me alone to get this job done." Mike shook his head and dropped his hands to his knees.

He turned to look toward the front of the wagon, but immediately regretted the action. There sat Garfield on the bedroll where Mike had made love with Abigail only a short while ago, a red gleam in his feline eyes.

"I should've known."

"Yeah, you should've." The cat's mouth moved with the words.

"You leave Wade alone." Mike tensed, imagining Slick in possession of Garfield and close to the innocent little boy all the time. "I'm warning you."

"Oh, I'm real scared." Slick laughed again and his eyes flared brighter, vermilion now. "Eh, I'm not interested in picking on rug-rats. I have bigger problems."

"Problems?" Mike actually laughed, though he couldn't quite believe it. *"You* have problems?"

Slick stood on all fours and walked slowly toward Mike, his tail curled elegantly over his back while those glowing eyes riveted Mike. "Yeah. The big guy—remember? And you sure aren't helping matters any by getting lost."

Mike couldn't withdraw his gaze from Slick's, though he wanted desperately to break free. Now more than ever, he wanted to fight Slick.

Why?

"Yeah, what's different now?" Slick stopped a few feet from Mike and sat down again, though the glow in his eyes never lost its intensity. "Porking the Southern belle bimbo again make you feel like a man, Mike?"

"Shut up."

"No way." Slick tilted his feline head to one side. "I don't want to. Tell me about her, Mike. Tell me about sliding it deep inside her and—"

"Shut up!"

"Gotcha." Slick's laughter was sick, maniacal. "She loves you. Ain't that sweet? And you're gonna kill the man she's planning to marry. Perfect. Just perfect."

Mike couldn't breathe. The air scorched him, though the flames remained contained within Slick's eyes. Every time Mike drew a breath, the flames of Hell seared his throat. Soon Slick would have Mike in the real Hell. Why couldn't he leave him alone for now?

Don't talk to him. Mike couldn't drag his gaze from Slick's, but he could maintain his silence. The devil's gofer couldn't make Mike talk if he didn't want to. Could he?

"I can do anything I damn well please. Haven't you figured that out by now?"

Mike gritted his teeth to prevent his retort.

"Next time you decide to dip your wick, I think I'll climb aboard for the ride. Might be fun."

"Eat shit."

"Ha! Made you talk, didn't I?" Slick's eyes flared brighter, boring into Mike. "You can't win, stupid. Give it up."

"No." What was it that made Mike keep fighting Slick? But he knew the answer—it was that Faricy pride. No matter how hard he tried, he couldn't bring himself to just surrender, at least not to this bastard. "Tell me more about your mother, Slick."

"Give it a rest, Mike. She doesn't matter."

"Sure she does, Slick. You told me you grew up in Denver and that's where we're headed." Mike searched his memory for every shred of information Slick had inadvertently passed along. "After all, you said you wouldn't be born until next year. She might be with your father right now."

The flames leapt from Slick's eyes, nearly blinding Mike

with the sudden, fierce flare. "I told you I don't know who the shit-bird is who did the deed, and I *don't care*. Now drop it, dickweed."

Mike summoned his strength and went on the offensive. "Sure you do, Slick. You care." He drew a deep, searing breath. "When's your birthday? What month?"

"Forget it, Mike."

"Tell me. I want to make sure I sing to you on your birthday. When?"

Slick laughed and shook his head, twitching his cat ears. "Suit yourself, but you'll be burning in Hell by then. May second, 1866. Happy now?"

"Maybe. Hey, wouldn't it be something to actually *see* your conception?" Mike laughed, though he had no idea where he'd found the courage or strength for the effort. "Denver. Hmm. Y'know, if you were born in May, then according to my calculations, your old man oughta be doing your old lady anytime now."

Blinded by the flames, Mike never saw the cat leap toward him. The claws raked his face, tearing Mike's flesh dangerously close to both eyes.

Screaming in pain, he clasped his face in his hands and felt the warmth of his own blood trickle between his fingers. Both the cat and Slick were gone now, leaving Mike alone with his pain and misery.

"What happened?"

Abigail's voice carved through the pain-induced fog which shrouded Mike's brain. He jerked open his eyes and pulled his hands away from his face and stared at his clean fingers.

"What is it?" Concern filled her voice.

"N-nothing." He felt his face again, then looked up at her. "Are there scratches . . . on my face?"

Frowning, Abigail leaned her head through the opening at the back of the wagon and peered at his face. "No." Her mouth fell open in obvious shock. "If you're implying that I—"

"No, no." Mike started to laugh, and he knew it was pure insanity that forced the sound from him. "No, not you. Garfield."

"I'm not laughing, Mike, and I saw Garfield with Wade and Rosalie just a minute ago. *Across* the river." Abigail drew a deep breath and he saw her stiffen. "The river's already starting to recede. I'd appreciate it if you could get us to Denver as quickly as possible."

Mike's laughter died and he felt dead inside himself. *Soon.*

"Sure. We should be able to bring them across tomorrow." He met her gaze and saw pain and regret in her blue eyes. Her distress was his fault—all of it.

"Very well. But tonight, I think it best if you sleep outside."

She turned and walked away from the wagon, leaving Mike to stare after her. He started to wish again that things could be different, then reminded himself that "if only's" weren't for him.

Only death and Hell awaited him.

And maybe . . . revenge.

Chapter Twenty

Denver.

Abigail shaded her eyes to stare down the dusty street. Tree-less mountains smudged the western skyline, while endless plains stretched to the east. At long last, they'd reached their destination.

She had no idea where the Landmark Hotel was located, but the center of town seemed a good place to start. Mike seemed to agree as he drove the wagon in that direction. He hadn't spoken more than a few words since the afternoon of the storm, nearly a week ago. Every time Abigail remembered the way she'd thrown herself at him, the way she'd ... ridden him, her face flashed with the heat of humiliation while her body throbbed with longing.

Mike Faricy had made her want the very things she'd feared before he came to Elysium. It seemed impossible, but it was true. She felt no fear at the thought of being with Mike, though she knew that would never happen again.

She was to become the bride of Casper Milton.

Bile rose in her throat and that old, familiar fear made her turn cold inside. How could one man make her want something another man made her dread?

Oh, but that was so simple, really. She *loved* Mike, and that made all the difference in the world.

She glanced askance at him and saw his jaw flinch. He was gritting his teeth again—one of the many things she'd learned about him over the past months. Soon, he would leave her with her new husband. Tears stung her eyes, but she blinked them away. Not now. It was far too late for tears.

Too late for everything.

"Mama?"

The sound of Wade's voice behind her brought Abigail back to the present and she turned to smile at her son's beaming face. His eyes were wide with wonder as he looked at the bustling crowd on the boardwalk.

"This is Denver, Wade," she told him, watching his smile. Determination welled within her. She would never allow him to learn of the sacrifice his mother had made on his behalf. Never!

"You gonna tell me now why we come to Denver?" Rosalie stuck her dark head out through the opening beside Wade's. "I been waitin' a powerful long time."

Heat flooded Abigail's face and she knew Mike was watching her now. She'd successfully avoided telling Rosalie of her wedding plans all this time. Now she had no choice but to reveal the truth.

"I'm going to be married, Rosalie." Abigail forced herself to smile when she met her friend's gaze.

"Married?" Rosalie shot Mike's back a look that broke Abigail's heart. Hope filled the woman's gaze when she looked at Abigail again.

"No, Rosalie," Abigail said quietly, thankful that the crowded street had forced Mike to look away. "Someone else— a man who needed a wife."

"Why don't you tell her the truth?"

Mike's question caught Abigail by surprise and she jerked her head around to stare in disbelief at the man. "Please, don't do this."

Mike met her gaze and she saw pain mingled with his hatred. He looked at her as if she'd betrayed him. *Had* she betrayed

him? Really? No, but he couldn't possibly realize that, because
he had no way of knowing Casper Milton was Wade's father.

No one did except Abigail. Even Rosalie didn't know the
name of the soldier who'd raped her mistress, though she'd
been there to bathe and console Abigail after the fact.

And she'd been there to help her bury a man later that same
night. Abigail forced the memories from her mind. She must
concentrate on the present—the past was something she could
never change.

Mike nodded, then turned to face forward again. For whatever
reasons, he'd decided not to press the issue. *Thank Heaven.*

What would Mike think if he learned she was willing to
marry a man who'd raped her?

Lord, I've lost my mind. I can't do this.

Her belly lurched and roiled; perspiration burst forth on every
inch of her body. Fear, commanding and powerful, gripped her
again, but she banished it and turned to face Rosalie and Wade
again. Her darling little boy . . .

Anything for Wade.

"I'm marrying a man who lives here," she explained to
Rosalie. "He owns a fancy hotel."

Rosalie's eyes widened. "We're gonna live in town? In a
hotel?"

Abigail gave her friend an indulgent smile. "That's right,
Rosalie. And we'll never be hungry again." She reached out
to touch her son's face, stroking his sunburned cheek and almost
white hair. "Wade will have food, clothes, and proper school-
ing. When he grows up, he'll inherit his fa—"

Biting her lower lip, Abigail realized her error. She couldn't
call the man Wade's father. What had she been thinking? Of
course, her husband-to-be might very well insist on telling
everyone the truth, though by doing so, he'd brand his son a
product of violence and sin.

Surely no man would want that. Not even a monster like
him.

"The Landmark Hotel. That must be the place." Mike's
voice sounded sarcastic and bitter. Abigail straightened and
stared in horror mingled with awe at the structure. Mike brought

the wagon to a stop and sat holding the reins in his lap for several seconds.

"Yes, this must be the right place." Abigail cleared her throat and blinked several times to remove the tears and grit from her eyes. She had to maintain control at all costs. The stakes were too high now and she was too near her goal.

Security for her son.

Food.

Money.

"I must look a sight." Abigail patted her hair nervously, knowing she didn't really care what her intended thought of her appearance. He hadn't taken her looks into consideration before having his way with her before.

"Married. I just don't believe it, Miss Abigail," Rosalie said in a wounded tone. "How could you plan this without tellin' me?"

Abigail turned and met her friend's injured gaze. "Please, try to understand. I'm doing this for all of us."

"Sans me, of course." Mike's bitterness made his voice harsh and gravelly. Without looking at her, he leapt to the ground and took the reins to lead the oxen to a watering trough. Then he set the brake and looked up at her, his expression carefully cloaked again. "Ready?"

For some reason, she had the feeling his question held more than one meaning, though she didn't have the time or the strength to decipher it now. "Yes, I'm ready." *No, I'll never be ready for this. If only you knew . . .*

As Mike slipped his hands around her waist to lift her to the ground, Abigail caught sight of a very old woman standing on the porch in front of the hotel. Abigail's heart slammed into the wall of her chest and her mouth went dry.

Was that his mother?

Her insides churned with remembered fear and anticipated terror. How could she go through with this?

Anything for Wade.

Because she had to. The only man she might have had a life with didn't want to make that commitment to her. *Don't love me, Abigail,* he'd said.

Though she couldn't stop herself from loving him, she couldn't allow that to prevent her from going through with what she must. Resolutely, she dragged in a breath as Mike let her feet touch the ground, then she swung her gaze back to the woman on the porch.

Her silver hair was pulled back in a severe style, revealing the widow's peak Abigail remembered on a man's face.

His face.

The woman's complexion was sallow, and she surveyed Abigail with faded blue eyes, filled with an undefinable expression. Leaning heavily on a cane, the woman stepped forward to the edge of the porch.

"You must be Miss Kingsley," she said in a quiet voice.

Abigail drew a deep breath and walked toward the steps, stopping on the first one to face the woman at eye-level. "Yes, I'm Abigail Kingsley."

Silence stretched between them, then the old woman's faded gaze looked beyond Abigail. A sparkle appeared in the blue depths and a smile crinkled the aged face.

"Lan' sakes, that must be the boy."

Fear shot through Abigail as she turned in the direction of the woman's gaze just in time to see Mike lifting Wade from the wagon to stand beside Rosalie. Would this woman and her son try to take Wade?

"My son," Abigail said quietly. "You . . . knew about my son."

"Of course, why do you think I sent for you?" The woman stiffened as she met Abigail's questioning gaze.

"*You* sent for me?" Abigail blinked as consternation turned her perspiration-soaked body to an icy chill. "I thought . . ."

"Yes, I sent you the letter . . . on behalf of my son." The woman lowered her gaze, then looked toward Wade again. "He's the image of his father."

"Please, he doesn't know." Abigail's voice was barely more than a whisper. "Please . . ."

The old woman's eyes were filled with compassion when she met Abigail's gaze again. "I understand, child. We'll wait awhile and things will turn out just fine. You'll see."

Relief and confusion nearly sent Abigail to her knees, but she quickly drew several deep breaths to allay her inclination to faint. Not now. She needed her strength and her wits.

This woman was kind and understanding. How could she possibly be that man's mother? It seemed utterly impossible, yet Abigail saw the resemblance. Here stood the woman who'd borne the man who raped Abigail.

Wade's father.

Soon, she'd have to face him . . . and her past.

"Introduce me to your companions, my dear. And I must insist that you call me Gertrude."

"Gertrude." The sound of that name made Abigail's head ache, but she sensed a possible ally in this woman. Where was Casper? Why wasn't he here to flaunt his victory? Mike stepped toward them and removed the hat he'd bought in St. Louis, before they started across the prairie. His dark curls hung in disarray across his forehead. The memory of running her fingers through his soft hair made her burn inside to feel him against her again.

No, stop! She couldn't do this—mustn't allow herself to think of Mike in that way anymore. Now they would part company and she would never see him again.

Her heart breaking, Abigail forced a smile to her face and cleared her throat. She noticed the hard glint in Mike's eyes when he looked at the old woman. Surely that was uncalled for. "This is Mr. Faricy, our . . . guide."

Mike's gaze shifted to Abigail for an instant and she saw again that he felt betrayed. Surely he didn't expect her to introduce him as her lover?

"Mrs. Milton."

Mike's voice sounded strange, as if he could barely control that deep anger she'd sensed in him before. Why was it surfacing again now?

"A pleasure to meet you, sir." Gertrude nodded and turned expectantly to Rosalie. "And you are . . . ?"

"I be Rosalie, ma'am." Rosalie curtsied politely.

"Fine. You'll be happy here, Rosalie," the old woman said warmly, though she looked at Wade as she spoke.

"This is my son, Wade." Abigail stepped forward and placed a protective hand on Wade's shoulder. "Wade, this is . . . Mrs. Milton."

"I'm going to be your grandmother, young man." Gertrude clumped down the steps toward the child with a broad smile on her wrinkled face. "And I want you to know right now, that I bake the world's best gingerbread. As a matter of fact, there's some cooling in the kitchen right now."

Wade stared at the woman with wide, puzzled eyes. "Gingerbread?"

The woman turned to Abigail with a stunned expression. "Don't tell me he's never had gingerbread before."

Tears stung Abigail's eyes again. "We've had hard times in the South, Gertrude." *The worst of times.* "Wade's never tasted anything even remotely similar to gingerbread."

Compassion filled the old woman's gaze, and she nodded in understanding. Abigail's heart warmed. If only she didn't have to face the woman's son . . .

"Well, do I have a treat for you, young man." She reached a gnarled hand toward Wade, who stared at it for a few moments, then cast his mother a questioning glance.

Abigail nodded and gave Rosalie a look that said "Protect him." Wade slipped his hand into Gertrude's and went up the steps with Rosalie following close behind.

Before the threesome entered the hotel, Gertrude turned toward Abigail. "Oh, my dear, you must forgive an old woman for being so rude." She touched her cheek in dismay. "I'll send the bellhop after your things, and my Molly will show you to your room so you can freshen up."

"Thank you." Abigail couldn't help wondering why Gertrude hadn't mentioned her son yet.

"And Mr. Faricy, there will be a soft bed and a warm meal for you tonight, too." Gertrude beamed at them all. "It's the least I can do to repay you for delivering my new family."

Confused, Abigail nodded. Why hadn't her future husband's name been mentioned in any of these plans?

"Mrs. Milton?" Mike's voice still held the harsh tone she'd noticed earlier. "Where's Miss Kingsley's . . . betrothed?"

Abigail held her breath, wondering why Mike was so interested in meeting Casper. Was he jealous? Did she dare hope?

Stop it, Abigail.

Gertrude's lips pressed into a thin line. "You'll all meet him
this evening at supper. We dine at six."

Abigail knew Wade would be safe with Rosalie close by,
and she breathed a sigh of relief. She had a short reprieve
before having to face that horrible man. A hot bath and some
clean clothes would do wonders.

She turned to look at Mike and saw his jaw twitching again.
His nostrils were flared and sweat trickled down his face. Then
he turned to face her and the expression in his eyes unhinged
her.

That haunted look of pure madness he'd worn the morning
she'd first found him, had returned with a vengeance. It was
as if he didn't even see her, though he was looking right at
her.

"Mike?" Then his gaze met hers and sent an icy tremor
skipping down her spine.

He looked as if he had the devil in him.

Mike took the wagon and oxen to the livery stable. He didn't
know whether Abigail would want them sold or not, though
she might need them after her husband-to-be died of unnatural
causes.

Guilt slithered through him like a venomous snake. The old
woman seemed kind enough. Maybe she would take pity on
Abigail and allow them all to stay with her after her son was
gone.

Of course, the old woman would grieve. What had she done
to deserve any of this?

He paid the man who ran the livery, then turned back toward
the Landmark Hotel, which more closely resembled a boardinghouse than a hotel. Still, it looked profitable enough. At least
Abigail and Wade might have a place to live in comfort after
Mike was gone.

Without him.

He walked stonily through the center of town. Denver was teeming with life—something Mike would have for only a short while. With a sigh, he wrapped his fingers around the coins in his pocket. He needed some clean clothes. Every man should have the right to die clean.

Abigail had insisted he take a salary for guiding them to Denver. *Yeah, some guide.* The memory of that afternoon in the wagon crept into his thoughts. Abigail had said she loved him.

Forget it, Faricy. It didn't matter now. He walked automatically across the street and into a store, where he purchased jeans and a blue chambray shirt. Carrying the paper-wrapped bundle, he left the store a few minutes later and looked down the street.

He needed a drink. In fact, he needed several drinks.

Mike crossed the street again, pushed through a pair of swinging doors and froze, staring at the rustic decor. Sawdust covered the floor and brass spittoons occupied several corners.

The tables and chairs scattered haphazardly around the large room, were rough and scarred. Mike lifted his gaze to admire the polished bar with its shiny brass rail, where several customers stood with their drinks. Behind it was a painting of a naked woman—a fat naked woman—lounging on her side with feathers half-concealing certain strategic areas of her anatomy.

As he turned to look at the rest of the room, he realized the higher he looked, the fancier the room was. The stairs and railing were intricately carved and highly polished. Plush red carpet covered the staircase. He looked higher still and saw three women leaning on the rail, staring down.

At him.

"Great." All he wanted was a drink, not a whore. Remembering how much trouble he'd found with Honey, he turned to leave, but something compelled him to glance back over his shoulder once more.

A dark blue uniform caught his attention. Suspicion crept slowly up his spine and he turned toward the soldier. It couldn't be.

But it was.

"Faricy, I see you finally made it."

Mike stopped beside Major Thiel and stared in disbelief. "What the hell are you doing here?"

"Waiting for you and the Kingsley woman." Thiel swung around to meet Mike's gaze. "Took you long enough. Did you get lost?"

"Maybe." Mike didn't know why, but he went to the bar and leaned against the brass rail.

"What'll it be?" A heavyset man stood behind the bar, polishing a glass.

"Uh . . . beer." Mike dug into his pocket and removed a coin. The bartender sat a beer on the counter and took the money. Apparently, it was enough.

Mike took a long pull of his beer and winced. Room temperature beer wasn't what he'd been expecting. But at least it was wet, and it *was* beer.

"Why are you here, Thiel? Pull a new assignment?" Mike didn't look at the soldier while he spoke. He stared straight ahead, because he knew—and feared—the answer.

"I told you back in Natchez I was investigating a soldier's disappearance."

Mike chuckled and shook his head. "Sorry, that still doesn't make sense."

Thiel sighed. "Suit yourself, Faricy." The major pushed away from the bar. "Like it or not, that Kingsley woman knows something about Denny's disappearance. Hell, she came out here to marry Denny's commanding officer. Doesn't that make *you* suspicious?"

Mike turned to face the major. "Only of you." And that was a lie. Remembering the day he'd learned Abigail knew a man named Milton, Mike's gut lurched and burned. He'd rationalized that as merely a coincidence, but was it? She'd traveled halfway across the country to marry the man.

Why?

Because he asked and I accepted . . . Her words returned to haunt him.

"All I can say is, you're one gullible son of a bitch." Thiel turned to walk away.

"Thiel."

The soldier turned around slowly. "What?"

"Nothing. Never mind." Suddenly Mike felt the need to think about everything. So many strange, apparently unconnected, pieces of a large puzzle . . .

"Suit yourself." The major started to walk away, but turned back to stare at Mike. "Tell you what—meet me here tomorrow night around eight o'clock. I have a hunch we both know more than we're admitting. That'll give you time to rethink your position."

"My position?" Mike couldn't prevent the bitter chuckle that burst forth. "Yeah, if you only knew the half of it."

The major's eyes narrowed to mere slits as he stared at him. "Tomorrow evening?"

Mike didn't know why, but he nodded in agreement. "I'll be here." *Unless I'm in Hell by then.*

The major left Mike standing alone at the bar with his empty beer mug clenched in his fist. Sighing in exhaustion laced with resignation, Mike turned and placed the mug on the bar. It was past time he settled things once and for all. He'd retrieved his gun from the wagon, and it was tucked safely in his shoulder holster under his jacket.

Time to end this nightmare.

"Hey, handsome."

Mike grimaced as he turned toward the feminine voice. He didn't need this right now. "I gotta—"

"What's your hurry?"

Mike stared in shock at the creature who literally sauntered toward him. Flaming red hair topped her head in an intricate network of curls. Feathers had been woven into the back and swished over her head when she moved like a crooked, beckoning finger.

The woman exuded sex for sale.

Mike wasn't the least bit interested, but he shot her a lopsided grin and allowed his gaze a leisurely journey down her full length and back up to her painted mouth. "Sorry, but I'm not in the market today."

"Hmm. Don't you like what you see?"

Mike frowned as he studied her face. He must really be losing it at this late date. This woman reminded him of someone. Shaking his head in a mental reminder that he had more important things to deal with, Mike started to turn away.

"What's the matter? Aren't you man enough for this much woman?"

Mike rubbed his eyes with his thumb and forefinger. A thousand miles of grit rimmed his eyes; his body ached with fatigue. The last thing in the world he wanted was sex, especially with a prostitute. "Not now. Just drop it, will you?"

He turned again to leave, but her angry voice sliced right through him.

"Suit yourself, dickweed."

Mike froze, then whirled around to face her. A snarl twisted her face into a mask of anger and resentment. He knew that face.

He took a step toward her. Was this another of Slick's games? If it wasn't, then this woman had to be . . .

I grew up in Denver, smart ass . . .

His memory of Slick's words penetrated Mike's fried brain. This couldn't be happening.

Mike stared long and hard at the woman's dark eyes, finding no sign of strange lights flaring in the pupils. Her eyes were a little bloodshot, but that was as far as the redness went. She was human—not Slick.

Could this be true?

"What's your name, peaches?" Mike asked in a patronizing tone. He didn't know why, but he had to know.

Her anger vanished and she became all business again. "Hattie. What's yours?" She moved closer and pressed her voluptuous breasts against him.

Her breath reeked of cheap wine, and Mike remembered Slick's comments about his mother's drinking problem. "Your last name. What is it, gorgeous?"

She sighed and rubbed herself across Mike's chest. "Dawson. Hattie Dawson. My room's right upstairs waitin' for us, honey.''

Dawson! It was all Mike could do to prevent himself from shouting in victory, though he didn't know what he'd won at this point. "No, I don't think so." Mike took a step back and she nearly fell on her face, but he reached for her shoulder to steady her. "I'll be back here tomorrow evening around eight to meet with someone. Can we talk more after that?"

"Sugar, I don't get paid to *talk.*"

Mike pitied the woman. She was pickled, and he suspected she probably went through life that way most of the time. Anaesthetized. "What if I agree to pay for your time . . . just to talk? Will that be all right?" Why was he doing this?

She laughed and staggered backward. "If you pay for it, you get whatever you want. Eight o'clock. I'll be here waitin'."

Mike watched her weave toward the stairs and he shook his head in incredulity. Slick's mother. When he'd taunted the little jerk about his mother, the thought of actually meeting her hadn't even crossed Mike's mind.

This was weird.

Mike turned to make his way out into the late afternoon air. He had to get back to the boardinghouse and take care of business, but now there was something else he had to take care of. Somehow, he had to protect Abigail from Major Thiel.

Maybe he'd take the old lady up on the hot bath and warm meal before he finished Milton. It wasn't as if he could put the new clothes on without a bath, and there was no rule that said condemned men had to go to Hell dirty and hungry. Besides, he had to wait for the right time to finish Milton, and there was one other matter Mike had to address before he could be sure of success.

He had to make certain Casper Milton didn't have any siblings, nieces, or nephews running around. And what about cousins? *Crap.*

The sense of urgency that had fueled Mike earlier vanished. Strange. He didn't know why, but for some reason, now that he knew the end was near, he no longer felt the need to hurry.

And if Slick butted in again before Mike finished his job, at least now he had some really powerful ammunition to unload on the asshole.

Slick's mother. *Sheesh.*

Maybe there really was a little justice left in this world.

Chapter Twenty-One

The Landmark certainly wasn't the sort of establishment Abigail had expected. It was really nothing more than a glorified boardinghouse, with only a few guests in residence, who took their meals in a separate dining room from the family.

Family. This was her new home. The sooner she accepted that fact, the better off she'd be.

Gripping the stair railing so tightly her knuckles turned white, she made her way down to the main floor. Gertrude had said Casper would be here this evening. Was he already in the dining room waiting for his bride-to-be?

Her insides twisted into a painful knot of dread. So far, arriving at the hotel and meeting her future mother-in-law had been an almost pleasant experience. With a sigh, she reminded herself of what awaited her—rather, *who* awaited her.

The monster—the man whose bed she must share for the rest of her life. *For Wade . . .*

She swallowed with difficulty and paused at the bottom of the stairs. It felt good to be clean, and the yellow dress was crisply ironed. Her braid wound around her head several times in a coronet. Though sunburned from weeks on the trail, she knew her appearance was now tolerable.

Not that she wanted to please Casper Milton—far from it, in fact.

Still, she had a role to play, and play it she would. Gertrude had shown them all nothing but kindness since their arrival. Being on time and neat in appearance was the least Abigail could do to repay her hospitality.

Wade was already sound asleep for the night. *Poor baby.* The journey had taken a toll on his young body, not to mention the entire pan of gingerbread he'd consumed this afternoon.

She couldn't prevent the smile that tugged at her lips. It was good to know her son would never want for anything, that hunger pangs would never disturb his slumber again.

Yes, she was doing the right thing.

"All dressed up for the occasion, I see."

Mike's voice shot through her and gooseflesh crept up her arms and neck. Abigail turned toward the sound, surprised to find him leaning against the door frame, freshly shaved and wearing clean clothes.

"I hope you don't mind, but I took a portion of my pay out of what you gave me for the livery." He straightened and took a step toward her, then stopped to look down at his attire. "Better?"

The grin he flashed turned her insides to liquid fire. How was she going to survive coming face to face with Casper at all, let alone in front of Mike?

A sinking feeling swept through her. Soon Mike would be gone from her life forever—a much more serious consequence than what she must face this evening. She drew a deep breath, vowing to maintain her composure this evening—no matter what.

"Well . . . ?" He held his hands out to his sides and looked at her. "Is this better or do you want me to go put on my dirty clothes again?"

"No, I'm sorry." She forced a smile to her lips, though tears pricked her eyes, threatening to spill down her cheeks with the slightest impetus. "You look nice."

"So do you." His expression grew somber as he stood staring at her. "Abigail, are you su—"

"Well, here you both are." Gertrude came into the room with a flourish. She was dressed in gray taffeta that rustled as she came across the room to take both of Abigail's hands in hers. "Supper will be served in a few moments. Shall we?"

Abigail gave a cursory nod and allowed Gertrude to escort her through the archway and into a dining room. Ruby-colored brocaded paper covered the walls, and a long cloth-covered table filled the room.

"Here you are, my dear." The older woman indicated a chair to the right of hers at the head of the table. "Mr. Faricy, if you'll just take that seat, I'll ring for Molly."

Mike and Abigail exchanged curious glances as they took their seats. His expression had grown hard again as he surveyed her from across the table, then he looked toward their hostess.

"Mrs. Milton, only three?" he asked in a quiet but intense voice. "I thought your . . . son would be joining us."

"No, Casper doesn't sup at table, Mr. Faricy."

Abigail frowned as Mike cast her a quick, questioning glance. Why wouldn't her husband-to-be take his meals with his mother?

"I . . . don't understand." Abigail jerked her gaze away from Mike's and looked at their hostess. "If he's changed his mind about . . . the wedding, please just te—"

"No, no, my dear. Nothing like that." Mrs. Milton sighed and looked down at her lap for a moment, then she met Abigail's gaze with unshed tears glimmering in her eyes. "Both of you, enjoy your meals and I shall tell you the entire, tragic story."

Tragic? Could Gertrude know about her son's heinous crime?

Abigail found Mike's gaze on her again when she looked across the table. His thoughts couldn't possibly mirror hers, though it was obvious they were unpleasant.

"As you wish." Abigail nodded toward their hostess, who rang a small brass bell.

Within a few seconds, Molly entered with a large tray. Abigail's mouth watered as a plate was placed before her and the cover removed. Fragrant steam drifted to her nostrils and she almost forgot everything else. This was *real* food, and there wasn't a morsel of fish or cornmeal to be found.

A thin slice of roast beef smothered in gravy occupied an entire half of her plate. How long had it been since she'd seen beef, let alone tasted it?

Wade had been too sleepy and full of gingerbread to eat supper. But if this was any example of the sort of fare her son had to look forward to, then Abigail had indeed done the right thing.

Though she hadn't yet paid the price.

A bitter taste invaded her mouth as she swallowed the burning sensation that filled her throat. The price for her meal? For her son's security? For this fine roof over their heads?

Casper Milton's abuse. His bed.

Stop!

"Aren't you hungry, my dear?" Concern filled Gertrude's voice.

Abigail nodded and lifted her fork. "Yes, it's just been a long time since I last saw so much . . ."

"I understand times have been hard in the South since the war." The older woman's voice was filled with compassion. "Pity, all the bloodshed."

Pity. That hardly seemed adequate to describe the senseless deaths, the misery, the destroyed lives . . .

Mike cleared his throat and Abigail looked up and realized he wasn't eating. He sat staring at their hostess, his expression hard, querulous.

"You were going to tell us why your son didn't join us?" he prompted, then reached for the wineglass in front of him and took a sip.

Abigail hadn't even noticed the wine. Absently, she imitated Mike's action and looked expectantly toward their hostess.

"I begged Casper not to join up to fight that stupid war." She shook her head. "He said he wanted a little adventure before he settled down to run the Landmark."

Adventure? Abigail's belly tightened into a vise. He'd wanted adventure? Her cheeks blazed and her hands trembled as she forced herself to listen in silence.

"My son was injured toward the end of the war, in the Wilderness Campaign."

Abigail put another forkful of roast into her mouth and chewed absently, praying she wouldn't choke on it while she listened to her hostess speak of the man Abigail hated more than anyone in the world. Swallowing proved even more difficult than chewing had, and she reached for the wine to wash it down.

"The doctors were amazed he made it home at all. They all expected him to perish there on that horrid battlefield, so far from home." She sighed and met Abigail's gaze. "My dear, I fear I've misled you."

"Misled me?" Abigail placed her fork on the edge of her plate and focused all her attention on Gertrude. Something peculiar was going on here. "How?"

"Casper didn't . . . answer your letter, or send the money." Her chin fell to her chest. "I did."

A wave of dizziness swept over Abigail and she gripped the table's edge for support. "You did? But why?" Did this mean there would be no marriage? Relief and fear blended inside her to form a new, undefinable emotion. "I don't understand."

"I know, and I'm sorry for that." Gertrude looked up, pressed her lips into a thin line and shook her head. "I shouldn't have deceived you, but Casper can't do these things for himself. I knew he would want you and Wade to come here if he could."

"Exactly what do you mean by he *can't?*" The brittle edge of disbelief tainted Mike's voice, prompting Abigail to look up at him.

"Just that, Mr. Faricy. Casper is . . . helpless." The older woman's voice broke on the last syllable and she covered her face with her napkin. "Please, forgive me." She drew a deep breath and dropped her napkin to her lap. "There."

"I still don't understand," Abigail said steadily, though she thought perhaps the situation was beginning to make itself clear. "Are you saying your son doesn't even *know* about me?"

"I'm afraid that's so." Gertrude sighed again, then reached for Abigail's hand and covered it with hers. "Casper hasn't spoken a word since they brought him home." A tear trickled down the woman's wrinkled cheek. "He just stares at the ceiling and sleeps intermittently. He doesn't move or speak. Ever.''

Abigail struggled against an onslaught of something she didn't wish to define. Something evil. Her heart thundered at a frantic pace. Part of her felt justice may have been served, while another, very selfish part wondered how this situation would affect Wade. And her.

What did this *mean*?

"Then there will be no wedding." Abigail avoided Gertrude's gaze and looked down at her half-empty plate. "Why did you send for us if . . ."

"Oh, but there *can* be a wedding." Gertrude's tone sounded unnaturally cheerful. "But only if you agree, of course."

"Milton's in a coma?" Mike's voice cracked with an odd inflection, prompting Abigail to look at him again.

He was staring at their hostess as if she'd just delivered a death blow. "Mike?" Abigail asked, suddenly frightened by the ferocity in his tone.

He looked at her once, quickly, then away again. His expression was unfathomable yet intense. Frightening.

"My God. You're saying he's a . . . a vegetable." Mike's tone sounded almost resigned now as he reached up to rake his fingers through his dark curls. "I don't believe this. Now what am I supposed to—"

He looked up sharply and Abigail saw genuine fear in his eyes, then he turned toward Gertrude again. "Is . . . is he your only child?"

Why in heaven's name would Mike care about something like that? Couldn't he see this woman was in pain? Abigail stared in horror at Mike, amazed by the intensity of his tone and expression.

"Yes. I had a daughter too, but she died of the smallpox when she was only nine."

"I'm sorry," he said quietly, though Abigail suspected that wasn't the case. Mike nodded stiffly and Abigail saw his Adam's apple travel up and down his throat several times before he spoke again. "Then there are no grandchildren either."

Abigail looked sharply toward Gertrude, who met her gaze

with sadness and a silent plea. "Casper's never been married." The older woman's tone was tight and clipped. "Until now."

Abigail gripped the table again as another wave of dizziness slammed into her. She felt, for a moment, as if she might fall from her chair, but the sensation passed quickly.

"I still don't understand how a . . . a marriage is possible." Abigail was afraid to look at the woman now, fearing her own emotions might be clearly displayed on her face.

"I've spoken to an acquaintance of mine—he's a judge here in Denver. He said he could arrange for the marriage to be legal, though, of course, it can only be in . . . name only." Gertrude's voice fell to a ragged whisper with the last words.

In name only. Abigail should feel guilty about the giddy swell of freedom which seeped through her. Slowly but surely, the knowledge that she would never be forced to endure that monster's touch again brought her a heady feeling of emancipation.

In name only.

She looked across the table to meet Mike's gaze. His eyes were hooded, but she was positive of one thing. He was looking right at her.

As if he could read her mind.

Rage and fear ricocheted through Mike as he watched Abigail. A stubborn and irrational emotion thrust itself into his thoughts.

She'll never sleep with him.

His relief was short-lived as realization waged a frontal assault. *Damn.* He'd thought this mess was nearly over—now this. A brick wall and a half.

If Milton couldn't father children, and he had no siblings . . .

"Mrs. Milton, did you or your husband have any brothers or sisters? Nieces or nephews?" He had to know.

Abigail's expression when she met his gaze was one of shock, but she'd get over it. A whole hell of a lot better than he would.

"Mr. Milton, rest his soul, was an only child, though I had four sisters and a brother."

But not Miltons. Mike slowly permitted himself to accept these facts. Cousins from her side of the family didn't count. He could grant them a reprieve.

"Of course, only my youngest sister is still alive." Gertrude sighed, then turned her attention to Abigail again. "I'll take you to see Casper after supper, if you wish."

Mike watched Abigail, wondering about the conflicting emotions he saw playing through her eyes. One moment she seemed almost relieved, then the next she looked terrified.

Why?

Give it a rest, Mike. It didn't matter. Nothing mattered except figuring out this final piece of the puzzle. Who was Frank Milton's ancestor?

Who was Mike's victim to be?

"Y-yes." Abigail bowed her head and her face reddened. When she looked up and met his gaze, a glitter of something undefinable flashed in her eyes.

Satisfaction.

Mike had seen that look before, on the faces of people waiting for a convicted murderer to be sentenced—usually the victim's family. Why did Abigail look like a woman who'd just seen justice done?

He frowned and rubbed his temples with both thumbs. The food no longer held any appeal for him. How could he end this nightmare without more information?

Slick.

Mike ground his teeth together, knowing the asshole would be waiting to rub it in, but when? Where? How? Slick would have to give Mike some additional information. *Oh, great.* That's all there was to it. Obviously, there was another branch of the Milton family somewhere.

Damn.

Still, he had to make sure. Mike couldn't completely dismiss this Milton until he saw him with his own two eyes. He had to see just how helpless Casper Milton truly was. He wanted guarantees.

"Shall we go up now?" Mrs. Milton looked at Abigail with a pleading expression.

Why did this woman want Abigail to marry her son? He stared long and hard at Abigail again as she nodded and pushed back from the table. Automatically, Mike rose and pulled out Mrs. Milton's chair as the older woman stood, leaning heavily on her cane.

Why Abigail? Why *any* woman? It wasn't as if a man in Milton's condition needed a wife. But there had to be a reason for Milton's mother to want him married.

"If you'll excuse us, Mr. Faricy, we'll go visit Casper now. Molly should be finished feeding him his broth about now." The woman smiled sadly. "If you'd care for port or brandy, you'll find it in the parlor. Please, make yourself at home."

"Thanks." Mike stared after the two women, noting Abigail's tension as she left the room with her future mother-in-law.

An old instinct surged through Mike and he followed at a distance. *Investigate.* He stepped into the foyer and watched the women go slowly up the stairs, then he took them in rapid, total silence until he stood alone in the dark, upstairs hallway.

A light shone around a partially open door at the end of the hall. His heart hammered the walls of his chest and made his head pound as he walked slowly toward the light.

For some reason, he felt compelled to do this. Was it his detective's instinct or Slick? Did it matter?

No.

Resigned, Mike inched his way along the wall until he was right beside the open door. Mrs. Milton's voice drifted into the hall as Mike leaned toward the crack and turned slightly.

A bed was the focal point of the room. He saw Mrs. Milton's small form standing on one side of it, while Abigail stood farther away wringing her hands. He'd seen her do that many times, but only when she was feeling particularly nervous about something.

Then he dragged his gaze to the bed itself and his heart swelled in his throat. The man's fair head rested against a stark white pillow, and his light eyes stared up at the ceiling. Slack-jawed, his mouth hung open and drool ran from one corner.

Mrs. Milton wiped it away with a rag, then stroked her son's forehead. Mike wanted to pity the woman, and did in a way. But he couldn't forget his mission.

The man.

He studied Casper Milton's expressionless face for interminable moments. As each second passed, he grew more certain. It couldn't be; none of this made sense.

As if this bizarre nightmare *could* make sense.

The resemblance between the man on the bed, and the pond scum Mike had arrested countless times in the future, was undeniable. Yet impossible.

How?

Frowning, Mike swallowed the bile burning his throat and forced his attention to Mrs. Milton. He had to hear her words. Perhaps then he could understand this ridiculous situation.

That man was Frank Milton's ancestor.

I don't think artificial insemination has been invented yet.

"So, Abigail, do you understand why receiving your letter seemed like the answer to a prayer?"

Mike shook his head slowly and waited for Abigail to answer. All she did was nod.

"Casper will never . . . be able to father children."

No kidding.

"I . . . I think I understand," Abigail said quietly.

Well, I don't. Mike gripped the door frame with his hands and waited. Sweat dripped down his forehead and ran into his eyes. He blinked and wiped it away.

"Yes, I'm sure you do." Mrs. Milton brushed the man's blond hair away from his face and sighed. "He was once such a bright, handsome man."

Abigail shuddered visibly and bowed her head. She didn't speak, but Mike could see her face reddening with each passing minute. What was it?

"It was very important to Casper's father that this hotel remain in the family." The older woman patted her son's shoulder and straightened, turning to face Abigail with that pleading expression again. "You do understand, my dear. Don't you?"

"Yes." Abigail's voice was a harsh whisper. "I do, but I'm not sure you do."

"I know it must be a disappointment to you to know there can never be . . ."

Abigail looked up sharply and Mike's confusion mounted, though something he couldn't quite define emerged from a dark place in the back of his mind. His attention riveted to her face as he awaited her next words.

Pay real close attention to everything she does . . .

Slick's words played over and over in Mike's mind as he watched the profile of the woman he loved. He'd almost forgotten she was the key to his mission.

He'd been distracted.

"No." Abigail's voice quavered and she shook her head. A tear trickled down her cheek. "I don't think you understand how . . ."

"Oh, my dear." Mrs. Milton walked around the bed and took Abigail's hand in hers. "Don't you concern yourself with the past. Things . . . happen. There was a war. You can't blame yourself for—"

"Blame *myself?*" Anger blazed in Abigail's eyes when she half-turned toward the open doorway and stared at Mrs. Milton. "Trust me, I most certainly do not . . . blame myself for *that.*"

Why the sudden change? Mike strained to hear Mrs. Milton's words, but the roar of his blood trumpeting through his brain made it nearly impossible.

"I'm sorry." Mrs. Milton shook her head. The older woman's back was to Mike, but he heard tears in her voice. "Please, forgive me, Abigail. I don't know what I'll do if you decide not to stay."

"I'm going to stay." Abigail bit her lower lip and closed her eyes for a moment. She drew a deep breath and squared her shoulders. "I have no choice. That's the only reason I'm here."

"The only—"

"That's right." Abigail's voice was stronger now as she

opened her eyes and stared at the older woman. A fierceness entered Abigail's eyes. "I had no choice."

"I remember your letter. Forgive me."

"Of course." Abigail cleared her throat, then released a sigh. "There are some things you're better off not knowing." She looked over her shoulder at the man in the bed, then turned to face his mother again.

The expression on her face was one of rage and hatred, but not for Mrs. Milton. There was no doubt in Mike's mind that it was the man in the bed who'd triggered such powerful emotions within Abigail.

Why?

"Will you stay and marry Casper?" Mrs. Milton's voice was clear and strong as she faced Abigail.

"Y-yes. I came here for that reason." She shrugged. "I'll see it through. Besides, as I said, I have no choice."

"My dear, I have to ask . . ."

"What?"

"About Mr. Faricy."

Mike tensed. His teeth gnashed and his gut wrenched. *All right, Abigail, what* about *Mr. Faricy?* How was she going to handle this one? It made perfect sense that the old woman would wonder about Mike. Who wouldn't?

And any suspicions Mrs. Milton might have were probably a lot less colorful than the truth.

Mike's gaze rested on Abigail, traveled down the length of her throat to where her pulse leapt at its base. The memory of how she'd looked sitting astride him in the back of the wagon assaulted him. A wave of desire struck him like a riot gun. Not that it would do him any good at this point.

"What is it you wish to know?" Abigail stiffened visibly and pressed her lips together.

"I think that must be obvious." Mrs. Milton looked down as she spoke. "Forgive me for being so forward, but I want some assurance that you won't grow bored here and run away with Mr. Faricy."

Abigail laughed—a sound that threw Mike for one hell of a loop. He stared at her in amazement mingled with respect.

Way to go, Abigail. His love for her surged within his heart, rivaling even the desire that pounded through his veins.

Her laughter died as suddenly as it had begun. "I won't be running away with any man."

Mrs. Milton nodded, then looked up at Abigail. "I'm sorry, my dear. Forgive me for being so rude."

"It's understandable." Abigail shrugged.

There was a shrewdness to Abigail's demeanor Mike had never noticed before. There was definitely more to this. She was hiding something—no doubt about it.

"After all, except for Wade and Rosalie, Mike and I have been alone in the wilderness for several weeks."

Color suffused her cheeks and he thought her even more beautiful now than before. Still, he had to ask himself why she was being so flippant about all this. The old lady had practically accused her of . . . the truth.

"That's true." Mrs. Milton nodded again and patted Abigail's hand. "I don't think we need to discuss this any further. Do you?"

"Are you convinced now that I won't run away with Mike?"

God, how I wish. Mike cursed himself for still wanting her, for still loving her. He should turn and walk away.

Mike had to ensure Barney's future.

Dammit. How? He raked his fingers through his hair and waited. There had to be something more. It couldn't end here, without him knowing for certain that there would be no more Miltons to beget Miltons to beget Frank Milton.

The bad seed's going to die with this generation.

"You've given me your word," Mrs. Milton said with confidence.

Abigail stared in silence at the woman for several moments. "Are you certain?"

"Why shouldn't I believe you, Abigail?" Mrs. Milton gave a nervous laugh and a red flush crept up the back of her neck.

"I can think of one reason." Abigail lifted her chin a notch and her blue eyes glittered with an emotion Mike couldn't quite define. "The reason you want me to marry your son."

Pay real close attention to everything she does . . .

Mike's body was wired. He felt as if he could leap tall buildings with a single bound. Superhuman. Why?

Pay real close attention . . .

"There is that. Yes." Mrs. Milton's words were barely audible. "We have a wedding to plan."

"Yes, I suppose we do." Abigail nodded. "I want your promise that you'll never try to come between my son and me."

Mike frowned and leaned farther into the open doorway. He was growing more confused by the minute.

"I wouldn't dream of it." Mrs. Milton clicked her tongue. "He's the reason I sent for you. I want him to be happy here."

No. Mike held his breath and watched Abigail's face, straining to hear the slightest whisper from her lips.

Abigail . . .

"All I ask is that you never try to take Wade from me."

"Take him from you?" Outrage filled the old woman's shaky voice. "How could you think such a thing?"

"Because it's Wade you really want here—not me." Abigail looked back over her shoulder at the bedridden man. When she met Mrs. Milton's gaze again, her nostrils were flared and her eyes glazed over with anger. "My son."

Oh, God, no.

The fires of Hell held nothing over the heat of anger and betrayal that swept through Mike. He shuddered deep inside himself as he watched the woman he loved speak the words that would destroy him.

Please, God. Not this.

But Mike knew it was true. This was just the sort of thing Slick would enjoy above all else. Why hadn't he seen this coming? If this Milton was Frank Milton's ancestor, then Abigail was . . .

"Your son." Mrs. Milton's voice rose. "Your son is Casper's son—his heir. You'll raise him here with me and he'll never want for anything again as long as he lives. Neither of you will."

Abigail released a shuddering sigh and silent tears streamed down her face. The look on her face was one of supreme defeat.

"Anything for Wade," she whispered.

And Mike saw—heard—it all through a haze of defeat.

His mission was clear.

Mike made his way down the hall to the room Mrs. Milton had shown him earlier. He couldn't breathe. This was killing him. Now what the hell was he going to do?

Kill Wade?

Chapter Twenty-Two

Mike burst through the bedroom door and kicked it shut, foregoing the lamp on the nightstand as he slumped onto the featherbed. God, he couldn't kill a little boy.

Especially not *that* little boy.

Wade's trusting eyes appeared in his mind's eye. Mike swallowed hard and flopped onto his back, laying his hand across his forehead as he stared up at the ceiling. *Wade.* God, why Wade?

"Mike, Mike."

Not that voice—not now. Mike squeezed his eyes shut and tried to banish the voice, knowing even as he did that Slick would find a way to force the issue.

"Well, well. You finally figured it out." A sigh echoed through the room. "I was beginning to wonder, Einstein. It sure took you long enough."

"Why?" Mike shook his head and slowly opened his eyes. He turned his head from one side to the other, but there was no sign of Slick in the dark room.

Or any possible hosts.

"Because that's the way it is."

Slick's voice was disembodied—larger than life.

"Larger than life 'cuz I'm dead, dickweed."

Dickweed. Mike squeezed his eyes shut again. "I saw your mother today."

"Yeah, I know. Big deal." Slick's voice sounded closer now. "That woman's so drunk all the time she doesn't know what she's doing. Besides, seeing her isn't going to do you any good."

"Maybe. So what? I can't see it doing me any harm either." Mike opened his eyes again. Still no sign of Slick in a physical form. "Why Wade? You know I can't kill a kid."

"Hey, it's your choice, Mike. If I'd brought you back to 1885 instead of 1865, Wade woulda been twenty-two years old. Would that have made a difference? End result's the same either way." Slick chuckled. "At least now you can be sure the little twerp hasn't spread his wild oats. Besides, in 1885 his mama will be less, shall we say, appealing. You have found a few perks along the way, haven't you y—"

"Shut up." Mike tried to regulate his breathing. In. Out. In. Out.

"Shut up? Me? Fat chance. It's time to pay the piper, Mike, whether you decide to dance . . . or not."

A strange sound prompted Mike to turn his head toward the window again. Garfield sat cleaning his paws in the windowsill. "Planning to scratch me again?"

The cat didn't turn toward Mike.

"Not yet. I'm not using the cat right now. Got a fur-ball last time." Slick's voice surrounded Mike, seeming to come from everywhere at once. "I don't need it. Like you said—I'm larger than life."

Slick's maniacal laughter filled the room.

As it subsided, Mike drew a deep breath while continuing to stare at the ceiling. "You still didn't answer my question, Slick."

"Ha! I told you it's *your* choice. That's it, bucko. This is the end of the line. Do or die." Slick laughed again. "Actually, you'll die whether you *do* or not. Question is—what'll happen to Barney?"

"Hate seems like such a small word right now." Mike looked

toward Garfield again. The small, furry creature lifted his head and stared right at Mike, his eyes rimmed with red.

"Shit."

"Gotcha." Garfield, hosting Slick, leapt from the windowsill to the bed, then walked up Mike's leg until all four paws were on Mike's chest. "You're mine now, whether you choose to finish your job or not. Makes no difference to me, but I sure can't figure out why you'd want to let Milton live. And Barney die."

Mike's gut burned and his heart swelled to fill his throat. The small cat felt heavier than lead right now, pressing into his chest with claws and paws. "Get the hell off me."

"Not a chance." Slick's eyes burned brighter as he inched his way up Mike's chest until his whiskers hovered mere inches above Mike's face. "Not until you make a decision. What's it gonna be, Mike? Hell with me now and let Milton live? Let Wade grow up to pork some broad and make more Miltons? Then those kids'll do the same thing in another generation. Before you know it, bingo. Frank Milton is born . . . and Barney Sloane is dead meat in Natchez, Mississippi."

"Why'd you pick this time to send me to? Why does it have to be Wade? Why, dammit?"

"Hey, the situation was classic." Slick's laughter grated on Mike's ears. "You were in a house where one of Milton's ancestors was born. Why go searching for another one when one was readily available, shall we say?"

Mike couldn't suppress the shudder that swept through him. Though Slick possessed him with his crimson gaze, Mike saw Barney's lifeless eyes. He imagined Carrie's grief at raising a child without his father, just as they'd been raised without parents.

Orphans.

"No." His voice sounded strangled. Broken.

"No, what?" Slick's voice rasped, cracked intermittently by a purr from Garfield's chest.

Talk about mixed metaphors.

"Say it, Mike."

Flames appeared in Slick's pupils and Mike saw himself there. Burning.

He was going to Hell, no matter what. But Barney. Carrie. Their baby.

"Damn."

"Damnation awaits you. Shall we hasten things right along now?" Slick pulled Garfield's lips back to expose sharp, feline teeth.

Why did the moon have to shine so brightly through the curtains? Mike didn't want to see Slick, though he knew no amount of darkness could prevent him from seeing those glowing red eyes. The flames.

Hell.

"Let's go. Makes no difference to me either way."

"No." Mike forced air into his oxygen-starved lungs. He released his breath very slowly, struggling against the hysteria that awaited even a hint of provocation. It would be so simple just to let Slick take him now and get this over with.

"Then you can live with your cowardice for eternity. Sounds fair to me. Just say the word." Slick sighed and tilted his head to one side, though the brightness of his eyes never diminished one iota.

"No."

"You keep saying that. Care to elaborate? We do have a contract, you know."

"I . . . I'll finish it." The roaring sound in Mike's ears grew louder and louder as reality thrust itself before him. There was no way out of this. He'd given up everything for this opportunity. Not only his life, but eternity as well.

For Barney. And Carrie.

"Good." The flames expanded from Slick's eyes and surrounded the cat's face. All Mike saw were red eyes and flames. "Now listen real close, boy genius, because there won't be any second chances this time."

"I . . . I'm listening." Mike stared, mesmerized by the flames. A sort of eerie calm descended over him.

Deadly calm.

"One day. That's it."

"One day?" The heat grew more intense and he felt his lips crack; every breath seared his lungs.

"That's it. Midnight tomorrow night, you and me return to Hell—this time, for keeps. Remember your last little visit?"

Mike tried to nod, but couldn't. "How could I forget?" The memory of his own flesh burning assailed him. Fear had no place in his heart now. Resignation had taken its place. "Midnight tomorrow night."

"Good." The intensity of Slick's eyes gradually diminished. "Midnight. Be there or be square."

Perverse, menacing laughter lingered long after Garfield had vanished from his perch atop Mike's chest. The evil sound swirled around and around, filling the room with deadly intent until a word emerged from the cackle.

"Midnight ... night ... night ... night ... night ... night ..."

Mike struggled into a sitting position and held his face in his hands. The air in the room gradually cooled now that Slick was gone. Soon, cool would be nothing more than a faded memory for Mike.

But Mike's real hell would start before the first flames seared his flesh.

He reached inside his jacket for the smooth butt of his weapon. Withdrawing it, he stared at it in the moonlight, admiring the way the silver beams reflected off the black metal.

He had two rounds of ammunition left. Only two.

But that was enough.

One for Wade ... and one for him.

Sunlight streamed through the lace curtains at the window, creating an intricate pattern across the dark wood floor. Just as Abigail finished closing the buttons at the front of her dress, a light knock sounded on her bedroom door.

Her heart leapt. Was it Mike? Would he leave them now?

Panic threatened her resolve as she crossed the room and opened the door just a crack.

"Miss Abigail?" Lines of concern etched Rosalie's dark face. "I gots to talk to you."

Wondering what had made her friend so nervous, Abigail swung the door wide and ushered Rosalie into the room. "Come over here and sit with me."

They sat facing each other on the velvet cushioned window seat. The sun felt warm against Abigail's back as she wondered why Rosalie looked so worried.

"What is it?"

"I knows who that man is."

Abigail's blood turned to an icy torrent. "What . . . man?"

"That man you come here to marry. That's who." Rosalie thrust out her lower lip and her brow furrowed. "You didn't think I saw him after he had his way with you, but I did. Lord help me, but I wanted to stop him, but I know'd you had the only gun in the house."

"Rosalie, don't—"

"You ain't gonna stop me from sayin' what gots to be said." Rosalie swiped at her eyes, then folded her arms across her chest; her chin quivered.

Abigail looked down at the floor. A single tear rolled down her cheek, but she paid it no heed. "Go on, then. Say it and get it over with."

"Yes'm, that's what I'm reckonin' to do." Rosalie drew a deep breath, then released it very slowly. "I seen that man leaving Elysium after . . . after he done what he done to you. I seen him, Miss Abigail, and I won't ever be forgettin' what he looked like. Never."

"Rosalie—"

"I ain't finished havin' my say."

"I'm sorry."

"You should be. How can you even think about marryin' that man? Ain't you got no thoughts for yourself at all?"

"I . . ." Abigail held her hands out in front of her helplessly, then met Rosalie's gaze again. "I'm doing what I think best for Wade."

"To marry that . . . that scalawag? Humph. Even that's too

nice for him." Rosalie reached out and grabbed both of Abigail's hands and held them fast. "You listen to me, Miss Abigail. That man's no good. I know he's just alyin' there now, but what if he wakes up?"

"He won't."

"What if he does?" Rosalie's voice grew higher and louder with each syllable. "Please, you can't do this." She pulled herself up straight and drew a deep breath. "I won't *let* you do it."

Abigail bit the inside of her cheek to quell the ragged sobs she felt pressing for release. "You can't stop me, Rosalie. I'm doing what's best for my son. Now he'll never be hungry again. He'll have a home and even a grand—"

"No'm." Rosalie shook her head and her face was set in grim lines of determination. "Miz Milton seems like a right fine lady, but that ain't enough. You ain't gonna raise that darlin' little boy in this house . . . with these people. I won't let you."

"Rosalie, please." Abigail blinked back the stinging tears. "I must do this. Don't try to stop me."

"I won't let you," Rosalie repeated. "I . . . I'll take Wade— that's what I'll do—and go far away from here. We'll go away with Mr. Mike."

Abigail felt as if someone had taken a knife to her heart. She wrenched her hands free of Rosalie's grasp and pressed them to her breast as if to stay the pain. But nothing could dilute this terrible feeling. She dragged in a shaky breath. "Rosalie, please, please don't do this. Try to understand why I have to—why I *must*—do this."

"Ain't no way I can ever understand this, Miss Abigail." Rosalie shook her head. "Miz Milton's woman, Molly, told me all about the man—that he never talked or nothin' since they brung him home from the war. Well, I couldn't figure out why you'd marry up with somebody like that, so I snuck myself up to his room to see for myself. I thought I done died right there on the spot when I seen that man's face. Oh, Lord. I'll never forget that night as long as I live."

"Nor shall I."

Abigail looked down at her hands, now clutched in her lap. "You won't try to take Wade from me. Promise me, Rosalie." She looked up, praying for the strength to reason with her friend in the midst of everything but reason.

Rosalie stared at her for several seconds. "No'm. I reckon you knows I don't got enough meanness in me to do somethin' like that." Her voice broke and tears flowed freely now down both cheeks. "That little boy loves his mama somethin' fierce . . . and so do I. You've always been family to me, Miss Abigail. Always. Your daddy asked me to look after you."

Abigail's heart broke, shattered into millions of brittle shards. The onslaught of pain was merciless. "Please . . . ?" Her voice broke and the sobs tore free.

Rosalie wrapped her arms around Abigail's shoulders and they held each other as they wept. Years of pain poured from Abigail, drenching her friend's shoulder with the salt of her tears.

After awhile, Rosalie held Abigail at arm's length. "Miss Abigail, please don't marry that man. Please, don't do this."

Abigail sniffled and dabbed at her tears. "I have to, Rosalie. Don't you see?" She met Rosalie's gaze and blinked several times to clear her blurry vision enough to realize no response was forthcoming. "I can't watch my son go hungry ever again. Don't you *remember* what it was like? Hearing my poor baby cry all the time and being powerless to end his hunger? I can't do that again. I *can't.*"

Rosalie gave an emphatic nod. "You knows I remember."

"Then why can't you understand?"

"Do you remember everything that happened that . . . that night, Miss Abigail? I don't see how you couldn't, but most times you act like . . . it never happened." Rosalie squared her shoulders and lifted her chin a notch. "And I do mean *everything.*"

A shudder began in the depths of Abigail's belly. It spread relentlessly throughout her body within seconds. Finally, she managed a nod.

"Well, so do I." Rosalie released Abigail's hand and stood beside the window seat. "Lord help me, but I'd do it all over again, if need be."

Abigail jerked her gaze up to meet Rosalie's. They stared at each other for interminable moments and she saw that it was true. Rosalie meant every word. She would do anything necessary to protect Abigail.

Again.

"It . . . won't come to that, Rosalie." Abigail stood on shaky legs to face her friend. "This will all work out for the best."

"No'm. I don't reckon that's so. Ain't no way any of this can be for the best." Rosalie pursed her lips, then shook her head. "There ain't no point in tryin' to talk sense to you, even if you and me both knows what man you *really* belongs with."

Abigail stared in numbed silence. She couldn't argue with that logic. No man would ever—*could* ever—take the place in her heart or her life that Mike Faricy had filled. No one.

"Why don't you tell that man you loves him?" Rosalie implored. "I know he'd take you and Wade with him. Please, just tell him. He loves you."

I already have told him. Abigail slowly shook her head, recalling Mike's words as if he'd just this moment spoken them. *Don't love me, Abigail . . .*

A moment later, she heard the door close behind Rosalie.

Abigail held her breath, struggling against the urge to follow. Rosalie wouldn't take Wade. Abigail had no choice but to accept that and proceed with her wedding plans.

Another knock at the door sent Abigail flying to throw it open, thinking Rosalie had returned to set things right between them again. Her heart fell at the sight of Gertrude's smile.

Abigail looked lower. Wade stood clutching the older woman's hand, a huge grin on his impish face. The sight of her son so readily embracing another adult gave Abigail pause. The one person she trusted above all others where Wade was concerned had just mentioned taking him from her. Perhaps that was what made her so uneasy about the budding relationship she saw before her eyes.

"Are you all right, dear?" Gertrude's brow furrowed with concern. "You're flushed."

"I'm fine." Abigail lowered her gaze and reached out to touch her son's fair head. "Come in." She stepped to the side as the pair stepped into the room. "I'm not normally such a lay-about. I'll be down shortly. Forgive me."

"Nonsense. You need rest from your journey." Gertrude waved her hand, summarily dismissing the notion altogether. "This fine young man just consumed a huge stack of hotcakes smothered in real maple syrup. I can't for the life of me imagine where he put all that food."

Wade giggled as the older woman chuckled happily, then she rushed ahead without giving Abigail a chance to speak. "I wonder if you'd permit me to borrow young Wade for a few hours this morning?"

"Borrow?" Abigail's heart thudded slow and loud in her chest. "I . . . don't understand."

"Forgive me." Gertrude laughed again and smiled down at a still-giggling Wade. "I'm expected to attend a sewing bee at church. One of the ladies has a son just about Wade's age who always accompanies her, and I thought . . ."

Abigail's face flooded with heat. Why was she so suspicious of everyone and everything today? "I'm sorry." She forced a smile to her face and looked down at her son.

He was the reason she'd come here. Now Wade could have opportunities like this one. A playmate! That was something she hadn't even thought of yet for her son. More mundane matters, like food and shelter, had taken precedence over all else. This only served to reinforce her decision. Surely Rosalie would come around in time. "Of course you may. When do you think you'll return?"

"Oh, by dinner for certain. Around one o'clock, I should think." Gertrude cast Abigail a warm smile. "I'm so glad you have faith in me, my dear. It means more than you can know. I thought I'd take your girl with me, though, if you don't mind."

Relieved, Abigail swallowed the lump in her throat and nodded, not trusting herself to speak. Rosalie would protect Wade, no matter what; her earlier threat had meant nothing, really.

Abigail bent to deliver a kiss to her son's cheek, unable to resist the temptation to pull him into her arms and hold him for just a moment. Her little boy.

Anything for Wade.

"I'll take good care of him. Now don't you worry at all." Though Gertrude still leaned on her cane, she seemed to move with more ease now than before. "You might go sit with Casper this morning. I usually do for a while after breakfast."

Casper. Abigail drew a deep breath and forced a smile to her face, hoping it didn't resemble a grimace instead. "You two have fun. I'll see you at dinner."

She stood in the open door to watch them walk down the hall together, hand-in-hand. Her heart swelled with love for her son, with the assurance that she had indeed made the right decision in coming here.

In agreeing to marry that man . . .

Everything would be fine.

Wouldn't it?

She stood in the hall for several minutes after her son and his grandmother-to-be had disappeared down the stairs. A sound from the far end of the hall caught her attention and she jerked her head toward it. There were at least ten doors separating hers from the one from which the man emerged.

But she'd know him anywhere, from any distance.

He turned to make his way toward the centrally located staircase, then looked up and saw her. His movements ceased as he stood staring. Eventually, he started to move. Purposefully.

Pausing in front of her, he captured her gaze with his and held her prisoner for interminable moments. She couldn't move, couldn't breathe.

"Mike," she finally whispered. Something clogged her throat and pricked her eyes, but she wouldn't cry now. It was far too late for tears.

He reached out and cupped her face with his large, work-roughened hand. Something inside her snapped and she turned toward his palm and kissed the warm flesh. It felt so good to have his hand on her, to kiss him.

Then why did it hurt so much to love him?

When she withdrew her lips from his palm, she again found his gaze, haunted and mesmerizing. The desperation flickering in his eyes unnerved her.

"What is it, Mike?" She didn't want him to hurt, though he had hurt her with his rejection. If only he could have returned her love. "What's wrong?"

His eyes glittered oddly and she thought, for a moment, the sheen might've been tears. But men like Mike Faricy didn't cry. Tears were a woman's curse in life, as she well knew.

"I wish . . ." He stopped and drew a deep breath. "I wish things could've been different."

"You're leaving me—us." Pain jolted through her, as surely as if he'd struck her with all the strength at his command. "Aren't you?"

He nodded very slowly. "I'm so sorry, Abigail." His words were barely audible. "So very sorry."

Abigail searched his face for answers. The last thing she wanted was for him to leave them—leave *her*. Yet she knew, considering her marriage plans, that it was for the best. Still, she couldn't prevent herself from wanting him to hold her, to kiss her, to make passionate love to her one more time.

Startling herself, she flung her body toward his and buried her face against the warmth of his denim jacket, vaguely conscious of his pistol beneath it, as usual.

Words wouldn't come. All she could do was wrap her arms around him and hold him.

If only she could hold him forever.

He reached down and cupped her chin in his hand, urging her to look up and meet his tortured gaze. Genuine tears rimmed his eyes now and one escaped to trickle down his cheek. Her heart swelled with love and admiration for a man who could actually weep. Mike Faricy was a rare man indeed.

But he was lost to her.

"Mike," she whispered again. How she longed to beg him not to leave or, better still, to take them with him. Instead, she lowered her lashes to veil her eyes from his probing, tormented expression.

When his lips brushed hers, she broke. Though his kiss was brief, its impact was all-powerful. The dam burst and her tears flowed freely from her eyes as he lifted his face and met her gaze again.

He stared at her for several silent moments as tears fell between them. She knew, gazing into the hazel depths of his eyes, that he loved her. Why couldn't he tell her? How could he let her marry another man, knowing she loved him, too?

Then he reached out to touch her face again, stroking her cheek with his callused thumb. "I'm sorry, Abigail," he repeated, brushing his thumb across her lips. "So very sorry."

Then he was gone.

Abigail brought her knuckles to her mouth and bit down hard to silence the sob which tore at her insides.

Mike was leaving her.

Panic spurred her feet to move and she started down the hall toward the stairs. The instinct which surged through her was simple and primitive. Survival. Deep in her heart, she knew Mike Faricy was the key to her future.

Mike was leaving her.

"No." She grabbed the bannister and started down the stairs, increasing her speed as she went. Yes, survival. She *needed* Mike; she loved Mike.

Rosalie had been right. She couldn't marry anyone but Mike. He couldn't leave her.

Her heart thundered wildly in her breast as she reached the bottom of the stairs. There he stood, his hand clutching the door handle.

"Mike," she called.

He froze, but didn't turn toward her. She stared at him, stricken with terror that he might walk out of her life.

Forever.

He looked down, then she saw his shoulders move as he drew a deep breath and turned the knob.

A strangled sound tore from her throat as she rushed toward him. She tried to form words, but none came.

Please, don't leave me.

"Miss Abigail!"

Rosalie's frantic voice and hurried entrance forced Mike away from the door. "Miss Abigail," Rosalie repeated, breathing hard, as if she'd been running.

"What . . . what is it?" Abigail found her voice, though she couldn't drag her gaze from Mike as he stood to one side as if frozen in place. "Where are Wade and Gertrude?"

"Miss Abigail, somethin' awful happened."

Abigail jerked her gaze from Mike and turned it on Rosalie. "What's happened?"

Mike moved toward them, and Abigail feared for a moment he would walk out of her life, but he didn't. Instead, he hovered nearby, between her and the open door.

Rosalie's dark eyes were round and frightened. "Miz Milton's dead."

"What?" Abigail shook her head in bewilderment. "I just saw her this morning. She seemed fine."

"Yes'm, I know." Rosalie's chin quivered. "When she took Wade out behind the church to see the ducks, she seemed right chipper."

"Wade." Terror seized Abigail and she grabbed Rosalie's shoulders. "Where's my son?"

"Sweet Jesus, Miss Abigail." Rosalie covered her face with her hands, then looked up to face Abigail. "I don't know where he is. The pastor found Miz Milton out by the pond, but there weren't no sign of Wade."

Abigail swayed and Mike reached out to steady her as she let her hands fall to her sides. "Where . . ." Her voice faded away as realization unfolded. "Lord have mercy. Rosalie, did you say pond?"

Rosalie nodded and tears streamed down her face. "The . . . the preacher got some men to search the . . ."

Frantic, Abigail tried to speak but no sound emerged. Her throat worked and struggled, but to no avail. Finally, she turned to Mike.

The expression in his eyes was tortured, but it served to

restore her voice. "Mike," she said in a strangled whisper. "Help me find him."

He looked as if she'd struck him and, for a moment, she thought he might refuse to help her. His jaw twitched and his mouth was set in a grim line.

"Mike, please."

Finally, without speaking, he nodded, then released her and walked out the door.

Chapter Twenty-Three

Mike walked toward the edge of town as if in a trance. He knew Wade wasn't in the pond. History proved the boy would grow to be a man.

To father children.

Mike's head ached from clenching his teeth. He remembered having seen the church on the edge of town when they'd arrived the day before. His pace quickened as he neared the structure and saw the gathering on the front steps.

One man in particular drew Mike's attention. He stood on the top step, talking in an authoritative manner to the small group. He had to be the pastor. Mike stopped behind the gathering and listened.

"The pond isn't deep, so if the boy's there Sam and Janx should find him." The man dragged his coat sleeve across his forehead; his bald head glistened in the warm sun. "But we have to organize a search party, just in case. He could've wandered away from town."

Mike followed the direction of the pastor's gaze, out into the vast plain which skirted the east side of Denver. His gut clenched, but he knew what he had to do.

Wade was out there somewhere. Instinct screamed from deep

inside Mike, forbidding him from shirking this last responsibility, no matter how desperately he wanted to.

"What happened to the old lady?" an overall-clad man asked from the group.

The pastor shook his head. "She was old. It was her time."

A murmur swept through the group and several heads nodded. "What about Milton? Her son?" one man asked.

"Mrs. Milton provided for his care," the pastor explained.

Mike turned away from them and looked out into the wilderness, beyond the trees and few buildings separating him from it. He had a mission to complete. Before midnight.

Hating himself more with each step, Mike walked away from the men. His gaze swept from side to side as he increased the distance between him and civilization. He didn't feel the least bit civilized right now. The stark plain suited him—suited the heinous act he was being forced to commit.

The execution of an innocent child.

He stumbled, but didn't slow his pace. It was almost as if some supernatural force drove him in this direction. He knew this path would lead him straight to Wade.

God help them both.

He lost track of time as he continued to walk, increasing his distance from town. The trail he followed was more like a cow path than a road; it twisted over barren hills and past an occasional farmhouse until there was nothing but emptiness.

He staunchly ignored the nagging dirt and small pebbles that filtered through the hole in the sole of his right shoe. Sweat rolled down his face and into the corners of his mouth and eyes.

Late in the afternoon, Mike stopped and looked around him. There was nothing in any direction but scrubby grass, dirt and tumbleweeds. He turned and looked to the west, where even the Rocky Mountains seemed to have vanished.

How far had he come? Squinting against the blazing sun, a thought took hold and refused to relinquish its hold.

Wade couldn't possibly have come this far on foot.

"Shit." Mike had been so blinded by his mission and the

torment in his soul that he hadn't paused long enough to consider anything the least bit logical.

Had Mike walked right by the boy? Was Wade somewhere
between the desolate patch of grass where Mike now stood and
the city of Denver?

His throat was parched and raw. He didn't even have water
with him, but neither did Wade.

Wade.

Mike dragged in a shaky breath and turned back toward
town. He had to find the boy. Midnight was mere hours away.
Nothing would prevent Slick from taking Mike to Hell with
him now.

Nothing.

Mike saw Hell in his mind's eye as he walked faster and
faster, limping from the stones bruising the bottom of his foot.
He saw his flesh burning, consumed by the greedy flames. The
pain was unbearable.

And never ending.

Then he started to run, blindly stumbling over rocks, barely
maintaining his footing. *Wade. Where's Wade?*

A macabre feeling washed over him. He felt almost as if he
was searching for Wade in order to rescue the boy, when
nothing could be farther from the truth.

Abigail's face appeared before him. That sweet look she
always had for her son rendered Mike's heart nothing more
than a mass of pulp. How could he take her son from her?

Yet how could he not?

Barney.

Mike ran faster, blinded by sweat and something more—
tears. Amazed that he had enough water left in his body to
produce sweat *and* tears, Mike ignored them both and continued
his stumbling trek.

Then he fell, face down in the dirt, almost as if someone
had stuck their leg out and tripped him. Grit filled his eyes,
nose and mouth. Lifting his head, Mike spit dirt from his mouth
and reached up to wipe his eyes with an equally dirty sleeve.

Then he heard it.

A faint sound drifted to him. The thundering of Mike's heart threatened to muffle the sound, but he drew several deep, dusty breaths until it quieted.

Crying.

Knowing he'd found Wade, indecision slashed through him again. God, how could he do this? How could he kill a little boy in cold blood? Especially a little boy Mike had grown to love as his own son?

Struggling to his feet, he thought briefly of the irony of his affection for Frank Milton's ancestor. If only there was some other way to prevent future generations of Miltons.

Only one way, other than death, that Mike could think of right now. The thought brought bitter bile to his throat. Even death was preferable to *that*, performed by amateur hands.

My kingdom for a surgeon—a urologist.

Blood trickled down his chin from his split lip as Mike staggered toward the sound. There he was, huddled beside a rock, his face buried in his hands as he wept.

"Mama," he cried.

Mike's heart broke. God, he couldn't do this. Why did it have to be Wade? *Why?*

"Wade?" Mike's voice cracked with emotion and dehydration.

The child looked up at Mike, his eyes puffy from tears. Dirt covered every inch of his small form. Where his tears had mixed with dirt, streaks of mud lined his impish face. "Uncle Mike."

More bittersweet words had never been spoken. Mike winced as the child stood and threw himself against Mike's legs and held on tight.

"Wade." Mike blinked against his own tears, then reached down to touch Wade's soft hair. Something inside him broke at the feel of the child's arms around his knees. He reached down and lifted the little boy, cradling him on his shoulder. "There, there, Wade. You're safe now."

Though Mike knew that was the greatest lie he'd ever told. Wade was far from safe in Mike's hands. This child trusted Mike, looked up to him, admired him.

Wade wrapped his small arms around Mike's neck and held him. "I want Mama."

Mama.

Mike squeezed his eyes shut, suddenly conscious of the gun in his shoulder holster. The weapon felt a thousand times heavier now than ever before. How he wished he'd lost the damned thing before now.

Before this.

He stood there, holding Wade in his arms for what seemed like forever. Unable to proceed with his monstrous mission, Mike rested his cheek against Wade's hair, savoring the feel of the small, warm body holding onto his with everything he had.

"Oh, dear God," Mike prayed, then he kissed the top of Wade's head. "What am I going to do?"

He remembered the night he'd first met Slick Dawson, and the deal he'd struck. The entire scene played over in his mind like a bad horror film, haunting and tormenting him beyond reason.

"There's something you want . . . name it . . . turn back the clock . . . anything . . ."

"Even my . . . soul," Mike whispered, jerking himself back to the present. Momentarily stunned, he looked around at the stark terrain.

Not once in his deal with Slick had Mike agreed to kill.

Confused, he started walking slowly toward Denver. What was he supposed to do? He had to prevent Frank Milton's birth, but he couldn't kill Wade. Not Wade.

In affirmation, he squeezed the boy tighter. Wade responded by hugging Mike's neck and lifting his face to look up at Mike.

The unconditional trust in the boy's eyes unhinged Mike.

Tears overflowed his eyes and trickled down his face as he forced himself to smile at the child. Somehow, he had to find another way.

"Let's go find your mama."

Wade smiled brightly and nodded.

Abigail, please help me.

* * *

Abigail saw them coming from her upstairs window and literally flew down the stairs to meet Mike and Wade at the front door of the hotel. After throwing open the door, she dropped to her knees and gathered her son in her arms, laughing and crying at the same time. "I knew you could find him. Thank you."

She smiled up at Mike, who looked tired and lost. The fierce glint she'd seen in his eyes this morning was gone. A sort of grim resignation had taken its place.

"Oh, Wade," she said, brushing his blond hair away from his eyes. "I was so worried. What happened? Why did you wander off like that?"

"I not."

Mike knelt beside them. "You didn't wander away?"

"No."

Abigail frowned and held her son at arm's length so she could see his dirty face more clearly. "Tell us what happened, Wade. Everything."

"Doggie." The boy's chin quivered. "Me thirsty. Hungwy."

Hungry. Her son was hungry. "Of course you are." She glanced at Mike, whose furrowed brow and twitching jaw told her he suspected something. "Let's go to the kitchen and wash up. I'll bet Molly and Rosalie kept dinner warm for you."

With a nod, Mike straightened and she sensed him following them to the kitchen. Thank Heavens. She needed him right now. Surely he would stay until she determined what was to become of them. Now, with Mrs. Milton gone, Abigail didn't know what was expected of her.

There certainly couldn't be a wedding now. The only catalyst for that event was gone from this world. Casper *couldn't* pursue the marriage, and Abigail didn't know how to proceed without Mrs. Milton's guidance.

Mike and Wade washed the worst of the dirt from their hands and faces, then sat at the kitchen table while Rosalie fussed over them both. Abigail looked on, trying not to allow that glimmer of hope to grow inside her.

But knowing marriage to Casper was no longer an option, she couldn't stop herself from hoping for a future with Mike. Anyone could see that Wade and Mike belonged together. They adored each other.

She adored both of them.

It seemed so right—so natural.

Would Mike agree?

"I'm goin' up to turn down your bed, young man," Rosalie announced, leaving the threesome alone in the kitchen.

"Tell me about the dog, Wade."

The sound of Mike's voice intruded on Abigail's reverie, jerking her back to the present, and to the unanswered questions surrounding her son's disappearance this morning. She poured Wade another cup of milk, then sat in a chair across the table from Mike.

She looked at Mike again and her gaze locked with his. For some illogical reason, she had the feeling he knew something she didn't. Well, that was entirely possible since she knew practically nothing. "Yes, Wade," she urged. "What dog?" Why did Mike feel this dog was so important?

"Him play."

Mike frowned, but Abigail knew what Wade meant. Suddenly, she felt frightened again, though she didn't know why. A dog wouldn't take her son into the wilderness and deliberately leave him there. *Ridiculous.* Then why did her heart pound with fear? "Did you follow the doggie, Wade?"

The boy nodded, then reached for his milk. Abigail exchanged worried looks with Mike again. What was going on here? Of course a little boy would follow a playful dog. Any boy would. But Mike's expression told her this situation wasn't nearly that simple.

"What . . . what did the dog look like, Wade?" Mike didn't look at the child as he spoke. He spread his hands out flat on the table's surface and stared steadily at Abigail.

The intensity of his gaze was unnerving. A chill passed through her and she shivered outwardly. "What is it, Mike?" she asked, unable to remain silent any longer. "What's so unusual about a little boy following a dog?'' She shook her head. ''I don't understand.''

Mike drew a deep breath. ''I'm going to tell you everything, Abigail, and you have to promise to listen until I'm finished.'' Then he turned to look down at Wade. ''But first, I want Wade to tell me about the dog.''

''Big dog.'' Wade's head nodded and he started to pitch sideways, but Mike reached out to steady him.

''Hold on there, partner.'' Mike slid Wade onto his lap. ''Now, tell me more about the dog. What . . . color were his eyes?''

Wade mumbled something unintelligible to Abigail, seated across the table, but Mike's face blanched. ''I was afraid of that.'' Mike's words were barely audible.

In silence, Mike pushed himself away from the table and rose, gathering Wade in his arms. ''I'll carry him up to bed, then you and I are going to have a serious talk.'' Mike looked away, then back again. ''An overdue one.''

Abigail nodded and followed them up the stairs. Her heart flip-flopped in her breast and her tummy felt queasy. Something important was about to happen. She knew it like she knew the time of day, the day of the week.

Abigail followed Mike down the stairs and into the small room off the parlor that Mrs. Milton had called her office. Though she'd known the woman for only one day, Abigail felt a sense of loss in her passing.

She walked into the room and paused before the window. The sun was beginning to set now, casting long shadows across the floor. When she heard the door click shut behind her, Abigail turned to face Mike.

''What is it, Mike?'' She took two steps toward him, then held her hands out away from her sides. ''Tell me.''

He moved closer and rested his hands on her shoulders. The contact reignited the deep hunger he always created with his nearness. Abigail wanted much more than this, but she knew there were other, more pressing, matters which commanded their attention now. ''Tell me,'' she repeated.

Mike's eyes glazed over and he looked beyond her, at something she knew only he could see.

"I'm from the future," he said soberly.

Abigail shook her head and stared at him. "What ... did you say?" She couldn't possibly have heard him correctly.

"The future, Abigail." He smiled sadly. "I was a cop—a detective. An officer of the law in the late twentieth century."

Impossible. But she nodded slowly and swallowed the lump in her throat. Could this explain his odd language, the strange shoes, the fastener he called a zipper ... ? "I'm listening." This was insane, but she had to hear this—every word.

"My friend, partner, my sister's husband ..." His voice cracked and he blinked rapidly. "Barney. He ... he was killed. A creep who worked for a drug lord named Frank Milton killed Barney."

Drug lord? Abigail's breath caught in her throat and she struggled against the urge to ask questions.

"I ran for my life—literally. Those thugs chased me until I hid inside an abandoned mansion on the edge of town." The haunted expression left his eyes and he locked his gaze with hers. "Your house, Abigail."

She shook her head. "I ... I still don't understand." None of this was possible. He couldn't be from the future.

"Of course you don't understand. How could you?" He gave her shoulders a squeeze, then brought his hands to her upper arms to massage them. "Abigail, none of this will make sense, but you must listen to all of it. Promise me."

"Y-yes."

"Good." He gave her a wan smile, then sighed again. "I hid in your house—Elysium. In the future, people will consider that house haunted, so no one ever went there during ... my time. I figured I'd be safe there." He barked a derisive laugh. "Boy, was I wrong."

"They didn't find you." She searched his face. "You're safe now."

"No, Abigail." Mike shook his head and that distant expression returned. "I'm not safe by any stretch of the imagination. As of midnight tonight, I'll be burning in Hell."

"Don't talk that way—you're frightening me." Abigail's mouth went dry and she tried to swallow but couldn't. For some reason, despite the voice of common sense that raged in her subconscious, she *believed* him. That made Mike's story all the more terrifying.

"It's true." His eyes glittered with a desperation unlike anything he'd displayed up until now. "Please, believe me, Abigail."

"I . . . I do." Heaven help her. "I don't know why, but I do believe you, Mike. But please, please tell me the rest. I don't want you to . . . leave."

A smile lifted the corners of his mouth. "Abigail Kingsley, I have no right to tell you this, or to drag you into this mess, but I'm afraid I have no choice." The smile vanished and a shudder racked his body. "The alternative . . ."

"Alternative?" She searched his face, desperately seeking answers to a barrage of questions. He'd asked her to believe the impossible, and she did. "What alternative?"

"You have to hear the rest of this, then I have to figure out what to do real damn fast." He took her hand and pulled her over to the settee near the window. "Don't you want to know how I got here? In 1865?"

She nodded, noticing that he still held her hand. Drawing comfort from his touch, she met his gaze again. "Please?"

"I was crazy with grief, Abigail." Perspiration trickled down his face and he reached up to rake his fingers through his shaggy hair. "Barney was dead, and I was willing to do *anything* to undo that. *Anything.*"

She knew that feeling well. *Anything for Wade.* Heaven help her, but only a miracle had saved her from spending the rest of her life reliving her worst nightmare. Yes, she could well understand the extreme remedies to which a human being could be driven.

"Then *he* came."

"Who?"

Mike's Adam's apple bobbed up and down in his throat and he tightened his grip on her hand. "Do you believe me, Abigail?"

The pleading expression in his eyes would be her undoing. She would deny him nothing now. "Yes." And she meant it.

"I sold my soul to the devil."

Her heart skipped a beat, then raced away. The roaring sound in her head was deafening for a moment and the room swayed. "W-what?"

"I sold my soul, Abigail." He leaned toward her, his expression frantic. "The devil will have his due . . . and he collects at midnight."

"Mike." Her voice was scarcely more than a strangled whisper and she shook her head. "I won't let you go. I won't!"

He lowered his gaze for a moment, then looked at her again. "And if it were in my power to stay here with you, I'd do it in an instant." He sighed, and squeezed her hands again with both of his. "There's more to this—things only you can help me with."

"Anything."

"Didn't you hear the name of the man responsible for Barney's death?" Mike's voice softened and his gaze continued to search hers. "It was Milton. Frank Milton."

"Oh." With a gasp, she straightened and pulled her hands from his warm grasp to cover her mouth. "Are you saying . . . ?"

Mike nodded, his expression stricken. She'd never seen a man more tormented.

"Yes," he confessed. "Wade is Frank Milton's ancestor."

She shook her head. "Mike, what are you saying?" Terror swept through her. Did the man she loved mean to harm her son?

He looked down for a moment, then met her gaze again with his usual determination. "I came to 1865 to do anything possible to prevent the birth of Frank Milton."

"Anything?" She felt as if the air was being squeezed from her lungs. Her body turned cold. "Mike, no."

He laughed bitterly. "I've spent most of the summer trying to find the Milton I was sent back in time to kill, only to learn yesterday that it's . . . it's Wade." He shook his head and a tear eased itself from the corner of his eye. Swiping at it angrily, he stood and walked across the room.

Abigail should hate him, but she didn't. She felt his pain—shared it. "Mike." She stood and crossed the room, gripping his arm until he turned to face her. "I know you won't harm Wade. If you could, you would've done so today. Wouldn't you?"

Mike closed his eyes for several seconds, then opened them with a slow nod. "Yes," he whispered, and her heart bled for him. "I . . . I have two rounds of ammunition left. I figured that was enough. One for . . . each of us."

With a strangled gasp, she gripped both his arms and absorbed his pain. "But you didn't. You can't hurt Wade. We both know that." How could she be so certain? She had no idea, but she was. Perhaps it was because she loved him so very much. "Tell me how we can fix this. What can we do?"

Mike shook his head and his shoulders slumped. "Abigail, if I don't . . . eliminate Milton's ancestor by midnight, Frank Milton will be born."

"And . . . Barney will die," she finished for him, nearly gagging on the words. Dear Lord, they were speaking of her son. "There must be another way."

Mike nodded. "My . . . deal with the devil is simple. I've sold my soul and collection time is midnight, no matter what." He sighed and clenched his teeth. "See? Slick gets his due, whether Milton's ancestor lives . . . or not."

"Slick?"

"The devil's assistant." Mike groaned and rubbed his forehead with his palm.

"I see." Abigail searched his face. "What can I do to help?" This was madness. "Just tell me and it's done."

He gripped her arms again and the desperation returned to his eyes. "Abigail, I'm dead meat—there's nothing we can do to prevent that."

Tears scalded her eyes. She shook her head, but words wouldn't come.

"Promise me you'll take Wade far away from here."

She nodded and the tears began to trickle down her cheeks.

"And that he'll never, never, *never* bear the name Milton."

She nodded again as the torrent continued. All she saw of Mike was a blur of color through a veil of bitter tears.

"Promise me, that he'll grow up to be a . . . a good man." Mike shook his head very slowly. "A good man who'll raise his sons to be good men."

Abigail nodded again, recognizing the direction of Mike's thoughts. "We can change history," she whispered, determined that it be so. "Knowledge is . . . is power."

Mike gathered her into his arms and she wept against his shoulder. "Abigail, there's something more I have to tell you."

She sniffled and burrowed her face against his soiled jacket. "You don't have to, Mike."

He lifted her chin until their gazes locked.

"You know, don't you?" His smile was sad and reassuring at the same time.

"I love you, too." She lifted her chin, silently challenging him to argue the point.

"Yeah, I guess you do know. I love you—your strength, your commitment to your son . . . and to me, no matter how crazy I've acted." He sighed. "I love everything about you."

"Enough to trust me with this?"

"No one else. Only you." He sighed and placed one hand on each side of her face. "And I hate myself for burdening you with this, but I had no choice."

"No, you didn't." She tried to swallow, but failed. God couldn't take him from her now that they'd found each other. It wasn't fair. "I don't want you to . . . to go."

Mike pulled his lips into a thin line of despair, then closed his eyes for a moment. "I know. I don't want to, but it's out of my hands."

He covered her lips with his and she tasted the salt of his tears mingling with her own. How could life be so cruel? When they parted, he searched her gaze with his for several silent moments.

"We can be together . . . for a while," she invited, feeling her face flood with heat. "Tonight."

He smiled. "I can't. There's one more thing I have to do before . . ."

Abigail's heart shattered. "Oh, Mike." A miracle had brought him to her—a tragedy and a miracle. All she could do was wait.

And pray for another one.

Chapter Twenty-Four

Mike glanced at the mantel clock. *Almost eight o'clock.* He had to get to that saloon to meet Thiel and Slick's mother. God only knew why he wanted to keep his date with Hattie Dawson, but he did.

For some reason, it almost seemed like a mandate from a higher power. One thing was for damned sure—it wasn't a mandate from a lower power.

He might be dead meat at midnight, but he was going to Hell with the assurance that Thiel would leave Abigail alone. That man had turned into a fanatic on this issue, which made no sense that Mike could see.

Of course, if all went as planned, Wade and Abigail would be on their way to a place far from Denver before Thiel could harass her again. But Mike couldn't take that chance. He had to make sure.

Abigail was his insurance . . . and the love of his life. .

Fate had a twisted sense of humor—that was for damned sure. Drag Mike back in time, introduce him to the woman of his dreams, then snatch it all away from him.

As if it had never happened at all.

He pushed through the swinging doors and into the saloon,

his gaze sweeping the area until he found the blue-clad soldier at the bar. Certain of the man's identity, Mike slowly approached, but hesitated when a redheaded woman sidled up beside the soldier to rub her voluptuous breasts against his arm.

A flash of memory jerked Mike from the present. Why now? He shook his head to rid himself of the image of Slick à la Garfield in the back of the wagon that day by the river, but it returned, insistent and in intricate detail.

"When's your birthday? What month?"

"May second, 1866. Happy now?"

"Get a grip, Mike," he whispered to himself, wondering why his mind had chosen this late date to start playing tricks on him.

Mike's gaze bore into the back of the soldier as he slipped his arms around the prostitute—Hattie, of course. That red hair was a dead giveaway.

Dead . . .

The scene with Slick played through his mind again. There had to be a reason for this unwelcome entertainment. He took another step toward the couple as the soldier turned to face Hattie, wrapped his arms around her and pulled her firmly against his lower torso.

Mike shook his head and sighed. Looked as if Thiel and Slick's mother would be busy for a while. Well, that was just too bad. They'd have to put their hormones on hiatus for a while. It wasn't as if Mike had time to be polite.

He took another step toward them and froze, his gaze glued to Thiel's profile. An eerie sensation trickled through him. Try as he might, he couldn't shake it.

Weird.

Thiel reached up and covered Hattie's breast with his hand, obviously sampling the merchandise. Hattie moved in for the kill; the vice cop in Mike recognized the signals. Thiel tilted his head to one side, then nodded.

Ah, they'd struck a bargain.

They stepped away from the bar and staggered arm-in-arm toward the stairs.

May second, 1866.

Mike shook his head, but the voice played again in his mind. *Think, Mike,* he commanded himself as the couple moved closer to the stairs.

Then it struck him like a canister of tear gas. "Holy shit," he whispered, suddenly positive of his suspicion. This was incredible, yet undeniable. He *knew* it, though common sense insisted he had no evidence—no proof. Still, Mike couldn't shake the certainty.

Thiel was Slick's father.

Son of a bitch.

Did that mean . . . ?

Mike shot his gaze up the stairs. They were near the top now. Did that mean that tonight was the night, so to speak?

Paralyzed, he watched them pause at the top of the stairs to embrace and kiss. Was he witnessing Slick Dawson in the making, revolting as the entire concept was?

Then another thought blasted through him and he moved hesitantly closer to the staircase.

Could he prevent Slick's conception?

And if so, would it—*could* it—make a difference? At midnight?

"Damn."

Mike reached for the bannister, his blood trumpeting through his veins. Poised, prepared to run up the stairs and tear the lovers apart physically if necessary, he heard a commotion from the saloon entrance. Instinctively, he turned toward it, stunned to see Lieutenant Brown push his way through with two other soldiers flanking him. The lanky young officer almost ran to the bar.

Mike's attention was diverted for a moment. When he looked back toward the top of the stairs, there was no sign of the couple.

His heart pounded mercilessly as he started up the stairs, wondering which of the many doors upstairs would lead him to Hattie Dawson . . . and Thiel.

But before he could take another step, Brown's voice stayed him.

"I'm looking for a soldier. Major Thiel," Brown said in an

urgent tone. "The hotel desk clerk across the road told me he thought he saw him come over here."

"I don't know nobody named Thiel," the bartender said in an impatient tone, dismissing the soldier's question and turning away.

Brown turned with his companions as if to leave the establishment, but Mike ran down the few steps he'd managed to climb and grabbed Brown's arm. "Lieutenant," he said urgently when the soldier turned toward him with a look of surprise.

"Faricy, what are you—"

"It doesn't matter." *But something else sure as hell does.* "Thiel's upstairs with Hattie Dawson. Ask the bartender which room. We have to stop them before it's too late."

A look of confusion crossed the Lieutenant's face, but he shrugged and turned back to the bartender. "Which room belongs to Hattie Dawson?"

Mike listened to the exchange, seeing images of the opening scene from *Look Who's Talking* in his frazzled mind. God help him, but if there was a sperm and an egg with Slick's name on it . . .

"Second door on the left," Brown shouted, then ran up the stairs, followed closely by the other two soldiers.

Mike followed, wondering briefly why Brown was so anxious to find Thiel. Shaking his head, he banished the thought and matched his stride to the rhythm of his heart.

Brown opened the door and entered without knocking, his companions following on his heels.

For some reason, Mike remained in the hall, almost afraid to look. The couple had been up there long enough to at least begin the act, depending on their mood.

A bitter taste filled Mike's mouth as he peered around the corner and saw a fully clothed Hattie Dawson pouring herself a drink. Thiel had his shirt and boots off, but his trousers were still in place.

Thank God.

But would it make a difference?

Mike swallowed hard and tried to overhear the conversation between Brown and Thiel.

"You're under arrest, Major," Brown said in an authoritative tone. "You're to accompany me to Washington to answer formal charges."

"What the hell are you talking about, Lieutenant?"

"*Cowardice.* Vicksburg. Do you remember that battle, Major? Do you remember riding away from a skirmish and leaving ten men to die? One of those men lived to tell the truth. Nine died, but one disappeared."

Thiel opened his mouth to speak, but his face reddened and he shook his head.

"Yes, Major. One man's body wasn't found, and you *know* which one."

"You're wasting your time, Brown, but suit yourself. The army can't prove a thing." The major reached for his shirt and followed Lieutenant Brown into the hall, pausing to stare long and hard at Mike.

"Faricy, tell that woman of yours she still has—"

Thiel's words seemed to trigger something that had been barely restrained inside Lieutenant Brown. The younger man grabbed Thiel by the arm and glowered down at him.

"You're in no position to make threats here, Thiel . . . *especially* about Lieutenant Denny." Brown's voice trembled in rage. "The military court closed the Denny case. He's just another dead soldier and you know it, but you had another reason for wanting to find him. For wanting to make sure he was really dead. Didn't you?" Brown thrust Thiel away from him as if he couldn't bear the sight of him any longer.

Then he turned to look at Mike as the soldiers escorted Thiel away. "I'm sorry, Faricy." He shook his head. "Denny disappeared after the episode near Vicksburg. Fortunately, he told the story of what really happened at Vicksburg before he died, whenever and wherever that was. That's why Thiel's been so determined to find out what happened to him. But it doesn't really matter now, does it?"

Mike slowly shook his head and tried to swallow, but his throat was too dry. "Why are you doing this?" He sensed that Brown was intervening for Abigail's benefit, that the soldier knew something more he hadn't yet revealed. Perhaps he never would.

The young officer shrugged. "Miss Kingsley's a nice lady, and Major Thiel treated her badly. She reminded me of my sister . . . who died." He blinked, then met Mike's gaze again. "I don't know what horrible things happened to her, or any of the folks around Natchez during the war, but it's over now. Time to let go."

"Amen." Mike shook hands with the lieutenant. Now Abigail would be all right.

Without another word, Lieutenant Brown turned and left Mike there in the hallway. Alone. Whatever secrets were buried at Elysium would remain buried now. The Civil War was over at last.

Mike looked in the room again. Hattie tipped her head back and drained the glass of its contents, apparently indifferent to her lost customer. Then she staggered to the bed, where she fell face down and began to snore almost immediately.

Mike felt numb from the inside out—afraid to even think of what he may have prevented, let alone the consequences. Did he dare hope?

Silently, he pulled the door closed on Hattie's room and looked toward the end of the hall. An image appeared, drawing him like a powerful drug. Mike walked slowly toward it, recognizing the translucent figure as Slick Dawson, in his true form. He'd just as well find out right now where things stood.

Slick was almost invisible.

Slick pointed toward the door Mike had just closed, then leveled his piercing gaze on Mike. The eyes flared red for a moment, but the flames merely sparked, before dying completely.

"Dickweed." Slick's strangled whisper was barely discernible as the figure faded even more. "Satan said he'd get even . . ."

Mike watched in silence as Slick grew fainter and fainter. This was incredible. Though he'd seen this creep put on theatrical performances before with his vanishing acts, Mike knew in his gut this was no show.

Slick was fading because he'd never be born.

And if he'd never be born, then he couldn't possibly have—

"My God."

But then, if Slick would never exist, how could Mike Faricy be standing in a Denver saloon in 1865?

Abigail waited near the front door, pacing and watching the clock on the mantel. Midnight was less than an hour away. Would Mike make it back in time to say good-bye?

To make love to her once more?

She bit the inside of her cheek to quell her panic. The household's few guests, Wade, Rosalie and Molly were all asleep for the night. Alone, she waited and wondered.

And prayed.

A sound in the kitchen prompted her to leave her post to investigate. Molly sat at the table with a cup of milk in her hand.

"Oh, I'm sorry, Miss Kingsley," she said, pushing away from the table and rising. "Forgive—"

"No, please sit down." Abigail tried to listen for the front door with one ear while she turned her attention to Molly. If she had to leave Denver with Wade, then she felt a certain responsibility to Mrs. Milton.

And her son.

"Do you know if Mrs. Milton made any . . . arrangements?" she asked. "I want to make sure that's taken care of, since we won't be getting married."

"You won't?" Molly looked up from the table, brightening for a moment. "Forgive me." She lowered her gaze again.

A suspicion formed in Abigail's mind and refused to leave her. "Molly, how long have you lived here?"

"Ten years." Molly shook her head. "My mother worked for Miz Milton when they first opened the Landmark. Mr. Milton died right after that, and we was like regular family." She looked down again. "Until the war."

Abigail drew a deep breath. "And after your mother died,

you stayed on?'' Molly nodded, and Abigail felt strengthened.
"Why, Molly?''

Molly gave Abigail a sad smile. "For Casper. I've always
loved him. I know he ain't . . . all here anymore, but I still love
him.''

''Ah.'' Abigail suspected Molly had no notion of Casper's
cruel side, but that was no longer an issue. Circumstances made
it impossible for the monster to ever repeat the crime he'd
inflicted on Abigail. "Then you should stay here to care for
him, and the Landmark should be yours.''

Molly looked up, startled. "Are you sure, ma'am?'' Her
eyes were round and hopeful. "I'd gladly give my life to care
for Casper. All of it.''

Abigail knew she'd do the same for Mike, and Molly obviously felt as deeply for Casper. However, Abigail couldn't
imagine why Molly would want to give up her entire life to
care for an invalid.

Still, she had no right to question another's priorities. She
knew that better than anyone, considering what she'd been
willing to sacrifice for the sake of her son.

Her belly clenched and burned, but she paid it no heed. "I'll
see what I can do to make sure you and Casper get to keep
the Landmark,'' she promised, and meant it. Before she left
Denver with her son and Rosalie, she would speak with Mrs.
Milton's friend, the judge.

Molly rose and walked around the table to stand before
Abigail. "You'll go to Heaven for your generous heart,
ma'am.''

Speechless, Abigail merely nodded as Molly moved toward
the back staircase. *Heaven? But Mike will be in Hell.*

"I think I'll go tell Casper the news. He likes to be read to
from *Les Misérables*. He taught me to read, before . . .'' Molly
said, then vanished up the dark staircase.

With a sigh, Abigail turned back to the front foyer to wait,
glancing again at the mantel clock. Only twenty-five minutes
remained.

"Oh, Mike,'' she whispered, despondent as she slumped into
a chair.

She heard a faint click and turned immediately toward the sound.

"Mike." She leapt to her feet and rushed to his side as he closed the door behind him. There was a strange, almost peaceful expression on his rugged face. "Mike?"

He reached out to touch her cheek with the back of his fingers. "Abigail, how I love you."

She threw herself into his embrace, savoring his warmth and strength. God couldn't take him from her now. They'd just found each other.

Without a word, she took his hand in hers and led him up the stairs to her room. Hurriedly, she closed and locked the door, then reached for the buttons at the front of her dress.

He reached out to still her efforts with his hand. "Are you sure?" he asked quietly.

Nodding, she watched him strip from his clothing and place his gun on the bureau beside the other unusual objects he removed from his pockets. He seemed so resigned, yet so at peace.

His demeanor both frightened her and gave her strength at the same time.

Naked and unashamed, she left the lamp burning and walked toward him, allowing her gaze a full feast of his magnificent male body.

Her body tightened in response, ready and aching for him. Desperation fueled her desire.

If the devil intended to take Mike at midnight, the demon would have to literally wrench him from her embrace to do so.

"Now Mike. Please hurry."

The urgency in her voice spurred him to action as he gathered her in his arms and carried her the few short steps. He eased her down to the bed as gently as a babe, though she wanted him to dispense with gentleness, and most of all, she wanted him to hurry. She needed to feel him inside her now.

This time would have to last them forever . . .

His kiss was urgent, seeking, demanding, and she answered him with her own exigency. He covered her and she wrapped her legs around his waist, urging him to take full and immediate possession.

With a groan, he sheathed himself, deep and sure. She gasped at the completeness. This couldn't be the last time she would feel him touch her, press himself against her, bury himself inside her.

She couldn't bear it.

Yet she knew she would, if she must.

Abandoning herself to the pleasures of the flesh, Abigail soared with him, savored each thrust of his body into hers. She held him with everything she had and gave back all she could.

For Mike, she would give everything. Anything.

She opened her eyes to see his face, but it was shrouded in shadow. The lamp's golden glow shone from behind him, casting an almost ethereal halo over them.

She lost herself as he pushed her over the edge into that delicious world she'd found before only in his arms. Swell after swell of fulfillment oozed through her, momentarily banishing all other thoughts as he claimed her as his.

Branded her for life.

He shuddered against her, releasing himself into her. She answered with her own acme as the knowledge that he would soon be taken from her assailed her anew.

"I won't let you go," she gasped as he cradled her against his chest, their hearts pounding as one in the afterglow of their love.

In silence, Mike kissed her forehead and eased himself onto his side. The night air washed over her, punctuating their separation.

Abigail hated the sensation. It was as if she'd had a limb amputated. She gazed into his eyes. No, not a limb—her soul.

"I won't let you go," she repeated, biting her trembling lower lip as she gripped his shoulders. "Heaven help me, but I ca—"

"Shh." He pressed his fingertip to her lips. "What time is it?"

She squeezed her eyes shut and shook her head. "I don't want to look. I can't."

She felt Mike turn toward the clock on the bureau. He sighed loudly and she felt his heart race again against her breast. "Open your eyes and look."

"I can't." She shook her head again. Maybe if she didn't look, this wouldn't be real.

"It's *after* midnight," Awe and incredulity filled his voice. "I don't believe it." He gave a nervous laugh. "Now you'll probably think I made the whole thing up."

Abigail's eyes shot open and she looked at the clock. "Twenty minutes past . . ." She gave Mike a searching look. "I told you this afternoon that I believed you. But how . . . ?"

"It's a very long story." Mike kissed her neck just beneath her ear. "But there's at least one baby that wasn't conceived tonight."

She gasped and pushed his forehead until he lifted his smiling face away from the sensitive flesh of her neck. "Mike, what does this mean? You aren't . . . going?"

"I . . . I guess not." He laughed quietly and shook his head. "God help me—well, I guess *He* already did."

"Mike." Abigail punched him on the shoulder. "Stop teasing and tell me what's happened."

"The devil's flunky—Slick?—will never be born." Mike's voice faltered and she saw his Adam's apple working in his throat. "And Major Thiel will never bother you again."

"Thiel? What does he have to do with any of this?"

"It doesn't matter now. He's out of your life forever." Mike's expression sobered and he stroked her cheek. "You've never told me all the nightmares of the war years, but I know—I've guessed—some. Maybe someday you'll tell me everything, but rest assured that it's all in the past. The war's over, Abigail . . . for us both."

The magnitude of Mike's words struck her and she blinked back her tears. "I'm not sure I understand any of this, but if it means you aren't leaving me . . ."

Mike shrugged and gave her a slow smile that made her melt inside, then his brow furrowed again. "Unless . . ."

"Mike." She pinched his arm. "Unless what?"

He frowned. "I have no way of knowing whether or not I'll be taken back to my own time." His voice was faint, uncertain.

"Do you . . . want to go back?" She was afraid to hear his answer.

He looked at her, and beyond for several moments, then shook his head. "It's strange, but I have a feeling of belonging here. Before, I didn't, but now I do. I can't explain it."

"You don't have to." She touched his face and smiled. "What about . . . Barney and your sister?"

"They'll be fine." Sadness filled his tone, but with no more dominance than certainty. "But I have to write one—no, two— more letters and send them to Saint Mary's. I have a feeling the first ones will never be delivered. But now that Slick's gone . . ."

"I love you," she whispered.

"And I love you, more than anything or anyone I've ever known." He kissed her soundly, then moved away to look at her. "Marry me, Abigail. Tomorrow."

She nodded and welcomed him into her arms again, praying that morning's light wouldn't declare this nothing more than a beautiful dream.

"Then we'll move far away from Denver and Natchez," he said quietly, nuzzling her neck as he spoke.

"Will that be enough? I mean, that Wade won't bear the name Milton?"

Mike sighed and lifted up on one elbow to meet her gaze. "Yes, we'll make sure of it. He'll be a Faricy." He grinned suddenly. "But, just to be safe, do you suppose we could convince him to enter the priesthood?"

Abigail smiled, though tears trickled down her cheeks. "There's one small problem with that idea, Mr. Faricy."

"Hmm. What's that?" Mike nuzzled her neck again.

"Baptists don't have priests."

"Ah, but I have it on good authority that they're wonders at chasing away the devil."

"Anything for you."

Epilogue

Present Day—Natchez, Mississippi

Barney stood at the altar at Saint Mary's with his newborn son in his arms and gazed lovingly at his wife. "I love you, Carrie," he whispered.

Tears sparkled in her eyes and she rested her cheek against his arm. "He's beautiful."

"With us for parents, he couldn't lose. Today would be perfect, if only . . ." His voice trailed away as memories assailed him.

"I know." Carrie cleared her throat and straightened. "I think they're ready to begin."

Barney stood straight and proud beside his wife, their son cradled protectively in his arms. Mary and Patrick Faricy stood with them at the altar, serving as both grandparents and godparents. Only one person with missing.

"Before we begin," Father Bennett began, "I have something for you."

He held a sealed envelope out to Barney, who passed the baby to Carrie before taking the yellowed paper. "What is it?"

The priest shrugged. "Father Perez left a note with this, saying it looks much like one he gave to Patrick and Mary many years ago. Do you remember?" The priest turned toward Patrick.

"How could we forget?" A frown furrowed Patrick's forehead. "It's all true, then."

"Let Barney read the letter," Mary said shakily.

Thankful they'd decided on a private ceremony, Barney opened the envelope, being careful not to tear the brittle pages inside. He recognized the handwriting immediately and his heart lurched. "Mike!"

"What is it?" Alarm filled Carrie's voice as she moved closer to her husband. "Read it, Barney."

In numb silence, he shook his head and passed the open page to Father Bennett. "Please, Father."

The priest cleared his throat and pushed his glasses farther up on his nose. "Very well. It's dated . . . Christmas, 1865."

"Dear Barney and Carrie, he read.

"If you're reading this, it means all is well. Barney's alive, and Mom and Dad are standing in the church with you and the baby. I said I'd give anything, and I meant it. Fortunately, I ended up with the woman of my dreams and a wonderful son for my trouble.

"I'm fine, living in Denver with my wife, Abigail, and our son, Wade. We're expecting a new baby in a few months.

"I've met Allan Pinkerton, and plan to hit him up for a job when he opens his agency. Remember when we used to play 'Pinkerton Agent' as kids? Hey, don't worry about me. I'm happy here and I still have my memories of life in the twentieth century.

"Strange, after I wrote the first of these two letters, I suddenly had another full set of childhood memories. It's almost like I got to be a kid twice. I know without asking that Mom and Dad didn't die in that car crash. Thank God for that. Ask them to explain how I ended up here. If they didn't believe my first letter, I'll bet this one will

*convince them. I wish I could see the baby. That's really
my only regret, but with any luck, he or she won't look
a thing like you. Give Carrie and Mom a kiss for me.*
  "Love, Mike."

Barney cleared his throat and blinked back his tears. "I think
we've decided on a name, Father."

The priest nodded and returned the letter to Barney. "I understand."

The ceremony began and Father Bennett dipped his fingers
in the holy water, then placed his hand on the baby's head. "I
christen you Michael Patrick . . ."

Dear Readers:

A desperate man and a desperate woman come together in *Some Like it Hotter*. It's unavoidable. It's destiny.

Think of it this way: If Dirty Harry met Scarlett O'Hara . . .

This is a book about love in the midst of crisis, and about priorities. Mike Faricy and Abigail Kingsley are two people facing life's most desperate challenges. They've both reached a point in their lives where something is so important, they're willing to pay any price to make things right.

I hope you enjoyed reading *Some Like it Hotter* as much as I did writing it. Write to me at Post Office Box 1196, Monument, CO 80132-1196. I love to surf the World Wide Web, so you can e-mail me at debstover@poboxes.com, or visit my home page at http://www.netforward.com/poboxes/?debstover.

May all your days include a bit of magic.

Deb

ROMANCE FROM JO BEVERLY

DANGEROUS JOY   (0-8217-5129-8, $5.99)

FORBIDDEN   (0-8217-4488-7, $4.99)

THE SHATTERED ROSE   (0-8217-5310-X, $5.99)

TEMPTING FORTUNE   (0-8217-4858-0, $4.99)

YOU WON'T WANT TO READ
JUST ONE—KATHERINE STONE

ROOMMATES (0-8217-5206-5, $6.99/$7.99)
No one could have prepared Carrie for the monumental
changes she would face when she met her new circle of friends
at Stanford University. Once their lives intertwined and became
woven into the tapestry of the times, they would never be the
same.

TWINS (0-8217-5207-3, $6.99/$7.99)
Brook and Melanie Chandler were so different, it was hard to
believe they were sisters. One was a dark, serious, ambitious
New York attorney; the other, a golden, glamourous, sophisti-
cated supermodel. But they were more than sisters—they were
twins and more alike than even they knew . . .

THE CARLTON CLUB (0-8217-5204-9, $6.99/$7.99)
It was the place to see and be seen, the only place to be. And
for those who frequented the playground of the very rich, it
was a way of life. Mark, Kathleen, Leslie and Janet—they
worked together, played together, and loved together, all behind
exclusive gates of the *Carlton Club*.